Praise for Marni Mann

"Great book."

—Rosie O'Donnell, actor/author

"A tautly written, complex, and emotionally charged love story that takes the reader on an unforgettable, unexpected, and deeply moving journey."

—*USA Today*

"A breathtakingly beautiful and deeply moving story. *When Ashes Fall* owned my emotions to the very last word."

—Jodi Ellen Malpas, #1 *New York Times* bestselling author

"Sucked in completely and jealous of such a clever story! You won't put this one down. Marni will have readers desperate for every soul-gripping page . . ."

—Rachel Van Dyken, #1 *New York Times* bestselling author

"If you're reading a book by Marni Mann, I'm warning you now: grab a glass of cold water because her spicy stories are going to set you on fire!"

—Monica Murphy, *New York Times* bestselling author

"Marni Mann is my spice queen! She delivers every single time. With smoldering chemistry and impeccable writing, her books are utterly addicting."

—Devney Perry, *Wall Street Journal* bestselling author

"This book is perfection, and that's not even a good enough word! Chef's kisses!"

—Natasha Madison, *USA Today* bestselling author

"If you're looking for your next wickedly hot read, look no further. Marni Mann will have you fanning yourself all the way through."

—Laurelin Paige, New York Times bestselling author

"Sierra-approved sexiness on every page."

—Sierra Simone, USA Today bestselling author

Mr. Wicked

The Agency Series—Erotic Romance

Signed
Endorsed
Contracted
Negotiated
Dominated

The Bearded Savages Series—Erotic Romance

The Unblocked Collection
Wild Aces

The Moments in Boston Series—Contemporary Romance

When Ashes Fall
When We Met
When Darkness Ends

The Prisoned Series—Dark Erotic Thriller

Prisoned
Animal
Monster

The Shadows Series—Erotica

Seductive Shadows
Seductive Secrecy

The Bar Harbor Series—New Adult

Pulled Beneath
Pulled Within

The Memoir Series—Dark Mainstream Fiction

Memoirs Aren't Fairytales
Scars from a Memoir

Mr. Wicked

MARNI MANN

 Montlake

Text copyright © 2024 by Marni Mann
All rights reserved.

Published by Montlake, Seattle

www.apub.com

Amazon, the Amazon logo, and Montlake are trademarks of Amazon.com, Inc., or its affiliates.

ISBN-13: 9781662515552 (paperback)
ISBN-13: 9781662515545 (digital)

Cover design by Caroline Teagle Johnson
Cover photography by Wander Aguiar Photography
Cover image: ©K.Yas / Shutterstock

Printed in the United States of America

To my ladies who love a filthy mouth and a wicked tongue

PLAYLIST

"Fall in the Fall"—Jelly Roll, Struggle Jennings
"Skinny"—KALEO
"Haunted"—Beyoncé
"I Need You"—Jelly Roll
"Pretty Bug"—Allan Rayman, James Vincent McMorrow
"Runs in the Family"—Matt Koziol
"Grave Digger"—Matt Maeson
"Keeper"—Reignwolf
"Moments Passed"—Dermot Kennedy
"White Horse"—Chris Stapleton

Spotify Playlist: https://geni.us/MrWickedSpotify

PROLOGUE

Grayson

Two months ago

She's coming home with me tonight.

That was the only thought in my head as I caught eyes with the waitress, easily one of the most beautiful women I'd ever seen. Since I came in with my best friends a few minutes earlier, I'd been watching her bounce around the bar. She hadn't come close enough to allow me to read her name tag, but whoever this woman was, she had the most incredible body.

Tight, petite, like a distance runner, not a sprinter. A set of tits that would fill my palms and an ass just thick enough to squeeze.

She had every physical trait that I looked for in a woman, that turned me on, even down to the dark hair—hers was black—and deep blue eyes that pierced mine from the other side of the room.

Goddamn it, she was gorgeous.

And her lips—fuck me—they were plump and pouty, glossy, dragging my attention right back to them every time my stare dived down her legs.

I wanted her.

I wanted to know how perfect that body looked under her tiny shorts and tank top. What color bra and panties she wore underneath.

Was light pink her thing, a shade that matched her rosy skin, or was she more of a magenta type of woman? Black or even dark green?

I wanted to know how she would smell when I bent down to inhale her.

The scent of a woman was one of my favorite things about them.

Floral. Fruit. Maybe something extra sweet, like dessert.

I would soon find out.

And I was positive that in order to make that happen, I'd have to approach her. I certainly wouldn't be lucky enough to be sitting in her section of tables. But after about ten minutes of waiting for a server, of watching this hottie prance around the bar, of trying to get my hard-on positioned just right in my pants, I saw her begin to head straight for us.

A smile tugged across her lips, like she knew I was visually fucking her, and it stayed there, frozen, as she stopped at the back of Holden's and Easton's chairs. "Welcome to Olives, gentlemen. What can I get you to drink?"

"I thought we were going to have to fend for ourselves," I replied.

She laughed, despite my sarcastic reply.

A sound that was light, cheerful.

Enticing.

And before she said another word, she locked eyes with me. There was something behind her stare that I was eating up. Maybe it was the intensity. Maybe it was that her smile had reached as high as her gaze. Maybe it was her confidence, a trait I found so sexy in a woman.

But within that silence, a long, drawn-out look seemed to pulse between us, hanging in the air, thickening, until she finally said, "I got tied up with an eight-top." She shifted her weight as if the moment had hit her just as hard. "Sorry it took me so long to come over."

"I think you need to make it up to us." I glanced at my best friends, knowing their order without even having to ask. "Vodka on the rocks for all of us—but why don't you make them doubles. For the wait. And you can also bring me a Coke. Can or bottle—but I prefer a bottle if you have it."

"You don't want a glass with ice?" she questioned.

"I want to hear the fizz when I open it. None of that fountain shit that's stale as hell. I like my soda sweet and bubbly."

She turned her head. "What did you just say?"

I couldn't tell if she really hadn't heard me or if she was just surprised by my request. "A Coke. I'd like one. Can. Bottle. Whatever."

"No, no. I mean the latter part."

My brows furrowed. If she weren't so cute and coming across so charming, I'd be annoyed. "I like my soda sweet and bubbly."

"That's funny. Someone else I know always says the same thing. Anyway"—she shook her head—"can I get you anything else?" Although she was addressing the three of us, her eyes were on me.

They hadn't left.

They were burrowing.

All the way down to my fucking cock.

I leaned my forearms onto the table, crossing my fingers. "Since you asked . . . how about your number."

Her cheeks flushed as she laughed again.

Red.

Now that was a color I really liked on her.

A color that would look incredible if it were in lace undergarments that I could tear off her with my teeth.

"My number," she repeated. "That's something you're going to have to work for." Before I could say another word, she added, "I'll be back with your drinks," and left the table.

Spunky.

Playful.

The opposite of me.

Easton put his hand up to his mouth, like he was about to cough, but chuckled instead. "Dude, seriously?"

"What?" I eyed him down, his dark hair spiked in the front, realizing we wore it the same way. "Don't even tell me you're about to give me shit. Before you started dating Drake, you were even worse than me.

You were looking for chicks everywhere. Hell, you used to bang them in the restrooms of bars because you couldn't wait to get them home."

And since Easton had shacked up with our director of app development and engineering at Hooked, the dating app Easton, Holden, and I had founded, he and Drake were practically inseparable.

But Holden and I weren't in the same situation.

We were single as fuck.

And fishing, a term we'd assigned to the courting of women we wanted to sleep with, was still a very heavy part of my life. The daunting step-by-step of small talk and drink buying and setting the agenda—all requirements for one-night stands.

"I was a dog, there's no question about that," Easton said. "But as for you, I'm surprised you want to shit where you eat—you know, since we come to this bar all the time, you're going to have to see her more than once a week, and I know that's something you won't like."

He was right. I wouldn't like that.

But I would make an exception if I got to lick that body every time I came in for a drink.

Now that was something I could definitely get behind.

Holden nodded at Easton. "Everything you just said." He glanced in the direction of the hottie as she waited on another table. "Jovana must be a new hire. I've never seen her here before."

"Who's Jovana?"

As Holden looked at me, he rolled his eyes, shaking his head. His hair constantly needed to be cut—golden, semi-curly strands that barely moved since they were already so windblown. Since becoming a single dad to Belle, the guy looked like the aftereffects of a permanently circulating tornado.

Not that it mattered, because women loved his messiness.

Where he was cuddly and approachable, I fucking roared like a lion.

"The woman whose number you asked for," Holden replied.

I'd been so distracted by her presence and that beautiful face and achingly seductive body, I'd forgotten to look at her name tag.

Easton studied me as if he were looking through a microscope and my face was on the other side of the glass. "You didn't even bother looking at her name."

He wasn't questioning me—he was judging me.

Teasing me.

They both were.

"Listen, motherfuckers, I was too busy looking at her lips." As I thought about her mouth, my exhale sounded like air hissing out of a tire. "Sue me for being distracted."

"Here's what I can't figure out," Easton said, clasping my shoulder as though he wanted to be sure I was listening. "We own the largest hook-up app in the country. Why are you out here looking when you don't have to?"

I could understand why he questioned my choice.

Years ago, while in graduate school at Harvard, the three of us had been in the middle of a bitch session, groaning about fishing, when the idea of Hooked was born—an app that would completely eliminate the need to fish. Since its launch, Hooked took only the completion of a psychological test and a few swipes of a finger before the user was paired with someone sexually compatible.

But the explosion of our business, the popularity the three of us had gained, was a problem we hadn't foreseen.

We were celebrities in Boston.

So the days of matching with random women weren't like they used to be.

"Out of the last three women I hooked with, all of them immediately recognized me. One asked if she could live stream our kiss on fucking Instagram. Another asked for a second date, even though I bailed on the first date the minute she asked for my autograph." I pounded my fist on the table. "My goddamn autograph, can you believe that shit? And the third woman, while I was taking her clothes off, said she wanted me to be her baby daddy and told me not to wear a condom."

That was why I'd returned to this method, in hopes that the women I met out in the wild, like Jovana, didn't know who the hell I was.

Wouldn't want to live stream our kiss or ask for my firstborn or want me to sign across her tits with a permanent marker.

Fuck no to all that.

"So, did you wear a condom?" Holden asked, grinning.

"You're serious?" I stared at my boy like he had three heads. "You think I'd actually fuck her after she said that? Hell no." I wanted to reach for my drink, but it hadn't been delivered, so I slid my hand through the side of my hair. "Hooked worked when we were nobodies. Now that I'm a somebody in this city, I can't take the chance." I got to the end of my strands and started over, raking just to keep my hand busy. "Don't get me wrong, I love the success, and once we launch internationally it's going to get even wilder, but as far as hooking up through Hooked goes, I miss the old days."

"You know what I find hilarious?" A sly smile lifted across Easton's lips. "You were the inventor of the marriage arm of our app. A guy who can't even fathom a second date, never mind a lifelong commitment. Out of all people, it was you. Now, how's that for irony?"

When we were brainstorming ways to grow our business, I came up with the idea of a new division. The marriage arm was designed for users looking for long-term commitments that would eventually lead to marriage—as opposed to only hooking up—where they could hook with other like-minded users. Once that arm was established, Holden came up with the same concept for single parents and people open to dating other single parents.

Every new user had to choose which arm they wanted when they first joined the app, and as their needs changed, they could move between arms.

As owners, we just wanted to ensure that we were catering to everyone.

But ultimately, each arm added users, which then expanded memberships and, in return, increased revenue.

"Listen, fellas, I created a pathway to cultivate people's happiness," I told them. "That doesn't mean I have to practice what I invent or even believe in it. Marriage isn't for me, but it's for you"—I used my chin to point toward Easton, and then shifted to do the same to Holden—"and probably you too." I looked away to scan the room, finding Jovana at the bar. She was putting our drinks on a tray, preparing to carry them over, pointing her ass in my direction. The tightness of those heart-shaped cheeks. The way she was bent over, like she was positioned for doggy style. It all made my cock throb even harder. "What's going to go down tonight with that one . . ." My voice trailed off as she turned around, her nipples hard and showing through her tank, like my tongue had just left them. "Shit, it's going to be epic."

"I don't doubt that," Holden said.

With each step, I surveyed her body as if it were the first time I was seeing her.

And now that I was getting a better look, I was even more confident in my analysis.

Jovana was fucking perfect.

What I wouldn't do to wrap that long hair around my wrist and tilt her neck back. To drag my tongue up her throat, tasting her scent, right before I turned her around and pulled her shorts down.

To check her wetness and make sure she was ready for my dick.

But aside from her perfection and adorable personality, there was something about this woman that gave me a raging hard-on.

That made me want to bend her over in a bar full of patrons.

That made me want her screams to fill my ears.

That made me think that having her once, like all the other women I'd been with, wouldn't be enough.

"Jovana," I said when she neared, setting the edge of the tray on the corner of our table. "Now that's a beautiful name."

"It's my mother's maiden name. She deserves the compliment, not me." She winked, then placed double vodkas in front of Holden and Easton. When there was one left, she held the glass for several moments, smiling, before she gave it to me.

"I thought you were going to take a sip," I said to her.

"And what if I did? Would it upset you if my lipstick stained your glass?"

I pushed my torso into the table, closing more of the distance between us.

She didn't back up.

She didn't cower either.

I wondered how she'd react if I told her the tip of my cock was where I'd rather have her pink, glossy lips.

Instead of testing that statement, I said instead, "You can put your lips on anything of mine, including my Coke, which you forgot to bring."

Her eyes narrowed as she turned her head to the side, giving me a profile view. I could still see her brain going into full-force thinking mode. "I forgot nothing." Her hand dropped to her waist, where she dug into her apron and pulled out a Coke, which she set in front of me. "Bottles are much better than cans."

I untwisted the top, hearing the fizz. "I'm surprised you had one. Most bars only have cans."

"You're right, that's all we have."

"Where'd you get this, then?"

"I gave you the one I brought from home that I planned to drink later."

She was already fawning over me like I'd given her an orgasm.

Very interesting.

She smiled. "What's your name?"

"Grayson Tanner."

The name she'd be shouting in a few hours when she got off her shift.

I held out my hand, questioning whether I'd made a mistake by giving her the truth when a lie would be less risky.

When she reached forward to clasp my fingers, the only look I saw staring back was of interest. If she was connecting the dots, she was doing a hell of a job at hiding it. But the moment we touched fingers, that look changed.

It deepened.

It grew to the point where the warmth on her skin began to turn hot.

And when her chest rose to take a breath, it didn't lower. It stayed high, like she was holding in all the air.

"Nice to meet you, Jovana."

She finally released my hand and inhaled once more before she said, "And you."

With my other hand, I held the Coke toward her. "Yours. If you want a sip, that is."

She sighed, the exhale like a song. "It's all yours now."

"How about a sip of the vodka?"

"If I wasn't working, I'd take you up on that offer."

"Then take the night off and join us."

As she breathed out this time, she made no noise. There was just the rise and fall of her chest and a wide, honest smile. "You make that sound so easy."

"Isn't it?" I licked across my bottom lip. "What if tonight turned into one of the best evenings of your life and you missed the opportunity because you wouldn't clock out."

She nodded, and I couldn't tell if she was in agreement or just following the beat pounding through the bar's speakers. "Grayson . . . you're fun."

"And you're gorgeous." I pointed at the space between Holden and me, a place that didn't currently have a chair, but I could easily fix that. "Join us."

She tucked the tray under her arm and put her other hand on her hip. "Here's a little tidbit about me—and it'll either make you rescind your question or want my number even more—but I fulfill my obligations. I don't drown myself in regret. If it's meant to be, you'll be here at the end of my shift. And if you are, maybe I'll join you and have a drink." She shrugged. "Or maybe I won't." She glanced over her shoulder before reconnecting our stare. "In the meantime, I have six other tables that need me. Let me know when you're ready for a refill."

And just like that, she was gone.

"Damn. I like her," Holden said. "She's a little fireball."

She was certainly that.

Confident as well. A woman who didn't cave, like most of the others I fished. She was making me work for it.

I liked that.

It made me want her more.

"I hope she's just as fiery in bed," I told him.

"You need someone like her to keep your grumpy ass in check," Easton replied.

"I don't need anyone. But do I want her? Fuck yes." I raised my glass into the air. "To getting shit-faced tonight."

The guys repeated my toast, one I'd voiced just to change the subject, and we clinked glasses.

As I took my first sip, I knew what I'd just told them was a lie.

There was zero chance I'd be getting drunk this evening. Not if I was going home with Jovana. And after that little episode she'd just pulled, I was going to do everything in my power to make that happen.

When it did, I wanted to remember every single detail.

What that spicy mouth tasted like when it parted for me.

What she sounded like when she came.

That was why, even though I requested a second and third drink, I nursed them. And in between rounds, I munched on fries and then nachos, making sure I had plenty in my stomach to soak up the booze. An added bonus was that each time I placed an order, Jovana had to return to our table.

An excuse to flirt with her again.

To see that breathtaking smile cross her lips.

To watch the way my words affected the flushness of her skin.

I was positive she felt my stare as she bopped around the bar.

I didn't hide it. There was no need to.

She had to be a fool not to know I wanted her.

So, when the end of the night rolled in, the guys tired and heading home, I saw Jovana walk toward the hallway of restrooms and I knew it was time to make my move.

I didn't want her to think I was following her.

Shit, I wasn't desperate.

I just needed a few minutes alone with her before she returned to her tables to make sure she bit the bait.

I waited, giving her enough headway to finish, and then I entered the hallway, timing it just right that she was coming out of the women's room as I was going toward the men's.

"I want to think this is a coincidence, but something tells me it's not." When she stopped, she blocked me from going any farther.

But that was with her body; her face told an entirely different story.

Her expression intriguing.

Her eyes enticing.

Her lips taunting.

This woman had powers like I'd never seen before.

"Everyone goes to the bathroom, Jovana. Even me."

"Mm-hmm." She crossed her arms just below her chest, the position making her tits look larger than they were. "But you've had all night to go pee and you just so happened to choose the same time as me." She nipped her lip. "Looks a little suspicious, Mr. Tanner."

Fuck, that sounded hot coming out of that gorgeous mouth.

What she didn't know was that I was an expert arguer.

No one won against me . . . unless I let them.

And Jovana, regardless of how fiery she was, wasn't getting a pass.

I slid my hands into my pockets, so I wouldn't be tempted to touch her. "Most people stop at the restroom before they're about to leave. Makes the walk home easier."

"But you haven't paid your bill."

"You haven't brought it."

Her arms dropped, and she began to play with the ends of her hair, fanning the strands across her fingers. "Hold on a second, let me see if I have this straight. You not only followed me in here, but you plan to skip out on your bill too?"

She was fierce, there was no question about that, but she was even sassier than I'd thought.

"Jovana, you don't have any of it straight."

"No?"

I shook my head. "No."

"Okay . . ." She smiled. "We'll have to agree to disagree, then." She took a step past me, our shoulders barely grazing, but they touched just enough that I felt something. Something that made my heart pound even harder. She turned around after a few paces and said, "By the way, I'm about to clock out."

"Are you saying yes to that drink?"

"Are you buying?"

Now that I was facing her, I stepped closer.

I needed to be nearer.

I needed to fill my nose with her scent.

Once I did, I was surprised at how much I liked it.

For someone whose comebacks bit like a habanero, her aroma was soft.

Lavender and vanilla.

I wanted to rub my nose across her neck and really take it in.

"Hold on a second, let me see if I have this straight." As I used her words, I rubbed my palm across the side of my beard, my eyes leaving hers to take a dip down her body. "You're accusing me of following you and skipping out on my bill. And you have the nerve to ask me to buy you a drink?"

Her lips puffed out like a duck. "Sounds about right."

"What if I had a better idea . . ."

As a woman came out of the restroom, Jovana moved out of her direct path by sliding over to the wall of the hallway. I followed, resting my shoulder against a spot about a foot from where Jovana was, positioning my body identically to hers.

The new placement gave us more privacy and less distance between us.

A win in my book.

"Tell me your idea, Grayson." When she said my name, she sounded breathless.

"Well, first, where do you live?"

She huffed out a burst of air. "That's forward, isn't it?"

My cock was fucking aching to be inside her.

I didn't have patience for this forward bullshit.

"I live two blocks from here," I told her. "Are you closer or farther than me?"

She tucked a chunk of hair behind her ear, showing light-pink nails and gold rings on two of her fingers. "I'm about a fifteen-minute train ride and then five blocks from the train station."

"That won't do."

She searched my eyes. "I'm confused."

"Don't be, Jovana. It's simple. Why have a drink here when I have plenty of liquor at my place? Your place was an option until I heard how far it was. Fifteen minutes and a walk—nah, that won't do." My brows raised as a thought began to nag at me. "Unless you're going to tell me you have other plans for when you get off work . . ."

"And if I do?"

A grin wanted to come through, but I wouldn't let it. "I won't believe you."

Although she checked her watch, I was positive she knew the time. She'd just said she was about to clock out, so she had a general idea, at

13

least. I assumed she just needed a break from my stare. "I was going to go home." She glanced up at me and took a breath. "You know, eat. Catch up on some things that I couldn't get done because I had to work tonight."

"There's an excellent pizzeria on the corner, one block away. I'll grab you a slice."

"How do you know I even like pizza?"

She was turning into quite the challenge.

Most of the women I'd been with didn't take this much finessing.

"Here's something you should know about me, Jovana. I don't compromise. Ever."

"But you're willing to stop and get me something to eat." As those words left her mouth, I refused to comment. "Interesting." She adjusted her stance, putting all her weight on her shoulder, and when she crossed her arms this time, she covered her chest. "And what are we going to do at your place?" Her mouth stayed unmoved, but her eyes were smiling.

Since my hands were no longer in my pockets, I reached forward, clasping the stray hairs that were teasing the corner of her lip, and slid them out of the way. When I did, I grazed her cheek.

That touch, that brief passing of skin, shocked me for two reasons.

The first was that she leaned into my hand, like she wanted it to stay.

And the second was how her skin felt. Not that I expected it to snap me. But I didn't expect it to welcome me with softness and warmth to the point where I wanted to touch more.

I fucking needed to touch more.

And I saw no reason to hide that from her.

"The moment you walk through my door, I'm going to lift you into my arms and sit you on the island in my kitchen, where I'm going to strip off this tank top." My hand lowered to her shoulder, bunching the cotton strap between my fingers. "Once that hits the floor, I'm going to remove your bra, and then your shorts, pulling them down your beautiful legs." I leaned back, so I could get a better view. "That'll leave you in just panties . . . unless you don't have any on?"

"I do."

Two words that weren't aimed to push me away.

They did the opposite.

They goaded me.

"While you're sitting, I won't be able to see your ass, and that's something I've been admiring all night and dying to touch. So, after I spread your legs over the counter and lick you, I'm going to lift you into my arms again, and while I carry you to my bedroom, I'm going to feel your ass the whole time."

Her body was lit.

I could see it.

Hell, I could smell it.

"Why?" She licked her bottom lip, paused, and swiped her tongue across it a second time, following the same route. "Why do you want me?"

"From the moment I saw you across the bar, before you even came to our table, I couldn't stop thinking about how you would taste. And then the moment your lips parted, all I could think about was sliding my tongue between them."

"No date. No small talk. No wine, even." Her arms dropped. "Just my body."

"I'll give you wine, if that's what you want."

"Is that another compromise?" She smiled.

I needed to get her back on track. "For the record, I don't beat around the bush, Jovana. I stomp right through it."

"It's a good thing I like that about you."

But she still wasn't convinced; I could see that in her expression.

My hand lifted to her cheek, and I took a step closer, our bodies aligned with just an inch of air between us. I pointed her face up at me, her scent even stronger now. "I want to kiss you."

"Are you asking for permission?"

"I'm warning you."

"Over a kiss?" She gazed at my mouth before locking our stares.

I rubbed my thumb over the corner of her lip. "If I just wanted to kiss you here, I wouldn't give you the warning. I'd lean forward and ravish you." My mouth now hovered above hers. "But these aren't the only lips I want to kiss, Jovana."

"Mister, you are wicked."

"And you're going to love that about me."

"Maybe I already do."

There was something else she was going to love, and that was how well I kissed—both sets of lips.

So I showed her, slamming our mouths together, holding her face to mine. As my tongue slid in, I inhaled the taste I'd been fantasizing about. The lavender hadn't made its way to her breath. What was on her tongue instead was a sweetness, like she'd been sucking on a cherry candy.

It made my fucking mouth water.

I wanted more.

So much so that I had to pull myself away, panting as I continued to hold her, staring at a face that was red because of me.

"Say yes."

She exhaled. "To what?"

"Everything."

When she smiled, her tongue folded over her bottom lip. "But you still haven't paid your bill."

I reached into my pocket, grabbed my wallet, and thumbed through the slots until I found my black Amex. "Sign my name on the receipt and give yourself a two-hundred-dollar tip." I pointed toward the exit. "I'll be outside. Waiting."

"Two hundred?" She laughed. "That's what you think I'm worth?"

My palm slid down her back, holding her against me, knowing she could feel my hard-on. "And I'm getting you pizza and I'm giving you wine."

"You haven't even been with me yet and I've already changed you." She winked. "What if I told you I was no longer hungry? Or thirsty?"

There was that mouth again.

The one I was finding myself unbelievably addicted to.

My hand lowered once more until it was around her ass cheek, the thickness, the shape, the feel—shit, this woman was going to be one hell of a good time tonight. "Hurry," I growled, squeezing harder, nodding toward the bar. "Go."

After she pecked my lips, she darted off to the bar, where I assumed she was going to close out my tab and charge my card. I went out the front entrance and moved off to the side, resting my back against the brick of the building. That was when I took out my phone and checked the notifications that had come in since I'd last looked.

Easton: Who owes who doughnuts in the morning?

Holden: Grayson hasn't responded. I'm assuming that means you won, dickhead.

Easton: I told you he wasn't leaving the bar unless he was with Jovana.

Holden: Yeah, yeah. Is a dozen enough or does your greedy ass want more?

Easton: More. Always more.

Holden: I might be late. I have a parent teacher conference at 9, but I'll be in after.

Easton: Sounds like you better place an order for pickup. We don't want them to sell out before you get there.

Me: Why are you talking about me like I'm not in the group text?

Holden: He responded! So???

Me: I can't believe you bet on me.

Me: Holden, don't you know by now that when I want something, it's a sure thing? For the mere fact that you bet against me, I think you should bring in enough doughnuts for our whole staff.

Easton: Hell yeah, that's my boy. Tell him.

Holden: I probably deserve that.

Easton: You do.

Me: I'll see you in the morning, gentlemen . . .

"Your card," Jovana said, causing me to look up from the screen of my phone. "And receipt." She placed both in my hand and I shoved them into my pocket, along with my cell, then wrapped an arm across her shoulders.

"I want to know something," she said as we began to walk toward my building.

I hoped this wasn't the start of small talk, something she'd mentioned that I hadn't given to her.

I couldn't stand a conversation that didn't have a point.

In fact, as far as I was concerned, Jovana and I didn't even have to talk.

Grunting, moaning, breathing—those were more than enough for tonight.

"All right . . ."

"Have you ever hooked up with anyone from the bar?"

That question, I could handle.

"Never. Why?"

"One of the other servers saw us in the hallway outside the bathroom and she mentioned you and your friends are regulars. But when she said it, she had a peculiar look on her face. Now, maybe I'm reading into things. Or maybe I'm not. I just thought it was important to ask and make sure I'm not stepping on anyone else's territory."

I laughed.

Hard.

"Territory?" I inquired.

Plenty of servers had eyed me down in that bar. None had enticed me enough to take her home.

And not a single one had anything on Jovana.

"Yeah, you know, like someone who may get jealous if they happen to find out we hooked up."

I pulled her closer to my side, my nose pressing against the top of her head, inhaling her lavender-scented hair. "First off, I don't kiss and tell, so no one is going to find out from me." The only exception to that rule was that I told my boys almost everything. But they were a vault and once information went into their ears, it didn't come out their mouths. "Second, I've never touched any employee at that bar."

She glanced up, a clever smile spreading across her mouth. "Aside from me."

"Aside from you." I wondered how far and deep that conversation with the server had gone. I didn't know if any of the employees were aware of who my friends and I were, but I certainly didn't want this evening to turn into a live stream on Instagram. "Was that all she said?"

"Yes . . . why?"

"No reason." Her expression validated her answer, and when I looked straight ahead, I pointed across the street at the high-rise on the upcoming block. "There's home."

"You weren't kidding, you do live close."

"And very soon you're going to realize why I didn't want to wait the fifteen minutes to have you."

Hell, it was more than soon.

Because once we went into the elevator of my building, which would take us to the penthouse, I guided her to the back wall, pressing her body against it while I devoured her lips.

My hands rose high above her head, my arms extended, creating a cage.

One I wanted to keep her in.

But one that, if she wanted to escape, she could.

Except that was the furthest thing from her mind, because she was moaning into my mouth and tracing my chest, learning the curves of my pecs, the ridges of my abs, feeling over my shirt the trail of hair that led to my cock.

I tasted her exhales, swallowing each one, experiencing the heat lift through her body until a chime echoed inside the elevator, letting me know we'd arrived, and I rushed her into my condo.

I wasted no time lifting her onto my kitchen island, spreading her legs over the stone so I could stand between them.

The moment she was seated, she began to look around the space and whispered, "What a magnificent kitchen. I would die to cook in here." As her gaze returned to me, it was filled with hunger and desire. "How about I make us a fabulous breakfast in the morning?"

I nuzzled her neck, moaning. "How about we just focus on right now?"

She giggled, and when I looked at her again, her gaze was filled with hunger and desire. "You're a man of your word."

"And I'm just getting started."

I gripped the bottom of her tank and pulled it over her head, letting the fabric fall to the floor as I admired her bra.

Red.

Satin.

The same shade she'd turned when I kissed her at the bar.

I couldn't have picked a better color myself. It looked incredible on her.

I unclasped the back, the bra joining her tank on the floor, and I instantly got to work on her shorts, popping the button, lowering the zipper, and shimmying the heavy material down her thighs.

Her panties matched her bra.

And my hard-on fucking raged.

Her body was even better than I'd suspected. Toned. Tanned. Tits that were small, perky, a size no bigger than my palm with light-pink, pebbled nipples begging for my tongue. A tiny, narrow waist with hips that dipped toward her incredible ass.

Curves I wanted to kiss.

Skin I wanted to lick.

A body I wanted to get lost in.

"My God, Jovana, you're perfect. Spread your legs," I ordered.

Her eyes hadn't left mine since her first piece of clothing had come off. "They're wide—"

"Wider."

She slid them apart more, and I took a step back to admire the view.

Bare.

Tight.

A pussy that didn't just demand my tongue but deserved it.

"You're like heaven."

As if she were inside my head, hearing my thoughts, she bent her knees, rolling her toes around the edge of the counter to give me an even better angle to look at her.

"And Grayson, it's all yours."

I wanted it.

I wanted her wetness on my face.

I wanted her clit brushing my lips.

And, goddamn it, I couldn't wait another second.

I gripped the insides of her thighs and dipped my face in between her legs. But before I gave her my tongue, I pressed my nose to the top of her clit, closing my eyes as I breathed her in.

The scent of lavender had made its way down here.

But there was something else.

A sweetness.

And, fuck me, that was where the vanilla came in.

This woman didn't just look like a dream—she smelled like one too.

And now that I'd begun to lick, I knew she also tasted like one.

"Grayson!" She slipped her hand through my hair and pulled the strands. "Oh! Yes!"

I'd planned on stopping after a few licks.

This was just an appetizer, a way to satisfy my need, my craving to know how she smelled, to make sure she was extra wet and ready for me.

But now that I was here, I couldn't get enough.

I needed to hear her scream.

So I licked until I made that happen.

Her clit hardened, her wetness thickened, and I flicked my tongue as fast as I could against that sensitive spot, earning the sound I wanted to hear, and it was just as hot and seductive as I expected.

"Grayson, oh my God!"

I thought her scent was perfection.

Her body.

But watching Jovana come was a sight I couldn't even describe.

A sight more beautiful than words.

As the orgasm rattled her body, her stomach shuddered, her legs crowded my face, her nails stabbed the top of my head.

"*Yesss!*" She sucked in some air. "Fuck!"

I didn't pause.

I didn't even slow.

I licked until I was sure every wave had passed, and then I lifted her into my arms and carried her into my bedroom.

"What are you?" Her body was limp and bendable as I held it against mine. "Some kind of unicorn?"

I had plenty of faults.

By the morning, Jovana would know what those were.

"I'm just a man who loves to give pleasure."

"Can I tell you something?" Her mouth was close to my ear, her breath warm on my skin.

"Yes."

"You've met your match."

My brows rose. "And why would you say that?"

"Because we share that trait." She paused. "I'm a woman who gets off on giving pleasure."

My match.

How fucking ironic.

I set her on the end of the bed, freeing my hands to take off my shirt. Once I had a few buttons loose, I lifted the button-down over my head and dropped my jeans. As I walked to my nightstand, grabbing a condom from the drawer, I slipped off my boxer briefs and stood directly in front of her.

"Grayson . . . my God." She looked slowly down my body. "I knew you were jacked. I could feel the muscles through your clothes, but I had no idea you looked like that."

I chuckled.

"And I certainly didn't know that was the size I'd be getting tonight."

I pumped my cock several times while her gaze was still on it. "Do you want it?"

Her stare lifted, finally locking with mine. "Yes."

"Show me how badly."

As I used my teeth to tear off the corner of the foil packet, she surrounded the bottom half of my shaft with her hand and parted her lips over my crown.

"Fuuuck," I hissed.

She could suck.

Harder and faster than I anticipated.

And she really did like to give pleasure, she wasn't lying.

But if she kept this up, I was going to be coming in her mouth, and even though that sounded good as hell, it wasn't what I wanted for this evening.

I let her have a few more bobs, watching her cheeks cave in as she took me deeper, her tongue swirling around my tip and down each side, using her hand to cover the parts her mouth didn't reach, before I pulled out. I aimed the rubber at my tip and rolled it over my length, making sure it was in place, and then I stretched her legs over my shoulders, lifted her ass off the mattress, and pointed my cock at her entrance.

"I'll go slow."

Once again, that was a warning I thought she needed, because even if she had plenty of experience, Jovana wasn't quite ready for me.

No woman was.

Her hand went to her clit, and she rubbed it as I entered. *"Daaamn."*

I didn't rush. I went gradually, listening to her sounds, watching her breathtakingly gorgeous face, looking for signs to make sure she wasn't in pain.

But I saw none.

What I saw instead was need.

Want.

Desire.

And that was exactly what I felt as I inched my way in, her tightness and wetness taking hold of me. "Goddamn it," I moaned, pausing when she had all of me. "You feel fucking amazing."

I gave her a few short pumps before I dropped her legs and climbed over her, my arms at either side of her face, my hips rearing back to take a full plunge.

Jovana leaned up on her elbows and connected our lips, kissing me as I increased my speed.

"Don't stop." She wrapped her arms around my neck, where her nails found my shoulders and dug in. "Faster. Please."

This wasn't stopping.

This was lifting her into the air while her legs straddled my waist and carrying her to the nearest wall, where I could finish what I'd started.

With her back pressed against the hard drywall, her hands held on to me. And as I resumed the relentless climb with only one goal in mind, her mouth released moan after moan.

"Grayson!"

That goal was to hear her scream even louder than she had in my kitchen.

I was almost there.

"You like that . . ."

Her head banged into the wall as I thrust deeper into her tightness. "Yes. I want more."

That was what I gave her—hard, relentless, agonizing strokes.

But while I watched her build and felt her narrow around me, there were sensations taking over my body. Alarms that were fucking ringing, enough so that I said, "You better come."

"I'm already there." By the time the last word left her mouth, her first yell was hitting my ears, her body contracting around my dick, and with that came a rush of wetness. *"Ohhh! Yesss!"* She filled her lungs and added, "Grayson!"

"Fuck!" I roared. The tingles shot through my balls and into my shaft, and with each dive, I could feel the condom filling more. "Yes!"

Our breaths mingled.

Our bodies were moving together.

Our shudders were rocking against one another.

And when the stillness took over, I set her on the mattress before I went into my en suite to trash the condom. When I returned to the bedroom, she was under the covers, propped high on a set of pillows.

Looking gorgeous as ever, but far too comfortable.

Before I climbed in next to her, I found my cell in the pocket of my jeans and brought it with me to bed, making sure the alarm was set for the morning.

"Jeez, that's early."

I looked at her, not realizing she was snooping on my screen. "I have a meeting I can't miss."

"I don't even know what you do for a living. Obviously something very profitable because your condo is kind of outrageous." She paused, smiling, assuming I was going to answer. When I didn't, she said, "So, does that mean no breakfast? I know a great little place, probably only a couple of blocks from here."

This was where things got sticky.

A meal would lead to her wanting another.

And another.

And feelings would be trickling in.

I couldn't have that.

But I also couldn't imagine never tasting her body again, never watching her beautiful face come.

That thought, that desire, took me completely by surprise.

Still, I chuckled and gave her the response that made me the most comfortable. "No. No breakfast."

That wasn't true. I'd be eating my weight in doughnuts once Holden arrived at work.

"How about dinner, then?"

She wasn't going to give up.

That meant I had to address the elephant in the room.

I set my phone on the nightstand and reclined in bed. "I don't do dinner either."

"You're telling me you don't eat?"

"Oh, I eat." I grazed her chin with the back of my hand. "I just ate you, didn't I?"

Her cheeks flushed, her grin not even close to fading. "That's not what I mean."

"I know what you mean, Jovana." I analyzed her expression, determining whether I had to tread lightly. I figured she'd appreciate my honesty over a bold-faced lie. "Let me tell you a little something about me." I folded my arms behind my head. "I work. I travel. I live my life exactly how I want. But I don't date."

She searched my eyes. "I don't understand."

"This"—I traced the air between us—"will end in the morning. One night, that's it, nothing more."

The confusion was gone.

In its place was a look of shock.

And that was confirmed when she shook her head. "You're serious?"

"I wouldn't bullshit you."

"Why?" She sat up tall, anger and disgust now building in her eyes. "Is it because I slept with you? Because I didn't make you take me out for dinner—"

"Let me stop you right there. It's nothing you've done. This is a me thing, not a you thing."

And that was because I didn't trust women.

I hadn't since I was ten years old.

Not after what the only woman in my life—who mattered at that age—had done to me.

I should have been her whole world, but I meant nothing to her.

She completely destroyed me.

That was why this—a few hours, an overnight tops—was enough.

"Jovana, you're perfect. I don't want you to take this personal."

"You just ate me out on your kitchen counter and fucked me and you don't want me to take this personal?" She sat up off the pillows and folded her legs in front of her. In that brief amount of time, I saw a change. A reset. "Maybe . . ." Her voice trailed off as she stared at me, her expression telling me she was deep in thought. "Maybe that's the way you've done things in the past, never willing to compromise on anything, so it's just been easy for you to move on. But I'm different." She put her hand on top of mine. "I'm not like the others. Something tells me you know that." Her warmth stayed until she moved her fingers to my chest, touching the center. It was a light graze, like a whisper in the wind, that I would have missed unless I was paying attention. "You feel it. I know you do."

So many had tried to fix me.

To turn me into someone I wasn't.

They'd all failed.

She'd fail too.

"That doesn't change what I'm capable of—or in this case, what I'm not capable of." She wanted a tomorrow, and I could only give her a right now. "I am who I am."

"Which is?"

I took a breath, curious if this warning was going to earn me a slap across the face or if she was going to fight me with her words. "A man who doesn't believe in commitment. Marriage. Or any of that shit."

27

"What you are is an asshole."

"But we had fun." I'd rather she hate me than cry. Her tears were something I couldn't deal with. "And there's no reason for that fun to be over. I have"—I glanced at my phone, touching the screen to check the time—"six more hours until I have to get up for work."

I would like nothing more than to devour her again.

To sink myself into her beauty and get the chance to savor her once more.

Something about her was so incredibly addictive.

She laughed. "Oh yeah, a straight-up fucking asshole. If you think I'd come anywhere near you after what you just said to me, then you must be nuts."

"We had a great time—at least I thought we did. I don't remember promising you anything but that and an orgasm. And I gave you both. I'm sorry if you felt this was going to turn into more."

She shook her head, staring at me like I was unrecognizable, before she got up from the bed and disappeared down the hallway. She returned fully dressed less than a minute later. Standing in the doorway, she raised her hand, showcasing her middle finger. "See you around, Grayson."

"You will. I'm at your bar at least once a week."

She sighed. "Just my luck."

"I'll call you a rideshare—"

"Don't bother."

Before I could say another word, she was gone, and I heard the click of my front door.

Using the tablet on my nightstand, I called down to the doorman and told him to make sure my guest got into a rideshare and to text me once she was safely inside one.

Just because I didn't do second dates didn't mean I was totally fucking heartless.

Parched, I got up from bed, but before I went into the kitchen to grab a drink, I picked up my pants from the floor, grabbing my credit card and the receipt that I'd shoved into my pocket when she'd handed them to me.

For some reason, I unfolded the small piece of paper, my attention falling to the bottom, where she'd signed my name and written the total.

Her signature wasn't even close to mine, but that wasn't what surprised me.

It was that instead of the $200 tip that I'd instructed her to leave, she'd written zero, giving herself absolutely nothing.

"Jovana," I said out loud, glancing toward my bedroom door even though she wasn't there, "you're right. You're nothing like the others."

CHAPTER ONE

Grayson

There was nothing like the deep blue waters of Saint-Tropez. That was why I'd chosen to come here when I started planning my celebration for the international launch of Hooked. A launch that had consumed our team of coders for months, all led by Drake from the moment we'd hired her as our director of app development and engineering. The roll-out that had just taken place a month ago. The result was an explosion in memberships, an overwhelming amount of press, and an income that had fucking skyrocketed.

Things weren't even close to settled at the office. Shit, there were still flames that needed to be tended to on a minute-by-minute basis. But after four weeks of living at my desk, working twenty-hour days, I had declared it time to party.

Holden had taken his daughter, Belle, to Disney. Easton and Drake were tucked into their love nest.

I wanted to be on the water.

So I rented a hundred-and-fifty-foot yacht and invited nine guests to join me for a weeklong cruise.

Of course, six of those guests were women.

We were only two days into the trip, and I was already having the time of my life.

And what made my smile grow even wider was that whenever I took a break from the fun and logged into Hooked's database to check how many new members had come in, the number had doubled from the last time I'd looked.

But according to the number I was staring at now, it had tripled.

Fuck yes.

"How about a refill?"

I glanced up from the screen of my phone. The butler was at my side with a freshly poured scotch on his tray.

I shot back the remaining sip in my tumbler and handed him the empty. "I'd love one. Thank you."

We exchanged glasses and I gazed out onto the Mediterranean, my phone now in my pocket, but the two million users who had come in over the last twelve hours were stamped on my mind.

This was power.

This was a level of success I hadn't anticipated when my friends and I had sat around the living room of our tiny apartment near Harvard, dreaming of the future of our app.

But now that we were already the largest dating app in the country and about to take over that worldwide spot, there was no going back. The top position was what I wanted and the only goal we hadn't yet reached. As chief marketing officer, I was going to make sure it happened.

That nothing stopped us.

That nothing got in our way.

Like a woman trying to slide into my life and slow me down, or another company attempting to steal our market share.

There wasn't anyone more single than me.

And as for the competition, we were currently in litigation with an ex-employee and Faceframe, the social media giant he had left us to work for. We were suing them for stealing our proprietary software and launching a similar type of app. But The Dalton Group, the set of lawyers representing us, assured us that we had the case in the bag.

Just two more reasons to celebrate.

And the yacht was an excellent place to do it.

The only thing that could make this vacation better was if my best friends had joined me.

But my other buddies who had come along were doing a fine job at making sure our time on this boat was well spent. They were in the hot tub now, waiting for me to join them, but I was just going to sit here off the port side, relishing in this view for a little while longer.

Not the sea, although it was certainly serene.

I was looking at them.

The six beauties tanning in lounge chairs only feet from mine. With their asses pointed high in the air, their skin oiled and glowing from the sun, a rainbow of string bikinis barely covering them.

Jesus fucking Christ.

France's scenery was something special, but it didn't compare to this view. A redhead, two blondes, and three brunettes, ranging from toned to curvy, tall to petite, gorgeous to stunning.

I was one happy man.

But as I attempted to make myself more comfortable, crossing my legs over the small table in front of me and sipping my scotch, digging for the cigar in one of the pockets of my swim trunks, something fucked up happened.

One of the brunettes glanced up and our eyes locked.

Within a blink, her face changed.

Her eyes now a bright blue.

Her nose small and sloped.

Her lips plump and pouty.

I knew that face.

It was one I couldn't forget.

One that, the last time I'd seen it, had accompanied her holding up her middle finger before she walked out of my doorway.

Jovana.

My legs dropped from the table, my hand gripping the glass so hard I thought it was going to break.

What the fuck?

What is she doing here?

Her gaze pierced mine.

Her nose scrunched, her lips pursed, like she'd whiffed something rotten, the same expression she'd worn before she fled my condo.

You can't be here.

I didn't invite you.

I don't even know how to get in touch with you.

My eyes were just playing tricks on me.

They had to be.

The brunette's name was Rachel or Rebecca or Rhonda—something that started with an *R*.

I blinked.

Again.

And again.

And finally, Jovana's face was gone.

Relief flooded my chest and I shook my head, rubbing my eyes with the backs of my hands, making sure her face didn't return.

It didn't.

Thank God.

But for that brief second, I swore it was her, and that was all it took for my heart to start pounding and my cock to turn hard.

What the hell is wrong with me?

Why am I acting like a fucking schoolboy? With jitters in my chest and a hard-on in my trunks?

I didn't want Jovana here.

I didn't give a shit about what she was doing or how she felt or the level of hate she had toward me.

I hadn't even seen her since the night she'd left my condo two months ago—the rollout had kept us so busy, the guys and I didn't have a chance to pop by the bar.

So I didn't understand why my brain was conjuring up images or why my body was reacting so strongly.

She was an ex-fish.

I'd moved on to bigger and better catches.

In fact, there was an entire school of fish on this yacht.

And I was loving it.

I was loving life.

But even though I no longer saw her face, the feeling hadn't left my body. There was this nagging ache inside me that made absolutely no sense. That I couldn't push away even with a hard swallow or by tapping my fist against my chest.

Or even by looking at the school of six.

Surely, alcohol could make it all disappear.

I downed what was left in my glass, the liquor just starting to burn my throat as I heard, "You all right, buddy?"

My friend Freddy stood by my chair, the dermatologist looking at me as if I were in one of his exam rooms. "Yeah . . . why?"

"You're a little flushed."

"Flushed?"

Damn it, I'd loved that color on Jovana.

Jovana?

Why am I still thinking about her?

"Nah, I'm not flushed," I told him. "I'm buzzed." I pointed at the sky. "And I'm hot as hell from all this sun."

He shook my shoulder before he took a seat beside me. "It's time to get some rays on that pasty New England skin of yours." He smiled. "But you do have sunscreen on, don't you?"

I laughed. "You can't help yourself, can you?"

"I'm about to go put some on the ladies. Looks like they've rubbed themselves in oil." He ran his hand over his thick, curly mop of hair before he tucked his arms under his head. "I wouldn't be a good doctor if I didn't cover them in better protection."

"Any excuse to touch them." I paused. "Am I right?"

I chuckled as he smiled.

The butler returned with another drink since, somehow, mine was already gone. I grabbed the new one off his tray and immediately brought it up to my lips.

"This is a marathon, remember."

I swallowed the sip and turned to my friend. "What, are you worried about me?"

"I was watching you from the hot tub and you looked like you needed to be checked on. Practically funneling booze, flushed skin—"

"I'm hot. That's all it is."

He nodded, the movement causing his aviators to fall, and he pushed them high on his nose. "I don't doubt that. But is there anything you want to talk about?"

Feelings. As if I had any.

But I didn't because emotions were bullshit.

Because they'd been sucked out of me at a young age and I'd never let them replenish.

"Things are good, my man." I positioned myself similarly to him, but with only one hand behind my head, the other surrounding my cocktail. "I'm here in paradise. Hooked is killing it. My dad's healthy. How could things get any better?"

He nodded toward the school of chicks. "I'm sure your answer to that question would be to bring those six women into a bedroom and see just how creative you can get when you have that many mouths and fingers and pussies at your disposal."

I moaned at the thought. "I like the way you think. But six is a lot, even for me."

"How about one?"

My brows raised as I nodded toward the women. "You mean one of them?"

"Sure. Or just one in general whom you spend more than one night with and, you know, you actually develop something with her."

"You have to be fucking shitting me."

He reached across the small space between us, flattening his hand on my chest as if to keep me in my seat. "Don't lose it on me. I know the mere mention of monogamy typically sends you on a shouty spiral—"

"Then why do you keep bringing it up?"

"Will you just hear me out?" When I didn't respond, his hand moved to my bicep. "Wouldn't it be nice to be able to go on double dates and vacation together as couples? Travel the world together—just the four of us, or six of us, where Easton and Drake could tag along too?"

Freddy had settled down a few months back. The motherfucker acted like he'd been married for ten years and could judge my single life when in reality this relationship—and any relationship—was new to him.

Since he'd gotten tied down, this was at least the second time he'd brought this up.

The first time, I'd ignored him.

But something was bubbling, and I was ready to fucking roar.

"Let me get this straight. You think it sounds good for the six of us to hop on Hooked's private jet and fly off to somewhere like Ibiza, where you can spoil your girlfriend in gifts and walk hand in hand in the sunset and declare every morning when she wakes up in your arms just how much you love her." I took a drink, still attempting to settle that unnerving feeling in my chest, but adding more booze to my bloodstream wasn't helping. "But from where I'm sitting, you look pretty content on a boat with six women who you're fucking salivating to touch." I adjusted my position so I could get a better look at him.

"I didn't say I was actually going to touch them."

I hissed out air, shaking my head. "But you want to, and you have a goddamn hard-on just thinking about it." I remembered the cigar I'd been searching for earlier and pulled it out of my pocket, the butler instantly appearing to light it. Once I had the tip lit, I asked Freddy, "Does your girlfriend know there are women on the boat? Or you happened to leave that bit out when you told her about the trip?" When he said nothing, I smiled. "Thought so."

"Do you know the argument that would ensue if she knew they were on this trip with us?"

"And that's one of the many reasons I'm not interested in the bull-shit." I blew out a mouthful of smoke. "Work is enough of a responsibility that consumes far too much of my time. I don't need a woman who's going to fight with me about everything and demand hours I don't have in my day and whine when she doesn't get her way."

He scratched the dark patch of hair across his chest. "Because we both know you don't understand the term *compromise*."

I understood the term, all right, and I'd made an exception—for Jovana.

I'd waited for her to get off work. I'd offered to feed her and give her wine. I'd even suggested a round two since I had time before I needed to leave for work.

She was the only woman I'd ever compromised for.

That memory, that admission, made my eyes narrow, and a lie growled its way out of my mouth. "You're right, asshole. I don't. Ever."

He laughed, his hands now in the air, like I was pointing a gun at him. "Just a suggestion, but it's semi-time to start thinking about what you want. A family. Kids. You're thirty now—you're not getting younger."

"You say that like I'm about to start collecting social security." I sat up. "You and your girl can live whatever kind of life that suits you—even if that means lying about who you're with. But don't you worry about me. I'm just going to keep on rolling with the way things are now. There's no reason to fuck with perfection." I stood from my chair, looking down at him. "You knew you weren't going to win that one."

"When have I ever won one with you?" He lowered his glasses, showing me green eyes that were aimed right at mine. "That doesn't mean I'm going to stop trying."

"You do you, buddy. I'm going to do me." I raised my glass high in the air and looked toward the hot tub where the other two guys were still soaking. Dudes who were as single as me. "Hey, motherfuckers!" I shouted in their direction. When I was sure I had their attention, their glasses lifted above their heads, waiting for my toast, I walked over to the school of women. I stood at the end of the long row of chairs and smiled at all of them. When my gaze reached the brunette whose name started with *R*, I waited for her face to change. For her nose to shrink, her brown eyes to turn blue, her lips to thicken.

But it didn't happen.

What did happen was the moment she grinned at me, there was a stab in my chest and a tightness that followed.

There was only one way to make that feeling go away.

I needed to get drunker.

"To fucking bachelorhood! Who needs marriage when you can have all of this!" I yelled across the top deck, and then lowered my glass to finish the rest of my scotch.

CHAPTER TWO

Jovana

"Girl, you're a lifesaver," Sloane, the bartender, said as I rushed behind the bar to clock in for my unscheduled shift. The moment I finished typing my code into the computer and turned toward her, she threw her arms around me, giving me a heavy whiff of her banana-scented lotion and weed—Sloane's signature scent. "I owe you everything and then some."

"Don't be silly. You know I'm always happy to come in whenever you need me."

Sloane was the reason I had this job in the first place. I'd known her since high school and throughout college. We'd even recently become roommates, which was the reason I'd said yes to this shift and all the others I'd been able to pick up over the last few months. I desperately needed the money for rent and bills, especially with my student loans on the verge of kicking in. When Sloane had gotten me this position, I was promised part-time hours. But because the other servers liked to call in sick all the time and do everything aside from coming to work, I had become their fill-in, basically earning me full-time status.

Once her arms dropped from my shoulders, I grabbed an apron from the bin and tied it around my waist. "Have I missed anything?"

"Oh, you know, the usual drama." She tore off the slip that had just come out of the printer that gave her a list of drinks she needed to make. "Two of the servers skipped out tonight, claiming they have the flu. Except I'm positive they're at the Jelly Roll concert."

I asked the same question every time I came in. Sloane, or the other bartender if my roommate wasn't in, would drown me in employee gossip.

Really, all I wanted to know was if Grayson was here.

In the two months since we'd slept together, he hadn't been in.

Not even once.

And part of me was relieved because I certainly didn't want to see that asshole, but part of me wanted to be in his presence because deep in my gut, I still felt something for him.

Based on Sloane's response, I assumed tonight was no different or it would have been the first thing she said.

I unscrewed my bottle of Coke, and as I heard the sound it made, I remembered the words Grayson had said that night about the soda.

I want to hear the fizz when I open it. None of that fountain shit that's stale as hell. I like my soda sweet and bubbly.

The words weren't identical—my mom wasn't as crude as Grayson— but she'd said something similar to my father the first time they'd met, and ironically, it had been over a bottle of Coke.

That also happened to be the same moment that my father knew he was going to marry her.

Whenever my mom described their meetup, she always talked about the way my father had made her feel. The way he had looked at her. The growing sensation she'd had in her stomach.

How she could barely breathe or respond.

I instinctively glanced at the table where Grayson had been sitting with his friends. Of course, he wasn't there now. All I had was the memory of him.

The way he'd looked at me when our eyes first connected.

The way my body had reacted, the swish of tingles that started at my feet and whipped across my legs and stomach and landed in my chest, where it simmered the rest of the night.

41

The way I'd been so consumed by his stare, it took me several seconds to even respond to him. To inhale and exhale without the tightness in my lungs.

The way my body needed to be satisfied by him, needed to be closer to him, needed to feel his hands on every part of me.

I didn't want to give him my number and wait for his call.

I didn't want to go home alone.

I wanted to do something I never did because my mind, my body, wouldn't allow anything different.

I sighed, attempting to push that memory and those feelings far, far away. "I wish I was at the Jelly Roll concert."

I wished I were anywhere except here, thinking about him.

She eyed me as she poured two different types of liquor into a mixer and began to squeeze in some fresh lime. "Don't even think about leaving me." Her hands moved so fast, all I could see was a blur of black nail polish and silver rings.

"I can't. I'm broke. Those tickets are far above what I can afford, which is absolutely nothing at the moment."

She patted my shoulder before picking up a martini glass. "All this hard work will pay off. I promise."

She reminded me of that at least once a week. But those words had nothing to do with my work here; it was the job I did at home—my passion—that seemed financially hopeless.

That passion was my dream of becoming the most well-known online influencer. I didn't just concentrate on fashion, fitness, or cosmetics. I was the go-to for women in their midtwenties who were looking for lifestyle inspiration. Like any other entertainer, I created a persona for my demographic. What I showed them, what products I pushed, what tidbits I revealed were all with the intention to strike curiosity. Most clicked that follow button because they wanted to live vicariously through me—they connected with me somehow, were fascinated with a life that was so different from their own. Perfecting this persona and nurturing her had been my focus for the last two years, and most recently, when I wasn't slinging drinks in the evening, I was making content, filming and digitally retouching my photos and videos.

As my numbers grew, so did the endorsements and brand deals, the kickbacks and commissions I received.

But my two hundred and fifty thousand followers weren't a large enough audience to pay my bills.

Not even close, in fact.

"Yeah, yeah," I groaned. My phone vibrated several times in my pocket, alerting me of incoming notifications. "And one day you're going to own this bar and I'm going to be able to pimp the hell out of you and make it the most popular spot in Boston."

She smiled, showing the diamond gem she'd bonded to her tooth this morning. "I'm so ready for that to happen." She wiped her hands on her apron, and as she took out her cell, she added, "Because it's exhausting to deal with . . ." Her voice trailed off, her eyes widening before she slowly glanced up at me. "*Ummm*, do me a favor. I know you just got the alert on your phone that I'm looking at right now, but I don't want you to see it. So don't check your phone, *'kaaay?*"

"Huh? Why?"

She put her cell away and grabbed the new paper that had just printed out, giving her the next order of drinks. "Because you just don't need to. So go greet your tables and find out what they want and do your thing for the rest of the night, but whatever you do, don't look at your phone."

"You're kidding, right?" As if I hadn't heard her, I slipped my phone out of my back pocket and held it at my side. "That's like telling me not to pee for a week."

She pointed at the hand that was gripping my cell. "Then look at your phone all you want—just skip over the Celebrity Alert that was just sent."

I couldn't imagine why she was saying this to me. How a Celebrity Alert would matter, considering I wasn't one myself and I didn't know any personally, at least not outside the influencer space.

But all her warning did was make me more interested, so I lifted my phone to my face, immediately hearing, "Don't do it, Jovana," as my eyes scanned the first notification on my screen.

Which just so happened to be the Celebrity Alert.

Groaning, "Fuck me," as I processed the words.

BREAKING NEWS: Boston's Biggest Bachelor Hooked SIX.

My hands shook as I tapped the notification, and then an article appeared with Grayson Tanner on a Megayacht with Six Unidentified Women as the headline.

I gazed up at my friend, my face turning as fiery as the blood swishing through my veins.

"What did I tell you?" She rimmed a glass with salt. "Put your phone away and skip the article. Seriously. It'll do you no good to read it."

I stepped back until I felt the edge of the bar and gave it most of my weight. "I need to be reminded of how much I despise him."

"You don't need an article to do that. I'm pretty sure you can just replay the last few minutes you guys were together and that's all the reminding you need."

The moment I'd gotten home from Grayson's place, I'd rushed to the fridge and grabbed the only booze I had—a bottle of champagne I'd been saving for when I reached three hundred thousand followers. I carried it to the couch, popped the cork, and that was where Sloane found me, hours later, taking the final sip. Within minutes of her arrival, I was purging every detail of my evening with Grayson. Given that he was a regular, she knew who I was talking about, and once I finished telling her everything that had gone down, she explained exactly who he was.

I hadn't slept with a man who worked a typical nine-to-five and was looking for a woman to spend the rest of his life with.

I'd chosen a man who was one of the founders of the largest hook-up app in the country and was allergic to dating. And who, according to

Google, had invented the app with his best friends because they were tired of putting so much time and effort into women.

As the days passed, I spent more time reading about him, locating articles that had appeared in different news outlets, interviews he'd done, reports that showed the growth and success of his business.

Instagram had been the most telling.

The forever playboy had quite an interesting life. He dined at Boston's top-rated restaurants, had box seats at every sporting event, was backstage and front row at concerts, was always shaking hands with celebrities, and traveled the world.

What I didn't see in a single photo was a woman.

Because he didn't care about them.

And that confirmed everything he'd told me had been correct.

A man who didn't believe in commitment. Marriage. Or any of that shit.

When it came to females, Grayson cared about only one thing.

Sex.

But looking back, aside from the way things had ended, the beginning and middle felt like so much more than a one-night stand.

They felt like the start of something epic.

Like the foundation of my parents' relationship.

Except, somehow, I'd read the situation all wrong.

I was too romantic.

That was why I needed to see the article. I needed to face that Grayson wasn't the guy I'd made him out to be. That what I'd thought we had wasn't real.

I released the air that I'd been holding in my lungs. "I have to read it, Sloane."

Besides, I was aware he was on a yacht. I'd seen the picture he posted of the giant ship. I just didn't know he was with other women.

Or six, for that matter.

God, I hated myself for stalking his Instagram profile, but I checked it every night before I went to sleep. I couldn't help myself, nor could

I stop myself. I didn't know if I found his life entertaining or if I was just obsessed with where he was and what he was doing and that he wasn't with me.

"It's going to sting."

"More than it already does?" I shook my head. "Impossible."

"Don't say I didn't warn you."

I hadn't listened to her first warning. I certainly wasn't going to listen to this one either.

I attempted to take a long, deep breath, and I began to skim the Celebrity Alert.

> Grayson Tanner, 30, cofounder of Hooked and inventor of the marriage division of the app, has been seen cruising the Mediterranean Sea aboard a 150-foot yacht, owned by Royston Wild, 36, founder of the largest restaurant group in New England. A well-deserved celebration for the cofounder as his app just launched internationally, instantly earning him the top slot of the most downloaded and used dating app in the world.
>
> One would assume Royston would be enjoying the waters of Saint-Tropez with his good friend, Grayson, especially given that it's Royston's yacht. However, that doesn't seem to be the case. The only people in attendance look to be Grayson and the women he's Hooked.
>
> Six, to be exact.
>
> Some like to celebrate in style. Some like to celebrate in large numbers.

Grayson appears to like both.

Our only question is: Why didn't you go for a whole dozen?

To use his own words, looks like bachelorhood is paying off . . .

. . . in many, many ways.

Have fun for us, Grayson.

Above the article was a series of photos, and I flipped through them, showing Grayson aboard the yacht in slightly different poses, wearing only a pair of swim trunks, his ripped abs on full display. The six women were in string bikinis, lying on lounge chairs, and ogling him.

I felt like I was going to be sick.

I didn't know why, because I'd definitely seen enough, but I clicked on the video below the article and the feed instantly showed a zoomed-in image of Grayson, holding a drink in the air, a cigar in his other hand, and a smile covering his face. That grin grew even larger when he shouted, "To bachelorhood. Who needs marriage when you can have all of this." The video lasted a few seconds past his toast, where he was walking toward the group of women before it cut off.

The second it stopped playing, I shoved my phone back into my pocket.

"Drink this," Sloane said, handing me a shot glass that overflowed with a clear liquid. When I hesitated, she searched the floor for our manager and said, "Don't worry, you're in the clear. He's in his office."

I brought the drink up to my lips and quickly swallowed, wiping my mouth as the liquor scorched the back of my throat. "Ugh, that was awful."

She held the bottle of vodka toward me. "Does that mean you don't want another?"

"What I meant was that the article and the pictures and the damn video were awful, and now they're burned into my head." I took the bottle from her and poured myself a refill, shooting that back before placing the glass in the sink. "Why did I read our situation all wrong and make the worst mistake ever?"

"It wasn't the worst mistake *ever*."

My brows rose. "How can you say that? I slept with a man who goes on vacation with six women because one isn't enough. I was dumb enough to actually think he was interested in me. But no, he told me instead that he'd never date me and things wouldn't extend beyond our one night together." I rolled my eyes. "Who does that?"

But he'd also told me he didn't compromise, yet he had.

That was something I couldn't make sense of.

Or why he would take me to his home—a place that had to mean a lot to him, where he wouldn't just want some random woman to know the address and location of—rather than just fuck me in the restroom or in the alley outside the bar.

Or why he looked at me with so much emotion behind his stare.

Grayson didn't gaze at me like I was something he wanted. He gazed at me like I was something he couldn't live without.

There was a difference.

And I felt it.

"Here's the thing about you that I love the most," Sloane said. "You have the biggest heart, and you trust so easily. But what that also means is that when it comes to men, even though it's only happened a few times in the past, you tend to fall fast and hard." After drying her hands, she tossed the rag over her shoulder, where it stayed and rested across her spaghetti strap. "So, when it came to Grayson—who we now know is a giant asshole, but how were you supposed to know that at the time?—you were just following that big heart of yours and seeing where it led you. You didn't know he was going to treat you that way, nor did you have any idea who he was." She paused. "Me on the other hand, I know, so I'd have no excuse"—she held up her hand before I could say a word—"not that he would ever try anything with me. He hasn't. I'm just saying I know his reputation, so I would know what to expect going in. You didn't and that's not your fault. Maybe if you'd gotten a warning or if I'd been working that night, things would have gone down differently."

I remembered the conversation I'd had with the other server that night when she saw Grayson and me kissing in the hallway outside the restroom. I'd thought she was questioning me about it because he'd dated someone at the bar and I was stepping on someone else's territory. What she was really doing was waving a handful of red flags in my face.

Why didn't I pick up on her cues?

Why didn't I ask her any questions?

Why did I, like an absolute fool, go to his condo and have the best sex of my entire life?

The answers were simple.

I was picking up on every sign he gave me and following my big heart to see where it led me.

But I was sure, even months later, as I continued to piece together everything he'd said and the way he'd made me feel, that I hadn't read things wrong.

It wasn't me.

It was him.

He was an asshole. One who didn't have the courage to explore what could happen between us.

Instead of letting me in, he pushed me out and slammed the door in my face.

Sloane was right—I fell fast and I fell hard when it came to men.

And I'd never seen a man more beautiful and charming than Grayson Tanner.

With the largest, most gorgeous alluring green eyes and hair the color of a dark roast blend, a beard that was thick and edged and just the right length. He towered over me in height, making me feel tiny and wanted, and he had muscles so big that I could see them through his clothes.

Muscles that could easily lift me into the air, that could protect me, that could dominate me in every way.

That had.

Oh God.

And then there was his smile.

White, straight enough teeth, with lips that were thick and powerful, like his hands.

Strong enough that when he kissed me, I felt it across my entire body.

With a mouth so talented, I wanted to marry him.

But that same mouth had told me, with zero regret, that I wasn't for him.

That we would never amount to anything.

"Sloane," I whispered. "For every single reason, I wish he was a nice guy."

She stopped making whatever drink she was working on and came over to me. "You'll find yourself one. I know you will. You're young, you're living in one of the most fab cities, and you're surrounded by hot, single men on the daily. Don't worry, it's going to happen. In the meantime, let's pretend Grayson doesn't exist. And let's not give him an inch of real estate in our brains, cool?"

Just as I was about to respond, my phone vibrated.

This wasn't a Celebrity Alert. Those were silenced. This had to be either a text or email or social media notification.

I pulled out my phone and what was on the screen made the bile in my stomach rise to my throat.

"What are you looking at?" Sloane asked.

I didn't tell her.

She would just grab the cell out of my hand and probably delete my Instagram app.

Instead, I clicked on the notification that told me Grayson had just posted something.

Why am I looking at this?

Why am I doing this to myself?

Why do I even care?

But I found myself watching the video that had just gone live on his profile. The video that showed him on a Jet Ski, riding the waves, sending him several feet into the air, having what looked like the best time.

His pecs and biceps bulged as he gripped the handlebars. His skin tan from all the sun. His hair wet and messy, his beard untamed.

That look on him . . . there was nothing sexier.

"Gimme," she said, tilting the phone toward her so she could see what I was looking at. Once she viewed my screen, she gazed at me. "You have notifications set up for his Instagram account?"

"No. Yes. Ugh." I exhaled a long breath. "I despise myself and him at this moment—just so you know."

She took the phone out of my hand and pressed the screen several times before she gave it back to me. "He's blocked. Don't even think about reversing it." Her hands went to my shoulders, which she squeezed and shook. "No real estate, remember. We're done with Grayson."

CHAPTER THREE

Grayson

The only thing worse than a vacation coming to an end was walking into the office the morning after you returned from the trip.

That was exactly what I was doing this fine, brisk Monday, wishing more than anything that I were still cruising the beautiful waters outside Saint-Tropez, that I were still hanging with my buddies, surrounded by the six gorgeous women and endless amounts of scotch and cigars.

There was certainly nothing warm or inviting or even gorgeous about the elevator in our building, where I was resting against the back wall, gripping the handle with both hands as it lifted me to the executive-level floor. I could only imagine the pile of papers waiting on my desk, along with an inbox that had thousands of emails needing a reply.

Aside from looking at the membership numbers, I'd done nothing while I was away. I hadn't responded to any messages. I hadn't even checked in with my partners.

I assumed that would earn me a lashing, especially given that these dudes were my best friends, but I had needed to unplug. I'd needed to focus on anything other than work, and conversations with them would have brought me right back to the place I was trying to avoid.

We all deserved a break after the most taxing period of our careers.

Mine just happened to come with zero communication.

The dreaded ding sounded through the elevator, signaling that I'd arrived, and I released the handlebar and stepped out, immediately catching eyes with our assistant, who was perched behind her desk.

"Welcome back, Grayson."

I nodded and mentally prepped myself for the walk down the hallway, knowing I had to pass Drake's and Easton's doors on the way to mine. I hoped to hell they weren't in yet, so I could go unseen and hurry to my office, where I'd lock myself in.

I was just about to step toward Easton's doorway when I heard, "Grayson?"

Did the motherfucker have a tracker hidden somewhere on me?

How would he know I was even here?

I stopped in the center of his doorframe and looked inside his office. Both of his arms rested on his desk, his face pointed down as if the weight of his head were too much to hold up. The gel was gone from his hair, his clothes wrinkled and disheveled, like he'd slept in them.

Or he'd been in the same position since yesterday.

Or the day before.

Fuck.

"Hey, bud." I swallowed, readying myself for the attack. "You're looking good this morning."

"I should fucking whip you." He stood from his desk and joined me. "Conference room. Now. Follow me."

I chuckled but didn't move. "You're bullshitting me, right?" When he didn't respond, I added, "But I just got in. I haven't even been to my office yet—"

"You'll go to your office after. The team needs to talk to you first."

"Does that mean I don't have time to grab coffee?"

"That's precisely what it means." He sighed. "If you weren't my best friend, I'd fucking despise you right now. Let's go."

I stayed in step with Easton as we rounded the corner, past Drake's office, mine, and then Holden's—all empty, which told me everyone was in the conference room already. "I get the feeling I'm grounded."

Easton laughed, but I could tell he wasn't finding me funny. "You deserve to get fired."

I winced. The air I sucked in was loud enough for him to hear.

"Do you know how many texts I sent you—"

"I shut off my phone." That was partially true. There were periods when I'd powered it down and moments when I'd had it on. The latter was unfortunately the majority.

"Was your phone off when you posted a picture of the yacht on Instagram? Or how about the video of you Jet Skiing? Or the most recent one of you sitting on the couch of Hooked's private plane during your journey home? Or are you going to tell me you hired a social media team while you were away and that wasn't you posting, it was your publicist?"

I halted.

As soon as Easton realized I was no longer walking, he stopped and faced me.

"I get it." I shoved my hands in the pockets of my jeans, unsure what to do with them. "I'd be pissed at me if the roles were reversed. But there's a reason I didn't respond and it's not a personal one."

Easton crossed his arms over his chest. "I can't wait to hear this."

I didn't know if it was anger or disappointment, but something was coming off his stare and hitting my goddamn chest like the pounding of a hammer.

"If I told you how hot the chicks were and all about the incredible food I was eating and the fun I was having, the conversation would have circled back to work." I shook my head, wishing the strands were wet and dripping from the Mediterranean Sea. "I needed a fucking break, man. I'd reached my limit. So I went off the grid, minus the posts on Instagram."

"You're fucking unbelievable." His stare narrowed. "If your silence was the only thing I was pissed about, I'd be getting over this quickly, but you created a hell of a shitstorm while you were gone, and Drake and I have been cleaning up the disaster you created. Hell, Holden even flew home early from Disney to help us."

My heart began to speed up as I processed his words. "A . . . *shitstorm?*"

His lips turned thin as he pulled them inward and roared, "Like I said, follow me."

I caught up to him, and within a few paces, we were heading into the conference room, where the entire executive team waited—Holden, Drake, our head of HR, our in-house counsel, and the head of finance.

All staring at me.

Their expressions aloof, but their postures stiff.

Bothered.

Ready for battle.

And as I looked at each one, I realized there was a face I didn't recognize. She sat at the head of the table, wearing a starched olive-colored suit with red glasses, her hair so stiff, it wouldn't move even in a windstorm.

"Grayson, meet Laura Day," Easton said once I found an empty seat. "She's our PR crisis manager."

I nodded at her and said, "Since when do we employ a PR crisis manager?"

"Since this." Holden held up a piece of paper. The words on the page were too small and too far away for me to see. "I'm sure you've read the article by now, so you know exactly what we're facing."

I took a seat, dropping my bag next to me, linking my hands on top of the table. "What article?"

"What article?" Holden mocked. "You're kidding, right?"

"If you don't mind, Holden, I would like to take over from here," Laura said. Her voice was as crisp and firm as her appearance. With Holden's approval, she started, "Your partners decided to hire me after two very serious and very alarming scenarios occurred while you were in Saint-Tropez."

"Alarming?" I repeated, eyeing the woman, who I believed was the queen of exaggeration. "I was on a yacht. In Europe. What the hell could have happened? I was off the grid—"

"This happened," Easton said. He was holding a remote, and within a few seconds, the TV began to play a video.

One that I hadn't seen, but I remembered the moment quite fondly. It was when I'd just finished chatting with Freddy and was standing on the top deck with a scotch and a cigar, toasting to bachelorhood.

"I didn't post that," I told the group once the video cut off and the room turned silent. "I don't know who did. It wasn't any of the women. They weren't allowed to have their phones on the boat and they all signed NDAs."

"We know you didn't post it. Whether it was one of the women or not, it doesn't matter, because it doesn't change the outcome," Laura said. "What matters is that someone took that footage and sent it to Celebrity Alert, and that video you just saw and some pictures of you were released to their entire subscriber list, along with an adjoining article that appeared on their app and website, having the potential to reach"—she glanced down at the tablet in front of her—"over eighty-five million people."

I couldn't fucking believe what I was hearing.

Who would have the balls to take that footage and send it in?

Why would Celebrity Alert—a site that focused on actual celebrities—give two fucks about me?

"What was the article even about?" I asked her. "And why would anyone care what the hell I was doing? And that I was toasting to bachelorhood on a yacht—"

"The reason they care, Grayson, is because you're now the cofounder of the largest dating app in the world and the inventor of the marriage arm—something you adamantly dismissed and basically dissed in your toast." Holden's voice wasn't raised, but I could see the steam coming off the top of his head. "This international launch has made Hooked one of the top twenty-five tech companies in the world." He leaned forward in his chair. "In. The. World." He repeated and enunciated each word as though I hadn't heard him previously. "That means all eyes are on us."

"That still doesn't answer my question." I looked at each of their faces, hoping I would get something, anything, that would clue me in as to why they were currently holding a meeting about me. What I did in my personal time—whether it went on the internet or not—was my fucking business. "Why do my extracurricular activities interest them?"

Laura held up her hand, claiming the stage, and said, "What the video and pictures don't show are any other male companions who joined you on the yacht. Your partners have informed me that there were three other gentlemen with you on the trip. But what this alert insinuates and what the article emphasizes is that you were alone with six women."

I laughed.

The editing that had been done to that footage and the conversation we were currently having and the looks I was getting from the people around this table were fucking hilarious. "You all know I was there with Freddy and Royston and—"

"It makes no difference what we know," Holden said, cutting me off for the umpteenth time. "It matters what they know. *They* being the entire world. And what they see is you on a yacht having an orgy with six women."

Maybe I should have read some of the texts that Holden and Easton had sent over the last week.

Maybe I should have returned their calls.

Nah, fuck that, I wouldn't have changed a thing.

This was absurd—on every level.

"So . . ." I exhaled. "What's the big deal? Maybe I was having an orgy." I smiled to make their blood boil just a tad bit more. "Maybe I didn't touch any of them. But what I do in my spare time has nothing to do with Hooked."

"Except it does," Easton barked back, the tips of his fingers white as he squeezed his hands together. "When you're the CMO of a top twenty-five tech firm that invented a dating app and, ironically, the division you founded was the marriage arm, what you do in your spare time reflects directly onto Hooked." He glanced at Drake and then Holden before he fixed his stare on me. "While you were out gallivanting in France with half a dozen women, shit was exploding here. There are ramifications to your actions, and the quicker you realize and acknowledge that, the quicker we'll be on the other side of this."

I wasn't sorry for what I'd done. I hadn't done a fucking thing wrong.

I was sorry that my best friends were here, while I was in France, and they had to clean up my so-called mess.

That wasn't fair to them.

But to understand how deep this went, what my actions had caused, I needed to know more.

I looked at Laura, the ringleader, who seemed to have all the data. "And what are those ramifications, exactly?"

"We'll get to that in a minute," she responded. "First, I need to address the other part of this PR crisis."

My eyebrows shot up. "There's more?"

"A lot more," Holden said. "There's also this." Still holding the paper, he pushed it toward me. "The day after your little bachelorhood toast aired, this article was published in the Boston College newspaper. A paper that's distributed to students and faculty and available on their website. We'll continue after you've finished reading it."

It didn't matter whether I wanted to read it; he wasn't giving me a choice.

Hooked for Life or Marketing Ploy?

If you've been online in the last twenty-four hours, then there's a very good chance you saw the toast Grayson Tanner, Boston's Biggest Bachelor and co-founder of Hooked, gave aboard the megayacht he's currently on. One can assume Tanner, 30, rented the yacht for the week, which comes—to my estimate— at a whopping price tag of $100,000 minimum. In the video, he's holding a tumbler, filled with an amber-colored liquid—if I had to guess, it's the Macallan 1962, which sold for $1.9 million at auction—along with a cigar—possibly a King of Denmark that goes for over $4,000 apiece. Why am I listing the possible price tags? Because given the timeline of events, I can assume this was the way Tanner chose to celebrate the international launch of Hooked, the company he started with Easton Jones and Holden Hayes while in their last year of graduate school at Harvard.

If you're not in the dating scene or you don't use technology to help aid you in that department, then let me tell you a little about Hooked. Within the last month, since its international launch, Hooked is now considered the top dating app in the world. When a user signs on to the app, there are three divisions to choose from: one that's just for people looking to hook up, another for marriage, and a third that's solely dedicated to single parents. According to Hooked's website, Grayson was the inventor of the marriage division. Isn't that ironic. For a man who, according to multiple sources, has never been in a relationship and, by the looks of it, isn't even interested in settling down.

So that brings me to the title of this article.

Tanner represents a brand, specifically the branch of the company that he founded, that promotes relationships, marriage, and monogamy. But any person who has access to the internet can clearly see that Tanner's promoting a brand he doesn't use. That Boston's Biggest Bachelor invented a software that's intended to match you with your soon-to-be significant other, someone you're, according to Hooked, statistically compatible to marry, yet he doesn't utilize it. Dare I say, Tanner doesn't even believe in it? Instead of practicing what he preaches, he would rather reap the benefits of his false advertising and spend the millions he's raked in from us—his members—to cruise the waters of France with a plethora of women. Half a dozen, to be exact.

So here lies the ultimate question: If the cofounder of Hooked doesn't believe in the service he's selling, is Hooked really a viable option for dating? Can this app fulfill what they're promising in their branding and messaging? And is it worth the monthly subscription fee Hooked charges, a fee that's affording one of the owners a vacation that most of us could only dream of? Or is Hooked nothing more than a marketing ploy to make the Hooked owners even richer than they already are?

Hooked users, if you've had your membership to the marriage division for more than, say, six months, I think it's safe to admit you already know the answer to that question. I know what I'll be doing the moment I submit this article to my editor. Bye-bye, Hooked.

It infuriated me that someone had the balls to write an article off the Celebrity Alert, sharing information that was only partially true, and omitting details that would change the whole direction of their story. Rather than track down the facts, the student, probably a senior, was looking for some notoriety and a job with a local news outlet that might see the story, like the *Boston Globe*.

Still, the anger pulsed through me.

I ground my teeth together before I said, "It's a school newspaper. Who gives a fuck about what they print. I'm sure only a handful of people even read it—"

"Seven million people care, apparently," Easton said. "That's how many times it's been shared as of this morning. Not to mention the hundreds of thousands of TikToks that have been made in your honor and how *Boston's Biggest Bachelor* is now a trending hashtag."

Seven fucking million?

Goddamn it.

"Who wrote it?" I asked.

"Who wrote it?" Holden mirrored, like the question was ludicrous.

"Yes. Who the hell wrote it." I hissed. "I want to know the name of the journalist, so when I call the paper and threaten libel—"

"One, you're not going to do that," Laura stated. "Whomever the journalist was, we'll never know since they published the article anonymously. After a little digging and pursuing some contacts, I learned that the name will never be disclosed. It was either a student or a faculty member, but it doesn't really matter. They have every right to voice their opinion. It's freedom of speech."

It did matter because I wanted to rip their fucking face off.

They had every right to share their opinion, if their opinion was only of me, but to bring Hooked into the equation and challenge the integrity of our business, that was where they crossed the line.

I mashed my lips together. "Tell me the ramifications of this, Laura."

She glanced at her tablet. "The marriage division is down over twenty percent." She looked up. "And it's dropping more and more every hour."

I shoved my hands under the table and squeezed them, my fingers bound like individual padlocks. "What about the other two arms?"

"Single parent is steady, but we suspect a decline to start immediately—today, tomorrow at the latest," Holden said, the tension obvious in his voice.

Easton pushed back from the table to cross his legs. "The hook-up division has decreased a bit, too, among our longtime US-based users. Those numbers are offset by the new international memberships that are rapidly coming in, but still, the cancellations are happening just as fast." He blew out a mouthful of air. "And there are a lot of them."

This business meant everything to the three of us.

It was our dream. Our livelihood. Our future.

When we started this company, we worked out of our apartment, which then led to the top floor of this building, and we'd recently bought the entire high-rise. We employed more than two hundred people. We had plans to keep growing.

The Celebrity Alert, the article in the school newspaper—they didn't have the power to ruin us.

I wouldn't let them.

But . . .

"*Fuuuck.*" I stood from my seat and began to pace the room, passing our head of finance, who hadn't uttered a single word, and our in-house counsel, who had remained quiet, and Drake, who had also stayed silent. I stopped near our head of finance and asked her, "I understand memberships have dipped, especially in the marriage arm, but are you seeing an overall change in our revenue?" I hesitated, the question burning the back of my throat. "How ugly can things get?"

"If the marriage sector begins to plummet even further and we continue getting this type of press, affecting the other two arms, it's hard to predict what things will look like in a week. Or even a month." She glanced down, away from my line of sight. "Stating the obvious, but I can tell you that at least for the marriage arm and quite possibly the hook-up arm, we're not going to see the growth we hoped for. Not at this rate."

My hands clenched, my feet pounding the floor as I walked across the room and halted behind Holden's chair, looking directly at Laura. "How do we stop this?"

"We can't stop what's already been done. The accusations are out there, and the rumor mill is worse than a California wildfire." She leaned back in her chair, her arms crossed. "There isn't anything people love more than a scandal that contradicts what's been promised. So all we can do is try to bandage the bleeding."

I gripped the back of Holden's chair. "How?"

A smile moved across Laura's lips. Something I didn't know she was capable of. "We have to give them another narrative."

My patience was already nonexistent, and it was running even thinner. "And that is?"

"Whether you realize it or not, you and your partners are the face of Hooked. How you conduct yourself, how you're seen in public, will matter even more over the next couple of months."

"You've made your point, Laura. The message of this meeting is loud and beyond clear." I looked around the room, connecting with each set of eyes that stared back at me. "It sounds like you all need to hear me say that I don't want to lose this company. Life is good. I want to keep things that way." I wiped my mouth. "You're telling me the narrative has to change. I'm asking you, How the fuck do I do it?"

The room turned even more silent. It was as if everyone in here had stopped breathing.

Laura shifted her gaze to Holden, to Easton, and then finally back to me. "You need to get married."

I laughed.

And it came out so fucking hard and loud, I snorted. "I . . . *what?*"

Laura nodded. "You need to show the world that you not only believe in the app and the service it provides, but you're the result of what the app is capable of."

I held the chair even tighter. If Holden weren't sitting in it, there was a chance I would pick it up and throw it across the goddamn room. "Are you joking? Because you have to be. This all has to be one big fucking joke."

"You don't have to get married immediately," she countered. "Whomever the woman is, you need to court her for several months. Have her move into your condo. Be seen with her in public." She framed her hands around her tablet. "We need to make sure the media knows that Grayson Tanner is off the market because Hooked and its incredible software was able to match you with your soulmate."

My fucking ears were on fire from her words.

My heart was pounding at a speed I couldn't control.

Sweat was beginning to pool from every crevice of my body.

"I would say by the four-month mark, you have a wedding," Laura said. "We'll drop the photos with several news outlets. We'll make sure there are shots of you two on your honeymoon. When you return home, we need to see the two of you walking your dog—if you don't have one, we'll get you one. A doodle or a Frenchie, something everyone coos over. We need you dining out together. Attending sporting events." She paused. "You get the point."

"A fucking doodle?" Heat was filling my face to the point where I had to wipe my brow. And possibly sit down, my feet suddenly no longer feeling steady. "No. No. No. And fuck no to everything."

"Like I said, we have to change the narrative," Laura added. "There's no better way to do that, Grayson, than to prove them all wrong. The world doesn't believe you'll ever get married. Let's show them you're not only willing to do so, but you've found the woman of your dreams. And because of Hooked, you're in the throes of love."

"The throes of love?" I snapped. "What the fuck is that?"

This was impossible.

It couldn't happen.

It wasn't even an option.

I didn't do love.

Commitment.

I definitely didn't do marriage.

The team had to have my back on this. They had to believe there was another way, a different route, a goddamn narrative that had nothing to do with me marrying a total stranger.

Still holding Holden's chair, I looked at each member of the executive team. "Do you all agree?" My voice was rising. "Do you really believe this is a good idea? Knowing how I am? And my aversion to relationships?"

Each head nodded.

Easton even said, "You fucked things up for Hooked. It makes no difference whether we think this is a good idea or not—it's decided."

And Holden contributed, "If I wasn't so angry and disappointed in you right now, I probably wouldn't find satisfaction in saying 'You're going to become a married man,' but it feels good to say those words because I'm hopeful it'll fix everything you've done."

My best friends.

These bastards knew why I felt the way I did, what I'd witnessed, how it had shaped me.

How dare they tell me to go against everything I believed in, to sacrifice my happiness, to do something so preposterous as get married.

I released Holden's chair and walked toward the middle of the room, my fingers pulsing, my throat tightening, the sweat soaking through the pits of my polo. "I'm not doing it, and fuck you all for thinking I should."

"But you are doing it, Grayson," Easton said. "Our company is losing money by the second. It's your fault. You need to mend what you've done, and this is the only way."

"If I was in the same position," Holden said, "I'd do whatever needed to be done, even if that was marrying someone I didn't love."

My head shook as I stared at the guys who were like brothers to me. "You've lost your fucking minds," I seethed, and I walked out.

CHAPTER FOUR

Jovana

"So don't freak out . . ." Sloane said the moment I rushed into the bar.

Tonight was another shift I hadn't been scheduled for, but when she called me in a panic, I'd stopped filming content for next week's social media posts and thrown on my bar attire and come right in.

I clocked in on the computer, turning to her as I sang, *"Okaaay . . ."*

"Grayson's here."

My eyes widened so large, they were on the verge of bulging out of my head. "Wait. *What?*"

"He walked through the door literally two minutes before you and sat at a table with his two business partners and two other women. I didn't even have time to call you and warn you, it happened so fast." Her expression was full of sympathy. "And babe, whatever you do, don't turn around. You're in his direct line of sight."

All I wanted to do was turn around. "Oh God."

"I know. Trust me, I know."

"Two other women?" I groaned. "He's the absolute worst." I held the apron that I'd grabbed from behind the bar in my hands, debating whether I should tie it around my waist or make a mad dash out of here. "How much would you hate me if I bailed?"

She faced me, holding a bottle in each hand. "Something tells me they're his employees or this is a business meeting because they all look kinda miserable and like they don't want to be here." She paused. "Does that make it better?"

"No." I shook my head. "Definitely not."

"It doesn't matter. You can't bail on me." She turned toward the row of shot glasses that lined the bar and began filling them with the two bottles. "I don't have another server coming in for two more hours."

My chest began to tighten as I realized exactly what she was saying. "So you're telling I'm responsible for every occupied table in this bar, along with Grayson's?"

"Pretty much." Her nose scrunched, emphasizing the silver loop that ran across the bottom of her nostril. "I owe you."

My hands went to my hips. "Like covering my half of the rent this month—we're at that level of owing."

She dropped the bottles in their holder, setting the shot glasses on a tray. "How about dinner? Followed by a night of complete debauchery?"

"Sloane, I don't know whether to cry or throw up at the thought of seeing him." I placed my back against the sink and looked at the wall of liquor bottles, ensuring I wouldn't turn toward Grayson. "I know it was only one night, more like a couple of hours, but I'm old-fashioned when it comes to this kind of stuff. I don't just sleep with anyone; you know this. I don't do one-night stands; you know this too. I would never join his app—it's not my thing." I gazed down at my feet, my arms wrapped across my stomach. "What happened between us . . . I know it meant nothing to him, but it meant something to me."

In fact, I could still feel the strength of his hands on my body.

The power in his lips when he kissed me.

His gaze devouring mine and the way it penetrated my chest, causing a storm of emotions.

"That's because your parents have the best marriage ever and you want the same thing."

Her statement caused me to look up. "You're right. I couldn't have better role models of love than them."

"And what they have, that's what you deserve."

When I'd decided to go home with him, it wasn't that I thought Grayson and I were going to instantly fall in love. That in the morning, I would wake to him on one knee, proposing. That would be ridiculous to even consider. I just hadn't expected things to end the way they did— or for them to end at all. For him to show me such a lack of respect.

For me to mean absolutely nothing to him.

"Yes," I whispered. "You're right."

She poured three different liquors into a metal mixer and began to shake it. "My advice, go march your hot ass over to his table and show him what he lost." She nodded toward the tray. "And please bring those to table four before you do. They've been waiting over fifteen minutes for that round of shots."

"That's the best advice you've got?"

"Listen, girl, men want what they can't have. I'm not saying you gave in easily, but you kinda gave in easily." A thin smile tugged at her lips. "If you want Grayson to regret being a giant asshole, then show him what he can't have. Show him you're unaffected by his presence. That he means nothing to you."

"Because I'm so good at that. My face will be a dead giveaway. I'm Miss Obvious, you know that about me."

She poured the mixed liquor into a martini glass and set her hands on my shoulders. "You film for hours a day where you're all smiley and upbeat, where you're acting and endorsing a product you most definitely don't believe in, but they're paying you, so you need to sound convincing. This'll be no different. Your uninterest in Grayson is the product and table twelve is the camera." She squeezed before she released me. "Now, go kick ass."

As she began to pour wine into a glass, I opened the apron and tied it around my waist, stealing a pen from Sloane's collection and a pad of paper. "I say this with all the love in my heart, but I want to murder you right now."

She winked. "But you couldn't live without me."

"That's debatable."

While I took the tray to table four, I kept my profile pointed toward Grayson, preventing myself from staring at him. It was safest to do that because if I happened to look at him, I wasn't sure I'd be able to glance away. This way, he didn't get a second of my attention.

He didn't deserve it.

But my body felt fiery as I delivered the shots. My skin was getting hot and—I was sure—red. My stomach jittery, my hands sweaty. I had to really focus on what I was doing so I wouldn't trip or spill, and the moment the last shot was on the table, I turned toward Grayson.

I expected to be able to walk the short distance to his table without having his eyes on me, giving me the chance to check him out while he was deep in conversation.

That wasn't the case.

Because his eyes were fixed on mine.

His stare looking right through me.

Like I was an animal he was hunting.

Like I was a taste that he wanted more of.

"This"—*he traced the air between us*—*"will end in the morning. One night, that's it, nothing more."*

That scene, those words—it all replayed in my head as I walked toward him.

With each step, I remembered what his mouth had felt like.

The sensation in my body when he'd caressed me.

How I felt when his arms were around me.

And I took in his face, how incredibly sexy it looked with a beard that was even thicker than before, skin that was tan, a smugness that dragged across his lips, reinforcing how cocky and confident he was.

I hate him.

That was what I told myself when the jitters began to shoot up my chest, when I found it difficult to breathe, when it was almost impossible to look away from his gaze.

I despise him.

The result of that night was a rideshare that I had to take alone, back to the apartment I rented with Sloane, in the middle of a heavy downpour.

The weather symbolic of how miserable I'd felt.

I resent him.

And that memory was painful enough that I shifted my focus to the women at the table and halted behind the two of them. One sat directly next to Grayson, a pair of bright-red glasses perched high on her nose, with an aura that screamed business. The other had her hair in a high, tight bun with a smear of freckles across her nose.

"Welcome to Olives," I said to the group. "My name is Jovana, what can I get you to drink?"

The ladies placed their orders first. I was too worked up to reach into my apron and grab the pen and pad, so I recited their wine preferences in my head before moving on to Grayson's partners. Their drinks were easy to remember; they were identical.

There was one person left.

One person I absolutely didn't want to look at.

That was a lie.

Shit.

I filled my lungs and gradually turned my gaze, my breath hitching as we locked eyes, my throat contracting, my arm feeling weak even though it was holding only the weight of the tray. "And Mr. Wicked, what can I get you?"

My eyes narrowed, my lips smiling.

This was how I'd look at the camera if I were recording content, a way to be flirty but not overly sexy. A way to make the audience feel like I was giving them all of me.

Even if I wasn't.

The salutation earned me a chuckle.

A sound that, when I'd previously heard it at his table and in the hallway outside the restrooms and during the walk to his condo and inside his place, I'd found so alluring.

Now, it almost stung.

Because it slapped those memories back into my head, reinforcing just how evil this man was.

"Vodka—"

"May I chime in," the woman in red glasses said, cutting Grayson off before she looked at me. She didn't receive an answer from either of us before she said, "Do the two of you know each other?"

I glanced from her to Grayson. "Somewhat . . . yes."

"What does *Mr. Wicked* stand for?" she asked.

An odd question, I thought.

Why hadn't she just asked Grayson, who was sitting next to her? Why had she directed the question at me?

My smile shifted to one that was a bit more polite than the flirty one I'd been aiming at him. "I'll let Grayson tell you that." And then I turned my focus to him and said, "Vodka on the rocks, like last time?"

The moment he nodded, I left the table, feeling his gaze bore through my back as I rushed toward the bar.

But it didn't just stay on my back.

I felt it on my ass.

My thighs.

Even my neck.

"How'd it go?" Sloane asked as I typed their orders into the computer. "He's ugly, right? And not worth a second of your time? And you're questioning why you ever went home with him? And we're going to practice how to shrink your heart to save yourself the heartache?"

I gripped the bar top with both hands. "Yep. Yep. Yep. And *yeeep.*"

I'm not going to look at him.

I'm absolutely not going to look at him.

I'm most definitely not going to look at him.

But I lost the battle.

And as soon as I glanced in his direction, our eyes locked again.

The hunger in his stare had doubled.

The passion exploded.

The need was beyond overwhelming.

So much so that I forced myself to look at Sloane, practically panting as I said, "I hate him."

What was it about Grayson Tanner that I couldn't get enough of?

That made me disregard the way he'd treated me?

That made me still want him so badly?

The answer to that was easy.

No man's gaze had ever made me feel the way his did.

She rolled her eyes, shaking her head. "You're right. You're Miss Fucking Obvious."

CHAPTER FIVE

Grayson

"She's perfect," Laura said the moment Jovana left the table.

I knew exactly what Laura was saying.

Who she was referring to.

And I agreed with every word.

That was why, *goddamn it*, I wanted the vodka already in my hand.

I wanted my fingers wrapped around the cold, condensation-covered glass.

I wanted the fucking burning in my throat as the liquor swished past my tongue on its way to my stomach.

All because of her.

Why was Jovana so hot?

Why was her personality so irresistible?

Why was her body so incredible? From the curve of her neck to the dip of her collarbone, from the arch of her hips to those toned, gorgeous thighs.

There wasn't an inch of her I didn't want to lick.

Bite.

Devour.

Why I physically had to force myself not to ask her to come closer, so I could wrap my arms around her waist and pull her against me.

What the fuck was happening to me—

"Grayson," Laura said, interrupting my thoughts.

Not only was I thinking of Jovana, but I was staring at her, too, as she stood at the bar, talking to the bartender.

"What?" I snapped, dragging my gaze away from her.

"Didn't you hear me? I said she's perfect," Laura replied.

I'd heard her, all right, and had only responded in my head, so I cleared my throat and said, "I agree with you."

"And that's why she's going to be your wife."

My head whipped toward Jovana and then back to Laura.

She raised her hand the moment my lips parted and said, "Let me tell you why I've come to that conclusion—"

I cut her off. "There's no reason to. She's not an option." As my arms crossed over my chest, I took a peek at Jovana's ass.

If there was ever one that I could wake up to every morning, that I could clutch every night before bed, that I could stare at every day for the rest of my life, it was hers.

It was flawlessly round.

Heart-shaped.

Grabbable.

Squeezable.

But that didn't change my mind.

I wasn't marrying Jovana.

A woman who wanted to cook me breakfast the next morning in what she had called my *magnificent kitchen*, and I'd squashed that dream when I'd told her I wasn't into dating or having a replay of our night together.

"Like I said," Laura continued, despite my attempt to shut her up, "she has a sweet, wholesome personality, which will offset yours quite well. She's young, but not too young. She has a relatable job that will resonate with the media. She's adorable and fit—the world will literally just eat her up the second we release photos of you two, especially when they see the chemistry you have."

Was this woman fucking nuts?

I knew we were here to discuss my future wife—a term I couldn't and wouldn't wrap my head around. The only reason I'd been able to convince the executive team to come here was because I'd told them if I had a drink, I might be more open to the idea.

But that was a lie.

I just needed a drink.

Still, I was semi-amused by her last statement and needed more clarification, so I barked, "What chemistry?"

"What chemistry," Laura repeated. "The way you two were looking at each other, I could feel the energy pulsing. I'm sure everyone at this table could too."

"Agreed," Holden said.

"I second that," Easton added.

"I third that," Drake said.

"You have to be shitting me." I dropped my hands on the table, unintentionally using a strength that caused a bang to echo around us. There was no way they could see the passion I had for this woman. I hid it well, I knew that. They were just filling me with bullshit so they could get me hitched to someone. "I'm not fucking marrying—"

"Before you finish that statement," Laura said, "I need you to listen to me." Her voice was sterner than it had been at the office. "When your partners hired me to clean up this PR disaster that you created, I made it very clear how I operate and conduct business. When I met with them and discussed my plan, everyone was on board. That's what I need from you as well, Grayson. I can't do my job effectively if you fight me every step of the way." She pushed up her glasses, her eyes enlarging as she gazed at me through the thick lenses. "I need you to trust me, to know that what I'm asking of you is what's best for your company. This is what I do, what I'm good at, and why your partners hired me." She placed a finger on her cheek, the rest of her hand sitting under her chin. "If you want me to save Hooked, then you need to be open to what I'm suggesting."

I turned my body toward her, my blood boiling to the point where it was ready to burst through my veins. "You need to listen to me, Laura. You think you're the alpha of this pack, that you're just going to come in and snap your fingers and all is going to be good in the Hooked world, but what you're telling me to do is impossible. I can't even stand the idea of a relationship, never mind the thought of getting married. It goes against everything I believe in." I smiled, the words like fire as they lashed off my tongue, and they felt so good to release. "So, no, I'm not going to get married. I'm also not going to lie on my back and do what you tell me to. I'm not a goddamn dog."

The group turned silent.

I was sure the head of HR wished she'd gone home, like our head of finance and in-house counsel had done.

But I didn't give a shit who was here. I wasn't going to tone down my response for anyone at this table.

"Grayson—"

"Don't," I warned Holden, knowing the motherfucker was going to try to smooth things out.

I didn't want smoothing.

I wanted things rough and bumpy, just like they were.

But Holden grabbed my shoulder as he sat on the other side of me. "I get it, man. I do. I know this isn't what you want, but I need you to think about Hooked and what we've sacrificed to build this company. The time you, Easton, and I have dedicated, all the long nights, the weekends." He squeezed, making sure I was listening, that I was hearing his words. "If that means you need to play house for a little while—say, a year or so—then do it for Hooked."

"Fuck—"

"Grayson . . ." Drake's voice was a surprise to hear, and it instantly quieted me. She hadn't said much at the bar and had been silent during our meeting at the office. With her being so analytical, I was curious about what she was going to tell me. "Like Holden said, you're facing an approximate one-year sentence. She'll live in your guest room. You'll pass each other in the morning before you leave for work and again at night before bed. You'll be seen in public with her a few times a week. Maybe the two of you will even develop a friendship and you'll enjoy your time together." She glanced at Easton. "In my eyes, it's much more difficult to keep a relationship a secret than to pretend you're in love with someone you're not." As she referenced her experience with Easton, she looked back at me. "From what I can tell, you've been staring at her since we arrived at the bar, and I'd say you find her quite irresistible."

Irresistible?

Was Drake somehow inside my head?

As though she heard me, her grin was small, careful, like she didn't want to be on the receiving end of one of my verbal hits. "I believe you when you say you don't want to marry her, but honestly, I wouldn't have thought that by the way you look at her, so you've fooled me. If the rest of the world is like me and can be so easily convinced, then this isn't going to be hard for you at all."

That wasn't what I'd anticipated Drake to say.

I wanted her to be on my side.

For her to admit this was comical and fucking absurd.

But what no one had addressed so far was the obvious roadblock.

"What if she says no?" I asked them. "Have you ever thought of that?"

"She won't," Laura countered. "Because you're going to offer her a package that she won't be able to refuse."

My brows lifted. "A package?"

"Well, of course," Laura said. "This is a business transaction with an NDA and a thoroughly laid-out contract. We need her completely on board with everything that we're asking to ensure there aren't any surprises, so yes, you have to offer her something."

"Un-fucking-believable." My hands dived into the sides of my hair while I checked the status of our drinks. Jovana wasn't at the bar anymore—she was helping another table, smiling at the group of three men she was waiting on, her tongue slowly leaving her mouth to swipe her bottom lip.

All three dudes were gazing at that tongue.

At that mouth.

At her beauty.

And they were thinking about what it would feel like if she were doing that same motion to their cock.

Just like I was.

Goddamn it.

I shook my head and roared, "What would that package look like?"

Laura took her tablet out of her bag, tapped the screen a few times, and said, "A onetime payment of one million dollars. If she has an apartment, you'll pay her rent for the duration of the marriage. You'll provide her with health insurance and cover all her expenses while she's living with you—food, utilities, a stipend for her cell phone, parking if she has a car, along with her car payment. Obviously, when the two of you go out and are seen in public, you'll cover all costs." She closed the tablet and looked at me. "As for the wedding and honeymoon, that's on you as well, including the cost of her gown."

As she read off each item, I felt my eyes bulge.

My hands fisted even tighter.

My pulse throbbed.

I had to be in another universe, or this was a fucking nightmare— anything that would justify what I was hearing, because there was no way what she was telling me could be the reality of my life.

"This is bullshit—"

"This is what's required," Easton said, "whether you marry her"—he nodded toward Jovana, who was still at the table of three—"or another woman."

"What's good about Jovana is that you've already slept with her," Holden said. "If Laura found you a total stranger to wed, think of how much time it would take to develop chemistry—if you even could develop it. You know, because you're this extra-warm and super-fuzzy guy that would just instantly cuddle right up to someone you don't know." He laughed.

But I didn't find this funny.

Not a goddamn word of it.

"Health insurance? A cell phone stipend? She's not a fucking employee." I let out a long exhale. "Maybe a stranger would be easier," I snapped at him. "Since Jovana already knows how much of an asshole I am, I'm sure she's immediately going to say no."

I watched her walk to the bar, relieved she was done with those guys, although I wasn't sure why.

As she set what looked like our drinks on her tray, her ass was pointed at me.

Her hips.

Those exquisite legs.

Fuck me.

I glared at Laura. "Besides, she's not the kind of woman who can be bought."

Not when she'd turned down the $200 tip I'd offered and left herself nothing.

"You have to make it worth her while, then, don't you understand that?" Laura asked. "That's why we're offering more than just money. And why I would encourage you to give her some emotional support—this isn't just about the finances, Grayson."

"You want me to pat her back and tell her I love her?" My words dripped with sarcasm. "All of you can fuck off."

"Assuming she's still single," Laura continued, ignoring me, "she's essentially going to be putting her personal life on hold while she heals your reputation. That's a job, Grayson, and it's a hefty ask of someone." She adjusted her position, recrossing her legs. "Also, something you probably haven't considered is that Jovana would have to tell her friends and family that she's marrying you. Her NDA would prevent her from telling them the truth, so she's going to have to make them believe that she's in love with you. And at the end of all this, the poor woman is going to end up divorced, unable to tell her family why, and I assure you that any kind of divorce is something most people don't want." Her voice softened as she said, "Take it from someone who's divorced—it's a hard pill for most to swallow. At least Jovana's young and, after you, she'll have time to find the man of her dreams. If she wants to have a family one day, she has plenty of years to do that."

Laura's facade had finally cracked, and I took that into account. Her mention of Jovana's friends and family and that they'd have to be lied to prior to our wedding and after our divorce was something even my hard ass could sympathize with.

She'd be helping to heal my recent wrongdoings. She'd be rebuilding my arm of the company, and that meant more to me than anything.

Laura was right—Jovana would have to sacrifice.

I sat back in my seat, processing everything that had been said tonight.

The benefits of going with Jovana, something I couldn't believe I was even considering.

But Holden had a point. If I was going to move forward—and I didn't know if I was—then marrying a stranger would create a whole new set of difficulties.

At least Jovana knew what to expect.

She knew I didn't want this. She would know that I was backed into a corner without a choice.

Therefore, she wouldn't expect a fucking rainbow after the Grayson storm.

That didn't mean I liked the idea of her moving into my place.

Of having to trust a woman.

Of being tied down.

Of not being able to fish because I couldn't risk getting busted and causing another media crisis.

Of getting married.

Of wearing a ring on a finger that I'd never planned to band.

"Shit," I hissed, turning my attention to Laura. "How would you do this? Sit her down? Give her the logistics? Whip out a pen and have her sign the contract that's probably already sitting in your bag?"

The crack in her appearance was gone as she said, "I'll pull her aside this evening and set up a time for her to come into my office. I would like the conversation to take place there, where she'll sign the NDA before anything is discussed, and you and your in-house counsel will be present, so everything is by the book and documented. We also have to get her on the app if she isn't already and have her profile specifically on the marriage arm, and Drake"—she looked at our director of app development and engineering—"you'll need to make sure the two of them are matched."

"I'm happy to do so," Drake replied.

"Before I leave this bar, the meeting will be set," Laura said, her stare intensifying. "What I need you to do is make sure you don't mess this up."

My neck tilted back as if she were tugging on the rear of my collar. "Mess it up? How in the hell could I do that?"

She signaled that Jovana was on her way over, so she couldn't answer, and I turned just in time to watch her carry our drinks to the table, working her way around the circle until she reached me.

That was when I got a whiff of her scent.

One I remembered licking off her.

Lavender and vanilla.

"I brought you all doubles," Jovana said quietly. "My apology for having to wait so long for your drinks." Once she placed the vodka in front of me, she tucked the tray under her arm.

"What, no bottle of Coke this time?"

She stared at me quietly. "Funny and wicked—you're quite the combo, aren't you." She instantly broke eye contact and said, "I'm the only server on at the moment, so things are taking a little longer than normal. I appreciate you being so patient with me."

We never caught eyes again before she left the table, something that oddly bothered me.

"See, I didn't fuck anything up," I said to Laura as though I needed to prove, out loud, that I could do this.

I didn't know why.

I had zero desire to move forward.

But I also knew I didn't have a choice.

There were certain things we did for Hooked, and this was one.

I just hoped these motherfuckers knew how much I was sacrificing for our company.

"You didn't," Laura said, "but you could have thanked her for the double. She is going to be your future wife and all."

"How can you be so sure she's going to say yes?" I asked.

Laura shrugged but smiled at the same time. "Oh, it's just a hunch."

I might have lain on my back for this one, but that didn't mean I was going down without a fight.

"Did the hunch also tell you that I was going to thank Jovana for the drinks?" I challenged.

"No, it didn't," Laura replied. "I just hoped you had some manners . . . and you don't."

I nodded toward Easton and Holden. "You picked a fiery one, fellas."

The two of them laughed.

So did Laura.

"And you know what?" Easton said. "She's going to save your ass, and she's going to save Hooked's ass too."

CHAPTER SIX

Jovana

I had no idea what Grayson was still doing at the bar, considering everyone he'd come here with had already left, but he was sitting in the same spot, nursing his latest round of vodka.

His fourth, to be exact.

It seemed that with each new glass I set in front of him, his stare intensified.

I felt it everywhere.

When I tended to the other tables, I swore his gaze followed me. When I went to the bar to pick up drinks, it burned through my backside. When I dashed down the hallway where the restrooms were located, I could even sense it there.

Though his eyes followed, he stayed put.

During the time he'd sat there alone, he didn't speak to any women. He didn't appear to be waiting for someone else to join him—at least there were no signs of that by the way he was staring at me. And with his large, well-stocked bar at home, he really had no reason to still be here.

Unless it was to watch me.

In that case, he was getting quite the show.

I'd taken every bit of Sloane's advice and made that asshole see what he was missing.

When I walked, I shook my butt a little harder than normal. When I approached my tables that were full of male patrons, I amped up the flirtation. When I brought Grayson and his party more drinks, I looked everywhere but at him.

If he wanted my attention, he was going to have to earn it.

But things had taken an interesting turn right before his guests had left. The woman with the red glasses, who had been sitting next to him, had approached me. The business card she'd handed to me showed she was a publicist with an office in the Back Bay, not far from the bar, where she'd asked if I would meet her this week. She wouldn't say why. She wouldn't say what she wanted. She was just adamant that we chat.

Since my interest was piqued, I'd told her I would see her tomorrow morning.

That was about thirty minutes ago, and I still couldn't figure out why someone associated with Grayson would want to speak to me.

It was that lingering question that made me want to join him and ask.

At least that was what I told myself.

I collected the check from my second-to-last table, the bar now almost empty, and I entered the tip into the computer. Just as I turned away from the screen to walk to his table, I felt him again.

His eyes.

A stare that deepened its way through my body. That dipped and rose, like the bouncing of a tennis ball.

A heat began to build between us as I made my way over to him. Once I arrived, I needed to do something with my hands and gripped the edge of the round wood table. At the very least, to keep them steady.

Why did he still have this effect on me?

Why wasn't I glaring at him while breathing fire like a dragon?

Why was his stare unlike any of the others I'd received tonight?

One that made me feel.

One that made me yearn.

"Jovana . . ."

My name sounded different coming out of his mouth compared to everyone else who had spoken it this evening.

A voice that was deep, gritty.

Far too sexy.

"Yes?"

"I want to know something." His arms landed on the table, his hands slowly crossing.

Those fingers. *Oh God.* I remembered them.

Their power.

Talent.

And even though I'd come here to ask a question, I was intrigued by his.

"Yes?" I shifted my weight, attempting to take a breath.

"Have you felt my eyes on you tonight?"

My face reddened, sweat now beginning to seep through my skin. "I have."

"The last time I saw you, you were flipping me off before you rushed out of my place." His exhales were raw, sounding almost like a huff, as if he were fighting to choose his words carefully. "Now that we're alone, why aren't you telling me to go fuck myself?"

"Well, for one, I'm at work."

"That's the only reason?"

I squeezed the table even harder, and somehow that moved me closer, his scent taunting the tips of my nostrils.

I already knew the smell. This wasn't the first time I'd inhaled it.

But like the first time, it hit me.

Nagged at me.

Almost tore at me.

The breeze of citrus was equally balanced with notes of amber, as if the freshness of a spring sky met the center of the woods, where the trees were the thickest.

That was Grayson's scent.

Full of confidence.

Sex.

And dominance.

"Believe it or not, I don't make it a habit to raise my middle finger unless the situation absolutely requires it, like that night." I tried not to label the color of his green eyes, because it shouldn't matter—no, it didn't matter. "Tonight, you're a customer, and my parents raised me to respect others. So my middle finger has stayed put unless it's raising to give you a drink." I laughed, the uncomfortableness tugging at all my edges. "Would I like to tell you just how you made me feel? Yes. Do I think it would make a difference?" I shook my head. "No."

He glanced at my hands. This was the first time he'd broken eye contact since I'd been standing here.

"I have a question for you." I took another breath, waiting for his gaze to reach me. I wasn't sure why I wanted it, why I missed the attention, but once I had it, I said, "Why does Laura want to speak with me?"

He studied my face. Looked at me as though he were counting my freckles and taking an inventory of each pore. And when he leaned to the side, I wasn't sure what had prompted the movement until I realized he was freeing up a pocket to remove his wallet. He slipped a card from one of the slits and held it out to me.

"What's this for?" I paused, waiting for a response. "Do you want me to bring you a check?"

"No."

"You just want me to run it for the full amount of tonight's bill?"

No one had paid before they left, so I assumed they were sticking him with the tab.

His eyes narrowed as he said, "That's why I'm giving you the card, Jovana."

There was my name again.

Just as coarse as it had been last time, with a touch of sarcasm, which I was learning that Grayson embedded into almost everything he said.

When I reached for the card, our fingers grazed.

Just that small movement, those few seconds of contact, and I was sucking in a mouthful of air, holding it, my pulse instantly hammering away.

The tingles now like tiny flames, licking me from the inside.

"I'll be back—"

"Add four hundred."

I blinked several times. "Excuse me?"

"Two hundred that you never charged me from before. Two hundred for this evening."

"But—"

"Four hundred." He nodded toward the bar. "Go."

I shook my head in awe. "Does everyone in your life just listen to your commands? Because—"

"We'll talk when you get back." He took out his phone and hit the screen, completely tuning me out.

That man.

He was unlike anyone I'd ever met.

Authoritative. Irritable. Yet charming in the weirdest way.

To the point where I found myself walking to the bar to run his card, perplexed at how obedient I was when it came to his demands.

Two hundred was an astronomical tip. I'd thought so last time, which was why I hadn't listened and had given myself nothing.

But it was more than just an outrageous number; it was an amount that had made me feel bought, as though that were a fair price to pay for me to go home with him.

Even now, knowing how much of an asshole he was, I felt uncomfortable as I looked at the tip line, the computer waiting for a total.

The difference between then and this evening was that I wasn't going home with him.

Period.

That was what made it a little easier to type in the four hundred. That I knew he didn't need it.

That I did.

I printed out his receipt, and while I was walking back to his table, it hit me. He'd never answered my question as to why Laura wanted to meet with me.

So, once the table was within reach, I placed the paper and pen in front of him and said, "I'm going to ask you again, Why does Laura want to—"

"Are you done for the night?" He signed his name across the bottom of the slip and dropped the pen.

I released a burst of air that was a mix between a laugh and a gasp. "No."

He glanced over my shoulder. "There's no one else here. I must be your last table."

"I'm closing." I crossed my arms. "That means I have a bunch of duties I need to get done before I leave."

He returned his card to his wallet. "Do you have a second to walk me out?"

"Walk you out?"

He slid his legs toward me, spreading them, so that even though I was a few paces away, it made me feel like I was standing between his thighs. "Yes, Jovana. Walk me out. That doesn't mean come home with me. It just means I'm asking you to come with me to the door. Can you do that?"

He made everything sound like a sexy argument, even a simple trip to the exit.

And a submissive side of me that I had no idea existed replied, "Yes."

He took the pen and receipt off the table and tucked them into my apron. The scrape of his fingers against my waist should have triggered nothing.

But it triggered everything.

A seductive explosion vibrated through me.

As it did, he laughed. "You don't mask your feelings well, do you?"

I couldn't when it came to him.

This was what he brought out in me.

What he stirred.

The amount of power his eyes and hands had over me.

But still, I played coy and said, "I'm not sure what you mean."

He was off his chair, towering over me. "I barely touched you and your reaction was as strong as if I'd cupped your face and dragged your lips to mine." His tongue gradually darted out, licking the top of his bottom lip. "Is it that you're not touched too often or you're just that turned on by me?"

I was positive my eyes bugged out when I snapped, "Dick."

Despite what had just come out of my mouth, something very different was happening between my legs.

A wetness that was taking hold of me.

That was what his directness did.

"Answer me, Jovana."

"I wouldn't give you that satisfaction."

He chuckled. "All right, we'll see." He took a step, which only brought us closer. "Follow me."

I stayed next to him, passing the tables, and when I assumed he'd head for the front of the bar, he turned and we began to go toward the hallway where the restrooms were located. At first, I was worried this was going to be a replay of our first night, since I couldn't understand why we were going in that direction, and then it became obvious.

Grayson wanted to leave through the back, the door that was nearest to his condo.

Once we reached the end point, he leaned into the glass while facing me. "Thank you."

"For what?"

He took several deep breaths. That was what I did when I was searching for words, but I didn't get the sense he had a hard time coming up with replies.

As his mouth opened, it pulled into a smile. "For not flipping me off."

"You haven't left yet. I still have time."

He laughed. "That's fair." He lifted his arm, holding the top of the doorway. "I have a question of my own." Still gripping the molding, he leaned forward, closing the space between us.

My muscles tightened.

My lips parted, drawing in more air.

He wasn't going to kiss me.

He wouldn't dare.

Not after telling me that nothing would happen following our one night together.

Because a kiss would be more.

And Grayson Tanner didn't do more.

But his lips were opening, his gaze locking with mine. "I want to know if I can feel it." As he spoke, his words hit my mouth, his breath soft, smelling of vodka and cologne.

"Feel what?"

He didn't answer. He just moved in a bit more, his mouth hovering above mine.

As the seconds passed, wetness pooled between my thighs.

My nipples tightened, hardening to peaks that I was positive were pointing straight through my bra.

I'd lost control of my body.

It was as if he held a string that dictated my reactions and was pulling on it.

With every ounce of his strength.

I had to force my hands to stay at my sides and stop my body from leaning into his.

"Us." His free hand lifted, his palm holding the base of my neck, tilting my face up, his mouth rising so that it didn't touch mine. "The chemistry that everyone says we have." His stare traced my eyes, nose, down to my lips, where his thumb moved across my pout. Back and forth. A speed so slow, it was making me yearn for more pressure. "Is that what this is?"

He hadn't earned this.

He hadn't even begun to grovel his way out of the hole he'd dug himself into.

But, my God, there was no way I could demand that now.

I was . . . lost.

"Yes. I feel it too." My voice wasn't any louder than a whisper.

"I can see how turned on you are." His teeth bared. "I can fucking feel it."

"Then what's stopping you from kissing me?"

His eyes closed, and his lips briefly grazed mine, like the passing of a windshield wiper, before he pressed our foreheads together. "Laura. That's who's stopping me."

My body was beating in a way that made it hard to breathe and impossible to process what he was saying. The only thing I could get out was, "What?"

His face pulled away, his hand moving to my chin, holding it while he replied, "You'll find out why tomorrow." He separated our bodies and opened the door and began to walk through it.

I grabbed the handle, keeping the door ajar while I watched him, dumbfounded, confused as to what had just happened, what he'd even said, and what this all meant. "Grayson?"

He didn't turn around. He didn't even look over his shoulder.

He just said, "I'll see you in the morning, Jovana," and it was loud enough for me to hear.

CHAPTER SEVEN

Grayson

"I called you in today to give you a proposition," Laura said, keeping her eyes focused solely on Jovana, who had looked like a deer in headlights since she'd arrived, especially when she was signing the NDA. "One that you're probably going to find rather unorthodox." Laura had her hands on top of a folder containing the contract, where every detail of our potential arrangement had been laid out.

My legal team had worked through the night to make sure every i was dotted, every t was crossed, that their verbiage outlined the duties the other party—whether it be Jovana or someone else—and I were responsible for.

And it set a term.

One year.

That was my sentence.

Admittedly, as I stared at Jovana from the head of Laura's oval table, it wasn't a bad sight to have to look at for the next twelve months.

Every time I saw her, she was even more gorgeous, and I found it impossible to pull my stare away from her.

But that didn't mean I was pleased with this proposition.

That I hadn't stayed up all night, contemplating a way out of it.

Or that I was going to be the ideal boyfriend and fiancé and husband.

I didn't give a shit how badly I wanted to kiss her last night. How hard my cock had been while I'd held her by the back door of the bar. How I'd gone home and jerked off in the shower, thinking of her incredible body and her tight, wet pussy and the softness of her skin and her incredible taste.

But this was a business transaction.

Nothing more.

And before she signed that contract—if she decided to sign—I planned on telling her that.

"I'm eager to hear what it is," Jovana replied to the crisis manager, her voice soft, her eyes darting to me and then back to Laura.

"I promise I'm going to get to that proposition soon, but before I do, I want to give you a little backstory, so you understand what prompted this meeting," Laura said. "I don't know if you've recently been following the media or if you've seen any of the articles or Alerts that showed Grayson on a yacht in Saint-Tropez?"

As Laura paused, Jovana's face flushed.

Oh, she fucking saw them, all right.

And I was sure if we weren't in Laura's office and if Jovana weren't so well mannered in front of my team, that would have earned me another middle finger.

"I subscribe to Celebrity Alerts," Jovana said, swallowing, "and, yes, I received the one about Grayson."

"Then you know exactly what I'm referring to and how that Alert—combined with the photos and videos and the subsequent article in Boston College's newspaper, causing an influx of TikToks and reposts—has implied that Grayson has a very strong opinion when it comes to marriage."

Implied.

Oh, she's fucking good.

Jovana nodded.

"Since you're not a member, I don't know how much you know about Hooked, but Grayson founded the marriage arm for the app, so the result of that footage going viral hasn't been very positive for the company. If I'm being frank, Hooked has found itself in a bit of a media storm."

"I've seen some of the things that have been shared online." Jovana's hands were under the table, but the way her shoulders moved, I could tell she was fidgeting. "I just don't understand why I'm here."

I didn't blame her for being uncomfortable. The whole fucking setting was stifling.

"Hooked has hired me to ease the media storm, and in order to do that, I have to create a different narrative that shows Grayson in a more"—Laura glanced at me—"relatable manner." She smiled at Jovana. "Once things shift and the storm calms and the media stops discussing Grayson's antimarriage announcement and his extracurricular activities"—she cleared her throat—"Hooked can continue to grow the way they intended."

"So, how does that involve me exactly?" Jovana asked.

Laura's hand touched the table, not far from where Jovana's bottle of water sat, the PR crisis manager's way of warming up her guest. "Dear, Grayson needs to get married."

Jovana's brows instantly rose. "Wait . . ." Her mouth dropped as she stared at Laura, her hand flattening against her chest, pushing as if she were trying to control the beating of her heart. After a few moments of silence, she looked at me and said, "Are you suggesting that person be me?"

"Yes," Laura answered. "After spending the evening researching you, learning you're an influencer, and seeing the presence you've established and the reputation you've earned among your followers, we feel you would be a perfect fit."

Jovana's eyes didn't move. They stayed on me. Her expression aloof, but her posture telling me that the news was shooting straight up her spine. I watched it circle in her head, the pieces clicking together, until she eventually focused on Laura.

Before Jovana could respond, Laura added, "But the marriage wouldn't happen immediately. Assuming you're interested in the position, which would be treated like a business transaction, Grayson would publicly court you for one to two months, and then he would propose. You would move in with him. A wedding would occur. Honeymoon." She tapped the folder. "Everything is spelled out in here, but I want to highlight some necessary requirements that I really want you to take note of." She pushed her glasses higher. "Remember, the purpose of this is to change Grayson's narrative, so you'd be required to go on dates with him in places where you would be seen. You would have to convince your family and friends that this is a man you're in love with. We would want him featured on your Instagram feed, even having a presence in some of your TikToks."

I knew all about influencers. We'd hired several in the past to market Hooked.

I just thought the bar was her only gig.

"You want me on fucking TikTok?" I burst out.

Laura glared at me. "Jovana has a large social media following. Having you appear in her feed would be a tremendous benefit for Hooked."

My head shook, immediately rejecting the idea.

The last thing I was going to do was dance to a goddamn song for the entire world to see.

Laura crossed her hands. "The most important part of this arrangement is that in everyone's eyes—and I'm talking the media, your family, friends, colleagues—this will look like a real, honest, love-filled relationship."

"You're asking me to lie."

Jovana's words and tone were as cold as the water sitting in front of me.

"We understand our request isn't easy, and you'll be well compensated for that." Laura pushed the folder toward her. "The top page summarizes the financial aspects of this deal."

Jovana didn't open the folder.

She took several deep breaths. "Why me?"

"The idea came to me at the bar last night. If I could have physically chosen a perfect partner for Grayson, it would be you, and that thought was only confirmed when I researched you. You're kind, Jovana, and that's the first thing I saw when I viewed your social media. You're also sweet. Humble. Wholesome. The media will love you—they already do, by the looks of your accounts and how much interaction you get." Laura took a drink of her coffee. "The moment you start hinting that you've fallen in love, you're going to get so much support from your following. They'll eat it up. Think of what that'll do to help build your influencer status. Women thrive off a beautiful love story, and I assure you, it's going to look like a fairy tale to anyone watching."

Where Laura had apparently spent the whole night googling Jovana, I'd drunk myself completely stupid until I barely remembered my name.

"So, you're an influencer?" I grabbed my water, swishing it around in my mouth, hoping it would help dull my hangover. "And a server?"

Jovana's stare slowly moved over to me. She leaned forward, her arms resting on the table. "You don't know anything about me, do you? Like, for starters, my last name."

"Let's not address Grayson's lack of—"

"No, she's right," I replied, cutting Laura off, not needing her to lie on my behalf and fill Jovana with bullshit that wasn't true. "I don't know your last name. I don't know where you live. I don't know—"

"Anything besides what I taste like," Jovana whispered. She was quiet for a moment before she addressed Laura and said, "I would like to talk to Grayson. Alone."

"Now?" Laura asked.

Jovana nodded. "Yes. Now."

"We still have so much to discuss," Laura said. "The terms of the contract, the responsibilities. I'd like to go over the legalities and make sure all your questions are answered."

"We'll have time for all that," Jovana said, pleading with the crisis manager. "It's important I talk to him before we discuss anything further."

Laura looked at Hooked's in-house counsel, like she needed her approval, which she ended up getting when the attorney nodded at her.

"We'll be right outside," Laura told us, and she left the room with the attorney.

Once we were alone, Jovana pushed a few inches away from the table and crossed her legs. "Did you know about this last night?"

"Yes."

She sighed. "And you didn't think it was important to say something to me about it when we were alone?"

I laughed.

And while I did, she looked at me as if she didn't recognize me.

"Listen, for one, I had to keep that shit under wraps or Laura and my partners would fucking kill me. Two, I couldn't say anything to you about it until you signed an NDA. Because what if I discussed it with you and then you went and gossiped to your friend behind the bar. That would defeat the whole purpose of us doing this. Get me?"

"Get you?" She held the edge of the table with both hands. "You made me follow you to the back door last night. You basically caged me in with your arms. You rubbed your lips across mine. For what, Grayson? To see if I would make a move? To test me? To decide if you wanted me to be your fake wife?"

Wife.

Goddamn it, that word made me fucking shudder.

"The team said we had chemistry. I wanted to know if they were right."

"Why?"

"What are you, five?" I barked, which was the same age as Belle, Holden's daughter, and every word that came out of that little girl's mouth was *why*, *why*, and more *why*. Hearing it from Belle was cute. Hearing it from Jovana was getting on my fucking nerves.

She either wanted to sign the contract or didn't.

"Because I don't know how to fake it." I pulled at my collar, wondering why the hell I'd changed into a button-down when I'd originally had on a polo. I certainly wasn't trying to impress her. "If I felt nothing toward you, the media would know, and then again, I'd be doing this all for nothing."

"You're telling me you felt something?"

I felt something, all right.

But it was more than just something.

I felt everything.

Every pulse.

Breath.

And all the emotions that churned inside her.

Because even though that was all happening in her, it had also been happening inside me.

"I felt how hot your body is," I admitted, unwilling to give her anything else.

Her eyes widened, her head shaking, her teeth bared as though she were about to take a bite of something. "That's all you're going to say? That my body is hot?"

"And you smell nice."

She laughed, and it got louder as each second passed, to the point where she covered her mouth with her hand. "And here I thought you actually felt something for me last night."

"I did." I swallowed, remembering it had taken every bit of my power not to kiss her in that hallway, not to beg for her to come home with me. "I felt the hard-on in my fucking jeans."

Her lips stayed open, forming an O as she gazed at me. "You're an asshole. Even bigger than I thought."

"Except you're wet right now . . . aren't you?" I smiled. "You're forgetting that I know your body and I can tell."

"Grayson—"

"No need to lie. I can see the truth all over you." I got up from the head of the oval and walked around to the back of her seat, where I held the top of her chair, turning the wood until she was fully facing me, and then I rested my hands on the armrests. "Let's get something straight right now. I told you the first night that we were together that I wasn't the dating type. It's not something I do. I'm never with women more than once."

"Unless you're on a yacht for a whole week, then sleeping with a woman more than once is okay, am I right?"

I smiled. "There were enough women on that boat that I didn't have to repeat."

"I despise you."

"Good. That means at the end of all this, assuming you sign the contract and accept the ungodly amount of money I'm going to pay you, you won't expect me to fall in love with you, because I promise love isn't at the end of this fucking rainbow, Jovana."

"What's at the end, then?"

"Divorce."

She crossed her legs, and her arms followed.

Silence ticked.

And as she kept quiet, I could see the goddamn wheels in her brain spinning.

"You know, this is actually kind of funny," she said.

"How so?"

"Your reputation is hanging on by a thread." Her smile turned sinister. "Your company is losing memberships by the second. Your team had to hire a PR crisis manager just to get you under control and flip your script. You would think that, considering *I'm* the one doing *you* a favor, you'd actually be nice to me."

I growled, "I don't do nice."

"Except you need me, and you know that and"—she slowly licked across her bottom lip before moving to the top, nipping the center with her teeth—"that fucking kills you."

"I don't need you."

But I did.

In every way.

My body screamed for her.

My hands ached for her.

"No?" Her posture became more relaxed, and the confidence she was clearly feeling caused her grin to grow even larger. "Not only am I the humble, wholesome girl who could save your reputation and help rebuild the marriage arm for your company, but with my following, I could grow that arm. When my followers see the happiness on my face and our lovey-dovey marriage, they'll be begging to sign up to Hooked." She sat up a bit taller. "So, let's get something straight." Her pause reinforced that she was using my own words against me. "I don't care how antirelationship you are, how the thought of marriage has you breaking out in hives, I'm not going to put up with your nonsense. Your nastiness. Or one of the things you do best, which is dismiss my questions so you can trump them with your own." She lifted her foot and placed it on the center of my thigh, pushing until I backed up. Once she was satisfied with my new location, about six inches from where I stood before, her foot dropped to the floor. "If you want me to even consider helping you, I need to know what's in it for me."

"Money."

"Do better."

The anger that was building in my chest made me spit, "You want fucking more?"

"Not money-wise, but yes, I want more."

"You're unbelievable."

My hands squeezed together so hard, I had to shove them in my pockets.

I didn't trust them. Not when I was around her. Not when I wanted to touch her this badly.

Shit, I no longer trusted myself.

Because that mouth, the spiciness, the rebelliousness that I was hearing, made me want to lift her onto the table and fuck her into submission.

With each new side she revealed, she got even more beautiful.

Even this side that was more aggressive than I'd ever seen.

But I couldn't concentrate on that right now.

Not when she had me by the balls.

No one ever had me by the balls.

But she did.

She knew that.

And she was loving every second.

My jaw clenched, my teeth ground. "What do you want, Jovana?"

"Where do I even start?"

"Don't get fucking smart with me." I took a breath, attempting to tame the hardness in my pants. "Tell me what you want so we can get this over with."

She raked her fingers through a few sections of long curls, unfazed by the rage that was boiling through me. "I want you to grovel."

Grovel?

And this was exactly why I didn't date or go at it with a woman for more than one round.

I didn't want the demands. The control. The emotions.

This wasn't going to work.

"Fuck that."

"Then there's nothing to discuss here. I'm just going to go home." A hint of a smile tugged at the corner of her lips. "Is that what you want?"

Every exhale got louder, my nostrils flaring each time.

She knew I didn't have a choice. That I was cornered.

That my hands were clenched because the domination was shifting, and I couldn't stand it.

"I didn't think so." She stood from her chair and took a seat on the sturdy table. "It'll pack a harder punch if we're a little more eye level."

She gripped the edge of the wood on either side of her. "Go on, I'm waiting."

"You're something else."

"Just wait, Grayson. You haven't seen anything yet."

I took a step forward, and then another, and I was instantly sucked into her scent.

The lavender, the vanilla—they came out of nowhere, even though they'd been here the whole time.

Aromas that were typically calming, but they were doing the opposite.

And I didn't just feel that sensation in my cock; I felt it in my chest.

My hands.

My fucking mouth.

"I need you, is that what you want to hear?" I halted, waiting for a response. I didn't get one. I just saw a satisfaction building in her eyes. "I can't do this without you." I drew in a breath, knowing the next sentence was going to fucking sting. "I'm willing to do anything to make you want to marry me."

What the hell has gotten into me?

Why am I doing this?

How is it possible that I'm even saying these words?

Fuck.

"Tell me what you want, Jovana." I took one more step, realizing how close we now were. My hands came out of their pockets and landed on her cheeks. Cupping them. Aiming her face up at me. "You want me to touch you softly instead of holding you with all my strength?" I gazed at her lips. "You want a man who's going to lick your pussy every night?" That wasn't part of the deal, it certainly wasn't in the contract, but I wouldn't be opposed. She had the best fucking pussy I'd ever eaten. "You want me to promise you the entire world?" I leaned my face toward hers.

Her eyes stayed open and scanned mine as my face continued to get closer.

I couldn't stop it. Not the movement nor the momentum.

The desire to taste her was far too strong.

If she was going to get something out of me, then I wanted something for myself.

Her lips.

Her tongue.

The sound of her moaning the second my hands glided to her tits.

But once I was only a hair's breadth away from her mouth, her fingers went on top of mine and she squeezed, stopping me from coming any closer.

"I don't want any of those things, Grayson."

"What the fuck do you want then?"

She leaned her neck back, presumably to see a wider angle of my face. "I want a man who's going to lift me over puddles. And a man who's going to order me an entire platter of desserts in my favorite flavor. And a man who's going to take my dad to a Red Sox game because my family is as important to him as they are to me." She pulled my hands off her cheeks and slid down from the table, moving away from me until she was at the head, taking the chair where I'd previously been sitting. "Send Laura in on your way out. I'll finish this meeting without you. And if I decide to move forward and sign, she'll let you know."

Jovana was now suddenly in charge?

While I stood here with a throbbing hard-on?

I didn't think.

"I'm not leaving—"

"Either you leave or I do," she said. "The decision is yours."

There was no decision.

Jovana knew that.

And she fucking loved it.

If I were as childish as she was, I would have flipped her off on my way out.

But I wouldn't give her that satisfaction . . . even though she knew she'd already won.

CHAPTER EIGHT

Jovana

"Because I refuse to drink alone," I said to Sloane as I walked toward our couch, handing her a beer from the twelve-pack I'd bought on my way home.

"Girl, you never have to convince me to drink, you know this." She took the bottle from my hand and clinked it against mine. "Isn't this a rare sighting—both of us home, on a Friday night. Can the bar even operate without one of us there?"

I sat down beside her and dropped my feet onto the ottoman, sighing. "Probably not, and at this moment I could care less. Everything hurts, even my eyes. I need a break."

"Same." She turned toward me. "But you do have this smile on your face that I noticed when you got home this afternoon." She nudged my calf with her foot. "What's that about?"

I rolled my head until I was facing her. "What, I'm not allowed to be happy?"

She laughed. "You're like a golden retriever. You're always happy and something is always wagging on your body. But today, you just seem the happiest. So, spill it."

She wouldn't have thought the same if she had seen my face the morning after my meeting with Laura and Grayson. But two days had passed since my talk with them. That gave me enough time to process the details and the contract. To really consider what they were asking of me.

To wrap my head around marrying Grayson Tanner.

Maybe I was making the worst decision of my entire life.

Maybe I was doing this for all the wrong reasons.

Maybe I was completely nuts to be confident enough to think that somewhere, deep down, Grayson had feelings for me, and it would just take time and patience for those feelings to surface.

But I'd sent Laura a text before I'd grabbed the beers from the fridge, telling her I agreed to the terms.

Within thirty days of signing, I'd be able to pay off all my debt. I could cut down on the shifts I was working at the bar to really focus on building my business and create constant content to pursue my dream of being a full-time influencer. I'd be able to flaunt my relationship with Grayson in my social media posts, adding another layer to my persona, and another reason for my followers to want to live vicariously through me. Laura was right: my audience would melt over a love story, and to watch one unfold would only increase my visibility and engagement and followers. I'd be able to plan for my future—save a ton and open an investment account, things my parents hounded me to do since they were unable to.

And, most importantly, I'd be able to help my parents. A factor that motivated me more than anything.

Their situation wasn't good.

I could change that.

I could give them what I'd always dreamed of.

But there was a massive downside to this agreement.

One that made my stomach ache.

That made my chest hurt.

That made me think of my parents and what they had and it made me want to cry.

I was marrying a man who wasn't openly confessing his love.

I wasn't even sure he cared about me.

The only thing I knew for sure—that I could feel every time I was in his presence—was that he was attracted to me. That it felt like he was doing everything in his power not to touch me, that he was straining to not kiss me.

In my gut, I believed there was more.

I just didn't have proof.

And I didn't know if things would change the more time we spent together. If it was even possible for Grayson to grow feelings when he was so anti-everything.

I just had hope.

But that hope was another reason I'd said yes.

Because despite how much of an asshole he was, I couldn't get enough of his gaze.

His attention.

The way he made me feel.

I couldn't stop thinking about him or scrolling through his social media, wanting to know everything about this mysterious, hard-edged man.

I couldn't stop myself from wanting more.

I couldn't ignore the feeling in my stomach, this foreign, nagging sensation that told me he was the one.

My goal, even if it felt outlandish and impossible, was to have Grayson fall in love with me.

To have the love that I saw every time I looked at my parents.

And that was the reason I'd shown him my sassy side when we'd been in Laura's office. My semi-shy, timid, submissive side hadn't gotten me what I wanted with him. In fact, if I had stayed the night, he would have rejected me the following morning. Possibly kicked me out. Most definitely turned me away. But once I laid on just a little sass, it appeared that Grayson didn't know what to do with himself. He didn't know how to handle a woman who talked back. Who stuck up for herself. Who had her own demands.

Still, those were two very important sides of me that held equal weight in my everyday life.

This was the real Jovana.

As authentic as it got.

And he was getting to meet all of me.

Even though it was hard to tell what he actually liked since he had only one side and that was grumpy, I had a feeling the sass had sparked something inside him.

It pulled at him.

It challenged him in a way where he hadn't been before.

Still, that didn't change the elephant in my life, and that was that I was going to be a wife.

In a fake relationship.

And somehow, I was going to have to convince my family, friends, and colleagues that this quick, whirlwind phase of dating that led straight to an engagement was completely normal. That I was falling right into love's hands. That Grayson was the man of my dreams. That a marriage to him was everything I wanted and needed.

That this was soulmate-level kind of shit.

And at the end of the one year, I would have to swallow the massive lump in my throat, along with my pride, and admit to everyone— mostly my parents and followers—that rushing into marriage had been the wrong thing to do.

I was sure that once my parents found out their only child was getting hitched, they were going to have a slew of things to say. Warnings. Advice. Words of caution. And once the divorce papers were signed, I could already predict how many *I told you so*'s were going to be thrown in my direction.

So I needed to be extra convincing.

I needed everyone to believe that if there was a man made for me, that man was Grayson. That I couldn't breathe without becoming his wife.

That there was nothing more solid in this world than our relationship.

And I needed to start now.

That was the reason for my smile.

Because first up was Sloane.

She wanted to know the cause of my grin, so I replied, "Well, I may have some news."

"I knew it. Spill the tea, girl."

I turned toward her after taking a long sip and tucked a throw pillow into my stomach, resting the beer on top of it. "You know how much I despised Grayson? And the way he treated me? And how painful it had been to wait on his party the other night, but how I was sorta hopeful by the end of it after I walked him out and we almost kissed?"

Her brows rose. "That would be hard to forget, yes."

"He reached out the next morning and took me to breakfast." I hated that I was lying. That breakfast was really a meeting with his PR crisis manager and attorney and that, somehow, this had become my life. Still, I had to roll with it.

"And?"

I chewed the corner of my thumbnail. "He apologized for everything—the way he treated me at his condo and the things he said to me, and that he regretted never getting my number so he could call me after and apologize."

"He didn't need your number. He could have just come into the bar to talk to you."

"True." I sighed. "But you're missing the point."

"Isn't the point that if he gave a shit about you and your feelings, then he wouldn't have rented a yacht with six other women? He would have asked *you* to cruise the Mediterranean instead?"

Sloane took zero crap from anyone and gave zero fucks.

I knew she was going to be a hard sell.

"We had one night together, Sloane. He wasn't about to invite me on vacation—"

"But he invited someone. Six someones, to be exact."

I set my elbow on top of the back cushion of the couch, holding my face with my palm. "What the Celebrity Alert didn't show was that there were three other dudes on that boat with him. He wasn't there alone with six other women. So, yeah, it was bad, but not nearly as bad as the way it was portrayed."

"And you believe him?" Her tone told me she didn't.

"He showed me photos of him and the other guys on the boat." My voice softened as I added, "Yes, I believe him. And he feels like the biggest piece of shit for everything that went down."

She guzzled at least half her beer. "So, let me see if I understand this. He met you for breakfast with his tail between his legs, and I'm assuming, by the way you're looking at me right now, that he wants a chance with you. Please, for the love of God, tell me you told him to fuck off."

"I didn't."

Her head shook while she stared at me. "Why, babe? Why are you giving this man even a second of your attention? He doesn't deserve it."

This was my chance.

An opportunity to make a Sloane breakthrough, especially since this was the part that wasn't a lie.

Every word I was about to speak was the truth that lived inside me.

"Because when I left his condo, I felt it. And as I stalked his social media between our first and second encounters, I continued to feel it. And when I waited on his table the other night, I felt it even more. And when he took me into the hallway by the restrooms and pressed our foreheads together instead of kissing me because he didn't think he'd earned the right to put his lips on me again, I felt it the most." I reached across the cushions and put my hand on her shoulder. "I've never felt anything like this, Sloane. Never, ever. And I know the start was rocky and much more turbulent than I wanted"—I swallowed, feeling my throat tighten as I said and really processed those words—"but I know in my heart that this is right. That I have to give him a chance. That I have to see where this goes or . . ." My voice lowered as I said, "I'll regret it for the rest of my life."

She was silent for several seconds. "Well, shit. I can't exactly fight you on that, can I?"

"I mean, you could. But that would be dickish." I winked.

As I pulled my hand back, hers extended and landed on the visor of my baseball hat, lifting it so she could really take in my eyes. "Does this mean I have to be nice to Grayson the next time I see him?"

"That's probably going to be very soon, and yes, that's exactly what it means."

She let out a long, drawn-out breath. "Fine. But I'm still going to give him an extremely strict warning that if he hurts you or breaks your heart, he's dead."

I smiled. "I expect nothing less."

"Good." Her eyes narrowed. "That doesn't mean I'm happy about this."

"You don't have to be. You just have to trust that I know what's best for me and that I'm following my heart and that Grayson Tanner— despite how much we used to despise him—is the perfect man for me."

Just as I finished speaking, a chime came from my phone, a sound specific to incoming texts.

I pulled out my cell and looked at the screen.

Unknown: It's Grayson. Laura gave me your number and said you were signing the contract tomorrow. That means we need to set up our first date. I'll be in touch with the details.

"That's him, isn't it?" Sloane asked. "I can tell because you have that goddamn smile on your face again."

I made sure she couldn't see the screen while I read his words once more and then shoved the phone back into my pocket. "I can't help it. He makes me swoony."

No matter what he said, like the professional text he'd just sent, or the directness that spewed from his mouth every time I was around him, it was all thrilling. Of course, sometimes more than others, but it still had the same result.

Grayson caused me to react—my heart, my body.

Every single bit of me.

"Swoony." She groaned. "For the record, that word should be banned. Forever."

I gently shook her shoulder. "Come on, you're going to love this and you're going to fall for him just like I have."

"Yeah, yeah." She finally gave me a smile. "We'll see about that."

CHAPTER NINE

Grayson

"Why the hell would you live all the way out here?" I asked Jovana as she climbed into the front seat of my car.

"All the way out here" was Somerville, a suburb fifteen minutes outside Boston that I never bothered going to. If I was going to leave the city, it was to go to one of its edges, like Cambridge, right near Harvard, and that was to grab some food I'd fallen in love with while in college.

It sure as hell wouldn't be to see a woman—whether I hooked or fished her.

Jovana was becoming the exception to everything.

Damn it.

"Wow, that's how you're going to greet me?" She wrapped the seat belt around her. "No, 'Hi, Jovana, you look nice tonight.' Or, 'Oh man, you smell terrific.' Or, 'I've missed you these last few days, it's nice to see you.'"

The thing was, she looked exceptional in the tight red dress that hugged her amazing curves, and seeing her prance across the sidewalk on the way to my car in those sky-high heels had made every part of me ache.

That was the reason I'd dug on her the second she opened the door.

To get my mind in a place of annoyance rather than pleasure.

But I wouldn't tell her that.

I wouldn't say anything that would trigger a conversation that had even the smallest chance of turning emotional.

The last thing that needed to happen between us was some type of connection.

I shook my head. "Again, why the hell would you live out here?"

"Why?" She laughed as she settled in the seat, placing her small purse on her lap. "Because it's semi-affordable, that's why."

I looked at the rows of apartment buildings. The convenience store on each corner, a nail salon, a Thai restaurant—all places she probably frequented, but in the city, the sidewalk between them would be packed, the road full of traffic.

Here, things were much quieter.

And there was no view.

Aside from her.

"You know," she continued, "most people don't make as much money as you. I mean, I sure don't." I watched her glance across the dashboard. "They don't drive fancy cars like this. They work two jobs because they have to, like me, and they still have to decide which bills they're going to pay since oftentimes they can't afford to pay all of them in the same month."

She knew nothing about me.

I wasn't surprised.

My childhood wasn't listed on my Wikipedia page.

For some reason, due to a feeling that came out of nowhere, I said, "Believe it or not, Jovana, I haven't always been rich."

"Have you forgotten the days when you weren't?"

"Hardly."

"Tell me about them. What did they look like? How did you live?"

I shifted into drive and pulled into the road that was far too lonely, gripping the steering wheel like the goddamn thing was about to fall off.

"Grayson . . ."

"What?"

"I'm going to marry you in two months. Don't you think it's important that I know these kinds of things about you?"

As I approached the red light, I gave her a look that told her I didn't appreciate the way she was digging.

Shit, I understood we needed to learn about each other to keep up appearances, but I didn't want to muddy the water. I didn't want her to grow feelings.

I definitely didn't want her to get too close.

But I also hated that she had a point.

That in just a couple of months, this stunning woman was going to be my wife.

That if her family or friends asked her questions about me—inquiries that would inevitably come up as she attempted to convince them we were the real deal—she would have to know the answers so our relationship came across as genuine.

"I don't mean to pry," she said. "Despite having a public job, I'm a very private person, so I understand how hard it is to reveal certain sides of yourself. But in doing that, it's just going to give me more of you, and regardless of how much you don't want that, it's necessary." Her voice was soft.

Far too fucking soft.

"How did you grow up, Grayson?"

I waited until the light turned green before I said, "I come from a single dad." As I released the words, I was glad I wasn't looking at her. It was easier to stare at the one car ahead. "He did everything he could to provide, and he did his best, but there weren't extras. Our vacations involved going three towns over for one of my basketball games." I took a breath. "I didn't have Daddy's credit card, like most of the kids I went to college with, so I worked while getting my undergraduate, and when I graduated with my MBA from Harvard, I had a fucking mound of debt. We were just launching the app and things were tight as hell for a while until we could afford to take money out of the business and pay ourselves. And when we did, it was almost nothing."

"See, that wasn't so hard, was it?" Her tone was now just above a whisper.

When I glanced at her, she was smiling.

I didn't return the expression.

"You're obviously making a boatload now, so when did that happen?"

I slowed at the stop sign. "It took a boatload to design the app, and we borrowed that money from Holden's and Easton's parents along with a few other private investors, so we had to pay them back. As we expanded, we had to rent office space, pay salaries. Advertise. Hire a social media team. By the two-year mark, we were able to pull a decent-size salary, and it just grew from there."

"What you guys have done, it's amazing."

"We worked our asses off. There were nights, more than I'd like to count, that I slept at my desk. But now . . ." I shook my head as my voice trailed off, thinking of the conversations I'd had with my best friends about the Celebrity Alert that had gone out about me and the media shitstorm that had followed. "Now things are falling apart a little and, fuck, I need to get the control back."

"You will."

I eyed her after I checked both directions and shifted to first. "Because of you?"

She nodded. "You're underestimating my abilities, Grayson. You think I'm just some gal who delivered drinks to your table and had enough pull to make your vodka doubles and enough memory to remember your Coke. I'm much more than that."

"To be honest, I don't know who the fuck you are."

"Do you want to know?"

"No." I ground my teeth together and shifted into second gear. Knowing would fill in the blanks, and I was afraid I'd like those answers far too much. "But I'm sure you're going to tell me. Just do me a favor, all right? Skip the boring parts. I don't need to know that you won a spelling bee in fifth grade and were the president of the knitting society and that you blew the RA of your dorm."

"You're such an asshole."

I glanced at her again.

Fuck, I liked when she looked mad.

The way her lips jutted out and her eyes got all fiery. How heat moved into her cheeks and turned them red.

How her skin was just slightly clammy from the tension, a sign that told me if I reached down and touched her pussy it would be wet.

She could deny it all she wanted, but the banter turned her on.

"I'm not an asshole, Jovana; I just don't take any bullshit. I have zero patience. For this, for you—for anything. This isn't what I want, so it's making me even wickeder than normal. You know this. Therefore there's no reason for you to act surprised."

"Oh, I'm not surprised. I'm just letting you know, you're a fucking asshole."

I smiled. Shit, it felt good. "Feel better now?"

"I won't feel better until the divorce papers are signed."

"Baby, that makes two of us."

As my reply hit her, I watched the top of her chest. Instead of rising and falling, there was no movement.

"Someone likes being called baby."

"Dick," she shot back.

I chuckled, waiting for more, but she was silent for a few moments, fidgeting in her seat, her legs uncrossing and recrossing before she said, "I got straight As in high school and was hoping to get an academic scholarship but didn't, so I graduated college with more debt than I can even stomach. I'm completely obsessed with music—I don't listen to a specific genre, I just love it all. The lyrics affect me emotionally, and the beats inspire me in the most creative ways. Lastly, since I know you're on the verge of snoring, I'm an only child, and with that comes a heavy burden. All I want to do is earn enough that I can get my parents out of the horrible, run-down apartment they're in, a place they've lived in for far too long, and be able to make their lives a little easier because, God knows, they've done nothing but struggle."

I understood her reasoning.

More than I even wanted to admit.

"That's certainly motivation," I told her.

"My parents deserve everything and more, and I want to be able to give it to them."

"What's the other reason?" When I didn't get an immediate answer, I looked at her. "What? Are you realizing that talking about yourself isn't as easy as you thought?" I huffed out some air and gazed through the windshield.

"It's not tough at all, Grayson. I just don't know how vulnerable I want to be with you."

"Fair."

More silence ticked until I heard, "The kids in my high school were mean. I'm talking downright cruel. I didn't have stylish clothes. I couldn't afford highlights in my hair. I wasn't one of the cool ones—far from it. I was picked on relentlessly and made fun of, and even though I had the brains and was smarter than all of them, no one thought I would amount to anything."

"What does that have to do with your success?"

"Everything." She faced me. "Do you know how satisfying it is to look in my Stories and see that girls from my class are viewing them? That when they get together and gossip, they're talking about the brand deals I've scored and the reach I have now, and my followers that are growing on the daily? I'm proving them wrong, and it feels fabulous."

"Why do you care what they think?"

"Why?" She let out a long exhale. "Because I'm sensitive. Because my heart aches when I think about the things they said and did to me, and it feels good to be able to show them exactly who I am now."

"The only person you have to prove anything to is yourself. What they think, what they say, what they did to you—that shit is insignificant."

"I get what you're saying. I really do. I just want the ones who dismissed me as unworthy to see me for who I really am."

"You're worthy, Jovana. Trust me. I see it in everything that you do, so I promise you they see it too. Whether they admit how powerful and incredible you are—that's a different story."

My comment left my lips before I had a chance to really think about it.

To process the impact of that compliment.

Silence ticked before she said, "That's the best thing you've said to me since we've met, thank you," in the softest voice.

I pulled up in front of the restaurant, leaving the car running for the valet attendant. "I wonder what those bitches are going to say when they find out you're marrying me."

"I'm sure they'll smile extra hard when I announce our breakup." She rolled her eyes and got out of the car before the valet attendant even had a chance to open her door.

I slid out as well and joined her on the sidewalk, my hand immediately going to her lower back as I walked her into the restaurant.

Laura hadn't encouraged physical contact. She'd said nothing about it, in fact. I just thought it would be a nice touch if there happened to be any eyes on us.

Once I put my hand there, her back straightened, and the muscles beneath my fingers tightened.

But that wasn't the only thing that happened.

I was shocked at how comfortable the placement felt.

At how badly I wanted to pull her against me and lock our mouths together.

I would give anything to know what she tasted like at this moment.

She turned her face toward my chest, and I hoped she was going to close the distance between us, but instead, she quietly said, "I'm warning you now, if you're not nice to me over dinner, you can forget that first kiss that's supposed to go down tonight."

It would defeat the purpose if she gave me one now. The kiss needed to be inside the restaurant, in front of the servers and dining patrons. Still, I was disappointed it didn't happen, which shocked my system again.

Since I came here regularly for sushi, most of the staff knew who I was and greeted me by name, and I hoped that rumors would start when they shared that they saw me with a chick.

A hot one, at that.

And that my hands and mouth were all over her—something I never did in public, so they were definitely going to take note.

I walked her into the hotel, the restaurant located along the left side of the small, intimate lobby, and whispered, "I know you're not threatening me."

"That's not a threat. It's a promise. I'm doing this for you and Hooked, *remember*?"

"I'm paying off your student loans and for your parents' new apartment, *remember*?"

She gazed up at me and smirked. "This is going to be the longest year of my life."

"And mine." I drove my teeth into my bottom lip, glaring at her beautiful face, and opened the door to the restaurant.

As soon as the hostess spotted me, she said, "Mr. Tanner, good evening. I see you have a reservation for two." She eyed up Jovana. "Let me bring you to your table."

The hostess, a student at Boston University, had been working here for the last six months. In that time, she'd done everything in her power to fuck me.

This was the best sushi restaurant in Boston, so I didn't want to make things awkward as hell when I came in once a week to eat alone at the bar. In addition, the chef and I were great friends.

So, there were actually times when I knew enough to keep my dick in my pants. This was one of those rare occasions.

"Yes, for two," I repeated, emphasizing the number while I stood at Jovana's side, gazing down her profile. I strengthened my grip on her back before I stepped behind her. The new position had her hair grazing the top of my chest, her locks giving off the lavender scent.

Even in a room full of food, I could still smell her.

And that smell increased the longing.

Fuck me.

"Follow me," the hostess replied.

There were two dining rooms, both small. I hoped she chose the larger, which would give us an audience of five or six more tables, and the potential of having all those extra eyes on us. Fortunately, when she turned to her right, I realized that was exactly where she was bringing us, and the table was in the center.

Perfectly placed. The hostess even earned herself a smile.

"Enjoy," she said, returning the grin while she placed a menu in front of me.

Once we were alone, I asked Jovana, "Have you eaten here before?"

She folded her hands on top of her menu. "I think the real question is, How long has it been since you've slept with the hostess?" Her eyes narrowed while she waited for a response.

My lips pulled wide. "Why? Are you jealous?"

"Not even close. I just couldn't tell what she wanted to do more—eat you or kill me."

I laughed, her description ironically very accurate. "I've never touched her." When I could tell she didn't believe me, I added, "I promise."

She sat on that reply for a few seconds. "No, I haven't eaten here. I've heard about this place, of course, but it's not in my why-do-you-live-in-Somerville budget."

"Smart-ass."

"Look at these prices." She was looking at her menu. "They're absolutely wild. Who would spend this for a spicy tuna roll?"

She'd never been spoiled.

She'd never tasted this quality of food.

I was going to show her the difference between this spicy tuna and all the others she'd had.

"Give me your menu," I demanded.

"Because you want me to stop looking at the prices?"

There was something so innocent about her, so refreshing.

"Yes, I want you to stop looking at them. When you're with me, price doesn't matter."

"But it'll always matter, Grayson." Her voice was soft, a side that didn't come with sass. She used this tone when she wanted me to see her core. "Even if I become a millionaire one day—"

"Are you forgetting how much the contract was for?"

She cleared her throat. "What I mean is, regardless of how much money I have now or when I build my business to the highest peak, I'll still count every penny. And I assure you, I would never spend that many dollars on eight tiny pieces of fish."

I held out my hand. "Give me your menu, Jovana." She did as she was told. "The other reason you don't need it is because we're dining omakase-style tonight."

"I have no idea what that means."

"Then sit back and enjoy yourself. Shit is about to get real fun."

"Grayson," the waiter said as he appeared at our table, the gentleman's face one I recognized as he'd waited on me multiple times. "It's great to see you back."

I shook his hand and thanked him.

"And I see you have a guest. Welcome," the waiter said to Jovana. "What can I get you both to drink? A bottle of your usual, perhaps?"

I nodded.

"And Pellegrino, I assume?"

"Please," I replied.

"I'll be back with both."

The second he was gone, a smile warmed Jovana's face. "They know your name. What you drink. Probably what you eat. I'm assuming that's why you brought me here? So these kind folks can spread the word that you have a woman in your life?"

"That, yes." I paused, my brows raising. "That *is* why we're sitting at this table together. Why I'm going to kiss you in about twenty seconds. And why we're getting married." I kept my voice as low as possible, the music playing throughout the dining room making it difficult for anyone to hear me anyway. "But I also brought you here because it's the best. That's what you deserve and that's what I wanted you to taste tonight."

I wasn't sure where that desire came from, but it existed and it was how I felt.

"Really?" She turned her head a little to the side, a heat entering her cheeks. "Sounds like an odd thing to want to give someone you resent and barely know."

That fucking smile.

I wanted to lick it off her face.

"Let's say I want to make things as comfortably cordial as possible."

"Cordial isn't kissing."

I set my napkin on my lap, clearing everything in the path of my wineglass, which was taking far too long to fill. "I suppose it can be if there's no feeling behind it. Just lips touching lips."

"Is that so?"

I leaned onto the table, moving closer to her. "I make up my own definitions, Jovana. People in power can do that."

"Ha!" She licked across her bottom lip, reminding me that we were on equal ground, despite how much I fucking hated that. "Don't forget my power, baby." She winked and my dick clenched. "I've got much more than you're giving me credit for." She glanced to her right and then left before locking our stares. "Let me remind you of something. We have an entire year together, and you're not stupid enough to jeopardize your reputation again, which means one whole year of celibacy. That's going to be quite the mindfuck—or, should I say, lack-of-physical fuck—for someone who likes to hook up all the time. That's what I call power."

I liked where this was going.

I liked it far too much.

"Are you saying you're going to give me your pussy?"

This time, she actually laughed. "Quite the opposite. I'm saying I'm going to make you wait an entire year to have sex. Once the divorce papers are signed, you can sleep with all of Boston. Until then, you're going to be a sad and very horny panda, I'm afraid."

"Is that so?" There was something about using her own words and seeing the way they affected her that turned me on. "You're going to go an entire year, most of it living in my home, without even thinking about my dick? Is that what you're trying to convince me of?"

Shit, this was becoming more fun by the second.

Because every sentence caused her cheeks to redden even more, her eyes to glare, her expression to intensify. She was trying to hide how she was feeling, but I knew.

Goddamn it, I could see it all over her.

"Before you attempt to do that, which you won't succeed at, let me paint a little picture for you. Every morning when you wake up in the guest room at my place, you're going to dream about sneaking into my bedroom, sliding your wet pussy over my cock. Riding me until you fucking scream." I halted, letting that really sink in. "And at night, when you're lying in the darkness, you're going to think about my tongue and how it felt when I licked you. You're going to be so needy and worked up from those fantasies that your hand is going to reach for your clit and you're going to stroke it the same way I licked you, swiping it up and down until you come. I may not be able to have sex for a year, but you're in the same boat, sweetheart. Just think of how easily you'll come after twelve months of not being touched. Fuck, it'll take nothing more than just blowing on your clit before you're shuddering."

"You're evil."

I leaned back in my seat, proud of what I'd just accomplished. "Power comes in all forms, baby. You may have yours, but don't forget the strength of mine." I chuckled. "How could you? I believe when you experienced it, it was the hardest you'd ever come. Am I right?" I read her eyes before I said, "I thought so."

"We'll see."

There it was—more fucking goading.

Oh, we'll see, all right.

I got up from my chair and stepped over to hers, leaning down until my mouth was just above her ear.

The closeness caused her posture to become erect and her to hold her breath, her chest no longer rising or falling.

Her scent wasn't the only thing that made my cock throb—the feel of her did too.

The way my lips were so near her flesh was nothing but a tease.

"Are you going to tell me that if I reached under your dress and slipped my fingers inside your panties, your pussy wouldn't be wet?" My whispered words caused goose bumps to rise across her. "That if I did, you wouldn't beg me to finger-fuck you?" I moved the hair off her neck and positioned my mouth along the side of it, halfway between her collarbone and ear.

"I wouldn't—"

"Whatever you do, don't lie to me. I can smell the sweetness of your pussy in the air, and I can see the goose bumps on your skin, which tells me just how wet and turned on you are." I brushed my lips over her skin. "But I want to hear it from you, Jovana. So tell me, just how wet are you right now?"

I knew I was playing with fire.

I knew I shouldn't be using my words to arouse her, that I shouldn't be standing this close, that I shouldn't be touching her, like I was going to lift her out of her chair and wrap her in my arms, but I couldn't help it.

There was something about Jovana Winters that made me want to do this.

That made me want to take her into the restroom and lock the door and fuck her against the wall. That made me want to then drive her to my place and strip her in the elevator and carry her inside my penthouse, where I'd sink into her tightness the moment we got inside, guaranteeing we'd both come again.

And again.

But I also knew that the eyes in this room were on me. I could feel them, and that was only going to help me and make this situation even more rewarding.

Jovana turned her head, causing our lips to align. She glanced at my mouth before my eyes. "You're not going to win this round. I assure you."

"You assure me, huh? But I've already won." I smiled. "One year is a long time to go without fucking. If you can handle the physical aspects without getting emotionally attached, I see no reason to keep our hands off each other. So, let me throw something out there for you to ponder. I know I'd love to ravish you, to make you feel incredible; I just don't want you to fall for me. If you can promise me that, then we have ourselves a deal." I closed the distance between us and breathed her in as my lips smashed against hers, my hand clamped on her neck, making sure she didn't pull away.

She didn't even attempt to.

Fuck, she tasted just the way I remembered.

Sweet.

Delicious.

Perfection.

I circled my tongue around hers, taking one final lap, and gradually pulled away.

Her eyes were slow to open, her skin the most flushed it had been all night.

I didn't want her to know how much I enjoyed this. How I would jerk off to this kiss when I was finally home and far away from her.

Those thoughts were staying vaulted.

Instead, I'd remind her of why we were here. The sterile technicalities of this arrangement.

I licked her off my lips as I pulled away and said, "First assignment—check. Now, let's eat so I can drop you off at home."

CHAPTER TEN

Jovana

Date two was coming to a close, and my heart was pounding even harder than when Grayson had driven me home from the sushi restaurant, where I'd eaten the best food of my entire life. Tonight had been Italian, and I'd never had pasta like that before. We'd eaten at a place in the North End that had a line out the door. Grayson took me straight inside, bypassing at least ten people standing in the rain. He smiled at the hostess, who greeted him by name, and we were seated at a table by the window, one reserved just for him even though the restaurant didn't take reservations.

I was learning what power looked like in all forms.

Grayson's was certainly impressive.

So was the way he kissed me, which happened seconds before he reached into the bread basket for a halved baguette. Soon after we finished our first glass of wine, his lips found mine again, and I could taste the burgundy on his tongue. The third time took place when we stood from the table to exit the restaurant. His arms briefly wrapped around me, and our bodies pressed together even after his mouth left mine.

He wanted us to be seen.

He'd accomplished that during both outings.

He wanted our dates to leave a lasting impression. If the other diners at these restaurants weren't convinced, then they just didn't believe in love. From the outside looking in, there may as well have been a camera in our faces and a script memorized in our heads.

We were that freaking good.

At least for me, that was because on the inside, every bit that was coming out was real. The tidbits of myself I revealed during conversation, the expression when I looked at him, the passion I put behind my kissing—that was my honest, raw emotion. Would I be able to be physical with him without falling harder? Could I give him my body without my heart?

Could I be intimate without being consumed by love?

I didn't have that answer yet.

All I knew was that every time I thought of the way this would end, the impending divorce in twelve months' time, my heart ached.

It didn't matter how shitty he acted, how difficult he could be, or how many times he deserved to be called a dick.

I wanted him.

I was deeply, endlessly attracted to him.

And I felt myself falling even more every time I was with him.

But could I change a man who didn't want or believe in us?

So far, I hadn't.

Now, as he wove through the city traffic on his way to Somerville, there was something I needed to discuss with him.

Something I was extremely nervous to do, but given that the timeline to our engagement was so short, this had to be done.

"Grayson . . ." I took a breath and looked across the dark space toward the driver's side, the headlights of the approaching car shining over the top of his face. "I want to put out a teaser on Instagram."

When he glanced at me, the light across his eyes had faded, leaving me with a glare that I felt through my entire body. "What does that mean?"

It meant that, after I posted, everything would change.

My content would have a whole new feel—my followers would be rooting for us. I wouldn't just be targeting my typical demographic; I would have an entirely new one. One that was only there to watch a love story unfold.

One that didn't technically exist, at least according to him.

The moment the car idled, I lifted his hand off the gearshift and placed it on my thigh. "It means, I want to take a photo of you doing this"—I tapped the back of his hand—"and post it to my Instagram feed."

"Jesus."

I wasn't entirely surprised by his response, but I was still taken aback by it.

"Isn't that why we're doing this? So the world sees you're a changed man? Or however Laura would word it."

"Yeah."

"Then what's the problem? You've now kissed me inside two of Boston's most popular restaurants and everyone and their mother watched you do it. Suddenly, you're all bothered that I'm going to post a photo of your hand?"

"I'm not bothered, Jovana. I just said *Jesus*. Calm down."

Except he was bothered.

And he was deflecting.

Maybe he didn't pay attention to me, but I listened, I watched, and I was learning him fast.

What I realized in that moment was that the weight of my post was really hitting him. It wasn't that his hand was going to appear on my social media. It was that this was really happening, that he was going against everything he believed in.

That we were soon going to be social media official.

"Don't worry." I sighed. "I'm not going to tag you. I'm just taunting my viewers, building the suspense so when it's time to reveal the identity of this mystery man, they'll go nuts."

And they would—both positively and negatively.

Everyone had something to say about everything nowadays. Some commented with the sweetest emojis. Some, like the keyboard warriors, would tear me apart, their words not only jarring but scarring.

When they found out the mystery man was Grayson Tanner, I suspected those keyboard warriors would remind me that he'd had a giant orgy with six women on a yacht. That he had a reputation for being Boston's Biggest Bachelor and he'd never settle down, even with me. That I was just after his money and his clout.

And when the divorce came, I could only imagine what they would say then.

The thought made me sick to my stomach.

"Is that what you're calling me? Mystery Man?"

I took out my phone and aimed it above his hand. "Or Dick. I'm happy to use that. Just tell me which you prefer."

His head shook while he hissed out several beats of air.

I smiled even though he probably couldn't see it. "Don't move." I pointed the phone at various angles, taking enough shots that I'd have plenty of options. "I'm good. You can have your hand back."

I expected him to immediately leave my thigh. He needed his hand to shift, after all, so even if he wanted to keep it there, he couldn't.

What I didn't expect was for him to not be in a hurry, to hold me for a count of three, to squeeze before he pulled away, the heat from his palm building to the point of sweat.

Normally, I'd have a sassy comment that I'd shoot off in his direction.

But I said nothing, scrolling through the library of photos, trying to get my mind off the way he'd just made me feel, how my skin instantly missed him now that he was gone. Each picture showed his rolled-up sleeve, the pattern on the cuff of his shirt, the dark hair that peeked out on his forearm. And just enough of my lap so that the viewers could tell I was showing them my thigh and the important placement of his hand.

I chose the best one and added my usual set of filters.

Cropped.

I then created a post, typing the following: Him.

I debated over an emoji and went with the red heart.

Oh God.

I filled my lungs, holding the air in as I clicked the button to share the pic. "Done." I exhaled.

His stare made me take another breath. "It's posted?"

"Yep."

"Are people responding already?"

My notifications were exploding, box after box appearing on my screen, an equal rotation of likes and comments. "Oh yeah. They're freaking out *aaand* . . ." I halted as I came across the first bit of nastiness, a woman telling me that my dress was far too short, and it was no wonder I'd landed a man. "Man, people can be ugly. I can't read any more."

"What did they say?"

"It was about me. Not you."

"Do you normally get a lot of hate?"

"I get a lot of everything. It comes with the territory." I slipped my phone back into my clutch.

"You should probably send the post to Laura." He turned at the light. "I'm sure she's keeping a folder on everything that's aired and she'll want—"

"Laura's one of my followers. I guarantee she set up notifications and just got alerted that I posted."

He chuckled. "Of course she is."

"You should be, too, you know."

"Yeah?" He didn't sound convinced. "And why's that?"

"Because it'll look awfully strange if we're in a relationship and I post pictures of us and someone clicks on your profile, checks your followers, and sees that you're not following me."

"Who the fuck would waste their time doing that?"

"Half the women in this world. You'd be surprised at what they do and the kind of information they want to find out."

"Jesus."

There was that word again, his tone telling me how bothered he was by this.

"I'm following you," I admitted.

Unless he had all his notifications turned off, he would have been alerted that on the date I'd signed the contract, I'd followed him on Instagram. That seemed like the only account he had, since I couldn't find him on TikTok or Faceframe.

His jaw clenched, like he was grinding his teeth. "Are you telling me I have to follow you back?"

"You say that like it's a death sentence." The man couldn't help himself. He had to make every situation so painfully challenging. "But yes, that's what I'm telling you." And the way I was about to shift the conversation, giving him another order, was going to turn him even grumpier. "What are you doing after you drop me off?"

"I'm meeting the guys at a strip club. Why?"

I had nothing against strip clubs.

I'd been to a few myself.

But everything about what he'd just said annoyed the hell out of me. From the pleasure in his voice to the instant reply to the thought of him getting a lap dance.

"Seriously?" I groaned. "And Laura approved that? What happens if one of the strippers snaps a pic of you and it goes viral—"

"I was joking, Jovana." He slowed for the stop sign and turned toward me. "But I'm glad you're so concerned with what the fuck I do." His eyes were on me again, and this time I felt them straight through my chest. "For the record, my actions don't warrant a lecture from you. You're not my mother and I'm a grown-ass man. If I want to go to a strip club, I will."

My blood was boiling.

"I'm sacrificing a year of my life to help you rebuild your name and your company's number of memberships. I don't care how much you're paying me—this is about you, not me. So, no, you're not going to risk this by getting caught at a strip club where the media will go bananas if they get their hands on a shot of you. This isn't the time to be rebellious or an asshole, *asshole*." I crossed my arms over my chest. "But you know what you will do? You'll come up to my apartment instead of just dropping me off, and you'll properly meet my roommate, Sloane."

He moved his hand to the top of the steering wheel and shifted into first, the car moving forward. "And here I thought you were going to take me upstairs and give me your pussy."

"That's the last thing you'll ever get from me."

He released a blow of air. "I assume the introduction is an order too?"

Satisfied, I let my arms drop. "In a major way."

"You've turned into quite the alpha, haven't you, Jovana?"

"Someone needs to keep your ass in check despite how grown you think you are."

"Jesus."

Third time.

But this time, I'd won.

He pulled into a spot beside my building and parked, the engine purring just before he turned it off.

Before he opened his door, I said, "Remember, this mission is to show Sloane how obsessed you are with me. From the moment we get out of this car, I need you to be Team Jovana. Got it?"

"As opposed to?"

"The dick you've been for most of the night."

That was a slight lie.

He'd been charming at the restaurant.

And irresistible.

And ridiculously sexy as he flirted with me from the other side of the small table, our knees touching every time I recrossed my legs.

But there was no way I would ever say any of that to him.

"Come on, let's go inside so we can get this over with," I told him, opening my door and meeting him on the sidewalk.

Like the two previous times we'd walked in and out of restaurants, I figured his hand would press against my lower back to lead me inside.

But as I took my first step toward the front of my building, his fingers linked with mine.

The gesture caught me off guard, and I found myself drawing in as much air as I could hold and not releasing it.

This was a different kind of power.

It was filled with lust.

Emotion.

A need that pulsed and radiated through my entire body.

When we got to the entrance, his hand dropped from mine to let me dig inside my clutch, searching for my set of keys. Once I found them, I waved the fob against the reader, and he opened the door for me. His hand then returned to mine, and we headed for the elevator.

"Top floor," he said the moment I pressed the button. "Does that mean you have a penthouse?"

I laughed. His comment was actually hysterical. "Absolutely. Wait until you see it, it's huge. Four beds, four bathrooms. We have the biggest unit in the building. It even comes with a butler who wakes us up with smoothies every morning and irons our sheets."

"Maybe I need to fire my housekeeper. Sounds like she's slacking compared to yours."

I shook my head. "You probably would too."

"Nah." He smiled. "I don't like smoothies."

"Who doesn't like a smoothie?"

"It does nothing for me. I need substance, like the smooth lips of a pussy or some scrambled eggs."

"I just gagged."

He moved closer, using his height and the broadness of his chest to back me up against the side wall. "No, what you did was remember the way I licked yours and instantly got wet."

"You're far too full of yourself."

I was beyond grateful that the elevator arrived before he was able to reply, and I stepped around him and moved us through the opening and down the hall, using my key to get us inside my apartment.

"Hey, hey," I called out to Sloane.

My plan all along had been to bring him upstairs, so before I left for my date, I'd already given Sloane the heads-up. This way, she'd be prepared and already wearing a bra, unlike the half-naked attire she usually lounged around in.

"Wine's in the fridge," she called out from the living room. "Bring me a refill, will ya?"

"I've got you," I replied.

As I made my way into the kitchen, Grayson stood near the sink, leaning against the counter. "It's good to see someone has the power to boss you around." He wasn't any louder than a whisper, so Sloane wouldn't hear.

I rolled my eyes at him and grabbed the bottle from the fridge. "Want a drink?" I scanned the shelves. "I have an IPA. Two summer lagers. And white wine."

"The IPA."

I glanced past the door of the fridge to look at him. "And if I told you that's the one I wanted?"

"You think that would change my decision?"

"You're such a gentleman." I grabbed the summer lager for myself, handing him the IPA. With the wine tucked under my arm, I said, "Follow me," and brought him into the living room.

Sloane was lounging across her favorite part of the couch, her feet extended over the ottoman, her socks pulled high to her knees. She wore her hair in a messy bun and hadn't bothered to put in her contacts, her thick black lenses sitting midway on her nose.

"Sloane," I said, stopping in front of the ottoman, where I handed her the wine, "I want you to officially meet Grayson."

For as grumpy as he was, she was equally as cunty. That was one of the things I loved most about her.

I couldn't wait to hear how this conversation was going to go down. If he thought I was snarky, he was meeting his toughest match.

But at the same time, I wanted this to go smoothly.

I wanted her to believe I cared about him.

I wanted her to see what I saw in him.

She poured the rest of the white into her glass and set the bottle on the floor, looking up just as Grayson's hand left my lower back to extend toward her.

"Sloane," he said, "it's a pleasure to meet you. I've heard a lot about you."

"Yeah?" She held the glass against her chest and shook his fingers. "Tell me something you've learned about me."

Oh, she was good.

Without pause, Grayson replied, "I hear you make a hell of a martini. Extra filthy. Just the way I like it."

I'd told him that over dinner tonight.

I couldn't believe he'd listened.

Most of the time when I was talking, unless the topic bordered on dirty, I was never positive I had his full attention. I just figured my words went in one ear and straight out the other.

But he'd heard me this evening. He'd processed.

I wasn't sure what to make of that.

Sloane looked at me, her eyes smiling even though her grin didn't reach her lips. "I'll make you one the next time you're at the bar."

"I look forward to it." He released her hand. "But should I ask you the same question?" He paused. "What have you learned about me?"

"You can," she responded.

"All right then," he started. "Tell me."

He was so incredibly charming in the way he spoke, how his stare stayed directly on her.

Nothing and no one made Sloane uncomfortable, but I noticed how she didn't remain still. She tucked her legs underneath her as we took a seat on the other side of the couch.

"Let's see . . ." She sipped her wine. "I know there were other men on the yacht with you. You're not as raunchy as everyone thinks." She winked at him. "I know you're one successful businessman. And I know that when my girl returns home from your dates, she has this wicked smile on her face." She nodded toward me. "The one she has on now. You may not know that smile, Grayson, but I do. She doesn't wear it often, so you must be doing something right."

"Hmm," he huffed.

I felt his eyes on me, but I didn't look at him.

I wished Sloane hadn't said that.

I liked that she'd noticed, but I didn't want him to know that he made me feel that way.

"Jovana tells me you want to buy the bar?" he said to her.

I gasped inwardly when his hand landed on my thigh, rubbing the inside and outside of my knee. He was definitely playing the part. Sitting close. Appearing attentive and present. Loving, even.

All of it was causing my skin to heat up.

I was sure he felt it.

And I was sure he was loving that he had this effect on me.

"I do," she replied.

Another topic we'd discussed over pasta was Sloane's desire to buy the bar and for my influence to make it the most popular place in the Back Bay.

"Except it's not for sale," she said. "I've been working on the owner and he's starting to open up to the idea a little. I'm not sure how I would get financing unless he gave me a loan, but my plan is to keep hounding him until he agrees."

"I'll talk to him," Grayson said.

She sat up taller, her feet moving to the floor. "You know Nate?"

"That's why my friends and I go there so often, aside from the fact that it's close to where we all live. We went to college with Cousins."

When I'd been online stalking Grayson, Google had told me he was thirty years old, and Nate Cousins looked to be the same age. Rumor was, Nate had bought the bar several years back and immediately hired a general manager to run it. Nate apparently had no interest in being a part of the day-to-day. He'd made no effort to market the place or expand the menu. He just had so much money, he wanted to add a bar to his portfolio.

"And what would you say to him?" Sloane questioned.

"That I have a party who's interested in buying with the possibility of owner financing."

She stared at him in awe. "It's that easy?"

"Of course." He sat with his legs open, the beer resting between them. "He's a businessman, just like myself. We like options. We also like to be presented with ways we can make money." His hand moved toward my hip, his eyes locking with mine for a single smoldering second before they returned to Sloane. "He'll profit off the sale, and if he's the one to hold the note, he's going to make plenty off the interest. Cousins has several other businesses that are more of a main focus to him."

"How much pull do you have with him?" Her body now faced us. "I mean, is this something that could actually happen?"

Grayson smiled.

Power was his love language.

She couldn't have asked a better question.

"I have a stronger chance of persuading him than you do."

Sloane drank half of her glass. "This could really be an option." She wasn't looking for an answer; she was saying the words out loud, like she couldn't believe them.

"Put together a business plan. If Cousins wants to move forward, that's the first thing he's going to ask for. It needs to be impressive, especially if he's going to finance the deal." He reached into his pocket and pulled out his wallet, slipping a business card from one of the folds. He held it out to her. "If you want me to look it over, I'm happy to."

She took the business card from his hand, reading the information printed on it. "You really don't mind?"

He chuckled. "I wouldn't have offered if I did."

She balanced the card between her pointer finger and thumb. "Wow." She swallowed. "Thank you."

He was so good when he wanted to be, and there was no doubt he'd won her over.

The only way to reward him for that was to let him leave. I was sure he was dying to. But before he went, it was only appropriate to show him around first. That was what any girlfriend would do the first time her boyfriend visited her apartment.

"Should I give you a tour?" I asked him.

"I would love one." His voice was deep, gritty.

It vibrated through my chest and down my navel toward that throbbing spot between my legs.

Why did he have so much control over me?

How could I make it stop?

"Come on." I pushed myself up from the couch, his hand dropping from my leg but pressing against my back as soon as we stood. That placement was somehow easier, less intimate. I cleared my throat and pointed toward the area where we'd stopped first when we came in. "The kitchen you've seen." I circled my hand in the air. "Living room, obviously." I gave Sloane a smile as I passed her on the couch and brought Grayson down the short hallway where the two bedrooms and bathroom were located. I flipped on the light and stalled in the closest doorway. "This is my room."

Instead of just peeking inside, he walked in, looking at the artwork on the walls, the pictures I had framed on my dresser. His hand skimmed across a few leaves of my Swiss cheese plant, and he moved on to the books piled on my nightstand. Once he conquered the full perimeter, he returned to where I was standing.

"What you were expecting?" I asked him.

I kept my voice down even though the TV was on in the living room, preventing Sloane from hearing me.

But before I'd asked that question, something had entered my mind. For someone who resented me, who wanted nothing to do with me aside from a signed contract and public outings, I found it extremely interesting that he took so much time exploring my small space. Why he hadn't just glanced in from the doorway, since that would have been far less personal.

"You want the truth. I was expecting more girlie." He broke eye contact to look around the room again. But his feet didn't move, they stayed put. Just close enough that I could smell his cologne, a distance that was making it hard to breathe. "This room isn't that."

"You mean like pink walls and a furry white desk chair and a diamond chandelier?" I laughed. "No, it's not that. That's not me."

"What's you, Jovana?"

That question hit differently.

It was like he was trying to see all the way down to my core.

"I like a space that's light on color, easy on the eyes, where I'm inspired by my mind and the brands I'm working with." I nodded toward the corner where my tripod and lighting were placed. "That's where I do most of my filming. It's important to me that my followers feel a warm, inviting atmosphere when they watch my videos or look at my photos. I don't want the space to compete with what I'm trying to endorse."

"Your face does that."

My brows couldn't climb any higher. "Excuse me?"

"You're fucking gorgeous. No one is looking at the product, Jovana. They're looking at you."

His compliment hit the top of my head and swished all the way to my toes.

Where is this niceness coming from?

"That's why you're good at your job," he continued. "You have a face everyone wants to stare at." He took a step closer and gave me his profile, his focus back on the room. "You've really thought about this. You've put time into it, haven't you?"

"I take my job as seriously as you take yours. It means everything to me. So, yes, I've thought about it. I've tested backgrounds and filters. I've worn different types of clothing to see what viewers connect to best. I change up the way I word my posts to gauge interaction. Nothing is random. It's all there because I'm either seeing if it works or I know it'll work."

"What about that dress?" Desire filled his gaze. "Would you wear that to film?"

I laughed. "No."

"And why not?"

I looked down my body. Even though I was covered, I felt naked. The dress was skintight and matched my eyes—the reason I'd bought it. It started just below my throat, the sleeveless bodice ending far above my knees. The material wasn't ribbed; there wasn't even bunching. The way it held me was all the design this dress needed.

"It's just too much," I replied, our eyes now locked.

"Too sexy, you mean."

I nodded.

"And seductive."

"Yes," I whispered, and that was as loud as I could speak.

"And so fucking enticing." His hand left his pocket, and he reached forward, cupping my waist.

His touch felt hotter than when he'd gripped my leg on the couch.

There was need in his palm.

Longing in his fingers.

"Do you know how many times I've tasted your lips tonight?"

Three.

I didn't even have to think.

"Yes," I replied.

"And do you know what that has done to me?"

"Grayson . . ."

He stepped forward again, his other hand raising and landing on the wall behind me. Our bodies were close, only breaths apart.

"You've been teasing me all fucking night, Jovana. Every time you bit your lip. Every time you tempted me with your eyes. Even when you put my hand on your thigh."

"That wasn't my intention."

"No?" He leaned his head down. "Then what were you doing?"

I took a deep breath. "Acting the part, like I agreed to do."

"Sure. We'll go with that." His hand slowly rose, halting at the very middle of my torso. "But I know something."

"And that is?"

"How badly you want me right now." His face dipped to my neck, his lips hovering above it. "I know how much it turned you on when I touched you on the couch and when I offered to help your friend. And when you watched me walk around your room. I felt it in your body then, and I feel it now." His lips moved lower, now at the base of my collarbone. "When you're lying in bed tonight, you're going to smell me in the air of your bedroom."

I tried to settle my thoughts.

The tingles that were spreading through my body.

But I couldn't.

His words were making them hum.

His touch was making those hums turn to screams.

"Sounds like that's what you want," I said softly.

When he lifted his head, I couldn't handle the way he looked at me.

The hunger. The tameless, feral eyes that stared back.

"Have you made me hard tonight . . . yes. More times than I can count."

Because there was another layer to this arrangement, the one he'd brought up during our last date, when he offered to keep me satisfied as long as there were no strings attached.

At the time, I hadn't responded.

I didn't know if I could handle it.

I still didn't know.

I just knew I wanted this man.

"Are you asking me if I've thought about your proposition? If I can be with you intimately and not grow feelings?"

Or more feelings, but I certainly wasn't going to say that.

His hand lifted again, this time just below the wire of my bra. "Yes."

Somehow, we were closer.

His other hand was lower on the wall, creating a cage.

Of Grayson.

"I just want to make you come." His lips were now on my ear. This time, they were touching the shell, his exhales like waves of pleasure that were spreading straight to my nipples. "Not with my cock. I want to give you my fingers, so when I go to bed tonight, I can hold them near my face and smell you."

Oh God.

My body was lit in a way that I couldn't extinguish.

There was a fire, and it was spreading.

"Are you going to tell me you don't want that?" He breathed against me, waiting a few seconds before he said, "Don't lie to me, Jovana."

I couldn't deny what he already felt.

There was no question, I wanted this man.

I wanted him to take me to a place where all I felt was him.

I wanted him to make every sound of lust pour from my mouth.

I wasn't going to answer his first question. At least not yet. Because it didn't matter what happened between us tonight—my feelings wouldn't change.

They were already there.

And they would still be there whether he got me off or not.

I also wouldn't think of the repercussions of this.

Or of tomorrow.

All I would think of was right now.

His fingers.

How badly I needed to be touched, since the last time that had happened, it had been him.

He'd given me the most mind-blowing orgasm.

Over.

And over.

And I wanted another right now.

"It's what I want."

A growl vibrated from his lips. "I thought so."

Before I could take a breath, before I could even take account of what was happening, he lowered his hand to the bottom of my dress, going far beneath it.

Until I felt the brush of his fingertips.

"Oh fuck," I hissed, the back of my head pushing against the wall.

"You're not wearing any panties."

"Surprise."

"You're saying your pussy has been bare and uncovered all night? What about the night we went for sushi?"

"Yes. Then too."

"Jovana," he roared against my lips. "You're one dangerous fucking woman, you know that?"

I didn't reply.

I was too swept up.

Because he was moving his fingers higher, teasing between my legs, climbing until he reached that sensitive spot at the very top.

Once he hit it, giving me the friction I craved, I was gone.

"Fuck me," he moaned. "You're dripping."

Thoughts were hard to form, but there was one thing I did know.

My door was open.

I was standing just to the side of the doorway.

At any point, Sloane could leave the living room and come down the hallway to use the bathroom. She'd reach my room first and she'd see.

"Let me close the door—"

"No. You're leaving it open."

"But—"

"You're just going to have to be quiet and"—his lips were on my ear—"quick."

He was evil.

And he was even controlling this—the environment, the way I came.

The speed.

Location.

But I couldn't fight it.

I didn't even want to.

He was rubbing my clit and I was doing all I could to hold on, my fingers suddenly digging into his shoulders, my legs spreading on their own.

My back grinding against the wall behind me.

"If I knew you were this wet, I would have fingered you over dinner and eaten you instead of that fucking pasta."

I could no longer concentrate on his words.

I heard them.

They hit my ears.

His breath traveled through my body.

But I couldn't respond.

The only noises I could make were tiny moans.

Especially as his thumb stayed on my clit and his hand turned, so his pointer and middle finger were rubbing my entrance. Dragging the wetness around in a circle.

I swallowed.

My mouth dry and scratchy.

"Grayson . . ."

"I know. I can feel how much you want it. I've been fucking dreaming about how tight you are." His lips were now in front of mine. "I remember. I haven't been able to forget."

And just like that, he was sliding into me.

"Goddamn it, Jovana." He rested his forehead against mine while he matched my sounds. "I can even hear how wet you are."

He wasn't going slow.

He wasn't savoring the moment.

He was pushing his thumb against my clit, moving back and forth, like he was swiping the screen of his phone, and at the same time two of his fingers plunged in and out of me.

"I can feel you getting close."

My fingers tightened on his shoulders, holding him as though I were about to fall.

But he wouldn't let me.

Neither would this wall.

They were both holding me, sandwiching me.

"Fuuuck," I cried, losing air.

Along with my ability to hold off this orgasm.

Things were building.

Rising.

It had been too long since I'd felt anything like this, and he was far too good.

Too consuming.

Too powerful.

"That's it," he whispered across my lips. "You're giving me exactly what I want."

He pinched my nipple.

Since I was staring into his eyes, I knew he was using his free hand and not his teeth.

"I didn't even have to order you to come." His voice quieted, his hands doing all the talking. "I can feel it . . . and there it is."

He was reading my body.

And he was dead-on because the surge was coming on fast, strong, whipping through me with such a force. I couldn't even distinguish the waves. They were just pounding all at once.

"Ah! Fuck!" I sucked in a breath and released it. "Grayson!"

He didn't stop.

He went faster.

Harder.

Owning me, dragging out each sensation.

Every drop of wetness.

And I clung to him, giving him all my weight, my moans, my air until there was nothing left.

Just silence.

And breathlessness.

He pulled his hand out from under my dress and it immediately went to his mouth. Our eyes locked while he sucked me off his skin. "Delicious," he growled, his tongue lapping his thumb, pointer, and middle fingers.

If I weren't so wound up, I would feel the heaviness of the guilt.

Possibly even regret.

But I was far too high to even consider those thoughts yet.

His wet hand moved to my face, and he pointed it up toward his. "I should go."

"Yes."

"You need to walk me out and kiss me at the door."

Sloane.

The role.

How ironic that he was the one telling me that.

"Right," I told him.

While he continued to stare at me, his expression began to change out of nowhere.

His breathing sped up.

His lips parted, hissing, "Fuck, that was hot," just before they hardened. His jaw flexed, and his Adam's apple bobbed, like he was forcing the emotion down his throat. "But I can't ignore the fact that you never answered my question. If you can be intimate and not grow feelings for me." He looked past my eyes, and I swear he was searching straight into my soul. "That's why I feel the need to remind you that we're not going to turn out like one of those books"—he pointed at my nightstand—"with a happy ending or any shit like that. Don't let your romantic heart make tonight more than it is. This was just me fingering you. My proposition is and will always be no strings attached. That's not going to change."

"Right," I repeated.

Which was as bitter a word as *fine*, but I'd chosen to go with the prior.

The latter sounded more like I was in agreement.

And I wasn't.

Because I wasn't sure if I could stop my heart from growing feelings since I already had them.

Maybe I could hide them from him?

Maybe I could set them aside in hopes that by being intimate, his would start to grow?

"I also don't need to remind you how badly I don't want to be tied down and how I don't want a fucking wife . . . *do I?*"

Where had this come from?

I thought we'd just shared something amazingly sexy, his walls finally coming down, but I was wrong.

Unless there was another side to this.

That he was deflecting because he couldn't deal with how he was feeling.

That he didn't want to admit it.

And that he was shocked at how badly he wanted me.

At least if it was the latter, I had hope. But how long would this continue? Would he ever let me in?

I had no idea.

All I knew was that he was an asshole.

The man who had come into my apartment and volunteered to help Sloane and toured my bedroom and appeared remotely interested in me—that man was gone.

Vanished.

And in his place was the side of him I despised.

He used a nasty attitude so no one could penetrate his exterior; he spit venom so no one would even get close enough to try.

I knew his type.

I wasn't an idiot. I could put two and two together.

The thing was, I also knew a hint of softness existed within him, like when I'd opened up about my family and the way the girls had treated me in high school, and he'd told me I was worthy. He could have torn me down. He could have come back with something sarcastic, like usual.

But he didn't.

He tried to build me up.

But that was only half of it. The other half were the quiet moments. The ones where his eyes did all the talking, like when we were in the hallway at the bar, the night before the meeting with Laura. When he was deep in conversation with Sloane at our apartment and stole glances at me. During our dates at the restaurants, when there was a stillness between us and he appeared so content, so glued to my gaze, that he did nothing to break it.

Those were the instances where I'd peeked below his shield, and I'd seen hints of what he was capable of.

He wouldn't want to hear that, to know I'd figured him out.

So instead I voiced, "I don't need the reminder. I know how badly you want my pussy—your hard-on gave that away—and just how badly you don't want my heart." My voice was as edged as I could make it.

We'd have the no-strings-attached talk at another time.

When I could properly think of the right approach and when I wasn't coming down from the orgasm he'd just given me.

"I'm glad we have that straightened out."

He moved into the doorway, where he took several deep breaths before he held out his hand. When I didn't immediately grab it, he roared, "Don't make me walk myself out. We both know that won't look good."

Bitterness was boiling through my body.

I hated that I had to act like nothing was bothering me so I could convince Sloane I was enamored with this man.

That he'd made me come so easily.

That I wanted him to make me come again.

And again.

That we were back to square one of Grayson being a complete dick.

I linked my fingers with his and joined him in the hallway, passing Sloane with an extra-wide grin on my face as we made our way to the front. I opened the door, and he released my hand, turning toward me after he made his way through.

"Good night, baby." He held the back of my neck and swept his mouth across mine, holding us together, breathing me in.

I didn't fight.

I didn't pull away.

Not with Sloane watching.

But when the kiss ended and he stalled for just a second before walking away, I noticed something.

Something that gave me a moment of pause.

Something I was having a hard time processing.

His smile.

CHAPTER ELEVEN

Grayson

"I don't want to fucking do this," I said to Holden and Easton as they walked into my office, a meeting I'd scheduled only seconds ago, when I'd stormed into the building and ordered them to follow me and to sit their asses down in the chairs in front of my desk. When they didn't respond, when they did no more than just stare at me from their seats, I added, "I'm not kidding, you motherfuckers. I can't do this with her."

"You have to do this," Holden said. He crossed his legs, lifting the bottom of his jeans and rubbing his bruised ankle like it was a goddamn cat.

I nodded toward his foot. "What the fuck happened to you?"

"I tripped over Belle's stool. She was helping me make dinner and I didn't see it. I went flying into the island and banged my ankle."

For a dude who was so athletic, becoming a single dad had made him a goddamn disaster.

"Anyway," I said, shaking my head, "you're wrong—I don't have to do this. I'm done. There has to be another way."

He blew out a long breath and crossed his arms over his chest. "Laura says you need a new narrative, and we agree with her. You can't be the inventor and promoter of the marriage arm and show the world you don't believe in it. What we have to show them instead is that it not only works, but it gave you this epic love story."

Oh, it was fucking epic, all right.

I couldn't get Jovana's sounds out of my head.

I couldn't get her taste off my fingers.

I couldn't get myself to forget the sight of her coming.

And the moment I'd gotten home, I'd used all three of those while I'd jerked myself off.

First in the shower.

When that wasn't enough, when I couldn't kill my fucking hard-on, I did another round while I lay in bed.

I would have thought the two orgasms were enough to knock me out for the night. But I continued to be restless for a few more hours until I gave up on sleep and went into my home office, where I worked until I arrived here just minutes ago.

What the hell is she doing to me?

And how can I get it to stop?

I dropped my hands onto my desk, the smack they made louder than I intended. "No." I pounded them again on the hard surface. "Fuck no." Every time I filled my lungs, the air burned on its way in.

"You can't say no," Easton said. "You don't have a choice about this."

"You realize how ridiculous that is, don't you? What you're asking of me—no, better yet, *telling* me to do. It's not like you're telling me to give a speech in front of a thousand people or take your grandmother to a goddamn doctor's appointment or go out with your virgin cousin because she's never been laid." I felt the anger boil in my throat. "This is marriage. A legal commitment. A fucking binding contract that isn't just going to go away. I'll be dealing with the ramifications of this for the rest of my life."

I wasn't just talking financials and the payout, the bills that I would be covering for her.

None of that meant anything to me.

I was talking about a much larger picture, and these assholes knew that.

They knew where I came from.

They knew the damage that had been done when I was just a kid.

They knew how I felt about all this.

"And what you're asking from me is bigger than probably either of you even realize."

While they looked at each other, thinking about what the hell they were going to say that would make this even a small percent better, I got up from my desk and went to the back of my office, where I'd had a wet bar installed.

I grabbed a bottle of vodka from the shelf and poured a few fingers' worth into a glass.

"It's eight fifteen in the morning, Grayson."

I turned toward Holden after I took my first sip. "I give zero fucks."

"So, your plan is to stay in your office and get completely shit-faced? And ignore the"—Easton pulled out his phone, tapped the screen, and looked up at me—"four meetings we have today?"

I sat back at my desk and kicked my legs up, resting them on top of a stack of papers that needed attention but were going to get completely ignored. "Yes."

"You're special, you know that?" Easton snapped.

I took another long sip. "What if I had told you that you couldn't date Drake?" I gripped one of the armrests, squeezing the cushion and fabric that wrapped around it, trying to hand off some of the rage I was feeling. "You know, when you came to us after the biggest scandal our company has ever experienced—and we're still experiencing, for that matter—and you said you were in a relationship with our director. I could have given you an ultimatum. I could have said it's either you or her, but you can't both work here. Or, in order for her to stay, the two of you have to separate."

"You're not comparing apples to apples," Easton said, in a tone far too relaxed for my liking.

"But it would put you in a situation you wouldn't like. That would make you question—"

"I'm going to stop you before you go on a tirade," Holden said. "You seem to have forgotten that you're in this position because of the situation you put yourself in. If that Celebrity Alert hadn't been released, then you could have continued having six-somes all over the world. But it happened and we're dealing with the fallout."

"No, I'm dealing with the fallout," I roared.

"We're equal partners with matching salaries. We're losing memberships, revenue is down," Easton said. "We're very much in this together, Grayson."

He looked at Holden, his brows raising. "I'm going to take a stab at something, and tell me if I'm wrong."

"All right," Holden replied to him.

"I have a hunch that this one's all worked up because he's feeling something for Jovana and he doesn't know what to do about it."

"Fuck you." My feet dropped from the desk, and I drained the rest of my glass. "Don't act like I'm not in the goddamn room. I can hear every word you're saying and I don't like any of them."

"But am I right?" Easton challenged.

"No." I got up and went back to the bar, bringing the bottle with me when I returned to my desk. I unscrewed the cap and said, "I've told you how this is all making me feel. I mean, fuck, look at me." I held my newly filled glass in the air.

Easton glanced at Holden again just as Holden said, "I think you're right."

I set the glass on the desk, staring at my best friends. Aside from my father, they knew me better than anyone. I needed to know what they were seeing. "What would give you the impression that I felt anything for her?"

Confidence was building across Easton's face. "Because I can't, for the life of me, figure out why you wouldn't be into her. She's hardworking. Smart, bubbly, charming. She wouldn't take your shit, and that's exactly what you need."

"She's beautiful," Holden added. "And she's just your type—petite, dark hair, blue eyes. When you're fishing, that's always what you go for."

"I can't deny that she's my type," I told them. "You got that part right, at least." I wrapped my fingers around the tumbler, not wanting it to be too far away. "But where you have it wrong is when you say she's exactly what I need." I glanced down toward the top of the glass, remembering how, back in the day, one of these had always been in my father's hand. When vodka would be his dinner, sometimes his breakfast. When I would go into his room as a kid and find bottles of it on his nightstand. "I don't need a woman in my life."

"And I get why you say that," Easton said, taking a quick glance at Holden. "We both do. But I still think that during the two dates you've been on with Jovana, you've had a good time. You've thought about her after you dropped her off. You've been surprisingly intrigued by the conversations you've had with her." He paused. "Am I wrong?"

I was ashamed that they'd come to this conclusion. That I'd somehow, through all the growling and anger and refusal, shown that I had feelings for her.

I let out a long, deep, drawn-out exhale. "She's interesting. I'll give you that."

"Hell, the girl is more than interesting. She's magnetic. Belle and I have watched some of her videos. Even my daughter was blown away." Holden ran his hand over the top of his hair, trying to tame his wild locks. "Jovana sure knows what she's doing when it comes to those little dance endorsement things she does."

I had to agree.

During the hours I'd lain in bed last night, unable to sleep, I'd looked up Jovana's Instagram and TikTok accounts.

I didn't go on Faceframe.

Fuck them.

We were currently in litigation with that company, and the moment we'd hired an attorney, I'd canceled my account.

But while I was on the other two, I checked out her posts. Some were just photos, like the one she'd released of my hand on her leg. That shot had collected more than eleven hundred comments.

It had been entertaining as hell to read them.

The questions.

Accusations.

Words of congrats.

But there was negative feedback, too, and that made me mad as hell. It took everything I had not to reply and tear into the commenters, giving them a piece of my mind.

How dare they speak to Jovana that way.

I didn't just stop at that post. I checked out her others as well, where she was showing off brands and products—whether it be some type of makeup or lotion for her face, clothing, or accessories. Sometimes she was even in the kitchen cooking from a particular meal service or using a special sauce or a specific kind of meat or utensil.

She had built a name for herself, and I could easily see that she was in demand.

Her followers wanted to communicate with her; they wanted whatever amount of attention she was willing to give them. When they bought something she endorsed, they returned to her account and told her. Even the assholes who had smart remarks were watching, and they were jealous, and their snideness reflected that.

Jovana wasn't just a face.

She was selling. She was making a difference.

And she fucking rocked at what she did.

Just like me when it came to my job.

"I would hope she knows what she's doing," I said to Holden. "It's her job." Every word bit my tongue as it came out.

I didn't know why.

Or why I found it so difficult to talk about her when it was easy as fuck to think about her.

But I wouldn't be thinking about her if I hadn't fingered her last night.

If I hadn't let my dick lead me instead of my goddamn brain.

I still didn't have an answer to my proposition, if she could handle a year of fucking without developing any feelings.

If she could, then this was going to be a tolerable twelve months.

If she couldn't, I'd have to go the whole year without touching her.

Without kissing her.

Without fucking her.

And I knew, without question, that I'd lose it.

That seeing her prance around my condo, smelling her in the air, making out with her in public, would be a tease that would send me right over the goddamn edge.

I brought the vodka up to my mouth and swallowed. Instead of a bite, there was a burn, and it continued as I drained the rest of the glass.

The room was quiet, all eyes were on me, and when I set the empty glass down, Easton leaned forward, his arms resting on the edge of my desk.

"Are you really going to tell me that you feel absolutely nothing for her?" he asked.

I mashed my lips together while images of last night filled my head again.

Or maybe they'd never left.

Shit, I didn't know.

But what I did know was that one of the only things I could think about while I was on the couch in her living room was how fast I could get my hand up her dress. When I'd volunteered to put a good word in for her friend, I knew it would score me points in the nice category—a category where I needed all the help I could get. And while I walked around her bedroom, I found myself soaking in the details, learning things we hadn't yet talked about, like her interest in reading romance, based on the books that were on her nightstand. How her closet, which had no door, was full of bright colors when her bedroom had only the hues of white and beige. How the pieces of art on her walls were photographs, printed in black and white, of different places around Boston. But they weren't the ones you'd expect, like the Tobin Bridge or the

Prudential Building or TD Garden. These were of tiny pockets around the city—the long strip of water in front of the Christian Science Plaza, the bridge across the pond at the Public Garden, the Paul Revere House nestled on Hanover Street within the North End.

What was ironic as hell was that I had similar photos in my home office, shots I'd taken with my phone and had framed. I was no photographer, but I enjoyed capturing a beautiful picture, and the ones I loved the most, I hung.

So, we both liked art.

Did that mean I felt something?

I was so disconnected from my feelings when it came to women, I didn't think I'd be able to distinguish a single emotion even if it were pounding against my heart.

All I knew was that at the end of the twelve months, I was walking, and that being in a fake marriage was the last fucking thing in this world that I wanted.

I looked at my best friend and replied, "I'm angry that I'm in this situation. That's what I feel right now."

He looked at Holden. "Oh, he definitely feels something."

"I'm getting pretty tired of you two acting like I'm not in this room."

"There's no acting involved," Holden said, tugging at his wrinkled polo. "We're just stating the obvious."

"Obvious?" I laughed and reached for the bottle, adding more to my glass. "What's obvious is that you two want me to get wifey'd up. That, for some reason, you refuse the idea of me being single for the rest of my life, like the status, for some reason, bothers you. That you want me to fall in love with this chick when she's only twenty-two years old."

"Now it's her age that's an issue?" Holden asked. "Or you're just reaching?"

I glared at him and downed the double shot that I'd poured.

"If we keep this up, he's going to be a wreck within an hour." Easton reached across my desk and picked up my phone from the receiver, pressed a few buttons, and held it against his ear. "Hey, it's Easton. I'm in Grayson's office. Can you go grab him a bagel? No, make that a bagel sandwich with double the eggs and cheese, and get some hash browns for a side with a huge glass of orange juice and the largest coffee you can find. Thank you." He hung up and then took the vodka off my desk. "Our assistant is running out to grab you food. Get it together. We have a long day ahead of us."

As he took a step away, proving that he was taking the bottle with him, I said, "You do realize I have a full bar in my office, don't you?"

Easton turned around just as Holden stood to join him, and Holden replied, "Do I have to father you, too, and bring you into my office to watch you all day and make sure you don't get into any trouble? Or can you act like a grown-ass man and actually process what you're feeling rather than bury those emotions under booze?"

"Get out. Both of you."

"Eat your breakfast," Holden countered. "We have a meeting in two hours. I better see you there."

I lifted my middle finger.

It earned me two smiles, but I didn't give one back.

CHAPTER TWELVE

Jovana

I was still getting over the whirlwind of our third date when Grayson walked into the bar to begin date number four. The moment our eyes connected, I somehow scored a smile, and it brought me right back to the evening we'd spent together three nights ago.

Grayson had taken me to a concert at the Garden. Imagine Dragons was playing, and Grayson and his friends had reserved an entire box. Not only had I experienced the VIP-ness of his lifestyle, but I'd also met his best friends. I'd hung with them the entire night, and even befriended Drake, Easton's girlfriend. They all knew about our situation, but never at any point did they make me feel like an outsider. They had been the warmest, most welcoming group.

During the small breaks between songs, I'd been so tempted to ask what they thought of our arrangement, to get a read on them individually. Especially since, every time Grayson touched me, I saw a smile come across one of their faces, and satisfaction in their eyes after Grayson and I would kiss.

Of course, our box had been extremely visible to the arena. There had been strategy behind every move we'd made.

Every kiss.

Touch.

Embrace.

We always acted as though there was a camera pointed at us.

At least that was what he was probably doing.

I didn't have to act at all.

Maybe one day I'd get to ask his friends why they seemed so pleased with what they saw, or I'd take Drake out for lunch and attempt to get her to spill.

The concert just didn't seem like the right time.

But the timing had been right for another Instagram tease. Although I'd shared plenty of live videos throughout the concert, before the show ended, I posted a photo on my main feed. A picture that Drake had taken of Grayson and me. We were standing in the front of the box, Grayson behind me, his hands on my navel, his face buried in my neck with a look of lust across my face.

The message couldn't have been clearer.

Especially when I included the bomb emoji along with the caption: Radioactive.

The comments had been streaming in ever since.

At the end of the evening, Grayson had hired a driver to take us to my apartment after the show. As the SUV pulled up in front of my building, Grayson didn't get out. He kept his hands completely to himself, unlike the last time we'd been together—something he hadn't brought up all night. When the driver opened the back seat door, Grayson leaned across the center seat and kissed me. A kiss that was slower, thought out, even more intimate than he'd been giving me during the concert. His exhales were just starting to scorch my cheeks when he pulled away and wished me a good night. The driver closed the door the moment I stepped onto the sidewalk, and I'd walked into my building alone.

For date four, we decided it was time I spent the night at his condo. With three dates and no sleepover . . . Sloane was going to start questioning if he'd turned into a prude.

We didn't want that.

So I'd brought an overnight bag with me to work, and since I was only scheduled to be here until seven, we were going to go to his place, order takeout, and go to bed in separate rooms. At some point before we went to sleep, I was going to take a picture of us in his bed, and that was what I'd post in the morning.

In just twelve hours' time, the identity of Mystery Man was going to be revealed.

Oh God.

But for now, my fake, delicious boyfriend was rounding the corner of the bar and had stopped directly in front of me. "Hey." His hand went to my lower back, pulling me until my chest was pressed against him. "You smell—"

I tensed. "Like the nachos and french fries I've been serving and the rum and Coke that I spilled all over myself, I know."

"I was going to say you smell incredible."

A compliment.

Huh?

Who is he tonight?

"I don't know how," I replied. "But thank you."

As for him, in the days since the concert, his beard had thickened a bit more, and I just wanted to run my hands through it, to feel the sensation of his rough whiskers, wishing they were scraping along the insides of my thighs. And as he stared at me, his eyes were deepening to a rich emerald rather than the light sea green they normally were, and I couldn't help but wonder why.

Or why he had to be so handsome.

Or why I had to be so attracted to him.

"Are you ready to leave?"

I swallowed, searching for my voice. "I just have a few things I need to finish so the girls who close tonight aren't swamped with duties. Why don't you sit at the bar?" I nodded toward Sloane. "She owes you a dirty martini anyway, doesn't she?"

His grip tightened. "I have to kiss you first . . . just in case someone is watching."

The way he was holding me would answer any question anyone would have.

But if he wanted to put his lips on me, I wasn't complaining.

"I'm sure they're watching, Grayson." I winked. "Give them a show."

His teeth scraped his bottom lip. "Are you doubting my abilities?"

I laughed. "No."

"Because I'd say I put on quite the show at the concert."

He'd kissed me more times than I could count in that box.

He'd grabbed my butt.

His hands had never been far from my body.

It was definitely a show.

"You were"—I sighed—"fine."

"Just fine?" He huffed. "Man, you're quick to dig."

"You deserve it."

"But I'm on my best behavior, Jovana." He leaned his mouth toward mine, his hands circling my waist, teasing my stomach with his thumbs. With each swipe, he was triggering the tingles to explode in my body. "I don't know how to be nicer than this. I even gave you a compliment."

"Kiss me." My voice was a whisper.

He dipped once again, his lips inches above mine. "Look who's being controlling . . ."

I was needy.

I was asking for what I wanted.

My insides were begging for pleasure.

This wasn't about control.

This was about desire.

"Please," I said softly.

He didn't let a single beat pass before he cupped my face and pulled us together, our mouths melding. Our tongues touching. All I could feel, all I could smell . . . was him.

Our kiss didn't last long. I was at work, after all, but it was enough. Enough to prove to anyone in this bar what we meant to each other. Enough to make me breathless.

His eyes scanned mine the moment we separated, and he thumbed my gloss off his lip. "I'm going to go get that drink."

I nodded.

And as his hand left me and he took a seat in front of Sloane, I hurried into the back, grabbing my pile of receipts to make sure all the tips were entered into the computer. I refilled the water glasses and checked the ice. I then cleaned up the soda station, and when I returned to the bar, Grayson was sipping one of Sloane's famous martinis.

"Girl, you're not going to believe this," Sloane said as I reached her, wiping my hands on one of her rags. "Grayson talked to Nate, and he's interested in hearing all my ideas. Nate wants me to set up a meeting where I can pitch him."

"If he's impressed with what she has to say," Grayson cut in, "they'll discuss owner financing."

My fingers clamped Sloane's arm. "Oh my God."

Her eyes were so big and emotional, her voice just as excited as her expression when she said, "I know!" She glanced at Grayson. "I'm going to work on my ideas over the next couple of days, along with the business plan that we discussed."

"Shoot it over to me when you're done. I'll review it and give you feedback."

She glanced at me. "I'm obsessed with your man. I don't even care how that sounds, it's the truth."

I pulled her into my arms and hugged her with all my strength. "I'm *sooo* happy for you right now. When I get back in the morning, I'll help. I'll type. Whatever you need me to do, we've got this."

"Don't rush back, it's your first night together. But if you get home before I have to go to work, plan on giving me your full and undivided attention."

I laughed. "You got it." My arms dropped from her neck, and I stepped back, giving her the biggest smile.

"This martini . . . shit, it's the best I've ever had in my life."

I looked at Grayson, who was scoring all the points tonight. "I told you, no one makes them like her."

"There's even ice crystals on the top. Damn." He took the last sip and popped a blue cheese olive into his mouth.

She asked him, "Do you want a roadie?"

He nodded. "Hell yes."

She laughed and looked at me. "I don't even have to ask you. I already know your answer."

As she began making our drinks, I said to Grayson, "I'm all ready to go."

He nodded toward the small bag that hung on my shoulder. "That's all you're bringing?"

Since Sloane was listening, I giggled and replied, "I plan on sleeping naked. That certainly doesn't require me to pack a lot."

"Fuck me," he moaned. He stood and took out his wallet. "What do I owe you, Sloane?"

"You're kidding, right?" She placed two to-go cups on the bar top. "Just be good to my girl and you'll never pay for anything while you're here. But *shhh*"—she held her finger against her lips—"don't tell Nate I said that. That's not very entrepreneurial of me."

"I won't say a word." Grayson smiled.

I grabbed both cups when she was done and met Grayson on the other side of the bar. "I'll see you tomorrow," I said to Sloane and waved.

"Have fun tonight, you two."

I waited until we were outside before I said, "I can't believe you talked to Nate for her. That was beyond sweet of you." That wasn't enough. I had to say more. I had to make him understand how big of a deal this was. "You have no idea how much that means to her . . . and me. Thank you."

He took the bag from my arm and held it while we walked, an act that completely took me off guard, but one that caused me to grin.

"You thought I was bullshitting when I first made her that offer?"

I shrugged. "I don't know what I thought."

"When it comes to business, I don't fuck around, Jovana."

"That only happens in your personal life, right?"

"Whoa, another dig."

I supposed it was.

I didn't mean for it to be. I just meant to point out the difference between his two sides.

"I'm sorry. That came out all wrong, but still, you didn't deserve that."

We said nothing for a few more steps until he broke the silence. "When she talked about buying the bar, I recognized her expression. It's the same one Easton, Holden, and I had when we wanted to start the app and had no money to fund it. It's the worst feeling. You don't know what the fuck to do, you just know you want it and you're helpless on how to make it happen." He adjusted the strap on his arm, and we slowed at the crosswalk. "Every time I come here with my buddies, Sloane's working. You know what that tells me?"

I looked up at him. "That she works her ass off?"

"Exactly." He nodded. "She'll make it one of the most successful bars in the Back Bay. And if you promote her, there'll be a line out the door."

I gently pushed his empty shoulder. "Is that another compliment?"

"I told you, I'm on my best behavior."

But I didn't understand why.

Whether he was nice or a raging dick, I still had to be here. I still had to go on dates with him.

I still had to stay the night at his condo.

That was all in the contract I'd signed.

I decided not to ask his motivation. It would be easier on my heart to just not know, but whatever was causing the change in his behavior, I dug it.

Less than a minute later, we reached his building and took the elevator up to his penthouse. The last time I was here, I'd been in only his kitchen, living room, and bedroom.

I hadn't forgotten what any of those rooms looked like.

But this time, when we entered the foyer and walked into the massive open floor plan, I saw his home in a whole different way. The sun was setting, casting a light glow, and the floor-to-ceiling windows showed just how large and tall and spacious the space was. I didn't know if he'd hired an interior designer, but whoever had picked out the furniture and artwork and decor had done an incredible job. His condo wasn't just masculine; it was warm and inviting—the opposite of his normal personality.

"The guest room is this way," he said.

The primary bedroom and massive en suite were on one side of the living room, but this was on the other, and there were a few doors in the hallway.

As we passed each one, he pointed and said, "Smaller of the three bedrooms. Guest bathroom. And now your room, which has its own en suite."

I stalled next to him in the doorway. "Wow. This is bigger than my bedroom at my apartment." The room was decorated in the same cool gray and black tones as the rest of the condo. A flat-screen hung on the wall. Art was above the bed. There was a chair in the corner and still plenty of area to set up a tripod and lighting.

He placed the bag on top of the beautiful light-wood dresser. "This is where you'll stay when you move in. If you want to leave anything here after tonight, do it. It's one less thing you'll have to bring later."

Why was it so hard to take a deep breath?

Was it the realization that I'd be spending every night under the same roof as him, only on the other side of his living room?

Or that this would be my room?

Or that this condo was about to be my new home?

Or that I wished I would be spending every night in his bedroom instead?

I felt his eyes on me as he said, "I'm required to make you feel comfortable while you're here. If there's anything you want to change or add or redecorate, I'll make sure it gets done."

I hadn't missed the way he'd worded that statement.

The coldness behind it.

He was still on his best behavior. I was just reminded that he really didn't want me here.

That once we hit the one-year mark, I'd be long gone.

"It's perfect." I turned toward him. "I don't want to change a thing." He stared at me silently, scanning my right eye and then my left. I needed a break. I needed to think. I needed to just be in a space where I didn't smell him. "Do you mind if I take a shower? I can feel work all over me."

"Yeah, sure. Room's all yours." He turned around and walked down the hallway.

I shut the door.

When that didn't feel like enough, I locked it.

And when my feet felt too numb to move, I put my back against the wall and slid down until my butt hit the carpet.

I didn't know why, but when I tried to take a deep breath, my throat felt even tighter than before.

"It smells incredible in here," I said as my nose filled with the scent of pizza.

I was padding my way across the hardwood floor of the living room, my hair soaking my tank top, my skin slick from the lotion I'd just rubbed across it.

Grayson was sitting on the couch, his back to me, ESPN playing on the TV. At the sound of my voice, he looked over his shoulder, his stare tiptoeing down my body.

With each inch, I felt it grow more intensely.

Especially when it rose from my feet and froze on my chest.

"I only brought pj's," I told him. "Hopefully, you're okay with that."

As my breasts bounced a little with each step, my nipples hardened in response to his eyes, which still hadn't moved.

But what did change was his expression.

He looked ferocious.

"Did you wear a bra to work?"

An odd question, I thought, as I came around the side of the couch and took a seat a few cushions down from him, noticing how delicious he looked in his gray sweatpants and T-shirt. "Yes."

"Then did you just forget to put it back on?"

Now I knew where he was going with this conversation.

"No. I didn't forget."

"Rule number one"—he turned down the TV as though I couldn't hear him over the commentators, but the balance of both volumes was just fine—"unless you're agreeing to my proposition and you're going to allow me to devour you on every surface of this condo, then you won't be wearing these tiny, provocative outfits around my place when you live here. Understood?"

"Tiny?" I glanced down my body. I was in cotton athletic shorts that I'd rolled once so they sat lower on my waist and higher on my thighs. They weren't like boy shorts. They covered me just fine. "And provocative?" I pinched the bottom of my tank and pulled it off my skin, the material snapping right back the moment I let go. This was a set I'd wear to the gym or out walking. It certainly wasn't racy or extra sexy. "I would hardly use those words to describe this getup." I winked. "But okay, I hear you."

"Rule number two, you'll wear a bra."

I laughed—two was even more ridiculous than one. "Let me just state the obvious. They're little, as you know. I don't really need to wear a bra most of the time unless I want to make them look bigger, which I don't. I'm fine with them just the way they are. Besides, you've already seen them, so I don't really understand the point of that rule."

"Do you want me to fuck you on this couch right now?"

Heat wafted across my body.

Of course I wanted him to.

But for now, I said, "You haven't earned the right to fuck me."

He glanced back at the TV. "Then abide by my rules. Got it?"

Nice Guy was gone.

Mr. Wicked had returned.

"Bra and snowsuit, check." I crossed my arms over my chest.

"I'm glad we have that straight." The side of his cheek flexed as he ground his jaws together. "As you probably guessed from the scent, I took the liberty of ordering us some pizza. It's in the kitchen. Help yourself."

My stomach growled at his offer. "Have you already eaten?"

"No."

I wondered why he didn't already have a plate. He must have been waiting for me.

"Would you like me to grab you some?" I pushed myself to the end of the couch.

His gaze slowly returned to me. "All right."

"Why am I not surprised . . . you like to be waited on, what a shocker." I tried not to look at him when I walked by where he was sitting, but I could feel the heat from his glare, and when I glanced in his direction, his eyes didn't meet mine.

Because his were on my chest.

And as I watched him, as I really took him in the same way he was observing me, I realized why he wanted me in a bra.

That man was turned on.

I had a feeling that he hadn't joined me in the kitchen or offered to get me any pizza because he didn't want me to see his hard-on.

I loved that thought.

It even made me smile.

Once I reached the kitchen, there were three pizza boxes on the island, a quantity I found odd given that there were only two of us. I lifted the lids, and inside were a plain cheese, a veggie, and a pepperoni.

Since the kitchen was completely open to the living room, I turned around to face him.

I was surprised that his stare hadn't left me.

It was just lower now, like it had been on my ass while I was looking at the food.

But it was rising and finally locked with mine.

Still smiling, I asked, "Are you expecting more people?"

"No."

"Do you just like a wide variety of toppings then?"

He lifted his beer, which had been sitting on a small end table beside him, and took a drink. "I didn't know what kind of pizza you liked. I guessed it would be one of the three."

"You could have asked."

"Jovana"—he shook his head before taking another drink—"I'm not a fucking moron. I tried to ask you, but your bedroom door was locked."

"Oh."

"Yeah . . . *oh*."

I glanced down at the open boxes. "Let me guess, pepperoni for you?"

"Veggie."

I laughed. "Veggie?"

"Don't sound surprised that I like vegetables on my pizza. There's no better combo on a pie than mushrooms and onions. At least in my opinion."

"I'm laughing because I agree. Nothing beats that combo, it's my fave." I went on the hunt for plates, checking the cabinets next to the fridge and sink, and when I finally found them, I grabbed two. "But I'm down for a slice of pepperoni here and there." I placed two pieces on his plate, two on mine, and opened the fridge, scanning the doors until I found the section where he kept his dressing. His ranch came in a jar, so I searched the drawers until I located the silverware and scooped some of the dressing onto my plate. I grabbed a beer as well, along with some napkins, and returned to the couch.

As I handed him his pizza, he was eyeing mine and asked, "What's the blob of white on your plate?"

"Ranch."

"You put dressing on your pizza?"

"I dip my pizza in it, yes."

"Who the fuck does that?"

"*Ummm*, me." I laughed again, and when I chose seats, I picked a spot closer to him this time, so only a square cushion separated us. "Sloane's family is originally from Upstate New York. Apparently, that's what they do there. I don't know, but she introduced me to it and now I'm hooked." I picked up my pizza, dipped the side, and took a bite. "She uses blue cheese, but the smell makes me gaggy. I'm Team Ranch all the way." I held my plate toward him. "Here, try it."

"No."

"*Try it*, Grayson."

"Jesus," he groaned. "But only because I don't want to hear your fucking whining." He ran the point of his slice through the pool of creamy dressing and took a large bite. "I don't hate it, shockingly."

I didn't move my plate. "Try it again. It takes a few rounds before you're sold."

"You want me to double-dip?"

"We've kissed a million and one times. If you have cooties, you've already given them to me."

Instead of commenting, he blew air through his nose, like a bull getting ready to charge. "The constant reminders, like this one, and the fact that I've seen your tits—not needed."

"I just like to get on your nerves."

"You're succeeding."

I winked. "I know."

He dragged the pizza through my dressing and chewed off the soaked end. "I'm not going to knock it. I can see the appeal."

"Do you want me to get you some ranch?"

He chuckled. "Nah, I'm good."

I finished off the pepperoni slice and dug into the veggie. "*Mmm.* Delicious. Thank you for ordering this."

He was quiet for a few moments, sucking the sauce off his fingers, and I handed him a napkin, forgetting that I still had both.

"What do you like to watch on TV?" he asked. "If it's something I can stomach, I'll change the channel."

"Whatever is fine." I shrugged. "I really don't watch much TV. I don't even have one in my room."

"I noticed when I was in there. Why's that?"

I wiped my mouth. "I never had one growing up, and I lived at home through most of college, except toward the very end when I moved in with Sloane, so I guess the lack of having one just carried forward." I picked off a piece of the crust and popped it into my mouth. "I've always had a job, even in high school, making time such a hard thing for me. I've never had enough of it—I'm always rushing somewhere. When I do have a few free minutes, I read."

"I worked through high school too." He finally looked at me again. "You know, to help my dad out."

He was opening a door and I didn't want to let it slam. Although Grayson had revealed tiny pieces of himself, there was so much more I wanted to know.

I sucked in a deep breath. "Can I ask you a super-personal question?"

"Maybe."

If I wasn't about to go deep, I would have laughed. "Where's Mom?"

"She's dead."

It felt like he'd just dumped a wheelbarrow of bricks on my chest. "Grayson, I'm so, so sorry."

"Don't be. I stopped talking to her when I was ten. She died shortly after we opened Hooked."

"Why?" I swallowed, my head shaking as I stared at him. "What happened between you two?"

He set his plate on his lap and lifted his beer, holding it against his chest. "I never talk about this shit. The people in my life know. They skate around it when my family situation gets brought up, but it's been a long time since I've gone into depth."

I kept my voice calm and gentle when I said, "Whether you like it or not, I'm a person in your life now."

"That doesn't mean I have to tell you anything." He finally sipped from the bottle, guzzling what was left until he set the empty on the end table.

"No, you don't." I placed the half-eaten veggie slice on the plate and rubbed the grease from my fingers onto the napkin. "But I would love it if you would."

He stared at me for what felt like hours until he broke eye contact and looked through the windows that were just to the side of me. "She took off when I was ten. She was done—being a wife and a mother. She wanted no part in either."

My throat tightened, but I said nothing.

He didn't need to be questioned. He just needed time to get it all out.

"I wrote her letters. I tried to get in contact with her. She didn't want to be found, and she didn't want to come back. But I was too young to understand that then." He finally looked at me. "As I got older, I found out she had an affair. Fuck, she really had multiple affairs. She'd disappear for a couple of days; Dad would catch her with some dude and bring her back because he didn't want to break up our family. He'd give me some wild excuse, telling me she went to a spa or a vacation with her girlfriends—things we couldn't afford. I should have known that." He wiped his mouth and threw the napkin on top of his half slice. "The last straw was when she cleaned out the bank account and stole all my baseball cards to pawn. That's when Dad decided not to go look for her. He said she could destroy him all she wanted, but the moment she hurt me, that was it." His chest rose but didn't fall. "That was the last time I saw her." He placed the plate on the table next to his empty beer. "She has a sister who my dad has somewhat kept in touch with, and a few months after we started Hooked, she showed up at my dad's place with an urn of my mom's ashes."

"How did she die?"

He got up and went into the kitchen, getting himself another beer, which he carried to the couch. "She was living in New Mexico at the time with a bunch of dudes. I guess she dropped dead of a heart attack right in the middle of the living room. The guys wouldn't pay to fly her body to Boston and my aunt didn't have the cash, so my aunt had her cremated in Santa Fe, not even knowing if that was my mom's wishes or not. She brought the ashes to my dad in case I would want them."

There were so many parts of our past that were identical.

All except for this.

My heart was shattered for ten-year-old Grayson.

I had no idea if this was the reason why he was so antirelationship or why he proclaimed he'd be single for the rest of his life, but I had a feeling his mother had a lot to do with it.

Not just in the way she treated his father.

But in the way she abandoned Grayson.

If he didn't settle down, he'd never have to worry about the woman leaving him. If he didn't develop feelings, he'd never have to worry about getting his heart broken.

I hated this for him.

But I also hated this for me.

"Do you have the ashes?" I asked.

"Fuck no. I want nothing to do with her. I especially don't want the remains of her." He took a long drink, holding the beer in his mouth before he swallowed. "My father is my best friend. We agree on almost everything, but when he kept those ashes and couldn't part with them, that's where we differ. I can't understand that after all the things she did to him, he couldn't let go. That he has such a goddamn soft spot for that woman."

I could hear the resentment.

How his father's softness hadn't been passed down to Grayson.

"Love never dies," I whispered.

He looked at me as he said, "I wouldn't know, and she's why I never plan to know."

Those words prickled my skin.

And once that phase ended, they stung.

And once that ran its course, they slapped.

Over and over.

I was right: she was the reason.

I supposed it made sense and maybe I would feel the same way if I were him.

Or maybe I'd want to find the opposite of what his parents had. I'd want to find my person, the one I could trust implicitly, who would become my forever, giving them every single part of me without any reservation.

After this conversation, I wished that over the last few dates and the time we'd spent together, I hadn't thought that person could be Grayson.

That I wasn't falling.

That I wasn't thinking these twelve months were only the beginning instead of the end.

But I was.

I didn't care that he was grumpy, growly, that he was impatient. Because underneath those sounds and layers was a guy who was completely and utterly wonderful. Who had the kindest, most giving heart.

Who owned my body and every physical sensation in ways that I'd never experienced.

But in thinking that, in dreaming, in mentally preparing for the future, all I was doing was setting myself up to become the one who would get wrecked.

It was that haunting realization that made me get up from the couch, stopping at the end table, where I said softly, "I know that wasn't easy." His hand was resting on the cushioned armrest, and I placed my fingers on top of his. "Thank you for sharing this with me."

He said nothing, just stared at me.

Neither of us blinked.

Or moved.

The moment was building, I could feel it in every part of me.

The angst.

Emotion.

There was so much I wanted to say.

So much I wanted to do.

And just as I breathed, "Grayson," he pulled his hand away and lifted the beer and began chugging it.

The moment was over.

I shoved every feeling down my throat and asked, "Are you done eating?"

When he nodded, I took my plate and his, along with our empty beers, into the kitchen. I dumped our half-eaten slices and napkins into the trash. The dishes went into the dishwasher, and the three pizza boxes in the fridge.

As I returned to the living room, Grayson was turning off the TV. Once the room was silenced, he stood.

"I'm going to bed," he told me.

"We have to take the picture."

"What picture?"

I crossed my arms over my chest, something I'd done more than once tonight. I didn't know why, I just suddenly felt so naked. "The one we're posting in the morning. You know, that tells everyone we're together."

"Right."

"My phone's in the bedroom. I'll go grab it—"

"We have to do this now?"

I could hear the annoyance in his voice.

"Don't be a dick, Grayson. It's just a picture. It'll take less than a minute and then I'll leave and you can go to bed."

He turned and walked toward his bedroom, roaring over his shoulder, "Hurry. *Fuck.*"

I sprinted toward my wing and got my phone from the nightstand. I tucked it under my fingers and rushed out into the hallway, across the living room, and entered his wing, halting at the entrance of his bedroom. From here, I could see into his closet, and he was in the middle of taking off his sweatpants.

I certainly didn't want to get caught staring, so I went over to his bed and pulled back the covers and slid underneath. While I listened to him rustle around in his closet, I took my time checking out his bedroom, something I hadn't done before.

The colors, the vibe, the mood—they were the embodiment of sex.

There was a fireplace directly across from the bed. Tiny lights in the ceiling above me that he'd dimmed to a light shadow. The artwork was abstract, but within the lines and dark hues were the visuals of a woman's body.

The textures throughout the whole space were smooth, silky, even. And the entire room smelled like Grayson, a heaviness of citrus balanced with amber notes.

This wasn't just his personal cave.

This was him—an equal combination of darkness and sexiness.

"That's my side."

The sound of his voice startled me, and I jolted up a few inches, sucking in the deepest breath. When I met his stare, it was as reprimanding as his words.

He wanted this over with.

He wanted me gone.

"Sorry."

While I slid to the other side, I watched him walk to the bed. He had on only a pair of boxer briefs that fit snugly over his dick, a part of him that was complete perfection, but what the tight cotton didn't cover was his incredible body. Cords of muscle rippled across his chest and down his etched abs, up his forearms and biceps, and crossed his shoulders. Small patches of dark hair the same color as his beard sprouted from some of those brawny sections, only adding to the power and strength that beamed from his body.

I knew this long before tonight, but something about this moment only reinforced how masculine Grayson was.

How the guys my age were still learning their rhythm, still finding their personalities, still building their bodies.

But not him.

This was a man full of experience and maturity.

And pain.

As he climbed into bed, I inhaled the deepness of his cologne, and I instantly felt the heat coming off his skin. And I sucked in another breath, waiting for him to get comfortable, then moved in next to him and held the phone in the air, directly above our faces.

"I'm going to take a few test pics first."

He said nothing as I pressed my leg against his and leaned into the side of his chest, tilting our faces together. I basked in his presence, letting the emotions take over my expression, and snapped a handful of shots.

"These are . . . *ugh*." I showed him the screen, swiping through the ones I'd just taken.

"What the fuck's wrong with them?"

"Everything." I held the phone in the air again. "I need you to look happy, Grayson. Like you're in love." When he didn't respond, I looked at him. "Please."

"Love isn't in my arsenal of emotions, Jovana. I told you, I don't do love. Don't be looking for it in these pictures because you won't find it and you won't find it in me. That's why you shouldn't fall for me."

There was that reminder again.

The one I hated every time I heard it.

The one that reinforced that I'd be a broken, dismantled mess at the end of this.

But I couldn't let him know that. I just had to keep going, so I said, "I know. I get it. But this isn't about me falling in love with you. This is about the world falling in love with us. So shut up, smile, we'll get the pic right, and then I can go to bed."

His arm had been at his side, a position that came across cold and uncaring and extremely detached in the test shots. After a few seconds of grumbling, he wrapped it around me and pulled me closer. In this new position, my head lay halfway between his chest and shoulder, the blanket pulled high enough that my lack of a bra wasn't revealed. He turned his face toward mine and I began to snap away, keeping my arm still, but moving my head just slightly, so there was a multitude of angles I could choose from.

"Jovana . . . I'm done."

With his voice a full-blown growl, the phone almost dropped from my hand as I lowered my arm.

I quickly clicked on the photos, scrolling through the twenty or so I'd taken.

With the right filter and a tiny bit of Photoshopping, eliminating the furrow between his brows, I'd have something good enough to post.

"I need you in your bed. Now."

His statement pierced my ears, stressing how close we still were.

As I turned toward him, holding the top of the blanket so I could lift it off me and get out, I paused. Something in his eyes wasn't letting me go. It was pulling me toward him instead.

Holding me.

Begging for me.

Was that why he wanted me to leave? Because he was having a hard time controlling himself with me being so close, physically forcing himself not to pull me on top of him?

Was he feeling everything that was flowing through my body?

Did he—

"Jovana . . ." His tone was different this time. Rather than being deep and gritty and demanding, it was almost needy.

He focused on my right eye and then my left, his grip tightening on my shoulder, his face moving toward mine.

Just when he was about an inch away, he hesitated.

And he stayed right there.

"Good night."

His words echoed through me, reinforcing that whatever I thought, whatever I anticipated happening, wasn't going to.

This was it—the finale.

He wanted me out.

Now.

"Good night," I whispered.

I pulled myself out of his bed and walked toward my wing, shutting the door behind me, and switching off the light before I climbed into bed.

I edited the photo as best as I could, smoothing out the elevens between his brows, adding a warm, crispy filter, and cropping the picture in a way that emphasized how he was holding me.

I didn't care what he said, I could see there was emotion in both of our faces.

That meant my followers would be able to see it too.

I uploaded the pic to Instagram and added the caption: Hooked him.♥

Instead of putting his name, I tagged him in the post and scheduled it to release at eight tomorrow morning. With my lack of makeup and messy, mostly dried hair, it would look like we'd just woken up together. That we were midcuddle when we decided to air our tea.

That we were just two people with very different pasts who had found each other on Hooked and had completely, utterly fallen for one another.

CHAPTER THIRTEEN

Grayson

The moment I watched Jovana fly out of my room, leaving her scent behind, I sat up in bed, recalling our last few hours together.

What the fuck is wrong with me?

I'd told her I was on my best behavior.

And I'd been doing so well until she asked me to open up about my mother and I'd purged the details of her taking off, followed by her death, and that was when I shut down.

When I couldn't eat another bite of food. When I couldn't say another word about my past.

When I needed darkness and beer and to be alone with my thoughts.

But, of course, that caring, nurturing woman wasn't going to let the anger I had toward my mother swallow me in a goddamn hole.

She was going to make me smile.

She was going to take our photo.

She was going to make me pretend I was in love.

And just when I had her in my arms, when I had every opportunity to pull her against me, mash our lips together, and bury myself in her pussy—things I was fucking dying to do—I reminded her how fucking awful I was for her and then I kicked her out of my bed.

What was left behind was a raging hard-on and my hands clenching to have her between them.

What was it about Jovana Winters that I couldn't get enough of?

That drove me fucking wild?

Despite how impatient she made me feel, how she tested me, challenged me, and a majority of the time made me want to scream, I enjoyed her softness as much as her sass.

I was enticed by her.

My thoughts were owned by her.

Fuck.

Why didn't regret come in waves, giving me a break between the crests?

Why did it have to continuously slam into me? Making me recount the last few seconds when I'd forced her out?

The whole scene made me feel like shit again.

It wasn't just weighing on me; it was eating away at me.

I wanted to be near her.

I wanted her scent filling my nose.

I wanted the softness of her words in my ears.

I wanted her.

In this room.

On top of me.

Riding my cock.

The only way this erection was going to go away was if I lubed up my palm and rubbed one out or if I walked across the living room and went into her room.

But even if I jerked myself off, I knew it wouldn't be enough. Not with her so easily accessible. Not with her so close by.

Not with my brain obsessing over every fucking detail of her.

Goddamn it.

I threw off the covers and stormed out of my bedroom, my cock pulsing with each step, my balls throbbing. As I entered the hallway of the guest wing, there was no light coming from under her door. There were no sounds either.

Whatever she was doing in that room, she was doing it silently and in the dark.

My hand paused an inch from the doorknob.

The last time I'd tried to turn it, it was locked. She'd been in the shower and didn't want me in her room.

Had she done that again?

I grabbed the handle and it immediately twisted. She'd left it unlocked.

In my head, she'd done that because she wanted me to come in, and she wanted me to cross that boundary.

Maybe under a different circumstance, I would have knocked. I would have given her a warning before shoving myself into her room.

But I had zero desire to pause.

To act like a gentleman.

If she was going to kick me out, it was going to happen to my face.

I walked through the doorway, the screen of her phone lighting up her face, so I could catch eyes with her while she lay in bed.

"What's wrong—"

Her voice cut off when I pressed my knee onto the mattress and crawled my way up to her, hovering over her body. My hand held her cheek and I aimed her mouth up to mine. "I want you and I can't wait another fucking second to have you. That's what's wrong."

She said nothing, just dropped the phone and circled her arms around my neck.

Once her grip was tightened around me, I devoured her lips, parting them with my tongue, and I slipped through the center, diving straight into her taste.

And what a fucking flavor that was.

One that I'd thought about since our last date.

But even then it hadn't been enough, and it wasn't now either.

I needed more.

I leaned up, putting my weight on my knees, and once both arms were free, I began tearing off her tank top. As soon as I had it over her head, I tossed it on the ground and reached for her shorts, yanking them down her legs.

I needed all of her.

With nothing separating us.

To be able to touch her wherever I wanted without any clothing getting in the way.

"Fuck," I hissed as I glanced down at her, the lights from the adjacent building creating just enough glow that I could view every bit of her skin.

Her perfect tits.

The arches and dips and curves of a body that was beyond gorgeous.

The present that was waiting for me between her legs.

A gift that wanted to be opened and licked and sipped from.

Although I could stare at her all night, the twinge in my cock caused my mouth to drag down her chest, halting at her nipple. I surrounded the peak with my lips before using my teeth to gently scrape the length, holding it in my mouth and biting around the base.

"Oh God!" Her hands slid through my hair, gripping the strands. "Grayson . . ."

As her back arched, she leaned even harder into me and I opened my mouth, taking more of her in, lapping her nipple several more times until I switched to the other side. While I gnawed on the small center bead, I wrapped her legs around me. The heat from her pussy soaked through my boxer briefs, especially as I ground my cock against her and pumped my tip forward.

It was nothing more than a tease.

A way to tempt me, as if this wait weren't already torturous enough.

"*Ahhh*, yes!" She guided my cock lower and moaned, "*Fuuuck!*"

But before I took off the last piece of clothing that kept me from plunging inside her, I lowered even farther down her body, kissing the flatness of her navel, the shallowness of her belly button, stopping when I reached her clit.

With her legs still circled around me, I held the outside of her thighs and pressed my nose against that sensitive spot at the very top.

And while I kept my face there, I breathed her in.

"You're everything I remember and more."

Her hand tightened in my hair.

"Jovana, how can you be this exceptional."

She had a scent that I'd been dreaming about.

A wetness that I hadn't been able to forget.

A flavor that I'd never be able to get enough of.

She didn't answer.

Instead, she spread her legs even farther apart, as if showing me more, giving me an even better view, silently ordering me to feast on her pussy.

I listened.

I soaked in every goddamn second of it.

I even smiled as I took my first lick.

"Yesss!" She gasped in some air. "Yes!"

My dick pounded as her taste exploded on my tongue and I swallowed some of it.

The moment it hit my throat, I just had to pause, the thoughts in my head completely overtaking me.

Oh God.

This woman.

What the hell is she doing to me?

How does she have so much power over me?

I traced my tongue up and down her clit, going as low as her entrance, making sure that was nice and wet, before I returned to the highest point.

The top was where I focused.

And I didn't go slow.

I didn't savor.

I didn't take my time.

I made up for all the days I hadn't been down here, when I'd kissed only her mouth. When I'd lain in bed, thinking about this to the point where I had to jerk myself off in the shower while fantasizing about a moment identical to this one.

"Oh God!" she cried.

I'd missed that sound. The way her pleasure hit my ears. The way she screamed out an orgasm.

Just like the one that was about to happen now.

I could tell by the way her clit was hardening. How her grip was strengthening. How her wetness was thickening.

"Grayson!"

And there it was.

A response that made me feel like a fucking king.

The first shudder rippled through her stomach, and her legs threatened to cave in around my face. I wouldn't let them, and I held them apart as I licked.

My tongue moved faster.

Harder.

Giving her the pressure I knew she needed.

"Fuck! Yes!" Her exhales were as sexy as her moans. "Grayson!" she shouted again.

As I continued to eat her, tasting her come, I stared up her wriggling body. I could see the tingles beating through her every time she rocked her hips forward, riding out each of the waves.

I waited until it all passed, when she was completely still, before I pulled my tongue away. "My fucking God," I groaned, gazing at her pussy. "If I didn't need you so badly, I'd do that again. And again."

She moved her foot to my boxer briefs and rubbed her toes over my crown. "I want this."

That was the hottest thing she could have ever said.

I pulled the tight cotton past my waist and shifted my weight to slide them off my legs.

"I've missed that." She was eyeing my shaft.

"It's about to be all yours." Once I tossed the boxer briefs onto the floor, I realized I'd left my bedroom empty-handed. I'd been in such a rush to get to her, I'd forgotten one of the most important things. "Give me a second, I'll be right back. I have to grab a condom."

"You don't need one."

Her words were a shock to my system.

They even vibrated through my chest, repeating within me as though I needed to hear them again.

"What?" I pressed.

I always wore one.

There were no exceptions to that rule.

"You're going to be my husband, Grayson." She allowed those words to settle between us. "In case you don't remember, it was stated in our contract that a form of birth control was required. Laura even requested a letter from my doctor to prove he'd inserted an IUD, which he'd done well over a year ago, but she wanted reassurance that it was in place, secure, and working properly. Maybe she'd manifested this situation, I don't know, but I really see no reason to use a condom."

Her husband.

Those were the words I'd concentrated on.

A title that weighed a thousand fucking pounds.

I couldn't let that thought get too far. I needed it to bounce right off me or I'd leave this room.

And I wasn't sure I'd ever come back.

She sat up, mimicking my position, even though her kneel wasn't as high as mine. Her arms rested on my shoulders, and she pulled our bodies together. "It's fine. Stop thinking about it, or worrying, or whatever you're doing." She gave me her lips, followed by a smooth swirl of her tongue.

I didn't know if it was her words or the feel of her body or her kiss, but she easily convinced me. "All right."

The moment she heard my approval, she fisted my cock and began to pump. "I don't know how, but I almost forgot how big and perfect this is."

I needed that touch.

The warmth from her hand, the speed, friction—all of it pulling me right out of my thoughts.

"Fuck yes," I hissed.

"Yeah? Good. Now fuck me, Grayson."

That demand.

So needy. Passionate. Sexy as hell.

I held her face, keeping her close, taking more of her mouth before I turned her around. While she faced the headboard, I placed her hands on top of it, securing them around the wooden edge, and I feathered my palms down her back to her ass. "You need to hold on."

It was a warning.

One she shouldn't take lightly.

Because for as long as I'd thought about eating her pussy, I'd also thought about doing this. That want had caused a burning desire to build inside me. I wasn't sure I could control the power of my strokes now that I was finally getting the chance to have her again.

I aligned her just right and positioned myself behind her, rubbing my hands over her ass, circling her cheeks. With each rotation, my cock got closer to her pussy.

A test.

A challenge, to see how long I could hold off until I thrust inside her.

But as soon as my tip swiped her wetness, I couldn't wait.

Neither could she.

Her moans were getting louder, the need amplifying within both of us, and once I was poking at her entrance, the slickness covering me, I fucking lost it.

"I can't fucking wait to have you." I gave myself just the smallest amount of her. It took only an inch before I knew this was going to be different from anything I'd ever had. "Fuck me, you feel so good."

Taking another inch, she bounced over my crown.

It was just the slightest movement, but it was enough for the heat to envelop me, the temperature catching me completely off guard. "Goddamn it," I growled. My head fell back, my mouth open. Without any protection, I could feel everything, and it was the most intense sensation. But her warmth wasn't the only thing that shocked the hell out of me, causing me to groan, "You're so tight."

"More." She was begging now. "Give me more, Grayson."

I held her hips and slid to the halfway point. I didn't want to hurt her. I certainly didn't want to break her. I knew she'd had me before, but it wasn't as if it had been yesterday, so she needed to be reminded of my size before she got all of me.

And as I worked my way in, I confirmed that she needed that reminder from the way she was pulsing against me, narrowing around my shaft.

"Yes!" In addition to her moans, she was fucking soaking me. "Ah!" And as I gave her more, she gave me, "My God." She reached back, her fingers landing on my abs, which she traced until she lowered to the base of my dick. She felt around it, like she was seeing how many inches were left, and continued to my sack, where she cupped my balls.

Each brush of her thumb had me fucking tingling.

"Give it to me," she demanded.

An order that didn't make me angry.

That, for once, didn't make me want to fight back.

I pumped my hips forward, earning myself a scream, and I stayed buried within her.

"Jesus," I roared. "This is fucking . . ."

But I didn't have a description.

I didn't even have words.

Because this right here—there was nothing better.

I tilted all the way back and took my first full dive, sinking into that hot, dripping pussy. And that was when I lost myself all over again. "God, Jovana, you feel so good."

My brain was occupied with pleasure. My body was overwhelmed. This was a feeling and a level I hadn't reached before.

I was sure that had everything to do with not wearing a condom. That had to be the case.

It couldn't be because I was getting the chance to have Jovana again.

Something that emotionally intimate wasn't possible. I wasn't even capable of conjuring those kinds of thoughts.

"Grayson!"

Her exhales were getting louder.

Her inhales were equally as erotic.

She wasn't telling me to slow.

She wasn't controlling me with her hands.

By the sounds she was making and the way she pumped her hips against me, she was telling me she wanted more.

This fucking woman.

She couldn't get enough.

Damn, I loved fucking her.

During the next set of dips, I swiveled my hips, circling inside her, giving her friction at every angle. She was nearing the edge she wouldn't be able to come back from. I could sense it, I could hear it. That was why I pulled out and flipped her on her back, the move taking her by surprise, even earning me an *"Ahhh!"*

Once she was settled, I stepped off the bed and stood on the floor, along the side, where I guided her to the very end of the mattress. There, I lifted her ass in the air and placed her legs over my shoulders, the new position giving me total access to her pussy.

"Ohhh."

She liked this.

And it was about to get even better.

Within a stroke, I realized how true that statement was for us both.

Because while I was giving her short, hard, deep pumps, I told her, "Touch yourself." I slowed my speed, pulling back to my crown, taunting her with my tip. All that did was make me miss her, which made me want her even more. "Rub your clit while I fuck you."

I wanted the vision of her hand on her pussy.

But I also wanted her to feel the combination of the two of us.

To experience what it felt like to be dominated by pleasure.

Her hand lifted from the bed and slithered down her navel until she reached her clit.

"That's it," I moaned, burying myself so the merger hit her at the same time. "Now go a little faster and tell me how you feel."

Her lips were already open. Her breath was coming out in pants. The backs of her knees pushed down on my shoulders, like she was urging me forward, and I bucked in.

After a twist, I did it again, my thrusts gaining more pressure.

Power.

Heat.

"Grayson!"

She gave me only one word.

That was because she was in that familiar place.

The one where she had lost control and the only thing she could focus on was the build.

I knew.

I could see it all over her.

I could feel it.

"That fucking pussy," I howled. "It's incredible."

The way it was sucking me in.

The way it was making me so damp.

The way it was contracting around me, almost holding me in.

And as she soared closer, so did I.

"Don't stop," I warned as her hand slowed. "No matter what, don't you dare stop."

"But I'm going to come."

"And that's what I want."

It was as if a switch had gone off the second I'd released that statement because she was instantly shuddering, clenching me from the inside, saturating me with her orgasm.

"God, yes!" Her screams pierced my ears in the best possible way.

I moaned while I listened to her, fighting off my own orgasm as I slipped in and out of her, even more easily than before. "Oh hell." She was tightening, quaking—things I could feel from the inside.

Things that were making it so fucking hard not to come.

I took a deep breath, holding it off while her body finally stilled, and that was when I pulled out and dropped her legs from my shoulders and let her ass fall to the bed.

Since she was still positioned in front of me, I leaned down and swiped her clit with my tongue.

"Ah!"

I chuckled before I did it again, gazing up her body to meet her eyes. "Sensitive?"

"In ways you can't even imagine." Her fingers dived into my hair. "But fuck that feels good."

She needed tenderness.

Softness.

Healing from the relentlessness I'd just given her.

So that was what I gave her, inhaling the scent I was starting to love so much while I flattened my tongue and dragged it up and down her clit.

I wanted to keep her wet.

I wanted to keep her moaning.

And I wanted to keep her desire thrumming through that perfect body.

Her legs spread wider, her knees bent, her feet pushing against the bed, and within a few more laps, she was moving with me.

Her exhales became desperate.

Her fingers dug my scalp out of need.

This greedy, beautiful woman wanted to come again.

And nothing pleased me more.

But this time, she was getting some of the control back.

I lifted my face and moved higher up her body, brushing my mouth over hers. "Ride me."

Her eyes opened after our kiss, her teeth giving her bottom lip a quick gnaw. "Now?"

"Yes. Now." I rolled onto my back, my legs dangling off the end of the bed. "Straddle me." I leaned up on my arms, watching her rise from the bed and move over me. Once both legs were on either side of me, I gripped her hips, guiding her toward my tip. "Do you have any idea how fucking hot you are?" I captured a nipple between my lips, roughing the end of it before I released it. "Or how sexy you look right now?"

Her hands were gentle when they landed on my shoulders, her head falling back as she took her first plunge. "No, but this is everything, Grayson." She lifted to my crown and lowered. "How do you feel this good?"

I could come this second.

That was how she felt to me.

What she was doing to me, what she was goading out of me.

But I needed to hold off just a little longer, to enjoy this for a few more moments.

I twisted her hair around my wrist. "Faster." I pressed my mouth against her throat and growled, "Fuck me like you want to come again."

"But I do."

"Then show me, Jovana. I want your pussy milking my cock."

She immediately went into overdrive, rising and falling, cranking her hips forward after every few dips, learning from earlier how it felt to have me hit every part of her.

The tightness was proving just how much she was enjoying it.

"Grayson!"

Ah, that fucking sound.

The one that told me she was close.

I reached down until I was grazing her clit, rubbing my thumb across it.

"Shit!" she cried, her fingers now squeezing my shoulders. "I. Can't. Breathe."

I released her hair and pointed her face toward mine. "You don't need to. You just have to kiss me. I want to know what your tongue tastes like when we're both coming."

"Just promise you won't pull out."

Her request came as a whisper, but the words were so fucking loud.

"I want to feel it," she continued. "I want to feel you."

Goddamn it.

I'd given her the power, but when a demand like that came in, I suddenly wanted it back.

"You want my cum?"

"Yes."

The hairs that I kept trimmed at the top of my shaft were pressed against her clit. With just a slight jerk of my hips, they would act like fingers, giving her clit the pressure it needed. To show her, I aimed upward and sensed the scrape against her most sensitive part.

"*Ohhh.*"

"You like that," I confirmed.

"I like everything you give me."

Then she was going to fucking love this.

"Just wait," I told her.

I was trying to give her notice that what was about to happen was going to rock her world.

But she was already screaming.

She was already so damp.

And she was already clamping me from the inside.

So I showed her no mercy, and while she stayed straddled around me, I pounded into her pussy, holding her back with both hands to make sure she wouldn't fall.

To give her all the strength I had in my body.

Enough that within a few strokes, the tingles shot from my balls into my shaft.

"Jovana!" She moaned my name at the same time. "Fuck!"

The way she was contracting, the way she was bathing me in her come, the way she was wrapped around me, her voice all I could hear, was sending me so far past the edge.

Jolts of shivers were moving through me, and with each influx, I felt myself empty into her.

A freedom that was so foreign yet so fucking amazing.

"Oh God," I rumbled, hardly able to hear myself because her sounds were so loud. "Yes!"

We held each other.

We practically clung to one another.

"Grayson!"

And as my movements slowed, our shudders began to lessen, and our breaths became louder than our moans until there was silence.

Stillness.

And just small, quiet pants of air.

My face had somehow, at some point, moved into her neck and I pulled away, locking our eyes in the dark room.

She traced a hand over my cheek and across my lips. "You are"—she exhaled—"kind of epic at that."

I laughed. "And last time, was that epic too?"

"Very much so. But this time was different in every way."

I didn't let that statement process.

It was too much.

Even now, even here, even after what had just gone down, I didn't want to put my brain there.

"I need to get you in the shower. You're full of me."

"Are you coming in with me?"

I'd never showered with a woman. That wasn't part of the normal process. I was usually long gone before that stage would even be considered.

But my skin was sweaty, and I liked the thought of having hot water wash my body.

I was even tempted at the idea of washing her pussy and then tasting her under the steamy spray.

"Would you like me to?" I asked.

She gripped me harder. "Of course."

I inhaled the skin right beside her mouth, my eyes closing as the lavender and vanilla mingled in my nose. "Then let's go get you wet again."

CHAPTER FOURTEEN

Jovana

"Mmm," I moaned as I began to roll over in bed, the warmth of the morning sunshine hitting my face, the movement a reminder of what had gone down last night. My muscles were sore and there was a tenderness between my legs. My God, that man knew just how to treat my body. My eyes flicked open as I faced his side of the bed and I uttered, "Good morning—"

But my voice cut off as soon as I saw the dent in the comforter where he'd lain in a towel last night after our shower. There was also a dent in his pillow where his head had been.

Except he was gone.

I reached for my phone on the nightstand, checking the time.

I was normally an early riser, where I'd get in a three- to four-mile walk before I started filming content for the day, but it was almost eight thirty.

That was extremely late for me.

And by the explosion of notifications, I knew the picture I'd taken of us in Grayson's bed had posted to my Instagram just like I'd scheduled it to.

As of thirty minutes ago, our fake relationship was out in the open.

I wondered how Grayson was reacting to that.

How he was processing this.

What his mood was like this morning.

I opened the app and immediately saw that he'd accepted my request to collaborate on the post, which meant the picture of us also appeared on his profile. That his forty-eight thousand followers were now mingled with mine.

And all of them were hit with the same bomb.

I was dating Grayson Tanner.

Boston's Biggest Bachelor.

I couldn't help but wonder if this, along with last night, was the start of something new.

Something wonderful.

Something I'd been wanting.

Was that how Grayson was feeling?

Or was this burst of attention setting him off?

My teeth bit into my bottom lip, and with *oh God, oh God* repeating in my head, I hurried into the en suite to use the restroom and brush my teeth. Since I'd fallen asleep in just a towel, I put on the shorts and tank I had on last night and rushed into the living room.

Once I got past the couch, I saw him in the kitchen, gripping the door to the fridge, peering inside, like he was scanning the shelves for something.

I didn't hesitate.

I didn't even say anything.

I just sprinted the remaining steps that separated us and wrapped my arms around his stomach, pressing my face into his back. I took a solo second to breathe him in before I asked, "Are you doing all right?"

I wasn't sure if it was the feel of me behind him or the words I'd chosen to speak, but he froze.

Stiffened.

He turned into a block of ice.

The door to the fridge closed, and with his hands empty, he clasped them on my arms and pulled them off his body. Once my arms fell to my sides, he reopened the fridge and removed the orange juice, side-stepping away from me to get a glass. "I'm fine."

His voice was sharp.

It bit me straight through the air while his eyes avoided me.

And where his limbs had unthawed, taking him to the other side of the kitchen, mine had turned to stone.

All I could do was watch him pour the juice to the halfway point in the glass and fill the rest with vodka that he'd gotten from the bar. He carried the bottle and juice container to the island, sitting in front of his tablet, which he swiped while he sipped.

He was either extremely mad at me for something or he didn't want to be touched.

I'd get to the bottom of that.

First, I needed to understand what kind of emotional state he was in and why he was going for the vodka this early in the day.

"Fine?" I said softly. "That's all you're going to say to me?" I walked a few steps closer. "No 'good morning'? Or, 'How does breakfast sound?' Or, 'How about a cup of coffee, Jovana? I learned during our Italian dinner date that you can't function without it, so I brewed a fresh pot.'"

He slowly looked up. "Coffee's over there." He nodded toward his fancy machine, which I didn't dare touch, it was so intimidating. "Help yourself."

When he attempted to glance down again, I replied, "Come on, Grayson. You've got to give me more than that. Talk to me. Tell me what you're thinking."

"What I'm thinking?" He laughed, a sound that told me he didn't find this funny at all. "I'm thinking my personal business is once again splattered all over social fucking media. I'm thinking the whole world is going to have a comment about our relationship and I don't want to know what they have to say—the good, the bad, or the goddamn ugly. I'm thinking I'm already over this and it's just started." He swished the contents around in his glass. "How's that for a little truth?"

Grayson was a private person. Sloane was too.

I could respect that.

Not everyone chose a career like I had that required so much transparency online. So I could understand why he wouldn't want his tea aired or to read the opinions of our followers.

The positive could be as heavy as the negative sometimes, and it was a lot to bear.

Maybe I needed to shift topics and discuss something that didn't make him want to drink so early in the morning.

Like addressing what had happened between us last night.

I moved to the island, stopping directly across from him, and poured myself a glass of juice. I was close enough that I could rest my hand on his shoulder, and after debating it for a few seconds, I decided that was the best way to enter this conversation and draped my wrist across his bulging muscle. "Want a little of my truth? I haven't slept that good or that late in years. That has everything to do with you. What time did you get up?"

"From your bed or mine?"

Huh?

"Mine," I replied.

"A few minutes after you fell asleep."

But I was positive he'd spent the whole night with me.

Of course, there was no way to know that—I'd been dead to the world—but I couldn't figure out why he wouldn't stay with me.

"Why did you leave?"

He shrugged my hand off, my fingers suspended in the air before I pulled them down to my side. "Because I shouldn't have even lain there after our shower."

Even though he looked away, I still searched his eyes, waiting for the answer to hit me.

And when he finally looked back at me, I saw the coldness.

The irritation.

The vulnerability that he showed last night was gone, and the side of Grayson that was completely shut off to everything except for the glass of vodka in his hand was back.

"I don't get why you'd say that."

He shook his head, sighing as if the conversation were wearing his patience down to the bone. "When I told you that you can't get emotionally attached to me, I couldn't have been any clearer. If you want incredible sex over the next year, I'm your guy. But, Jovana, I'm not someone you should fall in love with. I'm not built that way, and the second you climbed on that bed last night and wrapped your arms around me to cuddle—" He wiped some invisible wetness off his lips. "Shit, that's not me. That's not what I want." His eyes narrowed. "And that's not what this is ever going to turn into."

Each syllable he spoke caused my throat to tighten.

They caused my hands to shake.

They caused my feet to turn numb. I wasn't even sure how much longer they would hold my weight.

As much as it killed me to admit, he had been clear.

He had given me that warning.

But for some reason, I'd thought last night had changed things between us. I'd thought it was a new beginning.

I'd thought that he'd come into my room because he wanted more.

That the moments we'd shared when he'd opened up about his mom were the first step of him letting me in.

And maybe in that moment, that had been true.

But in this moment, he was deflecting. He was attempting to push me away because he couldn't deal with the way he was feeling.

Was it due to the conversation we'd had about his mom and the rawness he'd shown?

Or that he'd come into my room and we'd shared such a deep level of intimacy?

I didn't know.

But what I did know was that I was human. I had feelings. I was sensitive to words when they were spoken by someone I cared about.

And Grayson's hurt.

Especially since they were phrased to make me believe that I'd read the situation all wrong.

That he just wanted to fuck me.

That he wanted me to accept his proposition to keep this a no-strings-attached relationship, so he'd have someone to sleep with over the next year instead of jerking off.

That I meant absolutely nothing to him.

And as much as I tried, I couldn't hide the fact that his words were still affecting me. That they caused my stomach to churn as I whispered, "I wasn't trying to cuddle you."

"No? Then what were you doing?"

"I was trying to get warm. You wouldn't know this about me, since you know nothing about me, but I'm always cold."

"The guest wing has its own thermostat. Turn it up as high as you want."

God. He was such a dick.

"Noted." I smiled even though it took every ounce of strength out of me. And because I hadn't been emotionally tortured enough, I asked the question that wouldn't stop haunting me: "You're really going to walk away once the year is up . . . aren't you?"

Even with a low voice, the question dripped with angst.

"Yes. I am." He downed half his drink and reconnected our stares. "I'm Mr. Wicked. Mr. Good Time. Mr. I'll Fuck Your Brains Out. I'm not capable of love, and you can't change that about me. Don't even try, you'll just be wasting your time." He left his glass and clutched my rib cage, high enough that his palm pressed against the side of my breast. "But if you want to get naughty this morning, I'm fucking game."

I knew this was an act of masking his feelings. I knew that because there was absolutely no way he could look at me like this and feel nothing. That he could make love to me, like he had last night, and not care about me.

But if I knew this, then why was this conversation still stabbing at my heart?

Why had I woken up this morning with hopes that everything was going to be different?

That today would be the day he was going to drop his shield and toss it off the balcony of his penthouse?

Did I want to keep setting myself up to hurt like this?

Did I want to give my body to someone who admitted out loud—whether it was a lie or not—that we were having meaningless sex?

When I knew that after a year's time, I would ache even harder than I was right now?

Still, there was a chance things could go the way I wanted, that the risk would pay off, and Grayson would come around and choose us.

If that happened, if this man finally loved me, it would be the best thing I'd ever experienced in my life.

He grazed my nipple, rubbing the hard peak. "Feels like you are game." When he pinched it, the tiniest moan accidentally escaped my lips. "Sounds like you are too."

A wave of emotion catapulted through my chest.

He was seeking a reaction.

If I showed him how much this conversation hurt, he would know what kind of control he had over me.

Therefore, I couldn't react the way I wanted to, but I could give him all the sass.

"If you hadn't fucked me so hard last night, that answer would probably be yes." I lifted his hand off my body, the same way he'd done to my arms in front of the fridge, and placed it on his crotch. "This girl needs a little time-out, so you and Mr. Wicked down there can get well acquainted today."

"Too bad. Morning sex is my favorite." He refilled his glass. "I'm assuming you get what I'm telling you? That you're not going to get attached to me and you can handle that this is just sex?"

He couldn't help himself, he just had to keep digging.

But I still had yet to answer his question.

"Or should I stay far away from you?" he asked after a long pause.

No strings was impossible. So was unemotional.

Two parallel lives with no physical intersection. That was what I should have wanted.

But I wanted Grayson.

My body wanted him.

And I wanted him any way I could have him.

Because I knew, I felt, I was positive that at some point, that shield would drop.

No matter how many times he warned how our story was going to end, I wanted an epilogue.

One that I'd written.

One that I'd fantasized about.

And I wouldn't give up.

I wouldn't quit on him the way his mother had. He needed to know, to feel, to see that I wasn't going anywhere.

"Depends how nice you are to me," I told him. "If you're a dick, Mr. Good Time will have to keep it in his pants. But if you play nice, then maybe I will too."

This wasn't going to be easy.

Maybe I'd regret my decision when I was constantly searching for signs and gestures, my romantic mind turning them into moments of meaning when that simply wasn't the case.

Or maybe we'd become everything I'd ever wanted.

But I had to be realistic. There was no way I could stop myself from having sex with him.

Not when I wanted him this badly.

When we'd be together for twelve months.

When I'd be living in his condo, seeing him every day.

"It's funny . . . you didn't want a nice guy when I was licking your pussy. In fact, when I was doing it in the shower, I'm pretty sure you were telling me how dirty I was."

My cheeks flushed from the memory. "I like the balance."

"I'll remember that." He got up from his seat and headed toward his wing. After a few paces, he pulled his phone from his back pocket, stopping to read what was on the screen. He turned toward me. "Did you see Laura's text?"

I shook my head, not even remembering where I'd placed my phone.

"I guess a Celebrity Alert went out a few minutes ago. Hell, I know you subscribe to that shit, so you'll see it."

"What did it say?"

A smile tugged at his beautiful lips. "Looks like they found your post on Instagram and shared it with the headline, 'Hook, line, and locked down. It appears like Boston's Biggest Bachelor has gone from six to one.'"

I wished more than anything that were true.

But at least my post was believable.

"Laura must be ecstatic," I replied. "Everything she planned is coming true."

"We'll see how it affects our memberships." He took a sip, holding some in his throat before he swallowed. "You know, that's the real testament."

I knew the way my followers responded to my endorsements.

Grayson and I were a product of Hooked.

Memberships were going to soar. I felt that in my gut.

"The numbers will increase. Trust me," I said with confidence.

He brushed his fingers over his beard after putting his phone away. "Maybe that means we can cut our contract down to nine months."

Asshole.

"I'd prefer six if I'm being honest."

"Even better." He resumed walking toward his room, and when he neared the entrance, he said over his shoulder, "Don't bother me unless you've changed your mind about this morning."

"I haven't."

"Then go put on a fucking bra."

CHAPTER FIFTEEN

Grayson

"Don't you know how to knock?" I said to Laura as she walked into my office, unannounced, like she owned the place.

The smile on her face fucking irritated me.

I couldn't stand the whole I-told-you-so attitude. We'd hired her for a reason, so of course she was supposed to know how to fix what was happening at Hooked. But she didn't have to look so goddamn smug while she gloated.

"The door was open," she responded. "Besides, if you look at your calendar, I'm on it, so don't act so surprised to see me."

I glanced at my monitor, pulling up today's schedule. A two-hour time slot had been reserved for Laura. "Two fucking hours?" I barked. "What could you possibly need that would take that amount of time?"

"Didn't you read my email?"

"What email?"

She grabbed the back of the chair that sat in front of my desk. "The one that outlined why I'm here and what we're going to be doing."

Fuck.

In the last three weeks, everything had become such a blur.

Emails.

Conversations.

Outings with the guys.

The only details I could truly recall were the dates I'd gone on with Jovana.

Mostly because every one just teased me more, goading my erection.

Was that because she wore the sexiest outfits every time I was around her?

Because her nipples were constantly hard and showcased in every dress that she wore?

Because twenty-two days had passed since she'd given me her pussy after she turned down my offer of morning sex?

Shit, I didn't even know anymore.

I just knew that there were evenings where I had earned that happy ending. Where I'd been nice as hell during our dates and the moment we got back to my place, she would say good night and go into the guest room and lock the door. Then in the morning, she'd get up early and either film content at my place, her setup so intricate I could tell she didn't want to be bothered, or she'd go back to her apartment, and I wouldn't have a chance to touch her.

She was making me wild.

And not just when she was in my presence, but times when she was nowhere near me. During those moments, whatever I looked at, whenever I turned around, there was a reminder of her.

The way she left her scent all over my condo. How her sweatshirt now lived in my living room because she was always cold whenever she sat in there to read. How her cashew milk coffee creamer had a spot in the door of my fridge.

How her pictures and videos were constantly in my Instagram feed. Whenever I'd go on TikTok to bury myself in travel videos, places I wanted to disappear to in the upcoming weeks, there she was.

On my For You page.

Promoting a product.

Looking so hot, I immediately got a hard-on.

Even TikTok wanted me to see her.

Goddamn it.

I needed a break.

I needed her out of my head.

I needed Hooked to purge her from my brain.

And I was here, sitting at my fucking desk, attempting to do just that, and now Laura wanted something from me, and that brought my mind right back to Jovana.

I was done.

I pushed back in my chair, and just as I passed where Laura was standing on my way to the door, she said, "Where are you going?"

"Out."

"You can't leave, Grayson. We're doing a photo shoot that you're starring in."

I stopped walking and faced her. "I'm doing *what?*"

She was holding a tablet and aimed the screen at me. "If you'd read my email, you would know what I'm talking about." She pushed her red glasses to the highest point on her nose. "Going forward, please take the time to look at everything I send you. I don't write those emails for my benefit. I write them for yours."

I grabbed the tablet from her, flipping through mock-ups of cartoonlike figures of a male and female, posing in different areas of what I assumed was my office. There was copy written above each image, along with text conversations that were identical to the internal workings of our app. "Are these ads?"

"Yes."

"What are you going to do with them?"

She crossed her arms while another self-satisfied look moved over her face. "Since your dual post with Jovana went live, the marriage arm has regained over six percent of its loss. Just like I knew would happen." She grinned even harder. "We want to see if we can increase the results more rapidly if we start a marketing campaign that focuses on how Hooked helped you two find each other. The campaign won't launch for another month, after the two of you are engaged." She took out her phone and spoke directly into the speaker: "Remind Jovana to keep her left hand in a position where it'll be easy for us to digitally wrap a diamond around her finger. We debated about using a mock ring, but we decided to go the digital route so when you do propose, it'll match the one you give her, which I understand you haven't purchased yet."

I clenched my fingers together as I processed what she'd said to me.

An ad campaign, which I assumed would run internationally to capture our full demographic.

With my face plastered across all forms of digital media.

That would bring more attention to me.

More comments.

And now everywhere I looked online, I'd see not only Jovana but the two of us together.

"You're fucking kidding me," I barked.

She pulled the tablet from my hand, like she thought I was about to throw it. "I'm telling you, when I initially saw her in the bar, I knew she had the perfect presence for what I was looking for, but I didn't anticipate her being an influencer and having the reach that she does." She set her bag on the chair in front of her, as if letting me know she had no intention of leaving before our two hours were up. "Grayson, the response you received from that dual post was immense, along with the additional posts Jovana has made since then."

She tapped the screen of the tablet several times before pointing it in my direction. She was on Jovana's Instagram account, showing me the picture that Jovana had shared of us at a Mexican restaurant, where there were glasses in our hands, and us toasting. The caption read: spicier than a jalapeño margarita.

Laura scrolled through the responses. "Look at the comments."

There were thousands.

I already knew what the majority said because I'd spent enough time checking out her fucking account.

"And this one," she said, moving on to the next photo that Jovana had posted of us, which was against a brick building on Newbury Street, showing us in an intimate embrace. We'd been walking back to my place after eating at a seafood restaurant when Jovana suggested we take a photo. My lips were on her cheek and her eyes were closed. She'd aimed the camera high, capturing the tops of our heads and her full expression with the caption: In my I-can't-stop-smiling era. "Grayson," Laura said softly, "as one of the few people who knows the truth about you two, I have to say, I'm blown away by what I'm seeing. The both of you couldn't look happier or more in love. And that connection grows stronger in each shot, like in this one."

She was on the most recent photograph Jovana had posted a few days ago. This one hadn't been staged. I was shirtless, cooking eggs and bacon at the gas range in my kitchen. Just a few moments before, I'd asked her how she liked her yolks when she came up behind me, wrapping her arms around my stomach, whispering, "Don't worry, I'm not cuddling. I'm just thanking you for making me breakfast," and then her arms were gone, and she released me.

What I hadn't realized was that she'd put her phone on a tripod and set the timer to capture the scene.

The photo showed my head turned to the side as I looked down at her, the angle emphasizing my profile, a smile lifting from the corner of my lip with the caption: When he makes you breakfast.

Rather than using a heart emoji, which had become one of her signature endings whenever she posted about us, she used the smiley face with the three red hearts spaced around it.

"So you see," Laura said, pulling the tablet back, "you two are quickly becoming the hot couple. And we'd be stupid not to use that to our advantage." She waved her hand over the air, drawing an invisible arch. "That's why we've entered the capitalization stage and why we're going to launch these ads as soon as you put a ring on her finger. The public is already going nuts for you two. Can you imagine the explosion that's going to happen then?"

Why the fuck was I smiling in that photo of her arms around me?

Why was I gazing down at her like she made me the happiest man alive?

Why was Laura telling me that she could see our connection grow through each photo?

This was too much.

All of it.

And I didn't know if my fucking head was burning up in flames or if it was my chest, but there was a fire licking up and down my body.

This wasn't what I'd signed up for.

Neither was a photo shoot or an ad campaign.

And fucking emojis with hearts around a smiling face.

"This is bullshit—"

"Speak of the devil," Laura said, interrupting me as Jovana stepped into my office. "We were just talking about you."

"I'm the angel, not the devil, Laura." Jovana winked at Laura as she joined us and gave me a quick kiss, letting her lips linger on mine for a second too long before she whispered, "Your office door is open. Anyone can see us if they walk by. Act like you like me."

I didn't know if it was the three weeks of no sex or the close contact or her kiss that caused my cock to clench in my jeans. But it did and it was getting harder.

"And Laura, I have to be an angel to put up with this one." Jovana smiled at me while wiping her gloss off my lips. "How's the temper today? Are we on nice-guy mode or are we roaring like a tiger?"

Her scent.

It took hold of me.

It shook the hell out of me.

I wrapped my arm around her back and squeezed her ass. "Roaring."

Her cheeks reddened, her bright-blue eyes shining. "Why am I not surprised." She held out a garment bag that she placed across my arm. "I grabbed you a suit and tie to match what I'm wearing for the photo shoot." Her attention shifted to Laura. "I thought matchy-matchy would look positively adorable for the campaign."

Since she now had a fob that would get her into my building, the elevator, and my front door, she could come and go as she pleased.

I didn't care that she'd picked through my closet.

I cared that my dick was fucking throbbing.

That all I wanted to do was kick Laura out and bend Jovana over my desk.

"Oh, you're good," Laura cooed, eating up every word Jovana had said.

"I brought my camera, so I'm hoping your assistant has some time to film us during the shoot?" Jovana asked me. "I want to show my followers the whole preshoot and us getting ready. I think they'll love having behind-the-scenes access. Since I don't have an assistant, I figured it would be okay to ask yours?"

Before I could respond, Laura said, "I think giving your followers that kind of access is a fabulous idea, so if your assistant is too busy, then I'm happy to do it." She glanced toward the doorway. "Real quick, I just want to mention something before your office is bombarded with people and I don't have the opportunity to bring it up." She cleared her throat. "When are you planning on living together? I assume this is going to happen soon since the engagement photographer has been booked for"—she looked at her tablet—"four weeks from this Saturday."

The date had been nailed down over our French dinner a few nights ago, agreed upon between the foie gras and smoked salmon canapés we'd shared for an appetizer. I'd even had my assistant book movers.

"Jovana's moving in this weekend," I said.

"You are?" The excitement on Laura's face was extreme.

"With our relationship about to hit fast-forward—our engagement coming up soon, followed by the wedding—we thought it was the right time." Jovana glanced at me. "You know, it makes things more believable."

"Has the impending move been well received?" Laura asked, directing the question to Jovana. "With your parents and Sloane, I mean?"

Jovana took a long, deep breath. "My parents don't know yet. I'm going to tell them after we're engaged, I think. It'll be less shocking and better received if they know we're committed to one another." The tension left her face when she added, "Sloane is Team Grayson all the way. Especially since he's helping her buy the bar and it'll be hers in about a month. Of course, she gave me a little crap about it despite the fact that I'm covering my portion of the rent until our lease is up, but that's just her personality. She's cautious when it comes to me. And, ultimately, she just wants me to be happy."

"It sounds like we have nothing to worry about then?" Laura pressed.

The last thing our situation needed was negative press, and if her parents raised a fuss or Sloane decided to dedicate a TikTok to our relationship, shit would hit the fan.

"No, we're all good," Jovana confirmed.

"Great, then let's get going with this photo shoot. How about the two of you get changed," Laura told us. "My hair and makeup team should be here any minute. They'll do some quick touch-ups on the both of you, and then we'll take a few test shots to make sure we're on the right track before we really start shooting."

Was I even in this goddamn room?

Were they forgetting that I was part of this too?

That my fucking opinion mattered, and this was the last thing I wanted to do right now?

"Sounds perfect to me," Jovana responded, unzipping the bag that was still across my arm to pull out my suit and her dress. "Laura, before we call in Grayson's assistant, how about we get a little footage of the clothes on the hangers?"

"I love when I work with a professional who needs no directing," Laura said. "It makes my job a million times easier."

"Definitely not my first rodeo," Jovana said, laughing.

"Isn't that lucky for you," I growled, making sure both women heard me. "Because this is the first time I've done anything like this and I'm not fucking happy about it."

The room turned quiet.

"Find a home for these," Jovana said, giving the clothes to Laura, "and snap a few shots—the camera is in my bag. I'll handle him in the meantime."

"Sure thing," Laura replied.

Jovana set her arms on top of my shoulders, moving our bodies close together. "I know this isn't your favorite thing in the world, but it's what I'm good at, and I promise it'll go by fast." She combed the back of my hair with her fingers, her expression calm and sexy as fuck. "And then we can go grab something to eat and have a few drinks and forget this all happened. Deal?"

"You mean until the pictures are released, and then I'm going to have to see my face attached to an entire Hooked media campaign. And you know exactly how that's going to make me feel."

She sighed. "Yes. There's that. But let's focus on how this is going to increase memberships and make you *alll* the money."

My arms lowered until my hands found her ass. "No, let's focus on what we're going to do at my place after the food and drinks. Tell me you have something in mind for that too."

"Depends how nice you are . . . *remember?*"

"I've been nice, Jovana. I've been so fucking nice. All that's earned me is a locked bedroom door and a relentless hard-on." My hand rose to just behind her neck, tilting her head back to aim her lips at mine. "Are you looking for cuddles? Is that the problem? Because if that's the case, consider it done."

She poked my chest even though I didn't move back even an inch. "Just because you think you're being nice doesn't mean I agree. Why don't you try amping it up a little and see where that gets you. You never know, when you lay it on extra thick, you might just get lucky."

"You're pushing every button I have."

"Good." She smiled. "I'm sure when Laura's makeup crew comes in, that's going to push you even further."

I gripped her even tighter. "Makeup is a hard no. I'm telling you that right now—"

"We can't have you shiny under the lights that the photographer is going to set up. That won't look hot in pics. So, just some powder—you won't even know it's on." She mashed our lips together and wiggled out of my embrace, joining Laura at my desk, where they started videoing the hanging of our clothes.

I was so fucking tempted to go over to the bar in my office and pour myself some vodka.

The edge was nearing, and the booze would help settle every thought.

But I stayed put, watching the women move around the room, until Jovana was escorting Laura out and closing the door behind her and the two of us were finally alone.

"You don't have a restroom in here, do you?" she asked me.

"No. Why?"

She was wearing jeans and a tank, her hands holding the bottom of the shirt. "I would have gone in there to change. Since you don't, let's strip . . . I guess." Her shirt immediately came off, leaving her in just a bra.

The throbbing in my cock had turned to a full-on ache.

I nodded toward the lacy number. "It's nice to see you do own one."

"You should feel fortunate that I go braless around you. Not everyone gets the pleasure of seeing my nipples." She smiled as her hand dropped to unbutton and unzip her jeans. "I won't be wearing one for the shoot, FYI. The dress is too tight."

Her jeans were off, and she stood in just her bra, no panties. It seemed she no longer wore any since our first night together.

A thought that had haunted me.

God.

That body was something else.

Every dip expertly spaced out, each curve aligned so beautifully.

How could someone look as perfect as her?

"Are you trying to fucking kill me?" I groaned.

She connected our stares—hers bright and far too pleased.

"Kill, no. But I would like you to get changed into your suit."

I hadn't moved.

I hadn't even lifted the collar of my polo to drag the shirt over my head.

I was just standing here, frozen like a goddamn fool, staring at her as if I hadn't seen her body before.

As if I hadn't been inside her.

As if I hadn't kissed or licked every inch of her skin.

"I've just been . . . admiring you."

She moved over to my desk, where her outfit was hanging. She slipped it off the wooden hook and held the light-pink dress in her hands. "*Ohhh*, I see. Mr. Nice Guy has come out to play."

"There's nothing nice about those words, Jovana. They're the truth. I'm in love with your body."

She reached behind her back, and suddenly her bra was loosening from her tits. The white-laced cups, when pulled down, revealed the hardness of her nipples, the straps falling from her arms until the bra was on the ground. She unzipped the dress and stepped into it.

Three weeks.

It felt like three years.

"Then I guess I should thank you." She came over to me and gave me her back. "Would you mind zipping me in?"

She was even breathtaking from this angle. The muscles in her shoulders, the delicateness of her spine, the roundness of her ass—every bit was stunning.

Fuck me.

"Grayson, I know what you're thinking and I'm shooting you down before you even try. We don't have time for office sex, so get that out of your head right now. I need you to help me with this dress, and then I need you to slip on your suit. Laura is outside this door waiting for us."

"I just need two minutes," I growled in her ear.

She glanced over her shoulder. "We both know you need a lot more time than that." She went to take a step away from me and I stopped her, my palm pressed against her navel, my cock thrusting against her ass. "Looks like I need to have Laura zip me up."

She wasn't giving in to me.

Goddamn it.

"No." I exhaled in frustration as my hand found the zipper. "But you fucking owe me."

She turned around once she was securely in the dress and said, "I think you owe me. Must I keep reminding you what this campaign is going to do for you? How your rich ass is going to get even richer?" This time, when she tapped my chest, I felt the sharpness of her nail. "And don't forget how ugly this is going to get for me once this is over. My followers are going to lecture me nonstop about jumping in too quickly and saying yes after only two months and the whirlwind wedding we're going to have. So, while you're off cruising on megayachts, burying yourself in a million different women, I'm going to be picking up the pieces of what's left of my business." She bit her lip while she glared at me. "Do me a favor, don't ever tell me I owe you. Now, get dressed."

She could really fight when she wanted to.

And it was hot.

But she was probably right. I could disappear from social media.

She couldn't.

I could even deactivate all my accounts.

But they were her livelihood.

She wasn't going to have it easy at all.

"Yeah, yeah," I whispered, and I went over to my desk and stripped off my shirt and jeans, putting on the black suit and white button-down, along with the light-pink tie that went with her dress.

Just as I began to tie the knot, Jovana appeared, taking the silk from my hands and weaving it, like it was something she did every day.

"My dad taught me, in case you're wondering." The sharpness was gone, in its place a tranquil tone. "Every Sunday morning, I'd grab the black tie with the light-blue stripes, the only one he owned, and I'd stand on the bed and do this for him until I was tall enough to do it from the floor." A soft smile crossed her mouth. "He said my future husband would be impressed. I never forgot that."

I watched her eyes.

Her lips.

The freckle she had on the side of her nose that I'd never noticed before.

A collection of characteristics that were individually alluring, but combined they were just exquisite.

"All done."

I glanced down, holding the knot, feeling around each side. "You're better at this than me."

"I know."

"I am impressed."

She scratched the center of my chest as though it were the belly of a dog. "You should be." She left me before I could grab her, and she opened the door to my office. Laura walked in with my assistant directly behind her, holding Jovana's camera.

"Hair and makeup are running a few minutes late," Laura mentioned right before the photographer entered the room, immediately setting up lighting near my desk. "Why don't we start with the test shots and then we can touch you guys up when they get here."

"I love that idea," Jovana said.

She grabbed me by the hand and led me to my desk, guiding me into my chair. She took a seat on the wooden edge in front of me, facing me, with her phone in her hand.

"Let me just make sure my cell is on silent . . ." Her eyes widened and she laughed as she read something on the screen.

"What's so funny?"

"It's just one of my followers. His comments are always so funny." She was typing now.

"His?" I couldn't stop my brows from rising.

"Yes. There are lots of *he*s who follow me. I have a huge audience, don't forget."

I hadn't forgotten.

I'd spent enough time observing her accounts to know just how popular she was.

But most of the comments I'd seen were from women.

"What's he saying?"

"He's just talking to me about my last video that went viral. It was for a meal kit and he's a wicked foodie, so he's teasing me about the lack of spice that I used." She glanced up. "He likes his food extra spicy, and I'm more of a salt lover. He's telling me I could have added sriracha to the shrimp tacos instead of the smoked paprika that I sprinkled on. We'll debate this for a couple of days—that's just how we are."

"I bet that's the only reason he's talking to you." My teeth ground together. "You sure know a lot about your followers . . . don't you?"

"Some, yes."

"Like him?"

She continued to type. "Well, him and I have been talking for a while, so yes, I know things about him."

"Is he single?"

She finally looked at me again. "Does it matter?"

I kept my voice low. "Answer me, Jovana."

"Yes. He's single."

I held out my hand. "Let me see what he's saying."

Her neck craned back. "You mean you want to look at my phone?"

The fire was back, and this time it was in the back of my throat. "Yes."

"Grayson . . ." She turned her face to the side. "Are you trying to be my bodyguard? Or are you jealous?"

I couldn't tell if she was saying this because the photographer and my assistant were nearby or if she was really wondering.

Regardless, I didn't have an answer. I just needed to see the words that man had typed to her.

It was as simple as that.

"Give it to me, Jovana."

She placed the phone in my hand. "Here you go. I have nothing to hide."

I scrolled through the messages. There were hundreds.

And when I exited out of their chat box, there were thousands of other DMs from men.

Some were telling her how sexy she was. Some were asking her out on dates. Some were requesting and sending her pictures. Some begging for her number.

They were doing whatever they could to capture her attention.

"Jesus," I huffed.

"Welcome to my social media world." She'd moved behind me and was reading the screen over my shoulder. "Here's a good one . . . look." She clicked on a DM and a dick pic instantly popped up.

"Fuck, get that away from me." I handed the phone back to her.

"Too much?" She giggled as she returned to the edge of my desk.

"All of it is too much." *Fuck, how many times have I thought that today?* "There are literally thousands of dudes trying to get with you."

She shrugged. "It comes with the job. I just ignore them—at least the creepy ones. Some of the guys, like Jared, I've befriended."

"Jared is . . . ?"

"The spicy guy."

I'd reached my limit.

"I don't want to know any more."

Her smile grew. "You don't want to hear about Peter and—"

"Fuck no." I looked at the photographer. "Are you about ready to start?"

He was positioning what looked like a silver umbrella on the other side of my desk. "If you'd like, I can."

I turned my finger in the air and said, "Let's get this ball rolling."

Laura and my assistant must have heard me because they were suddenly at our side. My assistant was filming, and Laura was doting on the photographer.

Jovana was telling me, "Sit up straight. I'm going to put my heel on your chest. I need you to look like you're being submissive to me."

Submissive?

That was a role I never played.

I glanced at Laura. "Those are the kind of photos you want?"

Laura moved a few pieces of my hair and picked something off my collar. "We already know you're enamored with this woman. Now I need you to show that you're a simp for her. The world is going to go wild when they see that."

I still couldn't shake the thought that she was a woman loved by so many male followers.

Some were even lucky enough to get her attention.

To make her smile.

I didn't know why that thought made me want to lift my desk and heave it across the room.

I just knew if we didn't get this shoot over with soon, it wasn't going to end well.

And a goddamn fucking simp?

Because I'd gone from six women to one.

Boston's Biggest Bachelor was hooked, and what better way to emphasize that point than to have me under Jovana's shoe.

The boys were going to get an earful about this.

"Grayson," Jovana declared, "I need you to smile."

I wrapped my hand around her calf, another around the pointed heel of her shoe, and I gave her the expression she wanted.

The look everyone in this room was after.

I stared at her like I was completely, undoubtedly in love.

CHAPTER SIXTEEN

Jovana

"I can't believe you have this much shit," Grayson grumbled from the kitchen the second the movers left his condo.

I'd asked the men to stack my boxes in the living room. I couldn't have them place my things in Grayson's bedroom. I'd just have to move them all the way to the other side of his condo, and I didn't want to do that. At least the living room was much closer to the guest wing. I also didn't want the movers to know I wasn't going to be staying in his room.

Extra precaution was necessary when you were lying to the entire world.

"It's not shit," I told him, standing next to the six rows of boxes, each row five boxes high. "This is my entire life. Everything I own aside from my bed, dresser, nightstand, and bookshelf." I'd given all the furniture to Sloane since I couldn't bring it here. Once the year was over, I hoped she'd give it all back—a thought that caused a knot to lodge into my throat, causing me to whisper, "Be a little gentler with your words, will ya?"

He was leaning over the island with a bottle of water in his hands, the plastic making a crinkle sound as he squeezed it. "What are you planning on doing with it all?"

"Unpacking it. Obviously."

"When?"

I opened the nearest box, which was full of books. The guest room didn't have a bookcase or shelf. I was sure I had at least five more boxes that were just as full as this one. "Over the next couple of days, assuming I can get some shelves installed or something to hold all of"—I reached inside and pulled out the top title, showing him the cover of a shirtless man gripping the waist of a woman dressed in his button-down—"these."

He eyed the book. "You want to display those in your room?"

"Yes."

"Because?"

I placed the book back and tucked the folds to close the box. "I've told you my parents have been very inspirational when it comes to love and what I want in a relationship, but so has everything I've read. These aren't just stories to me. They're lessons. Tales about life and commitment and the hardships of a relationship. Every one that I've read means something a little different to me."

He shook his head. "You're setting yourself up for failure. You know that, don't you? Whatever goes down in those stories isn't reality. At all."

"You would say that because you don't believe in love. But I do and I'm not going to settle." I glanced toward the boxes again. "Are some of the novels a little outlandish, sure. But the point is that everyone deserves to be loved. Not cheated on. Not used. Not disrespected. Not constantly screamed at. There's someone for everyone, and I'm going to find my person."

As I glanced in his direction, he was slowly licking across his lips. "And who is that person going to be? Jared?"

I laughed. "Maybe. Or maybe one of my other followers. Or a man I meet in the elevator of your building. Or someone I find on Hooked. Heck, even Holden is kinda cute."

I'd seen Holden a few times in the bar and after we'd shot the ad in Grayson's office. He had this beautiful, golden-color hair that reminded me of honey, the most dashing dark-blue eyes, and the kind of smile that was infectious. And when he looked at you, you could feel it, sense it, a unique type of charm that was positively consuming.

But Holden wasn't my type.

I just wanted to get under Grayson's skin.

His top lip lifted, like he was about to bare his teeth, and he clenched the plastic so hard, the bottle bent. "Watch yourself. You're playing with fire right now."

"Why would you care if I dated your best friend? Or one of my followers? Or a man I met in your elevator?" I waited for a response. When he said nothing, I continued, "Do me a favor, Grayson. If you're going to warn me, at least have a reason to back it up. I'm the most patient person in this world, but empty threats get on my nerves."

"God, you have a mouth on you." He opened the bottom cabinet where the trash was located and tossed the water inside. "I'm starving. I'm going out to get something to eat. You can either join me or sit around and play with your ridiculous fucking books. Your call."

My stomach groaned at the mention of food. With the move, I'd accidentally skipped lunch, and the only things in me were several cups of coffee and a banana.

I glanced down at what I had on.

Yoga pants.

Tank top.

Sneakers.

And on my head was a baseball hat, my hair braided and hanging across my breast.

I didn't care if we spent the rest of the night arguing where I could prove how wrong and ridiculous he was. I needed to eat. "Will you go somewhere casual? And not bougie like usual? So I can wear this and I don't have to change?"

"And here I thought you were going to decline my offer." He'd left his wallet on the counter after tipping the movers and he shoved it into his back pocket.

"I know that's what you really wanted, but I'd rather torture you with my presence."

"Sounds like it's going to be the perfect dinner." He chuckled. "How about the pub across the street?"

"Yesss."

"Then let's go," he said, walking to the door.

I quickly grabbed my purse from the guest bedroom and rushed to meet up with him at the elevator.

The ride down to the lobby was silent. Fortunately, I kept my hat low, so I could look at him without being so obvious. His arms were crossed over his broad chest, his eyes on the door, his expression full of focus, like he was deep in thought.

I was so curious about what ran through his mind.

Did Grayson ever self-reflect on his choice of words? Did he ever regret the things he said?

Did he ever say one thing but mean another?

And I understood why he protected himself with a thick outer layer—after what he experienced with his mother, he struggled with trust—but I just wished he didn't wear a shield all the time. That there were more moments when he'd hang that metal coating in the closet and show me the softness that was underneath.

The elevator opened before we reached the bottom, and an older woman walked in. She smiled at us, and since we were standing against the far wall, she gave us her back to face the front.

I was focused on the screen that showed our descent, the number changing with each floor, when Grayson whispered, "I thought that was going to be your chance."

I tried to piece together his statement. "Excuse me?"

"Your future husband." He nodded toward the woman. "Too bad, isn't it?"

My God.

He didn't self-reflect at all.

The man was just a constant, relentless asshole.

I shot him my middle finger, and when the door slid open, we allowed the woman to leave first and quickly passed her in the lobby, exiting through the front and crossing the street to the pub. We sat at a table near the bar, and just as I was taking my phone out of my purse so I wouldn't have to make small talk with Mr. Asshole, a waiter approached.

"What can I get you to drink?" he asked.

"Everything," I replied.

He laughed. "Ironically, I can probably make that happen."

While I pondered, Grayson said, "Since she can't make up her mind, I'll take an extra-dirty martini."

My mouth watered at the thought of sipping something olive flavored. "I'll have the same."

"Coming right up—" The waiter paused midsentence, staring at me much more intensely than when he'd first come to our table. "Hey, you're Jovana, aren't you?"

I held the top of my hat while I glanced up at him. "I am."

"I follow you on Instagram. My girlfriend got me into you. Well, ex-girlfriend now. I dumped the girl but kept you around." He laughed as though he realized how weird that sounded. "I like your vibe. I even bought that fanny pack thing you've been wearing for the last couple of months for my sister. She loves it."

This wasn't the first time I'd been recognized.

Each time, I found it so odd. Fantastic for business, but still . . . odd.

Especially when I smelled like a goat without a swipe of makeup on my face and an outfit that I'd sweated through more than once today.

Regardless, he was a follower of mine. His purchase contributed to my income. And now that his sister owned the fanny pack, maybe she would become a follower, along with her friends.

That was why it didn't matter how I felt about myself in this moment. How bad I smelled. How gross I looked and felt.

I appreciated what I had.

And kindness was never difficult.

"What color did you get her?" I smiled.

"Same as yours. The pink one."

"Good choice," I replied. I read his name tag and held out my hand. "It's nice to meet you, Sebastian."

"You as well." His stare gradually shifted over to Grayson. "And you're the boyfriend. I've seen your pictures on Jovana's account." He gave Grayson his hand and they shook. "You own that dating app, right?"

Grayson wasn't amused.

He was also losing his patience.

"You mean Hooked. Yes, I'm a cofounder." Coldness was pouring off his face by the gallon.

"Yeah, Hooked, that's what it's called." Sebastian's focus returned to me. "It's cool to see you in here. I can tell my friends I met someone famous." He laughed to himself as he walked away from the table.

I connected my stare with Grayson's, who was now leaning back in his chair, his arms perched high on his chest, his gaze penetrating right through me.

"What?" I asked him.

"What do you mean, what? That dude was eye-fucking the shit out of you."

"No, he wasn't."

"He certainly was, and the kicker is that I'm sitting right here. That takes some serious balls." His expression became a little more pompous when he said, *"You're the boyfriend. You own the dating app."* He even tried to mimic Sebastian's voice and Boston accent.

Someone was hot and bothered.

And I loved that.

"What did you want him to do?" I rested my arms on the table. "Bow down to you?"

He glanced around the bar until he found Sebastian, his eyes turning into a glare. "How about treat me with a little respect. I'm your goddamn boyfriend."

I sighed. "Isn't that a loaded statement."

He mirrored my position and said just loud enough for me to hear, "On paper, I am, Jovana. And as far as that motherfucker knows, you're taken."

Except that paper was going to be shredded.

And in Grayson's mind, I wasn't his.

"It's funny to me that this even bothers you. You don't want love. You don't want to be tied down. You don't want emotions to be involved whatsoever. But you don't want to hear about the male friends I've met online, like Jared, and you don't want me to date your best friend, and you care about Sebastian striking up a conversation with me, which was all he was doing, Grayson." I knew the next thing I was going to say was a bold move, but I no longer cared. "If I didn't know better, I'd think you actually felt something for me."

"Do you know what I feel?" He ground his teeth together. "Blue balls."

I knew how long it had been since we'd slept together.

I felt the ache too.

But I wanted him to desire me in a way that went beyond a physical need.

I wanted him to crave me emotionally.

I wanted his care as much as I wanted his mouth.

I smiled as large as my lips would pull apart. "Get used to that feeling. It's going to be a very long time before anything down there"—I nodded toward his lap—"goes anywhere near me."

CHAPTER SEVENTEEN

Grayson

Once we returned to my condo after a hellish dinner at the pub, where I'd done everything in my power not to fucking strangle the waiter, who continuously flirted his ass off with Jovana during the entire meal, I went to the wet bar and poured myself a vodka.

Jovana disappeared to her room. She didn't even take a box with her. They were still all lined up in rows, untouched, making a goddamn mess of my place.

Move-in day.

It wasn't as bad as I'd suspected. She was already here almost every night anyway, leaving little things around my condo, so it couldn't get much worse than it already was. The only difference was that this was officially her place now. Her mail had been switched to my address. Her name was in the call box outside the front of my building. If she got mad and stormed off, she would still be here; she'd just be on the other side of the living room in her wing.

A question I'd been asking myself all day, from the moment the movers unloaded the first box, was if I really minded having her here.

Damn it, I didn't know why that was such a hard one to answer.

As I sat on the couch, I lifted the glass to my lips, holding it there long after I swallowed.

The answer wasn't as much of a debate as it was admitting the truth.

We bickered like siblings.

She annoyed the shit out of me.

She wasn't the neat freak that I was.

But I didn't mind watching her walk around my place, braless, in her short shorts and tiny tank tops. I didn't mind cooking eggs and bacon for more than one.

I didn't mind the lack of quietness, where she always started conversations even when I wasn't in the mood to talk.

I didn't know why coming to that conclusion was so difficult.

It should be as easy as thinking, *Yes, fuck, I enjoy being around her.*

But it wasn't.

It was hard.

Muddy.

Layered.

It took everything out of me to just let those thoughts pass through my head.

But they were there.

They existed.

And they were spreading, like the glass of water Jovana had dropped on my hardwood floors this morning that seeped into the cracks between the wood, expanding across several planks.

The water was gone once it was wiped away.

But even though Jovana wasn't in my line of sight, she was far from gone.

That had nothing to do with being surrounded by her things.

That was because she lived in my head, and I couldn't get her out.

Fuck, I didn't want to.

I drained the rest of my glass, and as I was getting up to pour another few fingers' worth, she came out of her wing, wearing a dark hoodie. She had in earbuds. Her hat was gone, her hair twisted high on my head.

As she neared the front door, I asked, "Where are you going?"

"For a walk."

I checked the time. It was past ten.

"At this hour?"

She slipped her phone into the pocket of her sweatshirt. "I didn't get to walk this morning and I need it. I'm feeling—I don't know what I'm feeling. So, yes, I'm going at this hour."

"No."

Her brows lifted and stayed. "No?" She added in a laugh.

"Yeah, no, you're not going. I don't care how safe this area is, you'll be out there alone, in the dark, and something could happen. That's not going to go down on my watch—not while you're living with me."

She shifted her weight between her legs. "And how exactly do you plan on stopping me from going?"

I chuckled, but mine was deeper and grittier than hers. "You really want to test me on that?"

"Why do you make everything so difficult?" Her hands went to her hips.

I had an answer for that.

But it wasn't one I was ready to share.

I could barely settle the words in my own head, never mind speak them out loud.

"There's a gym on the first floor. Go find your way to the treadmill."

She shook her head. "No. I'm definitely not doing that."

"Then I'm going on a walk with you." I waited for her to respond. "Your choice: Treadmill or having me as company? Pick one."

She rolled her eyes. "Hurry up."

I left the glass on the island in the kitchen and walked into my bedroom, changing into a pair of sweats, a sweatshirt, and sneakers, and joined her in the entryway.

"You had to go with the gray sweats, didn't you?"

I glanced down my body, trying to see what she saw. "Huh?"

"I don't expect you to understand." She released a long breath. "Let's go."

I followed her through the door and into the elevator and out the front of my building. Once we hit the sidewalk, her speed tripled, and I was suddenly rushing to keep up. "Jesus, slow down."

"You wanted to come, don't forget that."

It wasn't that I wanted to come; it was that I didn't want her to be alone.

But I wasn't about to explain that to her.

"No earbuds?" I said as I noticed they were no longer in.

"I didn't want to be rude."

"You're telling me you want to talk?"

She glanced at me as we approached the crosswalk. "Shouldn't I be asking you that question, since you're not one for a ton of conversation? But every time you do speak to me, you're either bashing me, snarling at me, or picking me apart."

Her admission hit my chest.

It didn't bounce off.

It stayed there, penetrating my skin.

She took it as bashing, snarling, and picking her apart.

But what I was really doing was pushing her away. Backing her up. Preventing her from getting too close because I didn't want her to see inside.

Or I didn't want to reveal what was inside.

I didn't know the difference or if there was one.

But once she saw, once I shared the way I felt about her, once I gave her that missing piece, everything would change.

The way I saw my future.

Me.

Us.

"I know."

She'd stopped looking at me, but her stare returned.

"I haven't been the nicest to you, Jovana. I'm acknowledging that."

We were at the start of the crosswalk. She didn't move even though she could and there were no cars around. "Whoa."

I laughed. "I'm not good at admitting things like that. I guess that's because I never think I'm wrong." I gave her a small smile. "But I haven't been the most gentle with my words and I'm sorry for that."

"You're apologizing? I feel like this is a moment that should be documented."

I nodded. "You're not wrong about that."

She pulled at her collar. "Where did this realization come from?"

My hands hung at my sides, and I shoved them into the large front pocket of my sweatshirt. "Now you're pushing it."

"I'm not. I'm just trying to understand this—and you. Did you have an epiphany on the way back from the pub? Or in your condo when I made a mad dash to my wing? Or when I told you I was going for a walk? What caused it?"

I searched her eyes. "Why does it matter?"

"Because everything about you matters."

Even though she was pleading with me, there was a softness in her eyes. In her posture. Even in her lips.

I started walking and she was right beside me, only inches separating us. I could feel her stare in my peripheral vision.

"Grayson . . ."

"I heard your question," I barked, aware that I was doing it again, and I found myself halting and facing her. "You're expecting me to say I had this shining moment when everything came to a head and I recognized the bite I always have with you, but I can't say that. It's just been . . . an accumulation of thoughts."

Situations when I became cognizant that I was smiling more than frowning.

When I'd bring orange juice and vodka into my room, telling her not to bother me, so I wouldn't regret pulling her into my arms or telling her that I cared.

When I read her conversation with Jared and watched Sebastian flirt his ass off, a beast of anger moving through my chest because these men were invading my territory.

When I viewed our photos together on Instagram and saw the way I looked at her.

Those were the moments when it hit home.

When I knew she was different.

That we were unlike anything I'd ever experienced before.

"What are those thoughts, Grayson?"

My hands clenched inside my sweatshirt, sweat rising through my skin.

My heart was fucking pounding.

I could even feel it in the back of my throat.

It was producing this sensation where all I wanted to do was run.

That was all I knew. That was why I'd hooked and fished, so I wouldn't have to stick around.

So I could stay uncommitted.

But this beautiful woman was staring into my eyes and she wanted the truth.

My truth.

Why is it so goddamn hard to say it?

"You're not going to let it go, are you?" I stared up at the sky, wishing for rain.

But it wasn't going to come.

At least not before I voiced what she wanted to hear.

"No. I'm not," she admitted.

When I looked at her again, her expression hit me just like her statement had earlier. "What do you want from me, Jovana?"

"I want you to say what I already know." She took a step closer. "I want to hear the words you've been holding back because you weren't ready to say them."

My stare dropped to the ground as a new feeling entered my chest.

It wasn't tightness.

It wasn't a throbbing.

This was different.

A beat that I hadn't experienced. An urge that was almost beyond my control.

When I gazed up again, she had moved once more, our bodies now almost pressed together.

"Say it," she whispered.

I wanted to fucking growl.

I wanted to fight.

I wanted to do what I did best and find something to use against her, pick her apart, or snarl in her face.

But that would get me nowhere—and that was a direction I'd been heading in for a long-ass time.

"Jovana . . ." My voice was quiet, almost unrecognizable. "I care about you."

She smiled. "See, was that so hard?"

I appreciated the sarcasm.

I even huffed out a burst of air before I said, "Yes. It was."

She grabbed the collar of my sweatshirt and leaned up on her tip-toes, pressing her lips against mine.

The kiss was slow, passionate.

Sexy as hell.

And when she pulled away, she kept her face hovered in front of me.

"I don't know what any of this means," I told her, "or how things are going to change between us or what I'm even capable of. I don't know how to do this. You know I've never done anything like it before." I paused, collecting myself to make sure I stayed and didn't start to veer. "But what I can tell you is that I'm happy you've moved into my home and the feelings I have for you are strong and extremely real and"—I stopped to kiss her—"I want more. With you, with us." I lowered my hands down her back until they were gripping her ass. "And, fuck, I want you."

"Grayson . . ." Her stare moved between my eyes. "I feel the same way."

CHAPTER EIGHTEEN

Jovana

As soon we returned to Grayson's condo, I linked fingers with him and said, "Follow me," before I took him through the guest wing and into my room.

It was an embarrassing mess.

Clothes were piled along each side of the bed. The dresser was covered in accessories. My framed photography was on the floor, resting against the wall. A giant bin of cosmetics was in the corner. I'd moved my filming equipment to make more room, and now that was scattered around anywhere there was an open spot.

I'd get it all cleaned up and organized.

But not tonight.

Within a few steps into the room, I turned toward him, wrapping my arms around his neck. And as I stared into those haunting green eyes, I thought of all the moments that it had taken to get here.

The moments that had been hard on my heart.

The frustration he'd put me through.

The way I'd forced myself not to give up, even though he'd told me countless times there was never going to be an us. That we would never grow into anything. That in the end, he was going to walk.

Of course, that could still be true.

So many things could happen within the next year.

But a feeling inside told me that deep down, he didn't mean the harshness he'd said to me.

That he needed to process and accept what he really wanted and come to terms with it—something he'd never done before.

And once he did, he would realize that I was everything he didn't know he wanted.

That was when he'd finally drop the shield.

He would let me in.

And we would have a chance to be us—to be whatever we were supposed to be.

Even though he hadn't voiced those same words, he'd told me he cared.

That he wanted me.

That was enough.

And despite the fact that he didn't know how to do this, I knew we'd figure it out.

Tonight was the start of that.

While I was stuck in my head, lost in these deep, emotional thoughts, he was gazing at my face, taking in my eyes, my lips.

A gaze that he'd had since the day we'd met at the bar, one that had always tugged at my gut, telling me there was emotion behind his eyes.

He was holding me tight enough that I couldn't move.

I didn't want to.

"You have me in here"—he gave the room a quick scan, a sexy grin spreading across those thick lips—"now what are you going to do with me?"

I brushed my thumb over his mouth, wanting the softness under my fingertip. "I need a shower. I was hoping you'd join me."

"*Mmm.*" His moan was deep, coarse. It even vibrated through me. "I have a better idea." His hands lowered to my butt. "Why don't we use my shower. It's bigger with a lot more heads."

"Take me there."

Instead of reaching for my hand, like I'd done to him a few minutes ago when I'd led him into my room, he lifted me into the air as though there were a puddle on the floor and he didn't want my feet to get wet. My legs straddled his waist, my hands gripped his shoulders, and my face immediately went into his neck.

We weren't even to the doorway before he stopped.

I could tell he was looking at something on the floor, and I followed his stare. "What's wrong?"

"I just noticed that photo. I didn't see it in your room at your old apartment."

He had to be talking about the picture I'd taken in the Seaport District of the city. The one where I'd captured part of the bridge with the rainbow lights underneath, the rest of the shot a long angle of the water with part of Boston's skyline behind it.

"That's because it's new," I told him. "I had it framed shortly after you came to our apartment. And, funny enough, a couple of days ago, I saw that you have almost the same picture in your home office." It hit me then that he'd never taken me into his home office. I'd discovered the photo during one of the mornings he was at work and I snooped around a little, peering into the rooms I hadn't yet checked out. "I've looked around your condo. Don't be mad. I felt like since I'll be staying here, I should know the whole space."

He smiled. "I'm not mad." And then he gently kissed me. "I think I'm a little bit in shock that we have the same shot—that's what made me stop and stare at it."

I giggled. "I'm not going to lie, I was a little dumbstruck when I saw yours too. What are the chances that we'd be standing in almost the identical location, taking basically the same exact picture, and hanging it in our homes." I held him tighter. "We have more in common than you think, Mr. Wicked."

"When I saw your photography, I thought the same thing."

"But you didn't mention it."

"No." His stare shifted between my eyes. "There were a lot of things I didn't say, Jovana."

The same was true for me.

I cupped both sides of his face and kissed him, breathing in his citrus and amber scent, taking in the feel of his beard as it roughed up my skin, circling my tongue around his. "I hope that changes," I whispered when I pulled away.

He didn't respond.

He just started walking, carrying me past the hallway and living room and into his wing, where he brought me into his en suite. He set me on the edge of the large, freestanding tub in the corner, and he moved over to the massive walk-in shower, turning on the multiple heads. Two hung from the ceiling, and at least five more shot out from the walls.

Within a few seconds, the glass began to fog.

"Get over here," he growled as he stood in front of the double sinks.

He was already tearing off his sweatshirt and dropping those delicious gray sweatpants, the crotch hitting him in a way that showed the outline of his dick. He slid off his sneakers, and once he was fully naked, a body full of muscle that was making me practically drool, he reached for me.

"I need you," he roared.

He lifted my sweatshirt over my head and peeled off my yoga pants, freeing my feet from my sneakers. I unzipped the front of my sports bra and he brought me into the shower.

As the water hit the top of my head, I tugged the elastic that was holding my hair, letting my long locks fall down my back. But I had only a few seconds to enjoy the warmth of the heavy stream before his hands were all over me.

His lips were on my neck.

His hard-on was pressed against me.

My neck tilted back, my mouth opening, my breath already coming out in short, hard pants. "Grayson . . ."

With our skin so slick, the movement was easy.

Uninterrupted.

Wetness on wetness, slippery pleasure that increased as his fingers dived lower down my body.

"God, I've fucking missed this." He spoke right above my nipple, now holding me against the glass wall, and once he silenced, he sucked the peak into his mouth.

"Yesss."

As he flicked the end, grazing it first with his tongue and then with his teeth, I gripped his hair.

I just needed to hold on to something.

Anything.

Because the sensation wasn't only in my breasts.

His hand was now between my legs, rubbing the length of my clit.

"Don't stop." I tightened my fingers around his short strands. "Oh God, yes."

His thumb was focused on the very top while two of his fingers were circling my entrance. "You're so wet."

It could be the shower, but we both knew it wasn't.

The second he touched me, I was instantly damp.

"I can't wait to be inside of you"—he slid in, turned his wrist, and pulled back out—"and to feel this tightness on my cock."

He moved to my other breast, and my head pressed against the shower wall, my hair sticking to my cheeks, my lungs filling with hot steam.

I was completely full of this man.

He was touching each of my most sensitive spots, forcing the pleasure to build inside me.

"What are you doing to me?" I cried, changing my grip to his shoulders, which I began to dig with my nails. "You're going to make me—"

"Come." He swapped sides again, surrounding my nipple, mumbling, "Now."

I was already there.

The tingles were in my clit.

My stomach.

Shooting higher as he thrust his fingers in and out of me.

But there was something about him demanding orgasms from me and the way he voiced those orders that sent me right over the edge.

I clung to his upper body, sucking in as much air as I could hold, and I braced myself as I was hit with the first wave of shudders. "Ah!" I gasped. Again. "Fuck!"

"That's it." His voice practically licked me. "Oh fuck, I can feel it."

I was gone.

Floating in crests of intensity, and each one that pounded through me became more intense.

"Grayson!"

His hand didn't slow.

His tongue didn't halt from lapping my nipple.

If anything, he was moving harder.

Faster.

Working the layers of spasms through my body until I completely stilled.

I drew in a breath.

My skin, my body, my insides—afire.

"There's nothing as sexy as watching you come." He pulled me off the wall and lifted me again, placing me on top of the granite bench. It was on the far side of his shower, away from the heads. "Get on your knees."

The bench wasn't high enough for any other position; doggy style was the only way this would work. But before I flipped over, I ran my hands up his hard, etched thighs and licked the tip of his dick, where a bead of pre-cum was waiting for me. My palms pushed higher, tracing his happy trail, rounding each of his abs, all the way to his defined chest.

Even the hair on his body was incredibly erotic.

"You're fucking killing me, Jovana."

"You've waited this long. What's another few seconds."

He leaned down and slammed our mouths together, the taste of his tongue as warm as the pre-cum I'd just swallowed. And while he kissed me, he lifted me by the armpits, getting me into a standing position so it would be easier for me to kneel once he pulled away.

Which he did.

And growled, "I can't wait a second longer."

I smiled as I climbed onto the slick bench, holding the edge where the stone wall met the glass. He was there, without hesitation, poking at my entrance. As he pushed in, dipping to his tip, I reached under and cupped his balls.

"Goddamn it," he hissed. "You feel so fucking good."

I glanced over my shoulder, and his expression filled with hunger and need. "Was I worth the wait?"

He tightened his grip on my hips and slid all the way in. *"Yesss."* His head fell back, his neck elongated, his Adam's apple bobbing. "Fuck me."

I looked forward, too absorbed in my own body to focus on his, and the first of many moans came from my mouth. *"Ahhh."*

Still so tingly from my orgasm, I didn't know how he could make me feel this good, this quickly. But the passion was increasing and so were his thrusts.

"Jovana, you're so tight."

He was moving hard, his strokes deepening. Enough so that I needed both hands to hold on, and I released his sack and clasped my fingers around the edge of the stone.

The moment I did that, he reached underneath me and began to play with my clit. His skin so wet, it felt like his tongue, especially as he flicked the top, working that spot like he'd done earlier.

"Oh shit!" I flattened my palm against the glass, pushing against it every time he reared into me. "Grayson!"

"If you keep moving your hips like that, I'm not going to last."

I was meeting him.

Arching forward and back.

Rocking to a rhythm.

The combination of wanting to help and please and urge my orgasm drove me to do it even quicker.

As soon as I stilled, he pulled out and turned me around, lifting me into the air and holding me against the wall.

This time, we were under a direct stream.

The water was pelting against his back, splattering my face and chest, the parts that weren't shielded from his body. As he burrowed his cock, I wrapped around him, my legs clinging, my arms clutching.

My body now bucking with his.

"Jesus," he moaned. "You're fucking amazing."

I mashed our lips together, the heat from his skin, the water, our intimacy—all hovering around me like a thick cloud.

I couldn't breathe.

But I didn't need to.

I just needed him.

And I needed . . . "More." I kept our mouths together. "Fuck me harder, Grayson. Please."

I could tell my begging and pleading turned him on.

But it also set a fire under him, one that came with more power.

Strength.

And screams, because as soon as the build began to trickle in, I couldn't stop them from leaving my mouth. "Fuuuck!" I swallowed. "Yes!" I silenced and then repeated *"Yesss"* as the wave crashed through me.

"You know what your pussy is doing right now? It's sucking the cum out of me."

Shudders were moving through my stomach, holding me hostage, keeping me from being able to respond.

"Fuck, you just got tighter." He was pumping me so hard, his words were broken up into syllables. "And wetter. Goddamn it, Jovana."

And that was when I felt him lose himself.

The first shot hit a place where I could feel the warmth. When he slid back and stroked in again, I felt the second shot.

The third.

And fourth.

"Fuck!" he yelled. "Fuck me!"

Even though I was releasing my own moans, my ride hitting its peak, I wasn't lost to the sexiness of his sounds, the feral expression on his face, the dominance in his hands.

It was a look, a feel, an experience I would never forget.

And once we both began to slow, our noises lowering, our exhales coming out as pants, he kept us against the wall, not even moving us after we were still.

We hugged one another.

And we breathed.

"You're sleeping in my bed tonight."

For a moment, I thought I'd spoken those words.

They were in my head.

Deep in my thoughts.

But when I drew my face back and aligned our eyes, I knew it was him who had said it.

Instead of responding, I kissed him.

Differently this time.

More passionately.

And with love fueling my lips.

CHAPTER NINETEEN

Grayson

"You wanted to talk to us?" Easton said from the doorway of my office, where Holden stood next to him, my best friends looking slightly fearful as they gazed in.

I couldn't blame them. I'd been exploding more than normal lately.

I pulled my hands away from the keyboard and wrapped them around my coffee mug. "Yeah, come in and shut the door."

The boys followed my order and sat in the seats in front of my desk.

I'd gotten here two hours before everyone else this morning to give myself some extra time to get shit done. Although I'd been working nonstop since Jovana had come into my life, I'd lost focus. My productivity had declined. There were days when I wasn't sure I'd returned a single email.

I'd originally agreed to this marriage contract because I wanted to win back the memberships that Hooked had lost and to continue growing our company. But my work ethic hadn't reflected that.

I'd been a goddamn mess.

I had a lot to catch up on.

"We have a problem," I said to the boys, lifting my mug, realizing there was only a sip left. I chugged the small amount and reached for my bag. I normally tossed a bottle of orange juice in there and drank it on my way to work. But as I unzipped the top of the leather, I realized

I'd forgotten to grab any juice this morning. Therefore, I wasn't sure why the green top of the bottle was staring at me from inside the bag.

I pulled out the juice and there was a small note taped to the side.

As if I'd ever let you forget. xo

Jesus, that woman.

She was adorable and so fucking good to me.

She'd gotten out of bed at the same time as me, leaving before I did to go for a walk, but when I got out of the shower, there was a cup of coffee waiting for me on the bathroom counter, a little cream added to the dark roast because that was how I liked it.

Small gestures that hit hard.

"Are you going to tell us what the problem is?" Easton joked. "Or just stare at your orange juice?"

I caught eyes with the feisty motherfucker and barked, "Would you rather be in here, relaxing with your best friend? Or fielding emails and sweating your balls off over numbers?"

"I'd rather know what the problem is, so I don't start sweating." Easton pulled at the short sleeves of his shirt. "It's never good when you call us in first thing in the morning."

I peeled off the note and put it in the top drawer of my desk, unscrewing the cap of the juice to take a long drink.

Aside from needing to get work done, one of the reasons I'd come in so early was that I hadn't been able to sleep last night.

There was too much on my mind. Too much eating at me.

Too much at stake.

The guys didn't know that things had changed between Jovana and me.

They didn't know that, in the last week, I'd told her I cared about her, and she'd been spending the night in my bed ever since.

That when she posted a photo of me kissing her cheek two days ago, that hadn't been a planned shoot. That was just feeling an overwhelming desire to lean into her face, needing the feel of her skin under my lips.

Her scent.

Her warmth.

I'd been dragging my feet about coming clean to them.

Like the asshole that I was, admitting I was wrong about wanting a relationship, that I'd blown the fuck up and lost my shit more times than I could count, that they were right and I was wrong—I didn't know how I felt about speaking those words to my best pals.

"As I was saying"—I cleared my throat—"we have a problem." My gaze focused on Easton's stare and then Holden's. "I don't think it's a good idea that I marry Jovana."

Holden pushed himself to the edge of his seat, holding both armrests. "We've already talked about this far too many times—"

"Hear me out," I said, cutting him off.

"We have," Easton countered. "We've heard you try to weasel your way out on multiple occasions, and brother, I don't know how many times we have to tell you that you're going to marry this woman. The contract is for one year. What you do after the twelve months is up to you." He sighed. "I honestly don't want to have this conversation *again*."

I huffed out a lungful of air. "This isn't the same conversation. It's something entirely different."

"It doesn't sound that way," Holden said.

I eyed him up. "That's because you're not hearing me."

"That's because you're not saying anything," Easton shot back.

It was rare that they got snappy. The dudes were typically as happy as goddamn yellow labs. But I knew this topic rubbed them the wrong way.

"I'm about to. Fuck." I took a long, hard breath, trying to push my ego aside so I could be honest and vulnerable with them. "I'm bringing this up again because . . . I care about her."

"Wait . . ." Easton immediately reacted, his brows so high on his forehead, I thought they were going to get lost in his hairline. *"What?"*

"You heard me correctly."

Holden looked at Easton, and when their eyes locked, he said, "I think I need to hear you say it again."

A few weeks ago, I would have marched my ass over to the bar in the back of my office and added vodka to this orange juice.

But I was good.

Real good, in fact.

I sucked in more air, holding it in for a second before I said, "I care about her." I paused, knowing this part was going to be even harder to say. "And I want more with her."

Easton's hands lifted into the air, and he groaned, "Praise fucking be."

"What the hell does that mean?" I asked.

"Just some show that Drake's been making me watch and it stuck in my head—it doesn't matter. What matters is that I'm happy as hell to hear this news."

Holden couldn't stop smiling. "I'm so pleased you finally came around. I knew you would, it was just a matter of when you were going to admit it to yourself."

My exhale was louder than I intended it to be. "It's been a long road."

"And not just with Jovana." Holden's voice was soft, his expression considerate as he inched his way to a topic I didn't want to discuss.

I appreciated the recognition and that he hadn't said my mother's name.

I rubbed my sweaty hands over my jeans. "So, now you know why there's a problem and how these feelings are causing this situation to be even more fucked up." I pulled a file off my desk, opening the top to show the spreadsheet I'd printed out early this morning. At the bottom, I'd circled three numbers in red, which were the current membership totals for each arm. "What Jovana and I are doing is working. These numbers prove that." I pointed at the red circles. "We've regained nineteen percent of what we lost in the marriage arm. The other two arms are going up as well." I clasped my hands together, folding my fingers. "But we're not fake anymore, fellas. What she and I have is real. And that changes the playing field. All this forced PR and an engagement and marriage—shit, I don't know how that's going to affect us."

Holden looked at Easton.

"Dude, you don't have a choice at this point." Easton rubbed his hand over his gelled hair. "You've got to keep going. I know it feels fucked up. I know things have changed between you guys. But this is the path we've decided to take, and we can't quit now."

"Hold on a second, I'm confused." Now I wanted a goddamn drink. "I've shown the world I can settle down. It's plastered all over my social media and Jovana's. Therefore, I've proven that Hooked works. Business is on the rise. And you're still going to make me follow through with this marriage?"

"Yes," Holden said carefully. "Because all you've shown so far is that you're willing to date. You have to show them that you've found the love of your life on Hooked, that you've proposed and gotten married—that's the whole point of this."

"Anyone can date," Easton added. "But not just anyone is willing to make a commitment that involves vows and deeds and beneficiaries."

Holden's expression turned sympathetic. "I know this seems monumental in your world—and it is, trust me, I get that. But as far as business is concerned, Easton's right: dating Jovana is not nearly enough."

I fell back in my chair, my hands flattening on top of my head. "This is the first goddamn relationship I've ever been in. The first time I've ever had feelings for a woman. And our relationship is now going in fast-fucking-forward." I pushed away from my desk before I lifted something off the top of it and threw it across the room. "I'm meeting her parents soon, and I have to pull her dad aside and ask for his approval to marry his fucking daughter." I squeezed my eyes shut. "Do you have any idea how hard that's going to be?" My eyes opened and I glared at my best friends. "To look him in the face and ask a question that I know I'm not ready for? To make promises to him that I don't know if I'm capable of keeping? To straight-up lie and say I want this marriage more than anything when I'm scared shitless and—"

"We understand." Easton's tone was calm.

Far too fucking calm.

"That's easy for you to say. You're not the one who has to do it," I roared.

"But you knew this going in," Holden pronounced. "You knew you'd have to ask her father's permission; you knew you were going to have to propose. You knew you were going to have to get married."

"I'm not denying that fact." I pounded my fist against the armrest. "What I'm stating is that it's fucked up."

Easton placed his hand on my desk. "Listen, we're doing this for Hooked—"

"But what about me? Why isn't that taken into consideration?"

Silence penetrated across the room.

"Grayson, you're still getting the girl." Holden slid back in his seat, crossing his legs. "We're not taking her away from you."

My teeth ground together. "You're missing the point."

"I think you want us to say we're going to drop the requirements so your relationship can progress the way you want it to on a normal timeline." Easton's hand left my desk and went onto his lap. "We're not going to do that. We can't. And I wish you could understand that."

"This is fucked up."

I knew I'd said that multiple times this morning, but each instance was with more emphasis.

Couldn't they fathom how this was going to put pressure on Jovana and me?

How being forced to take things to all these new levels would have us moving at a speed that was so far from typical?

That this could ruin one of the biggest things to ever happen in my life?

"Grayson, the international launch is a milestone we've strived to achieve for a long-ass time," Easton said. "The numbers are only just turning around, and we have no way to determine or control where they'll go from here. All it takes is one more article scrutinizing your wicked, philandering ways, and everything will blow the hell up. That's why we can't just let this play out."

"Again, this is fucked up," I repeated.

"I'm sorry," Holden said softly. "We want you to be with her. We want you happy. Hell, I've been waiting more years than I can count to see you in love."

That word caught me off guard and I hissed, "Holden . . ."

"But we won't change the plans just because the two of you are together now," he continued. "You're going to have to just keep going, my man. See where this all takes you. And at the end of the twelve months, you're either going to thank us or you're going to fucking hate us."

CHAPTER TWENTY

Jovana

Me: Guess what I'm doing right now . . .

Sloane: My guess would be having sex, but if you're texting me while you're doing that, then you're not working hard enough or screaming loud enough. Lol.

Sloane: I have no other guesses.

Me: Driving with Grayson to Brockton. He's meeting the parents today. *insert every emoji*

Sloane: You two are shacking up. I'd hope he'd be meeting the rents soon, so it's about time, girl.

Me: They don't know about that part. You know, they're a little old school when it comes to stuff like that. Baby steps. I feel like they'd want me to at least be engaged before I moved into his place.

Sloane: Maybe that's coming soon?!?

Sloane's comment came from a place of honesty. She had no idea about the contract—I was sure of that. She thought our relationship was purely organic, and she based that on all the things I'd told her, along with my social media posts and the times she'd seen us together, most recently last night, when we'd stopped by the bar for a drink.

But I wanted to at least mention the word to prep her a little. I didn't want my best friend to be so thrown off, she would think an engagement came out of nowhere. Yet it sounded like she didn't need the prepping, that the thought had already been in her head.

Me: You think?

Sloane: Have you seen the way he looks at you? It's the same way I look at chocolate. With all the love and adoration and sentiment that's possible for someone with a charred, stone-cold heart.

Me: Stop, you're the queen of warm and fuzzy.

Sloane: Then the queen of warm and fuzzy says Grayson is positively obsessed with you.

Me: Good. The feeling is mutual. But hopefully, the love will still be there after he comes home with me . . .

Sloane: You say that like your parents aren't shining examples of happily ever after.

Me: No, it's not that. It's just that he's the first guy I've ever brought home. He's going to see where I grew up and meet my role models and—come on, that's epic.

Sloane: He's going to meet Ernie fucking Winters. Enough said.

Me: Right? Let's hope Dad keeps his sense of humor in check. Grayson isn't the kind of guy who's going to LOL just to make Dad feel funnier.

Sloane: Did you bring wine?

Me: Duh.

Sloane: Then, open the bottle as soon as you get there and all will be good. Have fuuuun.

Sloane: And text me after, of course.

Me: Of course.

I tucked my phone into my purse and reached across the front seat of Grayson's sports car, placing my hand on top of his. "Are you doing okay?"

We were nearing the Brockton exit. The apartment complex where my parents had lived for the last twenty-four years was seconds from the highway, so we were close.

Maybe too close.

He quickly glanced at me before focusing on the road. "Yeah, why?"

"I don't know . . . because this is a mega milestone for our relationship and you're about to ask my dad an extremely important question and things are now going from zero to a million." I squeezed his hand. "And if this scenario were normal, I wouldn't know that you're asking my dad today, but I do, and that's nuts."

He let out a sigh.

It could have come from me, that was how hard I felt it.

And how I sympathized with the gesture.

"It's going to be all right," he said.

My heart froze for a second as I processed his response. "You really think so?"

He was quiet for a moment, downshifting as he turned at the exit. "We have no other choice. This is the process, whether it feels fucked up or not."

I pointed right, so he knew which way to turn.

"Most fathers, I assume, want to know that their daughters are going to be taken care of—even if they can take care of themselves." He gazed at me. "Which you can, we all know that. But it's what I'm going to promise him, and that as long as you're with me, nothing is ever going to happen to you. And that I'm going to care about you— always." He'd moved our hands to the gearshift, his thumb rubbing over my knuckle. "Those aren't lies, Jovana."

"I want to say *buuut*, but I'm melting so hard, I can't."

He came to the first light and left my hand to graze my cheek. "I've thought a lot about this. Shit, it's kept me awake almost every night this week. I've even talked to the guys about it."

"I didn't know . . ." I pointed to the left, having him turn into the complex.

"*Fucked up* is the only way I know how to describe it, but we can't tear up the contract—I tried suggesting that to the fellas, and it got shot down. So as strange as this all feels, we've just got to move forward."

The last thing I pointed to was the building just past the dumpster, the one directly before the pool, which no one ever used since the water was green more than it was blue.

He parked and turned the car off.

That was when I turned to him, a smile tugging across my mouth. "Look at you being Mr. Positive. I like this side of you. It needs to stick around."

He chuckled. "You wouldn't have said that if you were in my office the day I brought it up to the guys. I wasn't exactly soft and gentle about it."

"Mr. Wicked is allowed to rear his roaring head when he needs to." I slipped my hand around the back of his neck. "In all seriousness, you're right about moving forward. I'd rather do that than move apart."

Forward was the direction he'd been taking me since our late-night walk, but it was still a relief to hear him suggest that.

To know that, finally, this was what he wanted.

His gaze narrowed while he studied my lips. "I want to kiss you so fucking bad right now, but I'm about to ask your dad to marry you, and I can't walk into your parents' place with red lipstick all over my mouth."

I laughed. "No. You can't." I grabbed the cloth bags off the floor in front of the passenger seat. "Come on. We have three flights of stairs to climb."

Grayson took the bags from my hand as I met him on the sidewalk, and I used my key to open the front door, leading him to the stairs and up the three long flights. The final one ended directly in front of their door, and I gave it a quick knock, letting them know we'd arrived, before I opened it with another key.

"We're here," I sang.

Since the door opened into the tiny dining room, where the kitchen was on one side and the living room was on the other, a hallway in between that led to the bathroom and two bedrooms, it was easy to see where everyone was located.

Mom came out of the kitchen, wiping her hands on her pants, opening her arms to hug me. Dad rose from the couch, making his way over.

"Oh honey, I told you not to bring anything and it looks like poor Grayson has his hands full." Her hug was hard, but her voice was as soft as a cloud.

It didn't matter what time of day it was, she always smelled like cinnamon.

"I just threw together an appetizer. Nothing major. And wine—of course, I brought all the wine."

She kept her hands on my shoulders as she pulled away, taking an inventory of my face. When I was little, she used to tell me she was counting my freckles, checking to see if there were any new ones. Now that I was older, I knew better.

She was looking through me.

Seeing the secrets that I held inside.

"You look happy, baby."

I nodded, smiling. "I am." I turned just as Dad took the final steps to reach us. "Mom, Dad, meet Grayson."

"I'm a hugger, I hope you don't mind," Mom said to him, first taking the bags from his hands, and then wrapping her arms around him.

While they embraced, Dad gave me a look.

His brows were up, stretching beyond his forehead and into his semi-bald head, which was nodding.

He seemed impressed so far.

But that was just with Grayson's physical appearance. Once my father dug into Grayson's personality, that was another approval process.

Once Mom released him, Dad said, "I'm not a hugger," and he shook Grayson's hand. "Nice to meet you, son."

"Nice to meet you, Mr. Winters."

"Ernie, but I like effort." As their hands disconnected, Dad wrapped his arm around me and kissed the top of my head, my arm resting across his Santa belly. "Missed you, baby girl. You're so busy now, you don't come around as much as you used to." He nodded toward Grayson. "Looks to me like that's your reason why."

I grinned. "He's a lot of my reasons, Dad." I took the bag of wine from Mom's hand. "How about I open a bottle? What's everyone in the mood for, red or white?"

"Red for me," Grayson said.

"You know I don't drink that shit. Babe, grab me a Sam Adams, will ya? I need something cold going down my throat while I get to know this boy. Why don't you join me on the couch, Gray."

I was laughing on the inside at Dad making up his own nickname for him.

I squeezed Grayson's arm. "Have fun. I'll be there in a minute to save you."

"You act like I'm going to whip the boy," my father joked.

"Well, aren't you, honey?" Mom teased.

Dad's hand was already gripping Grayson's shoulder, bringing him over to the small couch, where I knew both men would be so crammed, their knees would be touching.

Unfortunately, I couldn't see them take a seat; there wasn't a peek-through in the kitchen.

So I hurried, grabbing the bottle opener from the drawer and pressing the metal spiral into the cork of the red.

Mom brought a beer to Dad and returned to the kitchen, taking out three wineglasses, whispering, "My goodness, he's handsome."

"Isn't he?"

"And so well dressed and put together. Every bit of the city boy I imagined you'd one day be with."

Brockton was less than thirty miles from Boston.

But aside from the accents people spoke with and the seafood served in the restaurants and the weather, it felt like continents apart.

"That's what you envisioned?" I poured some into two of the glasses and went to work on the bottle of white. "I didn't know that."

"Honey, we never expected you to marry a townie and stay here like your father and I did. We dreamed of big things for you, and you're doing better than we could have ever imagined." She pushed a piece of hair off my cheek. "And I don't just mean by dating Grayson." When I looked at her, there were tears just starting to fill her eyes. "You're almost at a million followers, and you've been able to quit the bar and focus on your passion full-time. Do you know what an accomplishment that is?" Her voice softened when she added, "We're so, so proud of you."

As soon as I pulled the cork out of the bottle of white, I threw my arms around her neck.

But this time, when I pulled away, her hands went to my cheeks. "When I called in to pay the rent yesterday, the property manager told me it had already been taken care of. I knew I was going to see you today, so that's why I didn't call and say this over the phone." The first tear fell past her eyelid, a reaction I knew she didn't want because she was so prideful. "Jovana, baby, you don't have to do that. Your father and I have always found a way to manage."

The reason my mom called in the rent was so that she could put it on her credit card. My parents never had enough in their checking account to cover all their bills.

It had been that way since I was born.

Paycheck to paycheck.

Another reason why they'd never moved from this apartment was because they couldn't come up with the first and last months' rent, along with the security deposit, for a new place.

But within the next few months, they were going to move to an apartment where they wouldn't have to walk up three flights of stairs. Where there was a pool that was more blue than green. Where their carpet wasn't torn. Where their windows actually opened. Where Mom didn't have to go to the basement to do the laundry or to a Laundromat since the machines hardly ever worked. Where their view wasn't of raccoons eating the trash that didn't make it into the dumpster.

They'd lived here for so long, they no longer had a lease and went month to month, but I'd still let the property manager know that within ninety days, they were leaving.

And if my parents didn't want to pick out a new apartment, then I would do it for them, making sure that there was an option to buy the property if they decided they loved it.

Because, long term, that was my goal too.

But no matter what, they were moving.

They were finally going to experience the freedom of not being weighed down by a monthly rent and being able to indulge a little. That was something I'd wanted to give them for as long as I could remember.

"I can afford it, Mom. I'm doing really well. And I want to help."

She shook her head. "I can't accept it—"

"You can." I squeezed her fingers. "I'm taking care of me, don't you worry. My student loans are almost paid off. Aside from that, I have zero debt. I'm saving and investing. I've built quite a little nest egg." Most of that had to do with Grayson's massive contract, but things were also starting to really pick up business-wise. And within a year, I estimated that I'd be earning close to what Grayson had paid me. "What I'm saying is, there's plenty of extra, and if this is something I want to do, let me."

"Baby girl . . ."

"Come on, you need to go spend time with my man before Dad gobbles him up and leaves just a bunch of bones in the living room." I laughed, quickly pouring her a glass of wine, which I handed to her, and then I lifted the other two glasses of red.

"Thank you."

I looked over my shoulder.

Mom was wiping her eyes, making sure my father didn't see that she'd cried.

"I love you," I said softly.

"I love you far more."

I rounded the corner of the kitchen, and the two men were facing each other, lost in a conversation about the Red Sox.

Or the Pats.

I couldn't keep up, as they seemed to be switching between the two.

I handed Grayson his wine, staying at his side of the couch, smiling as I listened to them, my eyes bouncing back and forth like a tennis match.

Mom had returned to the kitchen and brought out the charcuterie board I'd thrown together before we'd come, keeping it simple with a few of my dad's favorite meats and cheeses, fruits, and crackers. My mom placed it on the coffee table in front of the couch.

Dad made a sandwich with some roast beef and crackers, spitting a few crumbs in my direction when he said, "I like him." He even pointed his thumb in Grayson's direction to add emphasis.

"Have I mentioned that Dad is known for his bluntness?" I said to Grayson.

"I am, too, so I appreciate that," Grayson replied. "I also appreciate his knowledge of Boston sports."

"A topic he could talk about endlessly," I said. "As you just experienced."

"First boy you've ever brought home, baby girl. I had to give Gray the once-over, make sure his knowledge of sports met my approval."

I laughed. "I'm glad to hear that it does."

"Ernie, honey, take a napkin"—Mom handed him the one she was holding—"before poor Grayson is wearing your next bite."

My father wiped his mouth with the paper towel and took a slice of pepperoni, chewing it while he said, "You want to know something, young man. I was nineteen years old, working at the 7-Eleven down on Commercial Street not more than ten minutes from here, when the prettiest girl I'd ever seen came in for a Coke. I asked her if she wanted a can instead of the bottle she'd set on the counter for me to ring up. Cans were cheaper, and I was trying to save her money, or if she wanted to pour a drink from the fountain, which was also a little less than a bottle.

She told me she treated herself to a bottle of soda every day, even if that meant it was a couple of cents more. She said she liked to hear the fizz when she twisted off the cap, knowing the treat waiting for her would be fresh and sweet. The cans, she said, tasted like metal, and the fountain sodas sometimes came out stale." Dad looked at Mom as he spoke.

I looked at Grayson, wondering if he was connecting the story from the first night we'd met.

His eyes told me he had.

"That was when I knew she was going to be my wife," my dad continued. "She didn't wear makeup. She didn't have on fancy clothes or purses or any of that shit. She didn't need it. She was gorgeous just the way she was. But she knew what she liked, and it was that small, little indulgence that made her different than all the other girls." Dad smiled. "I asked her out right then and there. After three dates, we were married." He made another sandwich, this time adding cheese and a piece of apple, folding the salami in fourths before placing the cracker on top. He gave it to my mother, and while she took it from his hand, he said, "Best decision of my life." He looked at Grayson. "When you know, you know. Am I right, son?"

Grayson nodded, slowly moving his gaze over to me. "You're right about that."

CHAPTER TWENTY-ONE

Grayson

The moment had come. I'd just asked Ernie if I could speak to him alone and he'd brought me into Jovana's old bedroom. Since his and his wife's bedroom was the only other room, I assumed this space was less personal.

As soon as I stepped through the doorway, I wasn't shocked to find more romance novels on the shelves across from her small twin bed. There were a few pictures of her and Sloane and some with her parents—most of those taken at the beach. I assumed it was Nantasket, the same one my dad had always brought me to. There was a corkboard where she'd pinned her achievements, along with multiple acceptance letters from colleges she must have applied to. All the way to the left was a letter from Tufts University. Followed by Boston University and Northeastern University. The last one was from Boston College.

Fuck them.

I hated that school for what their newspaper had published about me.

I was happy as hell she hadn't gone there.

I shifted away from the board and checked out the few framed photographs on her walls that were of sites I wasn't familiar with, but they were just like the ones that had hung in the bedroom of her apartment.

The biggest thing I noticed was that this room lacked character. Warmth.

Color.

Things I now associated with Jovana.

Either this had been just a place for her to crash or Jovana hadn't developed her own sense of style until after she had moved out.

I took a seat on the bed while Ernie positioned himself in the chair in front of her desk. My hands folded in my lap, my lips parted, waiting for the right thing to say, planning how to best approach this.

It didn't matter how many times I'd rehearsed the words in my head or how I'd discussed it with the guys, which was supposed to help me lead up to this moment.

I'd forgotten everything—everything I'd planned to say, everything they'd coached me on.

And staring Ernie in the face, knowing the circumstances that surrounded Jovana and me, the revelations we'd recently had in our relationship, the contract that was still signed, the requirements that were necessary—those made it even harder.

My hands were sweating.

My feet were tapping the floor.

My heart was fucking racing.

"I have a feeling I know what this is about." He made a noise that sounded like a half cough, half clearing of his throat.

Taken aback by his comment, I said, "You do?"

"I saw the way you were looking at my daughter and the way she looks at you. I'm no dummy. I know what comes next, and given that I was once your age and felt the same way about my Caroline, I can say I've been in your shoes."

But he hadn't really.

He saw signs, I could agree to that.

But did he see the fear?

The apprehension?

The fact that I had no choice but to marry his daughter?

"Ernie . . ." I couldn't sit in this man's house and lie to him. I couldn't look into his eyes and feed him bullshit. He deserved respect and I was going to give it to him. "You're right. I asked to speak to you because I want to ask your permission to marry Jovana."

"But?"

I felt my forehead wrinkle. "Why do you say that?"

"Because I feel a *but* coming. Am I wrong?"

I shook my head. "No."

"Explain yourself."

My pulse was beating even faster.

This was when I was either going to make him understand or ruin any hope for a relationship.

"I'm not sure I'm ready for marriage—I know that sounds strange, given what I just asked you. I want to be with her. I want to take care of her. I want to promise her things I haven't even thought of yet."

He smiled, air slowly leaving his nose, whistling as it came out. "Like I said, I've been in your shoes."

"You had doubts?"

"I was a lot younger than you when I proposed. Nineteen compared to, what, you're around thirty, I'm guessing?"

I nodded.

"But I've been on my own since I was sixteen, and even though on paper I was still just a kid, in my head I was your age. I was having fun with the ladies. I was going out drinking with my boys. What I'm trying to say is that I was having a good ol' time. I wasn't looking for a woman, especially not a wife. I only knew how to take care of myself. I didn't know how to take care of anyone else." He scratched his forearm, the noise like Velcro as his fingers brushed over the hair. "At that time, I knew nothing about women—what they wanted, needed. What they were looking for. I just knew how to work and pay my bills and make just enough to score myself a twelve-pack on Friday nights." He glanced out the window, the inside clean but the outside so dirty, I could barely see through it. "Did I want to bring a woman into that life? Shit, no. I wanted to keep doing my thing and having fun and not have to worry about anyone besides myself. And then I met my Caroline."

His voice changed when he said her name.

His expression did too.

It softened him in a way that I hadn't seen before.

"She changed everything?" I asked.

"Everything." He twisted the gold band around his finger. "She wanted a family. She wanted to feel loved. She wanted a home. Things I didn't know if I could provide."

I pressed my thumbs together, stopping my hands from fidgeting. "Is that what you wanted?"

"It certainly wasn't what I was looking for. No, sir, I was content with the way things were. But you know what I learned the second she paid for that bottle of Coke and walked out the door of that 7-Eleven? That once the glass door closed, I already missed her. And whether we'd be drinking cans of soda for the rest of our lives because there was going to have to be sacrifice—I couldn't give her everything—it didn't matter. I'd be better off with her than without her."

My head dropped and I exhaled.

There was no question. Jovana Winters made me a better person.

She made me feel.

Want.

Need.

Desire.

Aspire.

"Let me tell you something, son. Something I learned within those three dates before I married Caroline was that we can give our heart and life to a woman and that doesn't make us weak. It doesn't make us feel weak either." He lifted a photo off Jovana's desk. It was of the three of them. He rubbed his hands over it. "We don't lose ourselves in women. We find ourselves. And that's what I did. I found myself in Caroline and she gave me my daughter—the best thing that's ever happened to me."

I glanced up, and that was when I saw the emotion in his eyes.

"We've had our ups. We've had plenty of downs. We've had to fight like hell. But you know what never changes, what stays the same, always?"

I saw the answer and whispered, "How much you love her."

"Exactly." He crossed his legs, hugging his hands around his knee. "I know you care about Jovana. I saw it when you walked in, and I see it right now."

I swallowed, a rough, knot-like rock settling right in my throat. "I'll never let anything happen to her."

He nodded. "I know that too."

Why did it feel like this conversation was pressing against my chest, like it weighed a million goddamn pounds?

"You know what else I know?"

I waited for his response, adjusting myself on the bed, feeling hot even though the room wasn't.

"I know that you've already found yourself in my daughter. You just don't know it yet. You will, though. Trust me." I went to look away and he added, "Gray." I locked eyes with him. "You have my permission to marry my little girl."

"But?"

He chuckled. "Now we're going to shift modes a bit and I'm going to tell you what happens if you hurt my baby."

CHAPTER TWENTY-TWO

Grayson

When I finally heard the door knock, I set my tablet on the coffee table and pushed myself off the couch, opening the door for Easton. As I stood in the doorway, staring at the tardy motherfucker, I checked my watch and said, "What took you so goddamn long?"

"You just love being a dick, don't you." He squeezed my shoulder on the way in and helped himself to a beer from my fridge. "Where's Jovana?"

Easton and I had both bought penthouses in the same building.

Only eight paces separated our entrances.

That was why I couldn't figure out how he could be ten minutes late.

"She's with her parents—" My phone vibrated from my pocket, and I took it out, checking the screen. "Give me a sec, that's her," I told him and answered, "Hey you."

"Hi! We just stopped to grab something to eat, so I wanted to call and see how everything is going?"

I held out my hand to Easton, signaling I wanted him to get me a beer, too, and he placed a cold one in my grip. "All is good. Easton just stopped over."

"Tell him I said hi."

I nodded toward my best friend. "Jovana says hi."

"What's up, J."

"Did you hear him?" I asked her.

She laughed. "Yep."

"Have you had any luck finding your parents a new place to live?"

She sighed.

I could hear the stress in her breath.

"Oh, we've found four places that would work great for them. I just can't get them to commit. They don't want me to pay for their lease, so Dad is intentionally sabotaging each showing, finding the smallest things wrong. Like the washer is a front loader instead of a top loader, that there aren't enough outlets in the kitchen, or that only one of the two bathrooms has a tub. My parents don't even have a washer and dryer now—Mom goes to the Laundromat since the one in the basement is broken a majority of the time, and Dad hasn't taken a bath since he was a child. Please make sense of this because I can't."

I twisted off the top of the beer and tossed the metal in the trash. "Pick the one you think they'll enjoy the most and sign the paperwork."

There was noise in the background, what sounded like several trucks driving by. "We have a few more places to look at after lunch. If they don't pick one of those, I'm doing exactly what you said."

"Don't get discouraged." I carried the beer into the living room and returned to my seat on the couch. "My dad acted the same when I bought him a house. Fought me the whole time. It's just in their nature. They don't know how to accept things because they've always been the provider. They'll come around, you'll see."

"I hope so."

Easton sat beside me, a cushion between us, and took out his phone, reading whatever was on the screen.

Because he'd been late arriving at my place, I knew my doorman was about to call at any minute, letting me know our visitor was here—the whole reason Easton had come over in the first place, so I wouldn't be doing this alone.

Since Jovana didn't know what we had planned, I wanted to wrap up our call before she got tipped off by hearing something.

"Go have a good time at lunch and order your dad a Sam Adams. Maybe he'll loosen up a little."

"You know, I really should have brought you. You would have been the perfect distraction and probably would have gotten Dad to agree to anything."

I crossed my legs, tucking an arm behind my head. "Oh yeah?"

"Dad's semi-obsessed with you. He's brought you up at least twenty times already."

I chuckled. "If you need leverage, offer up a Red Sox game. Box seats."

"Don't tease me, Grayson. Dad will literally go nuts if I dangle that in front of his face."

I knew that because I remembered the conversation I'd had with her about her father and the Red Sox.

I want a man who's going to take my dad to a Red Sox game because my family is as important to him as they are to me.

"I wouldn't have said it if I didn't mean it," I told her.

"Oh my God, he's going to go wild, and I know just how to play it—that man is going to be putty in my hands. I can't wait."

I laughed again. "See you when you get home."

"Thank you." Her voice had quieted and turned more serious. "No, really, thank you."

"I know just how you can thank me later."

Easton looked at me as Jovana said, "And you know I will," and we both hung up.

"Who the fuck are you?" he asked me as I set my phone next to my tablet.

"What do you mean?"

"I mean, I've never heard you talk to a woman this way. You're either snapping or growling. But you're never giving them advice, you're never offering up your Red Sox tickets to who, I assume, was her dad." He turned toward me. "Whether you're fishing or hooking, you're in, out, and you're done. But you know what I heard just now?" He searched my eyes. "A conversation between two people who sound like friends."

I shrugged. "I guess we are—or we're becoming, but yeah, we're moving in that direction."

"It's amazing to see, my man." He reached across the back cushion, clasping the area around my collarbone. "If you're talking a future Red Sox game, that must mean it went well when you asked her dad about marrying her?"

I guzzled several sips of beer, remembering the conversation I'd had with Ernie. "He gave me his blessing, and right before we left their place, he hugged me like I was already his son-in-law."

Easton's grip tightened. "That must be a relief?"

"Relief? No." I shook my head before I gazed up at him. "This whole thing is making me feel like shit." But at the same time, the realness I'd shared with Ernie also made me feel a bit lighter. "There's just so many layers to it and . . ." My free hand slid through my hair until I had enough to grab, and I pulled those strands.

Ernie had been so honest with me, and I'd been as candid and raw as I could with him.

I just respected him so much.

And Caroline.

And Jovana.

"You don't want to hurt her." His voice had softened. "Or hurt them."

I sucked in a deep breath. "That's the last thing I want. Especially now that I've met them."

"I know this is going to sound a little weird given the situation, but you don't have to rush things with her. Sure, you're putting a ring on her finger and you're getting married, but all that is is a piece of paper.

You guys can still take your time. Slowly get to know each other. Travel. Go on dates. It's not like you have to start a family and get a joint bank account and put the deed of your condo in her name, too, all within the next year."

"True."

When he released my shoulder, he gave it a small push. "Don't let the details get into your head. In fact, don't even think about them. Just enjoy this part."

"Easy for you to say, asshole." I waved my hand across the air, like I was smacking someone's cheek. "Your face isn't about to be plastered all over social media in an international ad campaign."

"Delete the apps off your phone or just don't open them—you do know how to keep yourself occupied without scrolling fucking TikTok, don't you?"

I reared my neck back. "And I'm the dick?"

"Dude, are you going to be crying this hard when your salary doubles and your bonus is in the millions?" He paused. "Holden would tell you the same thing if he wasn't tied up somewhere with Belle."

"My last bonus was two million. I expect this one to be a lot higher."

"Yeah? Then do us all a favor—post more, promote the hell out of your relationship. The world is loving it, man. Just give them what they want, and we'll all be a lot richer."

We were laughing when my phone rang, the caller ID showing that it was my doorman. I picked up my cell to answer and said into the speaker, "You can let them up," before I went over to the front door. I opened it just as the two gentlemen, both holding briefcases, were approaching.

"Thanks for coming over, fellas." I reached out my hand to shake theirs. "This is much easier than worrying about someone taking a picture of me in your store and sharing it everywhere. I don't want the surprise to be blown."

"It's our pleasure, you know that," Abraham said, grasping my fingers.

Once he released my hand, I shook Yaakov's. "Good to see you both," I said.

As they walked into my condo, Abraham replied, "We've designed several watches for you over the years, but never jewelry for any females. We're honored to be doing your engagement ring."

The Levi brothers not only owned the most successful jewelry chain in New England, but their designs were sold all over the world. They had a talent that I'd never seen before. And when it was time to pick out a ring, my friends were the only ones I would trust to make it.

I laughed. "I'm assuming you were a little taken aback when you got my call?"

"You could say that," Yaakov replied. "We knew you were finally dating"—the black hair of his beard hung over his top lip when he smiled—"but to hear you're getting engaged so soon, we didn't anticipate that."

"All it took was finding the right one and our boy became whipped as hell," Easton responded, standing to shake their hands. "Good to see you guys."

"And you," Abraham said. "You know, you're the next one we need to be designing a ring for."

Easton chuckled. "You're right about that. I'm just not tying the knot as fast as this one."

I gave Easton a look that was equally as loud as the snapping and growling he'd mentioned earlier, and I led the men into the dining room. Abraham and Yaakov laid their briefcases on the table, entering a series of codes to unlock the thick leather binding.

Once they were both open, Abraham said, "We brought a good collection of the higher-end pieces we had in our safe. All are custom and all were designed by us."

"Remember, anything can be changed, remade, added," Yaakov told me. "If there's something you like from one and something you like from another, we can combine the two elements into one piece."

Each case held about ten rings.

The diamonds were all different sizes, shapes; some were solo, some had diamonds on both sides of the center stone, and some even had them built into the band.

I reached for one in the middle that instantly caught my eye, lifting it from its holder.

Jesus.

I'd never envisioned this moment.

How it would feel, what it would look like.

Who would have been the recipient.

Now that it was happening, my body was reacting.

Sweat was lifting from my skin. There was an ache in my stomach. There was even a goddamn jitter in my chest.

"It's beautiful," Easton said.

When I looked at him, I could tell he was attempting to calm me. He wouldn't say anything—he wasn't going to blow my cover just because we were friends with Abraham and Yaakov. So he was doing it silently, a peacefulness spreading across his face while he nodded toward the ring or the beer that was in my other hand—I couldn't tell which one.

I glanced back at the ring. "Yeah . . . it's beautiful." My voice was just above a whisper.

"Do you think that's the one?" Abraham asked.

Square wasn't right for her. Neither was round.

Or gold.

"I like the shape of this one." I held it in the air, viewing the oval stone, the way it shone under the light. On either side of the diamond were two small triangular diamonds. "Get rid of the side diamonds— she's not a triangle type of woman." Jovana's hands weren't big. They were actually really small, her fingers thin and dainty. This diamond would probably take up the whole width of her finger. "I want the band to look like this." I placed my beer down and lifted another ring out of the case that had diamonds built all the way around it.

"Oval stone, our signature eternity band. That's easy," Abraham said.

I set both rings in his palm, my mind made up. "Except I don't want just any diamonds around the band. I want them to be black."

"Interesting choice," Yaakov said.

"And I want two small round diamonds on both sides of the stone, and I want those in black also."

"Making it nontraditional—that's one of my favorites to create," Abraham said, setting the rings back into the case.

I took a long drink, draining the rest of my beer. "If she's going to wear something I gave her, then it needs to be equal parts of the both of us. The diamond is all her—full of color no matter what angle you look at it. Gorgeous. Something you stare at in awe."

That was Jovana.

Without question.

"And the black diamonds?" Easton asked.

I walked over to the bar, grabbed a bottle of vodka and four shot glasses. When I returned to the table, I filled each glass and handed them out. "Come on, man," I said to my best friend. "You know the color of this soul."

Easton held his glass high in the air. "That's why you two are perfect for each other. Every relationship needs that balance. And yours . . . shit, it's going to last forever."

I was sure my best friend believed that, and he was attempting to make me believe it.

But it also sounded like a good toast to make in front of the jewelers, who knew nothing about the contract between Jovana and me.

"To forever," the brothers echoed.

And then we all drank.

CHAPTER TWENTY-THREE

Jovana

"That was"—I paused to rub my stomach over my dress—"literally incredible. One of the best dinners I've ever had in my life." I glanced around the dining room of the restaurant, taking in the stunning decor, which was something I'd done multiple times since we'd sat down for dinner. "It's just amazing here. The food. Atmosphere." I smiled as I looked at Grayson. "You."

"I'm glad you had a good time." He held the base of his vodka, turning it just enough that the ice rattled. "I've only been here once before, and I've been waiting for the right time to come back."

"And you chose to do that with me." I rested my arms on the table. "You're sweet."

He laughed, a sound that was quick and almost spicy. "I'm not sweet, Jovana. Not a single ounce of me is."

"I disagree."

"Yeah?"

When I nodded, a piece of hair fell into my face, and I tucked it behind my ear. "You offered Red Sox tickets to my dad, and you had lunch delivered to the condo twice this week because you knew I was so busy filming, I'd probably forget to eat. And you posted a picture on Instagram last night of me asleep in your arms that was completely melt-worthy. So, I'm sorry, but you're wicked sweet."

"Shit, then you're really going to love this." He pointed with his eyes to a spot over my shoulder, causing me to turn around to where a chef was coming toward our table with a giant, oversize plate in her hand.

"Grayson, it's nice to officially meet you," she said as she set the plate between Grayson and me. "I took all of your suggestions into consideration, and I made my own spin." She grinned. "I hope you enjoy the dessert sampler."

"I appreciate it, chef."

"My pleasure."

Once she was gone, my hand went to my chest, holding my heart as I said, "Wait a sec. You called the restaurant and had the pastry chef make us this?" There had to be at least fifteen desserts on the plate. All were small, enough for two to three bites, but the amount of effort was extraordinary.

"I didn't just want a massive piece of strawberry cheesecake or a slice of peanut butter mud pie, which was what I saw when I viewed their dessert menu. That's too much. So, yes, I called the chef, and we chatted about some options, and this is what she came up with."

"A sampler."

"Was it a little birdie who mentioned she wanted one . . . I can't recall." His stare grew more intense. So did his smile. "It's the best of everything, Jovana. Like you."

I gazed at him in amazement.

And while I took him in, I couldn't help but compare this version of Grayson to the one I had originally met at the bar and the one who had sat with me while I'd signed our marriage contract.

How much he'd changed.

How our relationship had grown.

How his attitude had simmered.

And out of nowhere, a pang of guilt began to break through my chest.

Did I deserve this man?

The alphahole who I had somehow tamed, no longer constantly battling me or finding things to tear into me about.

There was a kindness to him now. A patience that I saw during the most unexpected moments, like the day I'd brought him to meet my family.

I loved both versions.

I didn't doubt that.

I just wished that feeling weren't eating at the skin above my heart.

"Grayson . . ." I felt my cheeks redden as I looked at him. "I'm wild for you." I took a breath. "Completely and madly . . . wild."

He stabbed his bottom lip with his teeth, slowly loosening the grip until his mouth was free. "How about some champagne to toast to how wild you are?"

Before I could respond, our waiter was at our table, holding a standing bucket where the champagne was sitting in ice. He lifted the bottle and poured some into two flutes that he placed in front of us.

Once he was gone, Grayson lifted his glass.

"To us." I smiled.

"That's the best you've got?" His expression couldn't possibly be any sexier.

"Sometimes it doesn't take more than two words—or even three— to make an impact."

Even though I felt those three words, I wasn't going to voice them.

Grayson wasn't ready to hear them yet.

"How about to a future that's long and . . ." His voice drifted off, but his expression remained intact, as did his stare, which was looking right through me. "Everything we want it to be."

"*Mmm*. I like that." I clinked my glass against his and took a sip.

"You need to dig in." He ran his hand over his beard before he pointed at a dessert that was somewhat toward the middle. "That one I requested just for you."

I lifted my fork. "I honestly don't know how I'm going to eat another bite, but I'll try." Before I stuck the metal teeth into the dessert, I asked, "Why did you request that one for me?"

"I know how much you like strawberries."

I put them in my yogurt every morning for breakfast, and it was the flavor of ice cream I kept in the freezer. I wasn't sure he was into that kind of detail.

But I had to ask.

"And why do you think that?"

He leaned his arms on the table, teasing the edge of something chocolate with his spoon. "Come on, Jovana. You're not doubting me, are you?" He waited for a response. All I did was smile. "I've looked at the same foods in my fridge for years now. You think I wouldn't catch on when two new pints of strawberries appear each week or see the pink bowl of ice cream you eat every night before bed?"

My smile grew, spreading as wide as it would go.

"I notice everything about you—whether you think I do or not."

"I love that." I dipped my fork into the dessert, and I was immediately hit with the tartness of the fruit, followed by the creaminess of some type of cheese, all of it surrounded by a flaky, almost nutty shell. "Wow."

"It's good?"

"It's more than good." I took in another mouthful. "I could eat this every day for the rest of my life." I knew I had only a few more bites left in me, so I moved on, tasting a layered cake that had different hints of coffee flavor. "Can I ask you something?"

"Sure."

"When was the exact moment when it hit you that you wanted more to happen between us?"

He took a drink of his champagne. "What makes you think it was a moment and not a series of moments?"

"Well, it could have been, but I think at some point, something went off in your head and you went from 'Oh fuck, I want this girl' to 'Oh fuck, I think I want more with this girl.'"

"Is that your way of imitating me?" His grin was pure fire.

"How'd I do?"

He chuckled. "You did pretty well, actually." He set his fork down after he finished chewing. "I think there were plenty of moments, if I'm being honest. Whether I wanted to admit they were moments at the time . . . that's a different story. But I think it started during the photo shoot, when I looked at your phone and saw all those messages from those dudes."

"You felt threatened."

"No." His response came out quick, the word harsh as it left his lips. "Territorial. That's how I felt."

"Ahhh."

He leaned forward to get even closer. "I didn't want them creeping on what's mine."

"Yours." My brows lifted.

He nodded. "I didn't like the thought that they were getting your attention."

"But so were you." I twisted the stem of the glass. "Every bit of it."

"I didn't see it that way." He drained the rest of his flute. "I still don't, but I know I'm going to have to share you with your followers. That's part of who you are. I can't change that."

"Would you want to?"

He was silent for a moment. "No. And you want to know why?" He wiped his mouth with his napkin and called the waiter over, handing him his credit card. "When we were at your parents' place, after I'd asked your dad for his permission to marry you and we'd returned to the living room, he brought up one of the TikToks he'd recently seen you in, and how proud he was of you. Your mom too. She had the biggest smile on her face." He returned the napkin to his lap and mashed his lips together. "I know what it's like to do something a little out of the norm and build it from scratch. Shit isn't easy. And not everyone recognizes that, nor do they understand what it takes to get where you are. The fact that your parents do, that they acknowledge your hard work and your successes—that's something not everyone can appreciate. But I do and I'd never take that away from you."

I'd known before.

I'd felt it.

It was in my chest, trumping the guilt.

But this was the moment that the feeling was solidified.

This was the memory that I'd think of whenever I wanted to answer the question: When did you know you'd fallen in love with Grayson?

"The most heartfelt, emotional answer you could have ever given me," I whispered.

He reached across the table, putting his hand on top of mine. "We come from different towns, different family dynamics, but you and I—we have a lot in common."

"I've always thought that."

"And I've always believed it."

The waiter returned and Grayson signed his name across the bottom of the bill. "Would you mind bagging up all this dessert?" he asked the waiter. "My driver will be right outside. It would be great if you could bring it to him." He nodded toward me. "I'm going to take this one for a little walk."

"I'd be happy to," the waiter replied.

Grayson stood and took me by the hand and led me out of the restaurant. He glanced down the moment we hit the sidewalk outside and said, "How comfortable are those?"

I followed his stare, realizing he was inquiring about my heels. "I mean, I wouldn't run a mile in them."

"But you can walk?"

I laughed. "Yes, I can walk."

"Then come with me." He linked our hands and led us down the sidewalk.

The Seaport District was a busy area of the city, surrounded by sky-scrapers along each side of the water, and the lights from the buildings reflected off the harbor, creating a romantic glow.

The Back Bay had become home, and Grayson's condo was gorgeous and everything I could possibly want, but I could see myself, one day, living here.

Compared to our neighborhood, the crowd was slightly younger, the beat a little livelier.

It was as though they took everyone's taste in music and entertainment and restaurants and made sure it fit all our needs.

It certainly fit mine.

"I love this area."

He pulled my hand up to his mouth. "What do you love about it?"

"The water. It's so calm and pretty." I pointed at a residential building up ahead. "Can you picture yourself sitting on that balcony, sipping your coffee every morning? Eating dinner out there on the warmer nights? And going for walks along the water when you actually let me drag you out?"

He laughed. "What if I could make that a reality?"

"What do you mean?"

After a few more paces, he stopped us directly in front of the harbor where only a thin block of cement separated us from the water, but this was the spot that had the best view. The lights across from us were gold, the buildings navy, the current shimmering like tiny crystals.

Grayson stood behind me, his arms circling around my stomach, his face near my neck. "Do you see that bit of construction to your left?"

I followed the waterline, halting at the foundation that was just starting to take shape. "Yes."

"I met with the builder a few weeks ago to discuss his ideas for the penthouse. Since it's preconstruction, I can make any changes I want to the current design, which is something I'm interested in because I can customize it the way I want. I've been going back and forth over whether I should keep it as an investment or move into it. But if this is where you want to live . . ."

As I faced him, a breeze blew past us, and a chill ran through me, enough that I shivered. While my hands wrapped around him, he pulled me against his body.

More sweetness.

I searched his eyes. "Are you saying you would move here with me?"

"Yes."

I knew how much the rent was in this area. Sloane and I had looked it up before moving to Somerville, and it was thousands past our budget. Therefore, I could only imagine how much it cost to buy.

"But I wouldn't be able to afford a mortgage around here, especially a penthouse."

"What would make you think you'd have to?" He held me tighter. "I wouldn't want you to pay half, Jovana. Hell, I wouldn't want you to pay anything, nor would I let you."

"That isn't really fair to you."

His hands moved to my face, holding my cheeks. "We're going to be married . . . don't forget that." He slowly kissed me. "What's mine is technically yours."

He had a point—something I hadn't thought of.

And there would be a prenup involved that would protect him if we got divorced.

But still, despite how well I was doing, I felt like it wasn't nearly enough to afford the type of home he wanted.

Before I could say anything, he continued, "Do you recognize this spot?"

I was so deep in my thoughts and his stare that I had to actually pull myself out, gazing to my right, and then left.

As soon as I connected to the bridge and the rainbow lights and back to the water, I gasped. "Yes." I returned to his face. "This is where I took the photograph—where we both did, actually. The one that we love."

"Your favorite spot in the Seaport."

I nodded. "Yes. It is."

"And you would be living about twenty yards that way." He nodded toward the building's foundation. "With a balcony that would wrap around the whole top floor, giving you not only a full view of the entire city, but a direct line of sight to this very spot."

My head shook. I could feel it. I couldn't stop it. "Unbelievable."

"You know what would make this spot even more special?"

I felt my head tilt back when I laughed. "I don't think that's possible. You've covered every angle here."

"All but one."

He reached inside his jacket and pulled out a box.

It was small.

Black.

Velvet.

Oh my God.

Once he opened it, he stepped back just a few feet from me, and he knelt on one knee. "Jovana Winters . . ."

My hands shook.

My knees felt weak.

My fingers flew to my face, pressing against my mouth while I stared at him in awe.

"I know we haven't known each other for long and I know there's still so much to learn about one another. But in the time that you've been in my life, you've completely amazed me. You're the most breathtaking woman I've ever met. The inside of you is as beautiful as the outside. And every day we spend together, I find myself wanting to hold you closer. Wanting to touch you more. Wanting to wake up with my arms around you."

My heart pounded in a way I could feel in my chest.

My eyes were watering, making the background look blurry, the lights all blending into thin white lines.

He turned the box toward me, and the first drip fell down my cheek.

"This ring isn't just for you—it's a piece of me. Of what I was—of what I am. Of what we are together." He took it out of the box and held out his hand.

My left hand dropped from my mouth, and he captured it, holding the diamond in front of my ring finger.

The only thing I saw through my tears was a shiny, gorgeous blob.

"Jovana," he said again, "will you be my wife?"

I nodded, the movement unleashing the rest of my tears. "Yes. Of course I will."

I didn't let him stand.

Because I wanted him to know that we were in this together.

As equals.

So I got on my knees, the roughness of the pavement piercing my soft skin, and once he slid the ring on my finger, I threw my arms around his neck and held him as close as I could get him.

I squeezed.

I inhaled the air that was so full of his scent.

And I thought of the words he'd just spoken.

They hit me.

Hard.

Nothing about us was traditional. Neither was this moment, and how he'd never once told me he loved me.

But it was enough.

And it was our kind of perfect.

"I didn't know you were asking me tonight," I whispered, clutching him with all my strength.

"I wanted it to be a surprise."

CHAPTER
TWENTY-FOUR

BREAKING NEWS: Boston's Biggest Bachelor Has Officially Been Hooked

Grayson Tanner, 30, cofounder of Hooked, an international dating app, and Jovana Winters, 22, TikTok sensation and influencer, are now engaged. Sources tell us that Tanner popped the question in Boston's Seaport District around ten o'clock last night, and the pictures show Tanner on one knee, sliding the massive sparkler onto Winters's finger before she got on her knees, joining him in a hug on the ground.

Of course, this isn't the first time Tanner has found himself in a Celebrity Alert. No one can forget his trip to Saint-Tropez, when he was seen cruising the Mediterranean in a 150-foot yacht. His guests . . . all women.

Six, to be exact.

Shortly after returning from the Mediterranean, Tanner was spotted with Winters. Online reports state that they met within the marriage arm of Hooked, our sources confirming the pairing and that they've been together ever since.

That's quite the feat to whittle all those women down to one.

Seems like this one happens to be quite the catch.

Congrats, lovebirds.

CHAPTER TWENTY-FIVE

Grayson

"Have you seen today's membership numbers?" Easton asked me while I held the tumbler of vodka close to my lips, trying to ignore the notifications that were coming through my phone, causing it to vibrate in my pocket every few seconds.

If I weren't worried my dad was going to reach out sometime within the next hour, I would have turned the motherfucker to silent.

I leaned my back against the corner of the bar and replied, "I took a peek this morning."

I drained the rest of my drink and called over one of the waitresses who had been hovering near our group, assuming Sloane had given her that order when my friends and I had come in. I pointed at my glass and Easton's, letting her know we were ready for another round.

"Dude, we've regained eighty-nine percent of the members of the marriage arm. The hook-up arm is five percent over objective, and the single-parent arm is three percent over."

I pulled my phone out when a double vibration came through, thinking it was a phone call.

But it wasn't.

Just an explosion of alerts that came in so fast, my phone couldn't keep up.

"Look at this shit." I pointed my screen in Easton's direction. "Two hundred and eleven notifications from Instagram. All within the last twenty minutes." I scrolled through them so he could see what I was talking about. "First, our joint engagement post that blew the fuck up. Then, the goddamn Celebrity Alert that went out, gaining me even more eyes. Now Hooked is running ads with the pictures from our office photo shoot and that's igniting a storm. I feel like my fucking face is everywhere." I pulled up my profile to show him that my account was now verified and placed my thumb next to my followers. "Do you see that number? I've gained almost half a million in the last two weeks." I slipped my phone into my pocket. "Make it stop, man."

"Jesus."

I gripped the back of my neck, the pain starting there and shooting straight into my head. "That's half a million more than I want." I chomped on some ice. "I don't need this level of attention. I don't fucking want it." I squeezed and rubbed. "I get that Jovana needs it for her business, but not me."

"Why don't we focus on all the good that's come out of this?"

I took another mouthful of ice. "And that is?"

"Our business is on fire. We're making a shit ton of money. And you're happy as hell." He wrapped his arm around my shoulders, shaking me. "In fact, you're happier than I've ever seen you." He paused. "You're not going to deny that, are you?"

"Fuck no. I am happy. I'll give you that." I exhaled. Twice. "But this is a lot. It's a lot without all the media and attention. It's insanity with it."

"Hang tight. After the wedding, it'll all die down a little."

As he released me, I glanced toward the bar, where Jovana and Drake were standing next to Sloane. The three of them were smiling as they chatted it up with Nate.

As of last week, Sloane had bought the bar from him, and Nate had popped in this evening to celebrate with us.

I shifted my attention back to Easton. "Once she's my wife, it's not going to die down at all because everyone will be on baby watch. You know that's why they're going to think we got married so fast."

"Maybe." Easton shrugged. "Maybe not."

"Come on, man. That's how it works—they need to justify in their heads why a couple like us would do something so quickly, and a baby is the only thing that makes sense."

"So have her wear belly shirts in her posts so there's zero speculation."

"And allow them to see even more of her body? When she already shows them too much?" I lifted my hand from my neck, now holding the top of my head. "Nah. She'll wear belly shirts for me—not them. *Fuck.*"

"Sounds like someone's in a mood," I heard.

I turned, seeing that the speaker had been Holden, but he wasn't alone.

My father was standing next to him.

"Look who I found wandering the sidewalk outside," Holden said, referring to my dad.

I man-hugged my best friend while Easton shook hands with my father, and then I embraced my old man. "Glad you could make it, Pops."

"And miss out on the chance of finally meeting Jovana?" My dad smiled. "Wouldn't miss it, kid."

The waitress returned with our drinks, and Holden and my father placed their orders. That was when I glanced toward Jovana again, realizing her eyes were already on me.

A grin warmed her face.

I didn't really have the ability to read lips, but for some reason, I was so in tune to hers that when she said, "Excuse me a moment," to the group she was with, I knew exactly what she'd said.

Within a few paces, she was at my side and my arm locked around her, and as I glanced down, I had the best view of her body and the tight dress that covered it. "Baby, I want you to meet someone."

Her skin flushed as she gazed up at me. "I think I may already know who he is." She then looked at my father. "I saw you walk in. The two of you could be twins, the resemblance is so uncanny." She reached out both of her hands toward my father. "Mr. Tanner, it's lovely to finally meet you."

He opened his arms. "You're family, come here."

She wiggled out of my grip and fell into his.

"Introducing them at a bar where any onlooker can ask him a question about you two. You're ballsy, my man," Easton whispered to me.

I leaned my face toward his and replied, "He knows, and he's been prepped."

"You told him the truth?"

"He wouldn't have believed it otherwise." My stare told him what I wasn't saying. "He knows how I've always felt."

But he also knew how I felt about Jovana now.

Prior to the change that had happened between us, I had seen no reason for them to meet before the wedding. To unveil that part of me to her. To have my father grow feelings toward someone who would be in my life temporarily.

But things were different now.

There were feelings.

I wanted him to see that. And I wanted him to establish his own.

"*Ahhh*, now it makes sense," Jovana said, gaining my attention as she turned toward me but stayed next to my father. "This is who you get your charm from."

I hadn't listened to their conversation since I'd been preoccupied with my own, but I still replied, "My old man has always known how to charm the ladies."

My father glanced at Jovana. "You've done well for yourself, son. She's even more beautiful in person. Smart as a whip, too, I can tell."

"Thank you." Her skin flushed again. "But I'm pretty obsessed with your son, if you can't already tell." She laughed. "Speaking of which, I hope you know that he's the reason we're all here tonight. He negotiated the deal between my best friend and Nate, the previous owner of the bar. Without Grayson's help and coaching and mentoring, none of this would have happened."

I took a sip of my new drink. "I don't know about that . . ."

"He's being modest," Jovana countered. "I know my best friend, and that's why I can say with confidence that he's responsible for making her dreams come true."

"A conversation—that's all it was," I replied.

"No, no, no." Her goddamn grin was infectious. "He's telling you only half the story. Sure, it was a conversation. But in all actuality, it was multiple conversations, and he reviewed Sloane's business plan and gave her feedback and he helped facilitate all the financial arrangements of the deal."

She was bragging about me, and with each point she made, I could see my father getting deeper into the story.

"The reputation of an asshole, but a giant teddy bear inside," Holden said, clasping my arm.

"Don't say that too loud," I warned. "I don't want a single motherfucker in this bar to think I'm anything but an asshole." I winked at him.

And when I looked at Jovana, her entire expression had changed.

Because she wasn't just focused solely on my face.

She was glancing between my father and me, and eventually, she nodded at me, but continued to look at him as she said, "That one, I'm so proud to call him my forever."

"Holden, we're in the middle of a lovefest," Easton joked.

I shook my head. "Get over here," I said to Jovana. When she reached me, my arm went across her back, and I pulled her against my side.

I knew what she was doing.

Because I'd done the same when I'd met her parents.

I'd watched their faces while I'd talked about their daughter, the empathy growing in my fucking chest.

And when my dad said, "There isn't a day that goes by when I don't think I'm the luckiest man alive to have a son like him," she clutched my side.

She gazed up at me and whispered, "What a moment."

CHAPTER
TWENTY-SIX

Jovana

"How do you feel about everything we've accomplished so far today?" Jade asked Grayson and me while we sat across from her at her conference room table.

The black side hairs of her blunt bob had threatened to fall into her eyes during the whole two hours we'd been here. But even now, as she lifted her arms off the table and leaned back in her seat, the movement didn't cause a single strand to slide toward her eyes.

Jade Tucker even had full control of her hair.

Not that I should be surprised. What I'd learned since we'd arrived at her office was that she exceeded her reputation in every aspect. If you were having a function in New England with a hefty budget and a desire for the best, Jade was who you hired.

Event planner extraordinaire, with a name that stretched as far as Florida and a reputation for being poignant, creative, and inventive.

Once we'd chosen our date, there was no question about who Grayson and Laura wanted to hire to plan our wedding.

I had just never thought I'd be sitting in Jade's downtown office, listening to her ideas on the intimate, personal, lavish affair she was going to plan for us.

Of course I'd had fantasies about my wedding day.

But Jade had never fit within that mental budget.

I glanced at Grayson, wanting him to answer first, something I'd been doing since we'd arrived.

I wanted him as involved as me.

I wanted our wedding to be a combination of both of our tastes.

I wanted him to stand at the base of the aisle and to walk into our reception and be proud of what we had designed together.

He glanced at me before he responded, "I'm impressed as hell that on such short notice you'll be able to book the space we want. I really thought that was going to be nearly impossible."

A space we'd discussed over dinner the last few nights was a hotel we both loved. The ceremony would take place outside in their gardens, so while we exchanged our vows in the thick, green landscape and gorgeous botanicals, we would be surrounded by the city we were both so tied to. Once we went inside for the reception, we would have full views of its skyline.

Jade tapped her pen on the notebook she'd been writing on. "Nothing is impossible, Grayson."

The man sitting next to me had expressed his feelings for me.

He'd shown them.

She was right.

"I happen to have the right connections to pull off just about anything." She smiled as though extremely proud that she was able to make that statement. "My team will be able to pull off your requirements without a problem. Within the next week, I'm going to be sending you some mock-ups of the ceremony and reception designs. They'll include everything from chairs to charger plates to lighting, foliage, flowers to drapery—you'll be able to see the entire picture from the moment you spot your groom to the second you leave for the newlywed suite." She paused. "Once you have the visual, then we can change whatever you don't like, we can add more, take things away—you get my drift." She adjusted the arms of the sweater that hung over her shoulders, knotted in the center of her chest. "Given such a tight timeline, we'll have to make the adjustments fairly fast. I'll send you new mock-ups, we'll tweak again, and we'll continue that process until everyone is happy." She glanced down at the paper. "You'll have the next six weeks to finalize everything. Keep that in mind. Because after that date, there won't be room to make any edits. What exists is what you'll have to live with."

I stole another glance at Grayson.

His expression was aloof. It had been the entire meeting.

This was a lot for him, I understood that. It was a lot for me as well. Whenever I'd thought about getting married and my wedding, I had never pictured pulling it off in only a few short months.

Or marrying a man whose name was on a contract I'd signed that kept us together for a year.

That I'd be lying to everyone, including my friends and family, over the premise of our whole relationship.

Regardless, I cared about this man.

I wanted him.

And I loved that he was going to be my husband.

Because there was zero doubt in my mind about how much I loved him.

But even though he was going to spend a fortune on this wedding, and I had several carats of diamonds on my finger, there was something still looming in my mind.

A happily ever after that had the potential of not lasting forever.

After the twelve months were up, Grayson could end us in divorce.

Maybe he would realize I wasn't enough.

Or maybe he'd think I was too much.

That we just weren't meant to be.

That love—or my love—wasn't what he wanted.

Breakups were a possibility in every relationship, but ours was different.

His opinion was different.

His stand on marriage was different.

We didn't start this on equal ground.

The scale had been tipped and my feelings had weighed me to the ground.

I felt Jade's stare on me, and just as I glanced toward her, pulling out of my thoughts, trying to escape them, I felt something.

His hand.

It was under the table, on my lap, squeezing my thigh.

I set my fingers on top of his, the warmth of his skin instantly taking hold of me.

Could he hear my thoughts?

Read them?

Did he know I needed this?

Whatever his reasoning was, it meant everything to me.

A smile pulled at my lips as I said, "I don't see that being a problem. Grayson and I will review the mock-ups and immediately let you know if we have any changes. We won't be the ones to hold you up."

Jade nodded. "One last question." She looked at me as she spoke. "I know you want a white-and-cream color scheme. You've described the mood as romantic and intimate, sunset meets sunrise. There's going to be an emphasis on food and drinks, flowers, and lighting. You want your guests to leave with a lasting impression of love in their minds. But something I ask all my clients at the end of our initial meeting is this: If you could summarize your ideal wedding in one word, what would that word be?"

As I clutched his fingers, he held me back just as tightly.

Heat radiated from our hands.

But when I'd met Grayson, he was cold.

Ice.

A growly, grumpy asshole who did anything and everything to take away my sunshine.

That wasn't who he was anymore.

I felt that evolution every day.

And I felt it in his hand right now.

"Warmth." I looked at him. "I want to feel it. I want to see it. I want to smell it in the air." When I gazed back at Jade, I added, "I want it to be everywhere."

She wrote something on the paper and then addressed Grayson. "What's your word?"

Grayson's eyes were on me, causing me to look at him again, his stare so intense, I could feel it across my entire body. Tingles erupted inside me. And without glancing away from me, he replied, "Passion." He finally looked at Jade. "I want everyone in that room to know the passion I feel for Jovana."

"I'll make that happen." She set her pen down. "Unless you have any questions or anything else you'd like to discuss, then I think I have enough information to get started."

"I can't wait to see what you put together," I said. "But if we have questions in the meantime, we'll be in touch."

We stood from our chairs and met her at the door of the conference room.

While we walked down the hallway toward the exit, she said, "To give you a quick rundown of what's to come, you're going to have a full menu tasting that will include desserts and wedding cake flavors, along with a wine sampling. You'll need to listen to demos from the bands I'm going to recommend. We'll have meetings with the florist, photographer, and videographer. There's much more, but those are some of the main points." She smiled as we neared the doorway. "What I'm trying to say is that it's going to be a busy, but very exciting, time. How flexible are your schedules?"

"Since I work from home, I can meet whenever, wherever," I told her. "Grayson's days are a bit more strict, but we'll make it happen."

"Excellent," Jade replied.

We reached the main door, and she opened it. "Thank you for coming in. It's been lovely to meet you both. I'm honored you chose me to plan the wedding of your dreams."

Grayson's arm slipped around my shoulders, his stare holding mine for several seconds before he said, "We are too."

We shook her hand, and we walked out through the front, Grayson handing the valet attendant his ticket.

While we waited for the car, I wrapped my arms around him. "So, on a scale of one to ten, how badly did you hate that meeting?"

He laughed and kissed me.

And as though the first embrace weren't enough, he kissed me again.

"I didn't hate it. Jade was cool. She knows her shit. She's going to make sure the wedding is everything we want, and it sounds like she can make it happen even though we're hardly giving her any time to do it."

What I really wanted to ask was how badly he was freaking out over it.

But I didn't have the courage.

Or maybe I just didn't want to know.

"She's good. I've seen her work. I've been following her for a long time. I have a feeling we're going to be blown away with what she designs."

His hands lifted to my face, and our eyes locked. "I know what you're thinking. I can see every question in those beautiful, bright-blue eyes."

My voice lowered to a whisper as I said, "Grayson . . ."

"I'm standing right here, aren't I, and I haven't left your side once today. I didn't lose my shit during the meeting. I didn't walk out. I didn't have you go by yourself, or have you pick out all the colors and features and elements—I contributed and gave her my opinion."

"True."

He exhaled and I could hear the emotion in his breath. "Listen to me, you can't change what's going to happen or how we're going to feel once we're wed. Neither of us can. Nor can I tell you that every fucking moment is going to be perfect or what we're going to look like once we've fulfilled our contract. That's an answer no one can give you. We just have to be present and wait it out and trust that whatever happens, it's the best thing for the both of us." He rubbed his nose against mine. "What I can tell you is that I want to be here right now and I'd never let you do any of this shit alone."

He hadn't promised me a single thing, but for some reason, what he had given me was enough.

I pulled him in even tighter, hugging him against my body, his mouth pressing against the top of my head.

He broke the silence. "Your plan was to drop me off at home and then take the car to your parents' new place, right?"

There was still no reason for me to incur the expense of a car, even though it wouldn't cost anything to park in Grayson's garage. The last couple of times I'd driven out to see Mom and Dad, I'd just borrowed his.

I hoped that wasn't about to change for some reason.

I lifted my face off his chest. "I'd like to check on the move and see how it's going. Maybe bring my parents some lunch. Knowing them, they're so worked up about people touching their things and making sure no one drops anything that they probably haven't eaten a thing. That's okay, right?"

"Yeah, yeah. I was just checking."

The valet attendant pulled up and Grayson climbed into the driver's seat. I stood outside the passenger door while he put on his seat belt. "Shouldn't I drive?" I asked him. "It'll make dropping you off a little easier . . . no?"

He shifted into first gear. "I've decided to go with you." He smiled. "Unless you want to be alone?"

I climbed into the seat and instantly leaned across the center to kiss him. "Who are you?"

He chuckled and pulled into the road as I wrapped the belt around me. "What do you mean?"

"You just sat through a two-hour meeting with a wedding planner and now you're driving me out to Brockton to help me check on my parents' move. And your word of choice was *passion*. It wasn't *eclectic* or *unique* or *expensive* or even *extravagant*. It was *passion*—a word you used to describe us."

He stopped at the light. "And that's a bad thing?"

"It's just not a Grayson thing, so I feel the need to point it out. I can't help but get all wiggly about it."

"Wiggly?"

I leaned across the small armrest that separated us. "Yes. Wiggly. It's the way you make me feel. The tingles that erupted in my chest the second you held my hand during that meeting." I kissed his ear and over to his cheek, my lips buried in his beard, a sensation and scent I couldn't get enough of. "You've just been full of surprises today."

I could see his smile from his profile. "If you keep kissing me like that, I'm going to have us make a pit stop at the condo."

I giggled. "There's no reason to stop. I can do lots from the front seat."

"But I'm driving."

"So?"

He quickly glanced at me.

"Let's just say, you'll owe me when you get home."

He moaned, "My dirty girl," and his hand shot through the back of my hair, gripping my head. "But I'm already hard, so you better not be teasing me, Jovana."

"Oh, I'm not." I rubbed my palm over his dick. "I wouldn't do that to either of us." I found his button and popped it through the hole and lowered his zipper. "Because even though this is for you, it's just as much for me." Inside his jeans, he was wearing boxer briefs, the large opening in the front making it easy to poke his hard-on through, the tip glistening with pre-cum.

"I'm going to fucking devour your pussy the second we walk through the door."

I ran my tongue around the small hole, licking off the bead, swallowing the saltiness the second it hit my tongue.

"Fuck yes," he hissed.

"You have one job." I glanced up through the windshield and checked the windows on both sides of the car, knowing they were tinted enough that I couldn't be seen. "To not get us into an accident or this idea of mine is going to go downhill very fast."

"You have nothing to worry about. I'll get us there safely. Just don't stop." He moaned as I widened my lips around his crown and began to suck. "Goddamn it, you're good at that."

I gripped his base, squeezing the thickness, and while my spit ran under my fingers, I used it as a lubricant, spreading it across the bottom half of him, fisting upward until I met my mouth. Keeping my teeth tucked away, I lowered as far as I could go, stroking the skin I couldn't reach with my lips, concaving my cheeks while I sucked.

Up and down.

"Jovana," he growled.

He held my hair out of my face until it was time to shift, but he returned the moment his hand left the gearshift. That wasn't the only movement. He also had to use both feet to drive, so each time he pressed and released the clutch, his hips almost bucked forward, causing his cock to thrust into my mouth.

I loved it.

The taste.

The feel.

The control.

The way he breathed harder every time I went deeper. The way he made that noise—a half moan, half hiss—whenever I rose toward his tip.

The way I could feel his orgasm coming closer by how he was rocking into me, his dick growing even harder. His hand clutching my hair when it came back to my head.

"Fuuuck!"

Every time I dipped, I swirled my tongue around each side, adding more wetness, pressure, friction, and when I tilted back toward the tip, I gave that spot an extra suck.

Like I was urging the cum out.

Like I was begging for it.

"You're going to make me fucking come." He was moving with me. His breath so loud and heavy, I could feel it hitting the back of my head. "Is that what you want? For me to fill your fucking mouth with my cum?"

I didn't respond.

I just went harder.

Lower.

My hand picking up speed, rising to the center and back down, repeating that motion and altering the strength in my grip.

"Oh fuck. That's it. That's just how I want it."

And it was just what he needed, because his hips had stilled, his erection at its absolute hardest, and I could feel him on the verge of exploding. How the tingles were climbing through him, enough that it forced him to halt his movements and just take what I was giving him.

That lasted only a few seconds before he grunted, "Fuck me," and the first of his orgasm shot into my mouth.

The thickness pooled across my tongue, and it dripped through my lips as I lowered, even more so as he shot a second stream and a third. I held in as much as I could, trying not to cover him with it, swallowing what he was giving me so my mouth wouldn't fill.

"Jovana, my God." I didn't know if we were at a stoplight or he'd pulled over, but his hand was in my hair, guiding me across his length. "That feels so fucking amazing."

I continued to bob, my speed not letting up, my pressure as hard as it was before, and when I got the sense that he was done, that I'd drained him of every drop, that was when I slowed.

Cum had slipped from my mouth and slid down to his base and I wasn't going to let that dry, especially since we weren't going home. So I lapped up all the wetness, taking my time to lick and swallow around the bottom and up his cock, and finished at the tip.

With each second that passed, he gave me an earful—his breathing so erotic, his light moans making me even wetter.

And when I was satisfied with the cleanup, I tucked him back into his boxer briefs, tugged on the zipper, and put his button through the hole.

I was just lifting myself off his lap and wiping both sides of my mouth when he said, "Who the fuck are you?"

I smiled.

He'd used my own words against me.

As he looked at me, I mocked him and said, "What do you mean?"

"You know exactly what I mean."

We were at a red light, about to get on the highway, and he was holding the back of my head, leading me toward his mouth.

"Like I said, you make me wiggly."

"And sucking my cock like that took care of it?"

"Until we get home and I can ride you."

"Jovana"—he sighed, shaking his head—"you're something else."

I winked. "I know."

"But more importantly, you're mine."

Before I could respond, he was kissing me, owning my mouth in a way that backed up everything he'd just said.

CHAPTER
TWENTY-SEVEN

Grayson

Easton: Dude, have you seen the membership numbers this morning?

Me: No, why?

Holden: Of course he hasn't. His head has been between Jovana's legs all morning . . .

Me: Not a bad guess, asshole. But she's been wedding dress shopping and I've been assigned the task of picking out the band for the reception. I've been listening to goddamn demos for the last two hours.

Easton: Pause the music and look at our numbers.

Me: Holy shit, we jumped THAT much in just a couple of days?

Easton: The ads are working, my man. They love seeing your face all over their feed.

Holden: No, they love seeing Jovana's face all over their feed, let's be honest.

Me: You're absolutely right about that, motherfucker. It's all her, not me.

Easton: You know this means that the marriage arm is now 28% over our objective. We've not only made up for all the lost revenue and memberships, but we've exceeded our original goal.

Me: What's this we shit? I've made up the lost revenue while you two sat on your asses and ordered me around.

Holden: And you've loved every second of it.

Me: Oh yeah, getting bombarded on social media with endless notifications and comments is my fucking jam. I love nothing more in life than reading everyone's opinion about me.

Easton: But look where it got you.

Holden: And look who it got you.

Easton: And look who it's turned you into.

Holden: Did you see him at the office yesterday? He couldn't stop smiling all day. And I know it wasn't because Faceframe is offering us a settlement that's going to make us even richer.

Me: Fuck them. I'll happily take their money for the bullshit they pulled behind our backs.

Me: Regardless, you do know that I'm part of this text group . . . don't you? You're talking like I'm not even in here.

Easton: You're a man in love. It's good to see, brother.

Me: That's a big word.

Holden: Have you said it out loud yet?

Me: No.

Holden: You will. When you're ready. But you will.

Easton: But you do feel it, don't you?

Me: Fuck . . . yes.

Holden: My man, you've come a long way. How about you meet us for lunch? We have some celebrating to do.

Me: Jovana just walked through the door. Let me see what's up for today and I'll get back to you.

"Baby," I growled, setting my phone on the couch as she walked into the living room, where I was sitting. I held my arms open, and she sat on my lap. "How'd it go?"

She kissed me.

Slowly.

I could taste the champagne on her tongue. It was as strong as the lavender and vanilla coming off her body.

Her arms stayed around my neck even after she pulled her mouth away. "I found a dress."

"You did?"

She nodded. "And Mom really loved it on me, too, so they did a fitting today and they'll do one more a week before the wedding to make sure it hugs me just right for the big day." She traced my lips with the back of her thumb. "I can't wait for you to see it on me."

I'd never seen her in white.

Not a shirt, shorts, or jeans.

Not even a T-shirt or tank top.

It was a color she just didn't wear.

I held her cheek, holding her face in front of mine. "You're going to look fucking gorgeous."

"How do you know?"

"Because you do right now and you're barely wearing any makeup and your hair is in a nest on top of your head." As she smiled, I added, "It's not the dress or the makeup or the way you're going to have them fix your hair, Jovana. It's you. You're gorgeous no matter what."

She gave me another kiss, lingering against my lips. "Everything that comes out of your mouth is a ten on the sexy scale."

I chuckled. "But it's the truth." With my palm cupping her cheek, my fingers diving into her hair, I pressed my mouth onto the vacant side of her face and took a long, deep inhale of her scent. "There isn't a single woman I've ever seen who even comes close to comparing to you."

"You're sweet." Her hand clasped mine. "And now I need to go for a walk because all those women you just spoke about . . . they're going to be seeing me in that beautiful dress and I need to look my absolute best."

"You're going for a walk now?"

"Yes, now, and every day up until the wedding." She ran her hands down her sides. "It's tight. Sheer in some places. It shows every part of me and—ugh. I need to up the miles. Big-time."

"You need to do no such thing." I lifted her off my lap and set her in the corner of the couch, moving on top of her. "Your body drives me fucking wild. You know that." I moved in between her legs and kissed her before resting my chin on her chest. "The guys are meeting up for lunch today. I was hoping you'd come."

Her lips spread over her teeth, her nose scrunching. "Would you hate me if I didn't go?"

"You know I wouldn't hate you for that."

She combed my beard with her nails. "Go have a good time with them. I'm going for a long, long walk. We'll probably be back around the same time, and then we can plan something fun for dinner. Deal?"

I nodded. "Yeah, that works."

She gave me one more quick kiss and wiggled out from underneath me, hurrying into the guest room, where I assumed she was going to change her clothes. Even though she was spending every night in my room, she hadn't moved any of her things into my closet and I didn't push her to.

Things were working just the way they were.

As I moved into a sitting position, I found the last few demos I hadn't listened to and played them through the speaker of my phone. Once I finished, I attached my three favorites to a text and sent them over to Jovana.

Her phone dinged just as she walked into the kitchen. She glanced at her screen and said, "Looks like someone was busy while I was gone. So, these are your faves?"

I was no longer listening.

All I could focus on was her outfit, the workout clothes that clung to her body and the baseball hat she wore on her head and the long braid of hair that rested over her tit.

My dick started to fucking throb in my sweatpants.

"You're sure you have to go for a walk? I can cancel lunch and spend the rest of the day with my face between your legs."

Fucking Holden.

Regardless, it wouldn't be out of the norm to spend today that way, considering I'd spent lots of days doing just that.

Jovana grabbed a water from the fridge, her profile showing me she was still smiling. "I'm sure." And as she walked over to me, eye-fucking me the entire way, she continued, "But I'll be back soon and so will you and you're more than welcome to do that all evening if you'd like."

"I plan to."

"*Mmm.* I can't wait." She stopped in front of me. "See you in a little while."

I reached around and held her ass. "Yes, you will."

She leaned down and kissed me, and after she wiped off the ChapStick that she'd left on my lips, she headed for the door. Once I heard the lock click, I pulled up the group chat I had going with the fellas and typed a reply.

Me: Text me where and when. I can leave here in 20.

As soon as the message sent, I went into my room and changed my clothes, then headed for the en suite, where I gelled up my hair and brushed my beard and sprayed on some cologne. When I was walking out of my wing, a few texts came through, causing me to take out my phone. The first was from Holden, giving me the name of the restaurant they'd chosen. The second was from the front desk in the lobby of my building.

Front desk: Mr. Tanner, I've left your mail and packages by the front door.

A perk of living here that I fucking loved.

I opened the front door, and sitting in a small box on the floor were a package and about ten envelopes. I grabbed it all and set it on the kitchen counter, shuffling through the mail to see whether there was anything worth looking at.

A square envelope caught my attention. It was cream, made of semi-shiny paper with my name and Jovana's, along with our address, written in calligraphy.

When I turned it around and saw the return address, I knew what I was holding.

It was our wedding invitation.

Jade had the invitation company send us one so we could see the finished product.

I slid my finger under the thick, glued flap, where there was more cream and a hint of charcoal on the inside, and I pulled out the invitation. Jovana loved the simplicity of the design, how the actual invite was wrapped in a piece of clear vellum paper with a gold wax seal securing it shut and our initials engraved in the middle of the wax.

I didn't know why I didn't wait for her.

Why I pulled the wax off, unwrapped the vellum, and held the invitation in my palms.

But something made me want to see it.

Feel it.

Read the words.

Assess the heaviness as it sat in my hands.

Each invite was slightly unique since the flowers that ran along the side of the rectangle were all hand-painted by a local artist. The paper was then run through a printer with gold ink, where all the details were outlined, like our names and the location and time of the event. A small return envelope was included that requested the guest's response and choice of entrée, whether it be meat, fish, or vegan.

Only seventy-five people were invited.

A group that was just small and intimate enough, despite the fact that I could have asked colleagues and business associates and all my employees, having more than five hundred attend.

Neither of us wanted something large.

That wasn't because we were under contract and what would happen after the twelve months was in question.

That was because we wanted to share the day with those closest to us.

To have time to spend with our friends and family rather than making small talk with so many extra guests.

To have the ability to spend the night dancing with my wife.

My wife.

Goddamn it.

That word didn't feel natural, but it came out so easily as I stared at our names on the paper.

I'd told Jovana I cared about her.

That I wanted more.

That I wanted us.

And I'd informed the guys that there was love there.

And there was.

I felt it every morning when I looked at her, asleep in my bed. When I ran my hand down her bare back and kissed her shoulder. When I closed my eyes and inhaled the scent she'd left on my pillow.

I'd felt it when I'd reached around and grabbed her ass before she'd left for her walk. When she'd pressed her lips against mine. When she told me she'd see me after lunch.

When I knew I'd miss her while she was gone.

Like I did now.

I didn't know what she had done to me. What type of sorcery was inside that woman to make a man like me completely fall for her.

But it had happened.

And now I was marrying her.

I released all the air I'd been holding in my lungs and set the invitation on the counter, grabbing the package that I'd placed next to the mail. The box was rectangular and somewhat heavy, and as I read the words that had been printed on the invite, too consumed by it to pull my stare away from it, I ripped off the top of the box. Once it was open, I pulled out a thick piece of wood, the same shape as the packaging, and saw that there was an envelope taped to the top.

Unsure of what I was really looking at, I unsealed the envelope and read the handwritten note inside.

Jovana,

Every year, the department gifts a plaque to the student who receives the most views on their newspaper articles. This year, that student is you by a landslide. Admittedly, we've never had an article go viral. When I first had this plaque made, the article had only been published for a week; therefore, the numbers were outdated rather quickly. But given how well your article has done and the amount of attention it gained for our department, I decided to have a new plaque made (which is why this gift is coming so late). Now it shows a much more appropriate number range, which is an increase of over five million views from the original number I'd had printed.

Millions! I can't believe it!

Our little school newspaper reached such a vast audience and that's all thanks to you. I guess I shouldn't be surprised, as you were a star student from the moment you entered our department. That was why I never understood why you didn't want to take credit for any of the articles you wrote. Why you always published them anonymously. Now that I see the career you've built and your online presence, it certainly makes sense. Writing opinion pieces doesn't always mesh well when you're trying to gain popularity with brands as an influencer . . . and given your recent engagement, I assume that article is a skeleton you'd prefer to stay buried.

Don't worry, your secret is safe with me.

If you have any extra time or desire to do any mentoring, the students of the department, especially those who aspire to reach your level of success and emulate you, would enjoy it tremendously.

Like I said, I always knew you'd be a star. I'm thrilled that the world agrees.

Best of luck with everything—including your upcoming nuptials.

Jonathan Myers
Newspaper Director
Boston College

I set down the note, my hand shaking as the paper left my fingers.

Anonymously.

A word that wouldn't stop repeating in my goddamn head.

I didn't understand.

I couldn't make sense of anything.

Not the words that the man had written to Jovana.

Or the article that he had referenced many times throughout that note.

Or the plaque, which I assumed I was holding in my hands.

I glanced down at the front of the wood, realizing I had pulled it out backward, and I slowly turned it around.

My stomach tightened when I saw the name of the newspaper at the top of the plaque, the number of views the article had received.

The title of the article.

Hooked for Life or Marketing Ploy?

The byline.

Anonymous.

The first line that I remembered so fucking well.

If you've been online in the last twenty-four hours, then there's a very good chance you saw the toast

Grayson Tanner, Boston's Biggest Bachelor and co-founder of Hooked, gave aboard the megayacht he's currently on.

Jovana had graduated from Boston College? I knew she'd been accepted. I saw the letter in her childhood bedroom right before I asked Ernie's permission to marry her. But at the time and because there had been so many acceptance letters, it hadn't clicked that she'd gone there. I had just assumed she'd chosen one of the other colleges.

But why had I thought that?

And why had I never asked her?

Not that her answer would have mattered or sparked anything. I wouldn't have ever thought, out of the thousands of students who went to that school, she would have authored the article.

But she had.

Anonymous was her.

She had aired my laundry as badly as the Celebrity Alert had.

She was one of the reasons why Hooked had hired Laura.

Why the guys had forced marriage upon me.

Why I was in this fucking situation in the first place.

All . . . because of her.

I set the plaque down, my eyes shifting to the invitation.

Where our names were written.

Where, in gold, it showed that Jovana was going to be my fucking wife.

No.

Hell fucking no.

I took my phone out of my pocket, and I opened the group chat I had going with the guys.

Me: Change of plans. Come to my place. Now. And hurry the fuck up.

CHAPTER TWENTY-EIGHT

Grayson

I was pacing the living room with a tumbler of vodka in my hand when Easton and Holden walked in. I'd put in at least a fucking mile with how many passes I'd done so far, turning at the windows and again at the corner of the couch. Back and forth across the length of my living room.

With each step, I was piecing together the parts of the story that hadn't made sense earlier.

The progression of how it all unfolded.

The lies.

Now that I could wrap my head around it all, I swore there was fucking smoke coming out the top of me.

"Get a drink." I nodded at the bar as I made my way toward where they were now sitting. "You're going to need one."

Easton looked at Holden, but neither of them got up.

"What the fuck is going on?" Easton asked.

I halted at the windows, placing my back against the cool glass. That should have been enough to bring down my body temperature. To lower me from boiling to simmering.

But it didn't.

There was a fire inside me, and it wasn't letting up.

"I got an interesting package in the mail today—well, shit, it wasn't actually for me; it was for Jovana. But I'd just opened our wedding invitation that had also come in the mail, and I was so goddamn distracted that I didn't see her name on the package and assumed it was for me." I wrapped an arm across the middle of my stomach.

As Holden stared at me, his hands hung between his spread knees, a dumbfounded look growing across his face. "Okay . . ."

"It was a fucking plaque." I couldn't stand here. I needed to move. So I pushed myself off the window and went into the kitchen, where I'd left the gift on the counter and lifted it high enough for them to see. "Boston College sent this to her—the school where she got her bachelor's—as a gift because she had the most-read article in the school newspaper." I set my vodka down so I could grip the plaque with both hands, aiming it toward their faces. "You know, the article that was titled 'Hooked for Life or Marketing Ploy?' The one that went fucking viral? And was written by Anonymous?" The wood felt so acidic in my hands, I wanted to throw it across the room. I set it down before I whipped it like a Frisbee. "The writer wasn't so anonymous after all. It was Jovana."

"Hold on a second." Easton moved to the end of the cushion. "Let me make sure I have this straight." He clasped his hands together, and I could tell he was deep in thought. "She wrote the article that appeared in the school newspaper? The one that published right after the Celebrity Alert went out?"

Both of my hands clenched into fists. "Yes."

"And she never told you she was the one who wrote the story?" Easton continued.

"Correct." I cleared my throat, the sound like a growl. "And I'm positive she had no intention of ever telling me. My address isn't even on this goddamn package. It's her old apartment, but because they sent it through the mail, it was forwarded here."

"But you said it was a gift?" Holden inquired. "So Jovana didn't even know it was coming, right?"

"Right." I took a sip. "What's your point?"

"My point is, she wasn't hiding the plaque from you, because she didn't even know she was getting it."

"Insignificant." I waved my hand. "Moving on to the real point, which is that she signed a fucking contract to marry me. She then began to date me. And then I told her I had feelings for her, that I cared about her, that I wanted more with her. And the whole time"—I squeezed the glass as I walked back to the wall of windows—"she was fucking lying to me."

Holden shook his head. "Lying . . . no."

I paused midstep and glared at him. "Why the hell are you sticking up for her?"

"I'm not."

"But you are. I feel like you have been since I started this story."

"I'm just trying to make you see where she was coming from, something you're usually unable to do because you're stuck so far inside your head, all you feel is rage." Holden glanced around the room. "Where is she, anyway?"

"Out for a walk," I snapped, and kept marching across the floor until the windows were behind my back. "The article that she wrote was fucking nasty. You both know that. It was meant to tear me down and destroy me. And she didn't just come for me, she came for Hooked too. And then she signed that contract, knowing she shredded me, and she started promoting our company. Talk about being a conniving, backstabbing—"

"I'm going to stop you right there," Holden said, interrupting me. "You need to look at this from a different angle."

"Holden, I'm about ready to knock out your teeth."

He raised his hand. "Hear me out, okay?" He paused, waiting for a response, which I wouldn't give him. "You hooked up with Jovana the night we all went to the bar."

"So?"

"Jesus, Grayson, give me a second." Holden took a breath. "You had sex with her at your condo and things didn't end well, am I right?"

I shrugged.

"And then you didn't speak to her again until the night our executive team and Laura went to the bar to discuss your situation a bit further. And that was after the article was published and the Celebrity Alert aired, right?"

I moved the tumbler toward my mouth but didn't take a drink. "I still don't understand why any of this fucking matters."

"You're not putting yourself in her shoes," Holden said. "Jovana isn't a woman who sleeps around, I'm assuming. She felt something with you. A connection—whatever—and she went home with you. You guys did your thing. And then you basically told her you wanted nothing to do with her, and a relationship would never happen." He pushed up his sleeves. "For a woman who doesn't do one-night stands and wasn't even on our app, can you imagine how that could make her feel? How low? How shitty? How used?"

"I can't fucking believe what I'm hearing right now . . ."

"Fuck, Grayson, why can't you understand what Holden is saying?" Easton bellowed.

I gazed at Easton. "Don't even tell me you're on his side . . ."

"I'm not saying what she did was right. It wasn't," Easton replied. He tugged at the thigh area of his jeans, straightening them out to get more comfortable on the couch. "She should have told you, there's no question about it—it's definitely fucked up of her—but can you at least comprehend why she didn't?"

"No. I can't comprehend a goddamn thing aside from how mad I am right now." I tried to breathe but couldn't. "She should have told me before she signed the contract. End of story."

"True," Holden countered. "But if she had feelings for you then, and I suspect she did, then she knew she would immediately ruin anything that was going to happen the moment she said something to you."

My head dropped, staring at the floor.

Why is this so fucking hard?

"This is bullshit," I grumbled. "Complete, utter bullshit."

Silence ticked between us until Holden broke it. "Our favorite side of him is back."

"I can see that," Easton replied.

"Stop fucking talking about me like I'm not in the room!"

"Grayson . . ." Easton's voice was calm, but it had an edge to it. "I need you to listen to me. I need you to step back for a second and look at the whole picture." He let those words simmer between us. "Jovana had a motive to write that article. She was pissed—at the way you treated her, at the entire situation, and then at the Celebrity Alert that showed you on a yacht with six other women. Picture her face when that alert came across her phone. When she saw the photos of you. When she heard the speech you gave to bachelorhood." He paused again. "Now picture how she felt about all of it."

I frowned at my best friends. "You two are unbelievable."

"Can you fathom how that could wreck her?" Easton pushed. "Flip it around, pretend you were the one who had feelings for her. She told you she wanted nothing to do with you. She all but tossed you out of her condo. You don't see her again—and then, boom, she's on vacation with six dudes. Are you going to tell me that wouldn't sting?"

I continued to glare at them.

Without saying a word.

Easton grabbed a beer from the fridge, and on his way back to the couch, he said, "So, she wrote an article when she was in a vulnerable place. Hooked was already affected by the Celebrity Alert. Did the article hurt us more, yes. But there were other articles, Grayson. Jovana's wasn't the only one." He twisted off the cap and took his first drink. "We had Google Alerts set up and they were coming in by the dozen every hour, every day. Journalists thrive off negativity, and when they can throw their opinions into the mix, it only benefits their readership." He glanced at Holden, who was nodding. "Jovana wrote some strong words that were aimed at you and our company, pointing out that you represent the marriage arm and it's clear from the photos it's not something you believe in, so why would our customers want to believe in it. As much as I hate to say this, she's right. You didn't believe in it. What she said in that article wasn't a lie."

"And for all the bad that came from that article and all the others that were published," Holden said, "so much good has happened because of them too."

"You've got to be kidding me." I groaned.

"Business is stronger than ever." Holden held out his hand and started counting on his fingers. "We've recouped our losses and increased revenue by twenty-eight percent in the marriage arm. And then there's the two of you."

"The two of who?" I roared.

"You and Jovana." Holden smiled. "You said it yourself today that you love her."

"Loved," I clarified, shocked that I'd even said the word out loud.

"Oh, come on, man." Easton sighed. "You didn't fall out of love with her because she didn't tell you the truth about one minor detail. That woman doesn't have a malicious bone in her body. She's one of the nicest people I've ever met. I'm sure she assumed no one was even going to read the article. She was angry, bitter, and she used her words to fight back. And because you were in the news and the topic was hot, the story took off and went viral."

"Don't let this ruin the best thing that's ever happened to you," Holden said softly.

His statement hit me.

And I tried to fill my lungs.

I tried to calm the hell down.

I tried to sip the vodka that was still in my hand, but even the look of it made my stomachache worse. I set it down and said, "I'm blown away. By all of this."

"You went into this thinking that there are sides," Easton said. "That's how your brain works. You against the world. Always. But that isn't the case." He placed his beer on the coffee table. "This isn't us against you or you against her. When you're in a relationship, it doesn't work that way. You communicate the problem. You work through it. You move on. Now"—he cut me off as I was about to butt in—"I get that she didn't do that, but we've made it very clear why she didn't."

I wrung my hands together. "And that makes it okay?"

Holden nodded toward me. "You've been anti-everything since the moment she met you. She didn't give up, though, did she? She showed you who she was, what she wanted, what the two of you could have together."

"It goes deeper than that and we all know it." Easton's gaze softened as he looked at me. "She's not your mother, Grayson. You treated Jovana like shit, and she didn't walk, even though she could have at any point."

"You're right," Holden added. "What she did instead was show you that she loves you."

If she had told me she loved me, I would have pushed her away.

I would have used that as a reason to end things.

To terminate the contract.

To never see or talk to her again.

That was what I was looking for—reasons.

Because I didn't know how to do this.

Because I was so fucking scared of this.

Because I didn't want my future to turn out the way my father's did.

But the truth was, I wanted her.

I loved her.

"What do I do?" I looked at Easton, and then at Holden. "Do I repackage the plaque and pretend I never saw it? Do I bring this up to her and attempt to have a normal conversation about it?"

"Can you talk to her without losing your shit?" Holden asked.

Just as I was about to answer, there was a vibration in my pocket. A series of pulses that told me it was a phone call coming through, not a social media notification.

I took out my phone, my eyes widening from the caller ID that showed the largest hospital in Boston was phoning me.

"Why the hell would Mass General be calling me right now?"

"Answer it," Holden said. "What if—God forbid—something happened to your dad?"

Fuck me.

I swiped the screen and held the phone up to my ear. "Hello?"

"Hi, is this Grayson Tanner?"

"It is." I looked at my best friends, my heart racing even harder than it already was.

"This is Denise. I'm a nurse in the emergency department at Mass General. I'm calling because Jovana Winters was in an accident, and she just arrived by ambulance to our hospital. I was able to unlock her phone and she has you listed as her emergency contact."

The words weren't sinking in.

They were just hitting my ears.

And everything was ringing.

Followed by a numbness.

"She was . . . in an *accident?*" I flattened my hand against the glass behind me.

"Yes."

"Is she going to be all right?"

"She's headed into surgery now."

Surgery.

It felt like my chest was being cut open without any anesthesia.

"What surgery? What happened?" My voice was rising. "Is she going to be all right?" I repeated since she hadn't answered me the first time.

"All I can tell you is that they're wheeling her into an operating room right now. Unfortunately, I can't release any other information at this time."

"I'm her fucking fiancé."

"I understand. But there are HIPAA laws that we must—"

"I don't give a shit about HIPAA."

"Mr. Tanner, you're more than welcome to come to the hospital and wait for her—"

"I'll be right there," I said, and I hung up.

I slid the phone into my pocket and scanned the room, looking for something.

Anything that would help me.

That would explain how this could happen.

That would make this stabbing pain in my chest feel better.

"I . . . have to go." I pushed off the glass and headed for the door.

"What happened?" Easton asked from behind me.

"Jovana is headed into surgery. She was in an accident."

"What?"

I said over my shoulder, "And they won't fucking tell me anything else."

"Is she going to be all right?" Holden asked.

I could hear them following me, and I replied, "I don't know."

"I'll get us a car service," Easton said.

I opened the door, and they followed me to the elevator.

"You need to call Jovana's parents and let them know," Holden said. "Do you have their number?"

Did I have their number?

I couldn't think.

I couldn't wrap my head around what information I had and didn't have.

I couldn't feel anything aside from this heartbeat that was echoing through me, radiating like electricity.

"Grayson," Holden said.

I looked at him as I stepped into the elevator.

"Do you have their number? I'll call them if you want me to."

I shook my head.

I swallowed.

I felt the pain shoot across my chest again and into my throat. "What if I lose her?"

"You're not going to lose her—"

I pounded my fist against the elevator wall. "You don't know that!" I inhaled as deeply as I could. "You don't fucking know that."

"We're going there now, and we're going to be there when she gets out of surgery," Holden said.

He was calm.

Too goddamn calm.

"I was so mad at her." My voice was gone. Only a whisper was left. "Mad about the article. Mad about the plaque. Mad that she hadn't told me." The ache dived into my stomach and churned. "And while I was mad, she was fucking hurting. While I was screaming, she was on her way to the hospital."

Easton threw his arm around my shoulders, shaking me. "It's going to be all right, buddy. I promise."

But he didn't know that.

He was just filling me with false promises.

The only thing that would take this feeling away was seeing my baby, wrapping my arms around her, and having her look me in the eyes and tell me she was all right.

Silence stretched across the small room, but nothing in my head was quiet.

The guilt was eating at my skin.

The fear was knocking on every muscle.

The worry was slicing right through me.

"I promised her father," I whispered. I didn't realize I'd been staring at the floor, and I glanced up, looking at Holden's face since Easton was beside me and too close. "I promised him nothing would happen to her while she was with me . . . and look who the liar is now."

CHAPTER
TWENTY-NINE

Jovana

I was floating. Drifting through the thickness of clouds, my body completely weightless. There were no sensations aside from happiness. I felt like a living, walking smile. As if that emotion had been wrapped in a bow and were radiating through my body.

But as I was soaring through the fluff, there was something else.

Something that began to surface through the clouds.

Something . . . dark.

Cold.

That—suddenly—veered toward . . . *ouch.*

Oh God, it was so painful.

And I was bouncing between the two.

Until I couldn't.

Until my eyes were fighting to open, and my lungs were filling, and I was gripping something warm and dense, and I didn't know what that thing was—

"Hi."

One word was all I heard.

I blinked.

Hard.

And a face came into focus.

Eyes that were the most beautiful shade of green.

A sharp nose, thick lips.

A beard that I remembered.

That I'd run my fingers through so many times before.

I wanted to respond.

I tried to peel my lips apart.

But they were dry, like they'd been cemented shut.

It took every bit of strength I had to separate them. And once I broke that thick seal, my tongue felt like lead. "Grayson . . ."

"*Shhh.*" He was close. Enough so that I could smell his cologne. A citrus that was so crisp and clean, I felt like I was back in the clouds again. "You don't have to talk. Save your energy. I'm right here. I'm not leaving your side." Something tightened its hold on my hand, and I realized it was his fingers gripping me. "You're okay."

Okay?

Why wouldn't I be okay?

Why does it feel like something is extremely wrong?

Why do I hurt?

Where am I?

I glanced up and there was a long fluorescent light above my head. Walls that were pale, almost sickly colored. A door partially open with just enough light inside that I could make out a toilet and sink.

And there was beeping, a noise so loud it made the aches pound.

I turned my head to look at my side, each inch like a clock's second hand, the gears in my neck clicking as though they were ungreased.

But it brought me to the source of the beeping, which was a monitor that showed different lines and numbers.

And on the other side, a stand with several IV bags.

"You're in the hospital, Jovana."

My tongue was too heavy.

But my eyes widened. My chest, as tight as it was, began to rise. "You're okay."

Okay.

There was that word again.

The one that still didn't feel right.

"I don't know how much you remember—if you remember anything at all—but you were out for a walk," he said.

A walk.

That memory was a bit fuzzy, but snippets flashed through my head of my mom's smile and the dress I'd chosen and the champagne the sales associate had poured to celebrate, and then things got even hazier, but I remembered the sweat beading across my forehead while I'd been walking.

Why couldn't I recall returning home from the walk?

"You were only about six blocks from our condo when a woman ran a red light. In doing so, she caused a series of events, starting with a biker who was in the crosswalk at the time. To get out of the car's way, he veered into the sidewalk. He didn't turn enough, and he clipped you on your side. Since he was behind you, there was no way you could have seen him or moved out of the way. You had absolutely no warning."

I mashed my lips together, hoping to find enough liquid to move my tongue.

To respond.

To ask the questions that were pouring in so fast, I was overflowing.

"There were multiple witnesses," he continued, "and one was a woman who stayed with you until the ambulance arrived. She even came to the hospital to check on you, and she told me the whole story." He pushed the hair off my forehead, his fingers staying there, rubbing. "The impact of the bike punctured your spleen and caused you to bleed internally, which was repaired during surgery once you arrived at the hospital. That, along with the two ribs you broke, will take some time to heal, and you're going to have to take it easy. Your X-rays also showed a broken wrist, so that's been cast." His hand moved to my cheek. "The doctor says that as long as your vitals and blood work continue to stay stable, I'll be able to take you home in a day, two max."

A punctured spleen?

Two broken ribs?

A broken wrist?

I hadn't noticed the thick cast when I'd scanned the room, but it was there. Wrapped from the middle of my hand all the way to my elbow.

This was . . . so much.

"You'll have the cast on for at least six weeks," he told me.

Six weeks.

Why did it feel like something was happening within that time frame?

A nest of thoughts began to build in my mind, each layer weaving more pieces together until it hit me.

"Wedding," I croaked the second my tongue allowed me to.

"Yes, baby. You'll have the cast on for the wedding."

Emotion hit me out of nowhere.

In my eyes.

On my cheeks.

But it didn't stay long.

Grayson was sweeping away the wetness, cleaning what had fallen and stopping what was about to. "Listen to me, Jovana. You're alive. You're going to fully recover. That's what matters. Things could have been so much worse. Whether you have a cast on for the wedding or not, you're going to look breathtakingly beautiful."

I ached.

Not because there would be an ugly cast in all our photos, but because this had happened, because he was here to tell me the story, because he was under contract to marry me.

I loved this man.

I loved the way he stroked my cheek, collecting my tears, absorbing my emotion like he was trying to suck the sadness out of my body.

I loved that his eyes were the first thing I saw when I opened mine.

But did he love me?

"I want you to sleep." He kissed my forehead. "The only way you're going to get stronger is by resting your body, so that's what you need to do."

Sleep.

Something I couldn't imagine doing right now.

But with my eyelids so heavy, that was something I couldn't imagine fighting for a second longer.

Still, I had things to say.

Things I needed to get out.

Questions I wanted answered.

But my tongue—it hadn't lightened. It felt swollen and weighted, like an extra limb that didn't even fit in my mouth.

"Close your eyes," he whispered. "I'll be right here. I'm not leaving you."

"Are you in any pain?" Grayson asked from the open door of the back seat, where he stood just outside, an arm around my back and another on my uncast hand to help me get out of the SUV.

Even though the medication was helping, the pain was still present.

In my wrist.

On the side where I'd fallen, which was covered in dark-purple bruises.

In my abdomen, my ribs, and beyond, like I'd been hit with a hammer.

"I'm okay." I carefully turned toward the door and extended my legs across the side of the seat, my feet reaching for the ground, anticipating the sidewalk.

Once my toes touched down, I winced.

"Will you let me carry you inside?"

Something I'd adamantly refused when the driver had pulled up to our building and again when Grayson had opened my door.

"No." I took a breath and the motion—even though there was none aside from my lungs filling—felt like a jackhammer was cutting through my ribs. "The doctor says I need to walk as much as possible."

After two nights in the hospital, I had finally been discharged. My parents and Grayson had discussed this morning whether I should stay at their new apartment or Grayson's condo, like I wasn't in the hospital room while they'd talked about this or capable of making my own decisions.

There was no decision.

I was staying at home with my fiancé.

Grayson hadn't left my side once during the entire time I'd been in the hospital. He slept in the chair next to my bed, used the restroom in my room. He had the cafeteria bring him a tray when they delivered mine and had the guys bring him some fresh clothes.

When I closed and opened my eyes, he was always there.

I understood my mom's desire to want me under her roof, and I appreciated Grayson's insistence that he wanted the same. It was an amazing feeling to be cared for by everyone I loved.

But I was exactly where I was supposed to be.

I just needed to get past this sidewalk and through the lobby and into the elevator to go upstairs.

"Shit," I hissed after my first step.

"Jovana . . ."

"Don't you dare," I warned as he bent down to lift me. "I can do this." I glanced at the doorman, who had the lobby door already ajar for us. It was only ten feet away. "I have to do this . . . for me." I squeezed Grayson's hand.

With his arm around my waist, I slowly lifted a foot, holding my breath as I placed it back down, doing the same with the other leg, carefully making my way toward the door.

"Great to see you back, Ms. Winters," the doorman said. "I hope you start to feel better soon."

"Thank you," I replied.

As we passed through the entrance, Grayson said, "Jovana's parents will be stopping by later to bring lunch. Please send them right up. No need to call and notify us first."

"Will do, Mr. Tanner."

Grayson was bearing as much of my weight as I would give him, which I tried to keep to a minimum, but the closer we got to the elevator, the less energy I had.

Just a few days ago, I could walk miles without getting winded.

Now the journey from the curb to the elevator felt like a trek up Everest.

"You're almost there. You're doing great."

Great, no.

But encouragement was so out of the norm for him that I clung to his words and tried to focus on the remaining steps, estimating how many I had left, celebrating in my head every time I completed one.

The relief was immense when I crossed into the elevator and leaned my back against the side wall, giving me the perfect view to see the screen and watch the numbers climb once we passed each floor.

But as soon as Grayson pressed the button for the penthouse, he obviously wasn't pleased with my placement, and he slipped in behind me, holding me against his chest.

He wanted to be my wall.

To hold me up.

To make sure I didn't fall.

Oh God.

What did I do to deserve this man?

His care?

His attention?

I laced my fingers through his. "Thank you."

I wanted to say more.

I wanted to tell him how much I loved him.

But I kept my lips pressed together and took in the warmth from his chest and the strength of his arms as they enveloped me.

He leaned his face into my neck, and I felt him breathe me in. An act so subtle but so powerful.

Before Grayson, I didn't know the weight of an inhale, the heaviness of an exhale.

But his were as meaningful as words.

I felt them.

Through every part of me.

And when the door finally slid open, he helped me take the short walk to the front of the condo, where he waved his fob and guided me inside.

I filled my lungs with a scent I'd missed. "Home." I closed my eyes for just a second. "God, it feels good to say that."

"Does bed sound as good to you, because that's where I'm taking you." He walked me through the foyer and into the living room.

I glanced up at him just as we rounded toward the kitchen. "No . . . I need a bath first."

Actually, first I needed to catch my breath, so I halted us by the island.

"You're kidding?" He groaned.

Since I became conscious, all I'd been thinking about was dunking myself in some hot, bubbly water.

My skin begged to be clean. My muscles screamed for the heat.

I needed to wash this accident off me and my hair.

"I'm far from kidding. It's the only thing I want. Then bed. I promise." As I thought about it more, I added, "Will you join me?"

He let out a small chuckle. "An offer I can't say no to."

"Well, you could."

"But I wouldn't."

"I have one more request."

"You're really trying to test my patience, aren't you." He winked, but his voice was still a growl.

I attempted a smile before I glanced into the kitchen, seeing the cabinet where the mugs were stored, only about five feet from where we were standing. "I need some tea."

"I'll get it. Don't move."

He opened the cabinet, and while I didn't want to move, I did want to hold on to something, so I shuffled toward the island. My hands were just wrapping around the edge of the stone when a box on the counter caught my attention.

It wasn't the shape or the size.

It was that it was open, that it had been addressed to me.

That Jonathan Myers was listed as the sender.

The director of Boston College's newspaper.

Oh fuck.

My hands trembled as I lifted the box, and the moment I had it in the air, I noticed there was something underneath it.

A plaque.

With my name and the school newspaper at the top.

A number that showed how many times the article had been viewed.

Followed by the full article with **Anonymous** under the byline.

If the box was open, the plaque already pulled out, that could only mean one thing . . .

As I glanced up from the plaque, Grayson was looking at me, frozen, with a mug in his hand.

"Jovana . . ." He took a breath, and I watched him think of his next words. Silence beating between us, like the wheels of a bike. "I was going to seal it back up and pretend I never saw it, but the hospital called, and I left, and I haven't been back home."

Although his voice wasn't a growl, his statement was raw and emotional.

I couldn't tell whether he was leaning toward anger.

Hurt.

Sadness.

I just knew that everything inside me was throbbing, and it wasn't because of the accident.

It was from the guilt.

That I'd been holding.

"You know it was me," I whispered.

He nodded.

Of course he knew. Why else would Boston College send a plaque, if I hadn't been the one who had written the article?

"Grayson . . ." I pressed a hand against my chest to slow my heart down, hoping the thumping wouldn't break through my skin. "I'm sorry." When I sucked in more air, it sounded like a gasp. "I'm so fucking sorry. I was wrong. I shouldn't have written that article. I was just so hurt and—"

"Answer me one thing." He leaned his back into the counter. "Were you going to tell me before the wedding?"

My eyes were burning. Like my pupils had been replaced with rocks of lava, I couldn't stop the drips from rimming my eyelids. "I don't know." I glanced down at my hands. "Shit, I honestly don't know. I wanted to, but I didn't have the nerve."

"Why?"

"Because I knew it would make you hate me." I slowly gazed up at him. His expression made the knot in my throat double in size. It wasn't a look of shock that stared back at me. It was the look of someone who had anticipated this answer. And that hurt even more. "Because I was afraid that if I told you the truth, I would completely lose you . . . and I wasn't even sure I fully had you in the first place."

"Jovana—"

"No"—I swallowed—"I have to get this out." I flattened my hands on the stone, bracing myself for what I should have admitted a long time ago. "We're in this for twelve months. That's all that's been promised to me. Twelve months with the man I'm completely in love with. And after that, you have every right to walk away."

Why did his stare hurt this badly?

Why did it feel like we were already over?

"Since the moment I fell in love with you, Grayson, that's what I've been terrified of. That this isn't what you want, that I won't be enough, that in the end I'll be left with a shattered heart." I held up my hand as he attempted to speak. "You told me not to have feelings for you. Not to fall for you. Not to think of the future because there wouldn't be one. And I realize things between us have changed, that you've admitted that you care about me, but is it enough for you to stay married to me?" I shook my head. "I question that . . . far too often." The movement caused the tears to fall past my chin and I wiped them. "I've told you, I want the fairy tale. I want what my parents have. I want that kind of love that isn't based on money or materialistic things or vacations or success or work or even interests. My parents couldn't be more opposite. But what they have is a love that is deeper than anything I've ever seen. I want that with you." With the wetness passing my lips, I licked it off, immediately tasting the saltiness of my tears. "There have been moments, like today, like in the elevator, like the way you breathed me in, that I think we're there. That we want the same thing. That your feelings are as strong as mine. And then there are moments that I sense your views on marriage are bigger than us."

I pushed against my chest again, the pain so deep, but that didn't stop me.

It didn't prevent me from opening my heart.

And it didn't inhibit me from speaking my last piece of truth.

"I can't handle an end. Not with the way I feel about you. If that's what's going to happen after the year is up, then call off the wedding. Break me now before you completely destroy me." I balled my fingers into a fist. "I'll give back every dime. I'll tell my followers I jumped in too quickly and I'll spin the story so you and Hooked come out on top and I'm at fault. Whatever I have to do, I'll do it. Just don't let me walk down the aisle if the groom standing under our beautiful, flowered arch isn't completely in love with me."

CHAPTER THIRTY

Grayson

I can't handle an end. Not with the way I feel about you. If that's what's going to happen after the year is up, then call off the wedding. Break me now before you completely destroy me . . . Just don't let me walk down the aisle if the groom standing under our beautiful, flowered arch isn't completely in love with me.

Jovana's words had repeated in my head since the moment she'd spoken them.

I understood her request.

Her fear.

The reason she wouldn't want to fulfill the contract.

Pull the Band-Aid off now even if it left a scar. But at least, in time, the air would heal the wound, and despite thinking of me whenever she looked at it, at least she wouldn't have the adhesive snagging on her clothes every time a piece of fabric got close to it.

My girl wanted an answer.

Reassurance.

She wanted me to look her in the face and promise things I'd never voiced to her before.

Love.

A long-term commitment.

And while I'd gazed at her in the kitchen with the mug still in my hand, I had told her how the article had made me feel. How finding out that she had written it was such a huge fucking blow that I wasn't prepared for. How I'd discussed it with the fellas while she'd been out walking, and they made me see a side that I hadn't considered.

Her side.

But all that had happened before the phone call from the hospital.

Before I knew the details of the accident.

Before I held her hand that was pierced with an IV and kissed her cheek that no longer smelled of vanilla and lavender. Instead, she was covered in a smell I didn't recognize.

Remnants of the surgical room and rubbing alcohol and the tape that held the oxygen tubes in her nose.

Smells I couldn't fucking stand.

God, I'd almost lost her.

I'd almost reneged on the promise I'd made to her father that nothing would ever happen to her.

And while I'd told her about how I held her in that hospital room, I also detailed how I'd thought about her.

About us.

Jovana knew that my mother had shaped my view on relationships. How she had treated my father was the reason I never wanted to get married.

Why Hooked was so perfect for my lifestyle.

But what she didn't know was that I had learned something else from my mother.

Something vital.

Something I'd carried with me since I found out she had passed.

And that was the importance of time. How it wasn't promised. How it could slip through your fingers so quickly, you needed to grasp what was in front of you.

Hold on.

Never let go.

I dominated the shit out of that when it came to work, my friendships, and my dad.

Just not with women.

I was too angry. Bitter. Resentful.

I was never going to let a woman do to me what my mother had done to my father.

And I was never going to turn into the guy who consistently reached for a woman's hand even when it clasped another man's, who kept his ex-wife's urn on the mantel.

Fuck that.

But then this gorgeous, kindhearted, patient, blue-eyed woman came into my life.

She turned out to be the light I needed.

The light I never knew I wanted.

The light I didn't realize I could fall in love with.

Part of what she was asking of me was impossible. I couldn't promise a future. I couldn't tell her that after twelve months, or even twelve years, things would be perfect.

That I would always be everything she ever wanted.

That time wouldn't somehow come in and kick us in the balls, like the biker who had taken her feet out from under her and the health issues my mother had experienced that had ultimately caused her death.

But there was one thing I could promise.

One thing I was going to promise.

And the moment when I'd get to do it, when I'd be able to take her by the hand and say those words, was almost here.

I glanced toward the staircase, where Jovana was making her way down the steps. At the bottom, there was a landing that also happened to be the base of the garden. That was where she paused by the long bed of potted flowers.

She was giving me a chance to take her in.

To witness her beautiful smile.

To wipe the goddamn tear that had begun to fall from my eye.

No man should ever be this lucky.

To have someone who looked at me the way Jovana did.

But I had her.

The skin that glowed under the sun. The cast that covered her from wrist to elbow. The long, dark curls that hung around her exquisite face.

Every bit—all mine.

She was a masterpiece.

A vision.

And fuck, she made me breathless.

As she walked toward me, I thought about what I was going to say. Words I hadn't planned or rehearsed. It wasn't that I was an expert at public speaking; I just wanted to see how I felt in this moment. To let it hit me and simmer inside my gut before I purged the thoughts that came to me.

The emotions that surfaced high enough to be shared.

When she was within reach, I nodded at Ernie, silently thanking him for trusting me, for giving her to me, for not holding the accident against me despite what I'd promised him.

I took her hand from her father's fingers.

And then I led her under the flowered arch, where I'd been standing in my black tux.

"Jovana," I whispered, my gaze lowering down her perfect body, one that was wrapped in lace and satin, a dress that hugged her curves. It didn't come close to competing with her beauty, nothing could, but fuck me she was incredible in white. "You look amazing."

The smile grew across her lips. "So do you."

I didn't listen to the officiant as she started with an introduction, thanking our guests, or when she transitioned into her opening monologue.

I focused on the moments it had taken me to get here.

The fight.

The resistance.

The second-guessing.

The fall.

Each phase I had gone through since Jovana had come into my life. My thoughts ended at the promise I'd yet to make.

But she knew if I was under this arch, holding her hands, staring into her eyes, then I was completely, madly in love with her.

"As you know," the officiant said, "the exchange of wedding vows is not only a long-standing tradition, but it's the most important part of the ceremony. Words that the bride and groom use to signify the growth of their union and the promises they make to one another. Rather than going with traditional vows, our bride and groom have opted to write their own." She glanced up from the paper she held, adjusting her glasses while eyeing us at the same time. "I'm going to ask you now to look at each other and speak those sacred words." She signaled to Jovana, letting her know she should go first.

My soon-to-be wife stared at me while a wave of emotion trickled into her eyes. A smile that I knew was different from the other versions she used. It was an expression that had taken me months to analyze and understand, but now I knew the truth about it.

She reserved that smile for only me.

"Grayson," she began, "when we found each other—or hooked, however you want to call it"—she stopped to wink—"this was what I envisioned. Maybe not this setting. Or this dress. Or all the papers we've now signed our names to." She paused to inhale, her eyes telling me she was referencing our twelve-month contract, but our guests would assume it was something home or utility or marriage-license related. "But what I saw was this depth of love. The feeling of wanting forever. A desire to hold you and never let go. I could promise to always love you, but those are just words. I'd rather show you, so you can feel all the love I have for you." Her chin trembled as she continued, "What I can promise is that you will have all of me. The good. The injured"—the crowd chuckled—"and the days that are my darkest when I'll rely on you to find the light. I can promise you my heart. My commitment. And I can promise you that there isn't anyone who could ever fulfill my fairy tale like you. You're everything I've ever wanted, Grayson, and I promise I'll spend the rest of my life making sure you know that."

God.

That fucking woman.

She couldn't have crafted a more perfect set of promises than the ones she'd given to me.

I carefully squeezed her fingers, making sure I didn't hurt the ones sticking out of her cast, and said, "Jovana, I know, like our vows, our story hasn't been traditional. The way we met. The way we grew. The way we fell. Or the steps that took us here, to our wedding, where I'm giving you all my promises. But if I'm being honest, a traditional courtship wouldn't have led us here. A place where I can look you in the eyes and tell you how much I love you." The first tear dripped over her eyelid, and I released her hand to catch it. "I promise to do that every time I see you cry—and I hope—Jesus, I hope—those tears aren't because of me. Not when our love is this deep. Not when I know that whatever comes our way, we'll jump those hurdles together, baby." Now that I'd wiped her tear, I held out my fingers, waiting for her to grab them again. "I promise that you'll wake up every morning in my arms and that my embrace will show you not only the kind of husband you need but the kind of husband I want to be. I promise to do everything in my power to keep you safe and protected. No one will ever hurt you again as long as I can help it. Including me. And I promise to love you, not just in my soul, but to make sure you feel that love, to make you see it, and hear it. Not just now. Not for the next year. But forever."

As she interpreted my vows, her head shook, her thumb ran across the backs of my knuckles, and her lips mashed together, like she was stopping herself from responding.

Her eyes showed me everything she wanted to say but couldn't with the seventy-five guests in attendance.

Jovana and I had secrets that would never be unlocked.

But it didn't matter.

I'd obliterated her fears.

I'd given her what she wanted to hear, and I'd voiced every word I wanted to say.

This was the true beginning.

Of us.

"Beautiful," the officiant said. "Now it's time to exchange rings."

I reached to my side, where my three best men stood, first my father, then Easton and Holden. I didn't believe in choosing one to have a higher role than the others. The three were in my life for different reasons.

But each one meant everything to me.

My father handed me the diamond band I'd chosen for Jovana, and I held it in front of her ring finger.

"Repeat after me," the officiant said. "With this ring, I thee wed, and pledge you my love, now and forever."

As I looked into Jovana's eyes, I pushed the diamond circle onto her finger, repeating the phrase.

And when it was her turn, she turned toward Sloane to get the band she'd picked out for me, aiming it at my finger, and as she pushed the metal higher, past my knuckle, she repeated the identical statement.

"By the power vested in me by the Commonwealth of Massachusetts," the officiant said, "I now pronounce you husband and wife. You may now kiss your bride."

I cupped her face with my hands, and I leaned down, hovering my lips above hers, whispering, "I love you so much," before I locked our mouths together.

◆ ◆ ◆

BREAKING NEWS: Boston's Biggest Bachelor Is Now a Married Man

Grayson Tanner, 30, and Jovana Winters, 22, have

officially tied the knot. Sources confirm that the wedding took place in Boston, where their guests were overheard gushing over the lavish, fancy, pricey affair.

You can keep the overpriced caviar, we're gushing over the bride. She may be a Winters, but there's nothing icy about the way she looks in that dress.

Baby Hooked news coming next?

We hope so.

Good luck to the newlyweds.

CHAPTER THIRTY-ONE

Jovana

Even though Grayson and I had made all our wedding plans together, our honeymoon was one aspect he'd asked to handle alone. He wanted me to be surprised with the location, or locations—he wouldn't give me even that detail. My only request was that wherever we went and whatever he had planned, I wanted the use of both hands. So when my orthopedist scheduled my cast to come off two weeks after our wedding, Grayson booked Hooked's private plane to fly us out the following morning.

Delaying the trip gave us a chance to relax after all the festivities. To bask in the warmth of our marriage and get to know each other as husband and wife.

They said it was just a piece of paper, that nothing would change.

But Grayson and I knew something about paper—we'd had a contract between us since almost the very beginning. One that had kept us legally bound.

Our marriage license didn't do that. It could be shredded anytime we wanted.

But since we'd both signed the license, things had become so different.

The first thing he said to me every morning when we woke up was how much he loved me. He uttered the same words before we went to bed.

In the two weeks that had passed, he proved his wedding vows.

He showed his promises.

And there wasn't a moment that had passed when I didn't believe him.

How much I meant to him.

How much he cared for me.

How much he loved me.

Even if those gestures were subtle, like the way his arm hung over my shoulders and his lips pressed into the top of my head as we got out of the SUV and walked the short distance to Hooked's plane.

I felt the passion.

His attention.

His constant, irrevocable love.

And as I wrapped my arm around his waist, I could feel the warmth of his skin without a chunk of plaster separating us. I could wear a sexy dress for my husband without my skin covered in purple bruises.

I could take a deep breath and bear his weight on top of me without the relentless pain in my abdomen.

I was finally healed.

Our honeymoon wasn't just a celebration of our marriage.

It was a celebration of my life.

That I'd survived.

That I was physically and mentally moving on from the accident.

We boarded the plane, and my head was filled with dreams of what these next two weeks were going to be like. The food we were going to eat. The wine we were going to drink.

The beauty we were going to experience.

Inside the plane, the monitor in the cabin, which I assumed normally showed the flight path and destination, was blacked out. The flight attendant and the two pilots didn't mention anything about where we were going or how long it would take to get there.

I knew absolutely nothing.

But when we were about nine hours into the flight, one of the pilots announced that we were starting our descent, and not a minute later, a text came across my phone.

Sloane: I just looked over Saturday's sales numbers and it was a record-breaking night. Highest sales I've had since I've owned the bar. Can I hire you as a weekly guest bartender, PLEASE?!?

Me: I make terrible drinks. You don't want me.

Sloane: Stop that . . . I can teach you.

Me: Better idea—how about I come a few times a month and just hang behind the bar instead? I'll even post a TikTok to let my followers know I'll be there. Something tells me they'd like that better than if I charged them for drinks that I butchered and they hated (which they did, I saw their faces, omg, they haaaated them, and don't tell me it's because I only had one hand, we both know a second hand wouldn't have made them taste better).

Sloane: I'm not going to lie, that extra dirty martini you made me at the end of the night was pretty rancid.

Me: SEE!

Me: By the way, I knew things were going to explode once you took over the bar. Glad I can say I was right.☺

Sloane: A lot of that is due to you.

Me: No way, I'm not taking any credit. You know what the patrons are looking for and you've reshaped the whole place. It's nothing like it was when I worked there. It's a million times better. Your success is because of YOU.

Sloane: If I had even an ounce of sappiness in my body, I'd be aww-ing right now. But I don't, so I'm going to say, the second you return from your honeymoon, I better be seeing you.

Me: You got it. XO

"First stop," Grayson gently growled in my ear as I set my phone down, "is the Amalfi Coast."

I glanced out the window, the plane coming to a halt at the end of the runway. "Oh my God." I turned toward him. "You're kidding? This has been on my travel bucket list and—"

"I know. And for the next five days, before we move on to surprise location number two, you're going to experience every bit of it."

"Grayson . . ."

He cupped my chin, holding our faces close together. "Wife . . ."

I smiled. "God, I love you."

"I love you more," he roared before our lips touched.

The second we parted, we stood from our seats and made our way out of the plane to where an SUV waited for us on the tarmac.

But before I climbed in, I stood on the bottom of the plane's steps, taking in the sights and smells and emotions racking my body.

I'd found paradise.

In the way the leaves on the trees moved and whispered from the wind.

In the way the air smelled of the sun's warmth and a hint of lemon.

In the way that my husband held my hand.

How he looked at me as I faced him, like Italy didn't even compare to me.

This was love.

This was what a future with Grayson was going to look like, and I didn't want to rush it, but I couldn't wait for more.

We got into the back seat, and after a short drive, we pulled up to the home that he'd rented for our stay. Rose petals met my feet the second he opened the front door.

I took in the long trail of red that wove through the living room and kitchen, the only two rooms I could view from the doorway, and filled my lungs with a shaky, emotional breath. "This is magical."

With our fingers locked, he led me through the living room to show me the view outside the balcony. The home was nestled in a mountain, surrounded by others that were as beautiful and as colorful as ours, and below was the water.

Not like the dark, almost midnight blue of the Atlantic.

The Tyrrhenian Sea was teal, and in some places, it was so clear I could see the sand below.

"Five days." I sighed, still having a hard time fathoming that I would get to look at this view for that long. "I'm literally in heaven."

As he stood behind me, he held my stomach, his face in my neck. "Wait until you see the bedroom . . . and what I'm going to do to you when we get in there."

I giggled as he pressed his hard-on against me. "Show me. Now."

We followed the petals into a hallway where there was a large walk-in closet, an en suite, and a balcony off the bedroom where we could open the doors and listen to the waves below. The bed was decorated with more petals, and champagne sat on ice by the dresser. Vases of red roses were on every surface with candles waiting to be lit.

Despite the long flight and not having slept at all, I wasn't tired.

Adrenaline flowed through me as I thought about the first leg of this trip. I wrapped my arms around Grayson's neck, fantasizing about what he was now going to do to me in this room.

How loud I was going to scream.

How hard I was going to come.

"You have me," I whispered, my gaze dropping to his lips. "What are you going to do with me?"

He lifted me into the air and placed me on top of the wonderfully big, comfortable bed, where the softness of the petals grazed my skin.

"I'm going to fucking devour you."

His eyes backed up every word, and suddenly my dress was off and my sandals were no longer on my feet. My strapless bra was the only thing left, since I hadn't worn any panties, and that was now unhooked and flung to the ground.

"And the first thing I want to do is taste you." He spread my legs, his beard scraping the insides of my thighs as he moved between them. Before his tongue landed on me, his nose wedged between my folds, taking a long, deep inhale. "Mine." He breathed me in again. "God, you smell good." He slowly and gradually licked me from top to bottom. "Fuck yes, you taste amazing."

"*Yesss.*" My fingers dived into his hair, gripping his strands, needing to just hold on to something while he moved to the top of me, focusing on the highest point, licking it horizontally. "Your tongue . . . fuck."

Then vertically.

His pace stayed but the pattern changed as he sucked me into his mouth, flicking the end of my clit with his tongue, while he slipped two fingers inside me.

The combination was too much.

I couldn't hold off the orgasm.

"You're getting close. I can taste it."

Just as I was memorizing his rhythm, it shifted.

Again.

He wasn't going to let me come that fast.

Grayson liked having that control.

That he could send me over the edge whenever he wanted.

I squirmed from the sensations, unable to stay still, the pleasure far too much, and I tightened my grip on his hair, my other hand clasping the blanket beneath me.

It seemed every time I neared the place of no return, he would lower his tongue to my entrance to stop the build from happening. His fingers would slow. He would gather my wetness and lick back up, starting the process all over again.

I was breathless.

"What are you doing to me?" I gasped.

"I'm making you want it so badly, you can't think of anything else."

Except I was there.

I had been since the very start.

And I was positive he knew that. He was just overwhelming me with thoughts.

Needs.

Wants.

Because there was nothing in this world that felt as good as Grayson's tongue.

"Please," I begged.

My legs threatened to cave inward, my hips rocking, matching the momentum of his tongue.

And just when I reached a point where I couldn't stop, something changed.

Something . . . felt different.

Something was extra soft.

A quick look showed me he was holding a rose petal between his teeth, rubbing it against my clit like it was his tongue.

"Oh God!" Although it wasn't wet like his mouth, the feel of it, the silkiness, the softness, was incredible.

And it was enough.

More than enough.

Within a few swipes of the flower, I was coming.

"Grayson!" Tingles shot through my navel and up toward my chest. *"Ahhh!"*

The shudders came next, moving through my stomach in waves, each one consuming me, sending me further into my orgasm, where I was positive I'd stopped breathing.

I also wasn't squeezing his hair anymore.

Nor could I hold my legs apart.

I was lost.

Overpowered and overstimulated.

Soaking in every perfect second.

Until his tongue stilled, his fingers pulled out, and my body finally began to come down from its high.

He kissed me, my wetness on his lips. "Tell me how you taste."

"Grayson—"

"Tell me."

"God, the things you do to me." I smiled. "Sweet . . . is that what you want to hear?"

He reached around and grabbed my ass. "I'm far from done, baby."

He was moving me higher on the bed, my head eventually hitting a pillow, my legs spread over his shoulders as he knelt in front of me.

With his tip aimed at my entrance, he ran it up and down, like he was mimicking his tongue, soaking himself with my orgasm. After a few drags, he was sinking inside me.

Inch by inch.

Taking the little breath I had in my lungs and draining it.

"Oh. My. God." I moaned.

Once again, I reached for the blanket, fisting the fabric, feeling the petals at the same time.

"Goddamn it," he roared. "You're so tight and so fucking wet."

He was diving into me, stroking me with his famous speed and power, his hips turning when he reached the end of me, pulling out to his tip to do it all over.

My nails pierced his hips, urging him to go faster.

Harder.

Deeper.

I needed more—I always needed more.

But that didn't earn me any of the things I wanted. What it got me instead was Grayson pulling completely out and repositioning us at the side of the bed, where he sat along the edge with his feet on the ground and my legs straddling him.

"Ride me."

I circled my arms around his neck and lined my lips up to his. "That's what you want?" I teased his tip, dipping just enough that I took in his crown, so he could feel my tightness, before I hauled myself back and he slipped out. "You want me to ride the cum out of you?"

"*Mmm.* My wife talking dirty to me. I fucking love it." His fingers bit my ass. "And yes, that's what I want." He was gripping my hips, using his power to drive me down, burying his shaft inside me. "Fuck. Me." He pulled me forward and back, bucking me over him, giving friction to all sides of his dick.

He wasn't the only one moaning, the only one totally flooded with these mind-blowing sensations.

I was there too.

Captivated.

Adrift.

The build came out of nowhere, but each time I lifted and lowered, bobbing over his cock, it brought me closer.

"Grayson . . ." My voice was a whisper. That was all I could muster up vocally. I was just too lost in movements. But what I did have was my lips, and I used them, pressing my mouth to his, his tongue swirling around mine.

"You want to come together?"

I grunted out a sexy response.

"Then don't stop." He held me tighter. "Fuck me like you want to come."

I didn't have much left, but what was there, I used. I rotated my hips in a circle, holding him inside me, rising to gain more momentum before I plunged him back in.

"That's it, Jovana." He whispered in my ear, "Now faster."

Our breaths increased. Our sounds got louder.

Our tongues touched again.

And when I couldn't hold it off for a second longer, confining him within my walls, pulsing around him, I lost it.

"Grayson!"

There was something so erotic about watching the man you loved turn vulnerable and pound his orgasm into you.

About feeling the wetness shoot from his tip.

About absorbing each other's pleasure.

That was where we were—together. Hugging our bodies against one another.

Clinging.

Kissing.

Screaming out our orgasms.

"Fuck yes!" He continued to hold my ass. "Jovana! Damn it, yes!"

The peak of my pleasure was drawn out, causing me to shudder over him, clutching him from the inside until I turned sensitive.

Grayson's trembles lasted as long as mine, and I inhaled his moans as he exhaled them over my face, holding me like I was going to slip away.

Draining ourselves until only stillness was left.

His hands held the sides of my face and he gazed into my eyes.

Several seconds of silence passed before he broke it. "I'll never have enough of you."

"I'm never going anywhere, so you can have me whenever you want me."

"You know what that was?"

My brows rose. "No?"

He pressed our noses together. "The best answer you could have ever given me."

EPILOGUE

Grayson

"Are you going to get in?" I asked Jovana as I swam up to where she sat on the edge of our rooftop pool, her legs dangling in the water. Every time she lifted her foot out, a set of droplets fell from her toes, making circular ribbons across the pool's surface.

"Maybe."

I placed my hands on her thighs and threatened to pull her in. "Maybe, huh?"

She laughed, ending the giggle with her teeth on her lip, dragging them across the bottom, my favorite of the two. "I don't know if I want to get wet."

Our new penthouse in the Seaport had just been completed last week, and it came with our own private pool. One of the many benefits of being this high up with dark glass surrounding each side of the massive balcony was that clothes weren't required.

Which was why I didn't have any on and why I intended to get Jovana naked in the next few seconds.

"If I reached between your legs, I guarantee you'd be wet, baby."

The warmth from the sunset glowed across her face, enhancing her smile. "That's a different kind of wet."

"How about we experience both kinds tonight?" I pushed myself out of the water, taking her lips.

"Mmm." She moaned. "You're relentless."

"Only when it comes to you."

She ran her fingers through my soaked hair. "How about I go grab us some drinks and check on our food, and if I see that dinner has another twenty or so minutes in the oven, then I'll negotiate with you . . ." She gave me her profile and the biggest grin. "You can get me wet if that means the hot tub instead of the pool."

"Deal."

She laughed. "I thought so. Be right back."

I watched her walk through the sliding glass doors of our condo, a place we had designed together. We'd agreed on every detail, ones as small as the fixtures in the bathrooms and as big as the interior layout and the furniture and decor our designer had chosen.

The first condo we'd lived in had been mine.

This place was ours.

A week in and we were already in love with it.

I swam to the side where I'd stored my phone and checked the screen for the notifications I'd missed. I'd learned months ago to turn off my social media, especially since Jovana was including me in so many of her posts, like the goddamn TikTok she'd had me film with her last week. The only time I was alerted was when she posted a new picture on Instagram or a video on TikTok.

I couldn't compete with her following. They saw her shit long before I did, but I still wanted to check out her posts as fast as I could.

To show my girl support.

She was fucking killing it online, creating a career that was everything she'd ever dreamed of. By her next birthday, she'd be a millionaire. Not many people as young as her could say that.

What was on the screen of my phone wasn't anything from social media or one of Jovana's posts.

It was a text from Laura.

Laura: Call me when you can.

The last time we'd spoken was the night before our wedding. She hadn't been a guest. The three of us had decided it would be best if she wasn't seen as an attendee. But she had called to talk about the details of the event and how she planned to give the photos to the media.

I couldn't imagine what she wanted to discuss now.

I held the phone to my ear and waited for her to answer.

"Grayson," she said after the second ring. "How are things?"

"They couldn't be better."

Damn it, that was true.

Hooked was fucking exploding. Our advertising agency was still using our ads across every channel and medium, now showing our wedding pictures, and all three arms were on fire. We were up 30 percent from our objective, and Drake was about to launch a new version of the app, estimating that with an enhanced interface that was more user-friendly, our sales were only going to rise.

"Excellent, excellent," she said. "I'm reaching out because I was just looking over my calendar and I realized that today is an extremely important date."

"Yeah?" I walked the phone back to where Jovana had been sitting, giving me a better view of our living room. "Why is that?"

"It marks twelve months to the day from when you and Jovana signed the contract. According to the terms, the both of you have technically fulfilled all your requirements. Which means you're no longer obligated to stay married to her or pay her insurance or bills. Grayson, you're financially free of Jovana Winters—if you choose to be."

I didn't like the sound of that at all.

In fact, the words made my free hand clasp into a ball.

"Laura, watch it. You're talking about my fucking wife."

"You're saying you choose her, then?"

I could hear her smiling through the phone.

"Yes."

"I've waited for what feels like forever to hear you say that." She paused. "Sending my love to the both of you. Always."

I hung up, not offering a goodbye, and watched Jovana come through the slider with a vodka and a glass of wine.

"What's wrong?" She handed me my drink. "What's the face for?"

"That was Laura on the phone."

She took a sip of her drink. "And?"

I walked up the short flight of steps, onto the pool deck, and moved over to the hot tub, getting right in. I set my drink on the side, waiting for her to take a seat on the edge and place her wine down before I pulled her into the hot water.

She squealed. "I knew you were going to do that."

"I need you in my arms. Now."

As her legs circled around me, I kissed her, owning her mouth, sucking the end of her tongue.

It wasn't enough.

Fuck, it would never be enough.

But I separated our faces and stared into her eyes.

"Are you going to tell me what Laura wanted?"

I handed her the wine, clinking my glass against hers. "To twelve months."

"Twelve . . ." Her voice faded, but the realization suddenly came over her, her eyes widening in response. "I completely forgot."

"So did I, but Laura reminded me."

She placed the wine on the pool deck and tightened her grip around me. "What else did she say?"

"You know, the required bullshit. That we've fulfilled our obligations. That if either of us want to call it, we can, contractually."

I didn't want to say anything about the financial responsibilities.

That would imply that Jovana wasn't supporting herself, and that wasn't the case at all. Even though our new condo was out of her price range, Jovana insisted on paying all our utilities, and she could most definitely afford a nice place in the city, with a lifestyle as lavish as she wanted.

"Interesting." She shifted. "And how did you respond to that?"

I hovered my lips over hers, inhaling the vanilla first and then the lavender. "I told her I choose my wife."

"God"—she shook her head—"that title never gets old."

My hands lowered to her ass, and I lifted her a little higher. "She sends her best."

"I mean this with all the love in my heart, and it's nothing against Laura, but I really hope I never have to see her again."

I chuckled, feeling the same way. "You won't."

"Why do you say that?"

"Because you're mine." I kissed her collarbone. Her neck. Her lips. "Nothing will ever change that."

She pressed her mouth against the side of my beard, leaving it there while she grumbled, "And what about my family? And Sloane? Are we ever going to tell them the truth?"

"Do you want to?"

She was quiet for a moment. "No."

"Then they'll never know about our contract or the obligations that brought us here."

She moved her face in front of mine, smiling. "Can you imagine what they'd say?"

"You mean how much of an asshole they'd think I am. No, I can't imagine. I'd like to bypass that whole conversation with them if possible."

"You mean how much of an asshole you *were*, not *are*." She kissed me. "You've come a long, long way . . . Mr. Wicked."

ACKNOWLEDGMENTS

Nina Grinstead, our journey is one that can't be described. In fact, most of the time, I don't even have to say the words—you're already inside my head, knowing everything I'm thinking. I'm sure here, in this moment, is no different. You can see the tears in my eyes. The smile on my face. The subtle shaking of my head. You've made this all come true. And *thank you* and *love you* will never be enough. Team B forever.

Nicole Resciniti, the way you have my back, the way you fight for my success, the way you open doors I thought would be locked forever, you're constantly making my dreams come true. You're the best agent in the world.

Maria Gomez, I've never met anyone who fights for my nondairy meals like you. 😊 Gah, I just heart you so much. Thank you for your patience and understanding—there were lots of hurdles that came during this book, and you were so compassionate with me the whole time. I'll never forget that. Ever.♥

Lindsey Faber, meeting you confirmed everything I already knew: we're kindred spirits. 😊 I absolutely adore you and cherish the time we spent together at BB. All these months later and I can still hear your voice in my head—the things you've taught me, the things you've made me aware of. I'll forever be a stronger writer because of you. As I said before, it's the biggest honor to work with you on this book, and I can say that again. XO

Ratula Roy, 2023 was the year of us. In ways I wasn't anticipating, but in ways that have made me the happiest. You stepped in and saved me like a true friend would. I owe you everything and I love you endlessly.

Sarah Symonds, you've been here since the beginning, and you'll be here until the end. Thank you for being my everything, always. Love you to the moon and back.

Brittney Sahin, I never would have typed THE END on this book if it weren't for you. You held my hand through the hardest times; you listened; you gave me words that I needed to hear. You motivated me. Inspired me. And like I told you the day you showed me your dedication, you were a light in a roomful of darkness. Thank you for always being here. I love you.

Kimmi Street, my sister from another mister. There's no way to describe us; there's just something special when it comes to our unbreakable bond. Nothing and no one will ever change that. I love you more than love.

Extra-special love goes to Monica Murphy, Devney Perry, Valentine PR, Kim Cermak, Christine Miller, Kelley Beckham, Rachel Brookes, Jan and Pang, Tracey Waggaman, and Jennifer Porpora. I'm so grateful for all of you and I love you so much.

My Midnighters, my ARC team, my Bookstagram team: You are such a supportive, loving, motivating group. Thanks for being such an inspiration, for holding my hand when I need it, and for always begging for more words. I love you all.

Mom and Dad, I love you.

Brian, I am me because of you, and you are the best part of me. There is nothing I love more than our love.

MARNI'S MIDNIGHTERS

Getting to know my readers is one of my favorite parts about being an author. In Marni's Midnighters, my private Facebook group, I post covers before they're revealed to the public and excerpts of my current projects, and team members qualify for exclusive giveaways. You can join Marni's Midnighters at https://geni.us/MMFacebook.

Newsletter

Would you like a free book? To qualify for exclusive giveaways and be notified of new releases and sales? Then sign up for my newsletter at http://marnismann.com/newsletter/. I promise not to spam you.

SNEAK PEEK OF *The Playboy*

Are you interested in reading a sizzling grumpy/sunshine, boy-obsessed, one-night-stand romance that's dripping with chemistry and scorching heat? Check out *The Playboy*, book one from my Spade Hotel series. Turn the page for a sneak peek.

Editor's Note: this is an early excerpt and may not reflect the finished book.

PROLOGUE

Macon

Seven Years Ago

"Six beers deep before noon. Now that's a style I can get behind," Cooper, my middle brother, said as he stood in the doorway to my room.

He was wearing a black suit and light-blue tie. His golden-brown hair was styled and gelled and looked so put together, I almost had to shield my eyes.

He walked in and slid the chair away from my desk. Rather than turning it around to face me, he straddled the wooden seat and sat backward.

I could smell his cologne and cleanliness all the way across the room from my bed.

"I suppose I can stop being such an ass and offer you one." I grabbed a beer from the twelve-pack on the nightstand. "Here."

"I'm good. I'm headed to work in a few. Uncle Walter would lose his shit if he smelled beer on my breath."

Uncle Walter, my father's brother, was the founder of Spade Hotels, a high-end, super-exclusive, luxury hotel brand with locations all over the world. Until my father had retired, he'd been partners with Walter, who had eventually bought him out. But that didn't stop the next generation from working for the family business. My oldest brother, Brady, had an executive role. Now that Cooper had graduated from the University of Southern California, he was employed there, too, and he'd be moving into his own place in a few weeks.

I was the baby of the family.

Once summer was over, I'd be starting my junior year at the University of Colorado, and upon graduation, I'd follow in my older brothers' footsteps and join the brand within the next two years.

"Suit yourself," I replied. "That just leaves more for me."

Instead of putting the beer in the pack, I twisted off the cap and took a sip of drink number seven.

Cooper rested his arms across the top of the chair. "You want to talk about it?"

"Talk about what?" I flung the metal cap across the room, aiming for the small trash can by the desk, hearing it clink to the bottom when I made the shot.

"The reason you're drinking, in bed, and it's not even"—he looked at his watch—"eleven in the morning."

"No. I don't want to talk about it."

"Come on, Macon. What the fuck is going on with you? You're grumpier than normal. You took off all day yesterday, didn't answer your phone, and you didn't get back until, what, two this morning. And now I find you like this."

I stared at the trash can that held all seven metal beer caps.

But inside, it also held something else.

A picture.

One that had traveled with me to school the last two years.

One that I'd brought home for the summer and had planned to pack up and take to Boulder when I headed there for fall semester.

Had planned—but didn't plan to anymore.

My parents' housekeeper would be coming in sometime this week, and she'd empty my trash can, dumping the picture into the bin that would be pushed out to the curb.

I couldn't wait for that day.

I never wanted to see that fucking picture again.

I took a long drink, wiping the leftover liquid off my lips. "What do you mean, *like this*? Drunk?" I sighed. "I'm far from that."

"You're making this difficult when it doesn't have to be."

I lifted my phone, scrolling through Instagram, done with this conversation.

Until I heard, "Is this about Marley?"

My hands shook from the sound of her name.

My stomach ached.

My heart beat a rhythm that was far too fast.

I glanced up at my brother. I didn't like the expression on his face.

Shit, I wanted to wipe it away and never see it again.

"So that *is* what this is about," he said. "Yeah, now it all makes sense." He lifted his chair and moved it closer until he was about a foot away from my bed, resting his feet on the end of my mattress. "You guys break up?"

There it was.

The statement that had been pounding through my chest since I'd left Marley's house two nights ago.

There was no reason to hide the truth.

It wasn't a secret.

It just hurt—to think about, to say out loud.

To come to terms with.

I took another drink. "Two fucking years of my life . . . gone."

He clasped my shoulder, shaking it. "What happened?"

"Nothing happened. That's what is so fucked up about this. She just couldn't deal with everything—the long distance, the unknown at the end of the night whenever I went out with my buddies, even though I assured her every single fucking time that I wasn't hitting on anyone and there wasn't a chick in my bed." My head dropped, hanging low. "The idea that something could happen became too much. I wouldn't cheat on her, Coop. You know I wouldn't. I loved that girl . . ." My voice faded, my hand gripping the bottle so hard, I was waiting for it to smash. "But her jealousy took over and created scenarios that didn't exist." I tapped the screen of my phone, the background a picture of us when she'd visited last semester and I'd taken her skiing.

I tossed my phone. I couldn't stand the sight of it.

Marley and I had begun dating our senior year of high school. Not the best timing, considering I was heading off to Colorado for college and she was going to Florida, but we'd made it work. We'd visited each other as often as we could. We talked all the time. Texted nonstop. We spent every summer together.

Until now.

She was going to London tomorrow to start her semester abroad, and for the last week, she'd been telling me we needed to talk.

All we did when we were away from each other was talk.

We were finally together again; a conversation was the last thing I wanted.

I was talked the fuck out.

But Marley forced a discussion, and her emotions spiraled as she explained how she'd been feeling the past two semesters and told me she couldn't do it anymore.

She was giving up.

Two years in . . . and she quit.

Us.

Cooper tapped his foot against my shin. "You know, if Brady was here, he'd say, *I told you so.*"

I rolled my eyes. "That asshole told me from day one not to get tied down before I went off to school. I should have listened to him." I adjusted the pillow behind my back and sat up straighter. "In fact, now I'm going to do exactly what he's done all these years." I pulled at my shirt, getting a strong whiff of beer and day-old clothes. "Fuck feelings. Fuck being tied down. Fuck any kind of relationship. I want no commitments. No emotions. I want—"

"To be a playboy."

"Yeah," I replied. "That."

Because there was no way I was ever going through this again. No way I would ever allow myself to feel this way.

To hurt this badly.

To want something—and someone—I couldn't have.

I would never give my heart to another woman.

Ever again.

Cooper chuckled, like he actually found my reply funny. "I'm not Brady. That's not even close to what I'm going to say." He adjusted his cuff links, his arms returning to the top of the chair. "Instead, I'm going to give you the best piece of advice anyone will ever give you."

"Sure you are."

His brows rose. "You don't believe me?"

"You're only two years older than I am, Cooper. What the hell do you know about life and women at this point?"

"More than you."

I downed the rest of beer number seven, added the empty to the pack, and took out number eight, missing the trash can when I tossed the cap in its direction.

Maybe I was starting to feel buzzed.

I groaned. "I can't wait to hear this."

"There are women who will come into your life who are there just to have fun. Like some of the dudes you go to college with—they're a blast when it comes to partying, but after you graduate, you won't see or hear from them again." He paused, like he was letting that sink in. "Then there are women who will come into your line of vision and the moment you see them, they'll blow your fucking mind. You'll do anything to be near them. Talk to them. Hear their voice." He closed his eyes and shook his head. "Smell their skin." When he opened his eyes again, he added, "Those are the women who will completely change your life."

Like Marley?

Fuck that.

I hissed out all the air I'd been holding in. "I don't believe it. That shit doesn't exist —at least not anymore."

"All right, we'll see about that. But when a woman has the power to make your grumpy ass smile, and I'm talking really smile, where it starts in your stomach and goes up your chest and you feel it deep in your bones, you'll know she's the one."

I chugged half my beer, not bothering to wipe my lips. "Bullshit."

He smiled in a way I hadn't seen before. "Just you wait and see, brother."

ABOUT THE AUTHOR

Photo © 2021 Moments by Jade Photography

Marni Mann is the *USA Today* bestselling author of more than thirty novels, including *Mr. Hook-up* in the Hooked series and the stand-alone novels *Even If It Hurts*, *Before You*, and *The Better Version of Me*. Marni has known she was going to be a writer since middle school. While other girls her age were daydreaming about teenage pop stars, Marni was fantasizing about penning her first novel. She crafts unique stories that weave together her love of darkness, mystery, passion, and human emotions. A New Englander at heart, she now lives with her husband in Sarasota, Florida. When she's not nose deep in her laptop and working on her next novel, she's sipping wine, traveling, boating along the Gulf of Mexico, or devouring fabulous books. For more information visit www.marnismann.com.